"Maybe we shouldn't be walking off together."

"Why not?" Simon raised his eyebrows, wondering what she thought would happen if they took a walk together.

"Because your aunt and my grandmother are watching us."

He glanced toward them. Sure enough, they had their eyes on him and Lydia, and they were talking in low voices.

He shrugged. "So what?"

"Matchmaking," she said darkly.

He couldn't hold back a chuckle. "Come to think of it, I have seen a twinkle in Aunt Bess's eyes when she looks at us. But so what? They won't bother us, even if they chatter."

"You don't know them as well as you think if you believe that," she said, wrinkling her nose. "Once the two of them get started, they'll drive us crazy."

"All we have to do is ignore it, and they'll stop."

She paused and looked at him, her gaze pitying. "You poor thing. You really believe that."

They looked at each other, laughing a little, and he realized he felt a connection again, just as he had when she was a pesky little kid.

A lifetime spent in rural Pennsylvania and her Pennsylvania Dutch heritage led **Marta Perry** to write about the Plain People, who add so much richness to her home state. Marta has seen over seventy of her books published, with over seven million books in print. She and her husband live in a beautiful central Pennsylvania valley noted for its farms and orchards. When she's not writing, she's reading, traveling, baking or enjoying her six beautiful grandchildren.

An Amazon top-ten bestselling historical romance author, **Tracey J. Lyons** was a 2017 National Excellence in Romance Fiction Award finalist. She sold her first book on 9/9/99! A true Upstate New Yorker, Tracey believes you should write what you know. Tracey considers herself a small-town gal who writes small-town romances. Visit traceyjlyons.com to learn more about her.

MARTA PERRY

&

TRACEY J. LYONS

Unexpected Amish Match

Previously published as *A Secret Amish Crush*
and *The Amish Teacher's Wish*

LOVE INSPIRED
INSPIRATIONAL ROMANCE

LOVE INSPIRED®

INSPIRATIONAL ROMANCE

Recycling programs for this product may not exist in your area.

ISBN-13: 978-1-335-42694-9

Unexpected Amish Match

Copyright © 2022 by Harlequin Enterprises ULC

A Secret Amish Crush
First published in 2021. This edition published in 2022.
Copyright © 2021 by Martha P. Johnson

The Amish Teacher's Wish
First published in 2021. This edition published in 2022.
Copyright © 2021 by Tracey J. Lyons

For questions and comments about the quality of this book, please contact us at CustomerService@Harlequin.com.

Harlequin Enterprises ULC
22 Adelaide St. West, 41st Floor
Toronto, Ontario M5H 4E3, Canada
www.LoveInspired.com

Printed in U.S.A.

CONTENTS

A SECRET AMISH CRUSH

Marta Perry

This story is dedicated to the one who walks with me through the storms of life: my husband, Brian.

Many waters cannot quench love,
neither can the floods drown it....
— *Song of Solomon* 8:7

Chapter One

Lydia Stoltzfus had gotten only a mile down the road toward town when the first huge wet flakes began to fall. Several spattered Dolly's black coat, and the mare lifted her head, sniffed the air and gave a soft whicker.

"I know," Lydia said, as much to herself as to the mare. "We weren't supposed to get so much as a flake today. Maybe it will stop as soon as it started."

Driving another few hundred feet along the road was enough to convince her that hope was futile. The flakes had begun by melting on the narrow country road, but now they were sticking, and the sound of Dolly's hooves was muffled by their coating.

Should she keep going or turn back? Daad and Mammi would worry, that was certain sure, but how could she fail Elizabeth? Elizabeth Fisher, the elderly owner of the coffee shop where Lydia worked, had been sick off and on for most of the winter. She'd be relying on Lydia, and Lydia couldn't let her down.

Keeping a firm grip on the reins, Lydia tried to discourage Dolly's excited reaction to snow after what had been a fairly mild March. Those who had proclaimed an early spring in Lost Creek were going to be sadly disappointed, she feared.

"Komm, Dolly. Act your age." The mare was nearly as old as she was, and at twenty-five, Lydia was seeing even her best friends begin to use the word *maidal* in connection with her. Old maid.

A car went past, moving slowly in response to the increasingly slick road, and a sliver of apprehension slid through her. Still, Dolly was sure-footed, and she certain sure didn't get excited about traffic at her age. As long as they kept a steady pace, they should be fine.

Lydia had about three minutes to think that before she heard the sound of a car behind her—a car coming fast. She hugged the side of the road, hoping for the best. The driver was going much too fast for conditions, but there was plenty of room for the car to pass—

Without slowing, the vehicle rushed up on her. It was going to clear…but then, at the last possible moment, it clipped her wheel. She felt the buggy slide to the right and urged the mare back to the left, but it was too late. Lydia's right rear wheel slid off the road, and she felt the jolt of dropping down to the berm. Dolly, with a sudden return to good sense, came to a halt and there they sat, half on and half off the road.

Breathing a silent prayer of thanks that they were both unhurt, Lydia assessed the situation. Would Dolly be able to get the buggy back onto the road or not? Shaking the lines, she tried to speak with more assurance than she felt. "Walk up, Dolly." She clucked at her. "You can do it."

Dolly made one half-hearted try and the buggy slid even farther. The mare halted, her ears back as if listening for a better idea.

"Stubborn creature." Lydia anchored the lines with a quick turn and slid cautiously down onto the wet surface. Slippery, very slippery underfoot. She moved slowly around the mare, patting her, to the offside.

"Komm along, girl." Grasping the headstall, she urged the mare to move forward. Dolly pawed with her forefeet, nervously testing the surface.

"Komm." Lydia tugged, the mare danced, the buggy rocked. And then Lydia's feet slid out from under her, she tried to right herself, and she landed flat on her face in the snow.

For an instant she lay there, stunned. Dolly reached down to nuzzle her, blowing warmly on her already wet face.

"Enough." Lydia pushed the mare's head out of the way and sat up. At least, she tried to sit up. It took two tries to make it happen, and then another three to get her up to standing.

Clinging to the harness, she caught her breath and tried to wipe the snow from her face. She hadn't quite finished when her ears caught the sound of another buggy coming up behind her. Relief swept through her. Help had come. Anyone with a buggy would be someone she knew.

The driver pulled up and slid down from the seat. Enos Fisher, who had the farm next to Daad's, came hurrying toward her, followed by another man.

"Ach, Lydia, what happened?" Enos reached her, slithering a little on the wet surface.

"She's got herself into a pickle."

The swirling snow hid the other man's face, but she recognized the voice even though she hadn't heard it in years, and something in her jolted to attention. It was Simon, Enos's son. Several years her senior, he'd been the object of her schoolgirl crush back when she was a skinny kid and he was courting Rebecca Schultz. They'd married and disappeared out to an Ohio settlement, and she hadn't seen him since.

And now he was back, and his first impression of her would be that of a sopping wet female who couldn't even keep her buggy on the road.

Hoping her mortification didn't show in her face, Lydia glanced up, snow whirling between them. "We heard you were coming back, Simon. Wilkom." She hesitated, unsure of whether to mention the death of his wife or not.

Enos broke in before either of them could say another word. "Komm, Simon. We'll push, and Lydia, you get in and take the lines. We'll soon have you on the road again. You want to go home?"

She shook her head as she swung up to the seat. "I'm on my way to work. Elizabeth will be needing me."

"Gut. We're going there ourselves, so you can follow us. We'll see you there safe, won't we, Simon?"

Simon, looking to Lydia's eyes as if he'd rather do anything else, nodded and put his shoulder against the rear of the buggy. With both of them pushing and her urging Dolly on, she was back on the road in moments. Before she could even express her thanks, they'd gone back to their own buggy. Trying to ignore her wet clothes and the hair that was straggling from under her kapp, Lydia fell in behind them, and they were off.

The snow kept on coming down, but with another buggy to follow, she realized that both she and Dolly felt more comfortable. In another ten minutes they'd reached the coffee shop, driving down the alley alongside to the shed where the horses could be safe and comfortable.

Lydia had Dolly taken care of quickly, and as she moved past Enos's buggy, she spotted something she hadn't before. Or rather, someone. A little girl, bundled up in a winter jacket and mittens, snuggled under a carriage robe in the back seat. Simon's little girl, she'd guess.

She stopped next to the buggy, smiling. "Hello. I'm Lydia. What's your name?"

Wide blue eyes stared at her from a small, pale face. Then the child turned and buried her face in the seat.

Before Lydia could come up with a word, Simon appeared next to her. "Her name is Becky. She doesn't like to talk to strangers."

The words could have been said in a variety of ways—excusing the child or expressing encouragement to her and thanks for Lydia's interest. Instead Simon made it sound as if she were at fault for intruding, and his disapproving expression forbade her from trying again.

The imp of mischief that never failed to lead her into something she shouldn't do suddenly came to life, and she responded with a cheerful smile.

"I just thought Becky might like to have a mug of hot chocolate to warm her up. I'm going to have one. What do you think, Becky?"

Simon's displeasure loomed over her, but she focused on the child, holding her hand out and smiling. For an instant she thought it was no good. But then a small hand found its way to hers, and she lifted the little girl to the ground. Hand in hand they headed for the door, and Lydia knew without looking that Simon was still frowning.

* * *

Simon watched them walk away, not sure whether he was pleased or annoyed. Of course he was happy to see his shy daughter willing to reach out to someone in what was a strange place to her, if not to him. But if she was ready to warm up to someone, did it have to be Lydia Stoltzfus?

He remembered Lydia. The pesky little kid next door, she'd been twice as much trouble as any of his younger siblings. She'd been an expert at leading the others into mischief, but she'd always come up smiling, no matter what. Everything had been a game to her.

Following them into Great-aunt Elizabeth's shop, he reminded himself that she was an adult now, but he wasn't quite convinced. Not when his first glimpse had been of her sprawled face down in the snow at the side of the road.

Aunt Elizabeth rushed to greet him, and he forgot Lydia in the warmth of her welcome. It had been too long, he thought. Too long since he'd been surrounded by people of his own blood, tied to him by unbreakable bonds of kinship. He and Rebecca had made good friends out west, but with her loss the longing had grown in him to return to Lost Creek, back where he could raise his daughter in the midst of family to love and care for them.

When he finally emerged from the hugs and exclamations, it was to find Becky installed at a table near the counter, with a mug of hot chocolate topped with whipped cream in front of her. With Lydia's help, she seemed to be trying to decide between a cruller and one of Aunt Elizabeth's cream horns.

"I think you'd like this one," he told her, pointing to

the cream horn. "Aunt Bess fills the whole thing with yummy cream." His old name for his much-loved great-aunt came automatically to his lips.

Becky looked at him, then seemed to look at Lydia for approval. When she smiled and nodded, Becky's hand clasped the cream horn, squirting out cream as she put it on her plate. She seemed confused for a moment, and then she carefully licked the cream off her fingers. Something in him eased at Becky's enjoyment, and his gaze met Lydia's for an instant of shared pleasure that startled him.

"Ach, this is our little Becky." Aunt Bess beamed down at the child. "Lydia is taking gut care of you, ain't so? She takes care of everybody, even me."

Before he could wrap his mind around this unexpected relationship between Aunt Bess and Lydia, the older woman surged on. "Lyddy, why don't you show Simon the extra storeroom? He's going to put some things there until his new house is ready."

Lydia, busily putting mugs of coffee on the table, looked up and nodded, while Simon's daad sat down next to Becky with every appearance of settling in for a bit. Before Simon quite knew what had happened, Lydia was leading him behind the counter to the cluster of rooms that made up the back of the building.

"I don't want to take you away from your work," he said. "This could wait."

Lydia shook her head. "Don't you remember? It's always best to listen to what Aunt Bess says. Otherwise she'll just keep after you and after you."

He couldn't help smiling at the accurate description of his great-aunt. "From what she said, it sounds as if she must listen to you. What did she mean about you taking care of her?"

"Ach, that's nothing." A flush that reminded him of peaches came up in Lydia's creamy cheeks. "She had a bad bout with pneumonia this winter, and since she insisted on staying in her apartment upstairs, everyone had to gang up on her to keep her out of the shop. That's all."

She opened one of the doors off the kitchen. "Here's the room she was talking about. We didn't know what you might need, so I just cleaned it out and left it empty."

A quick glance told him there was more than enough space for the furniture and belongings he'd had shipped home. "Denke, Lydia." He felt a bit awkward, as if he'd lost his footing in trying to fit back into the life he'd left behind. "I wouldn't want to trouble you. I could have taken care of it."

"It's my job," she said simply, but there was a twinkle in the deep blue of her eyes that suggested she understood his discomfort.

There didn't seem to be anything else to say. "Denke," he repeated. This new, grown-up Lydia confused him. At moments she seemed to be a calm, poised stranger, and then he'd get a quick glimpse of that giddy, naughty child. He could only hope that everyone he met wouldn't be equally confusing.

He discovered he was not only returning her smile, he was appreciating the effect of eyes more deeply blue than the depths of a pond and the honey gold of her hair, whose tendrils, loose from her kapp, were drying in tiny curls.

Oh no. He backed off those thoughts abruptly, turning away so sharply that he feared it must look rude.

Still, that was better than any alternative. He had lost Rebecca only a year ago, and he had no thoughts to spare for another woman, even if he had room in his heart. His goals were clear in front of him—to raise Becky among his own people, to build a home for them on Daad's farm, establish his clock- and watch-repair business so he could run it and look after Becky at the same time.

No, he had no time to spare for women. And especially not for one who still contained sparks of the frivolous, pesky child she'd been.

Lydia told herself she was just as happy when Simon returned abruptly to the table to sit with his family. After all, she had work to do. She didn't have time for a man who could look at her with obvious approval one minute and change to a glowering frown the next.

Still, she welcomed the sight of Frank Pierce, one of her regulars, coming in and stamping snow from his boots, his cheeks as red as apples and his white hair standing up in tufts when he pulled off his cap.

"Frank, what are you doing out on a snowy day like this? Doesn't your sister have any coffee for you at home?" She helped him off with the heavy winter jacket he wore. Frank lived with his equally elderly sister a block or two down Main Street, and his usual exercise was walking to the coffee shop every day to sit with several cronies and solve the world's problems.

"She's always telling him it'll stunt his growth," one of his buddies spoke up, making room for him.

"And she's not as pretty as our Lydia," another said, winking at her.

"Ach, you're all terrible, that's what you are." She

gave him the answer she knew he expected, and went to get the coffeepot and another mug. They were all proud of themselves for braving the snow, she could tell, and if pretending to flirt with her made them happy, she was glad to oblige.

Unfortunately, someone didn't seem to agree. Lydia caught a definite scowl from Simon as she turned back from another round of refilling cups and chatting. She whisked behind the counter and pulled out a poster on which she was listing the week's specials. If Simon didn't approve of her, that was just too bad.

A moment later she was chiding herself for her unkind thought. Simon might have been frowning about something else entirely. The good Lord knew he'd plenty to worry about in his circumstances.

Bending over the poster, she was able to study him, thinking about how he'd changed from the boy she remembered. Not in coloring. His hair was still the deep brown of the buckeyes they used to find and shine, with dark brown eyes to match. Simon had always been quiet and serious—introverted, although she hadn't known the word at the time. He was the oldest, and took on all the responsibility that went with being the oldest son in a large Amish family.

Her thoughts flickered to her own brother. Josiah had certainly been very aware of what was expected of him, but no one could call him introverted. Or quiet. He was always only too likely to yell if he caught any of his younger siblings doing something he didn't think they should.

Maybe the truth was that Simon's early tendencies had just been intensified by grief and the responsibility for a motherless child. Those had carved the lines in his face that hadn't been there before and given his eyes the look of one carrying too heavy a burden.

Elizabeth looked up from the discussion and gestured to her, so Lydia seized the coffeepot and headed to their table. "More coffee? Hot chocolate?"

Enos slid his mug over for a refill. "Looks like the snow's about done. You shouldn't have any trouble getting home."

"That's good." She hadn't even noticed, but she looked now and saw that the snow on the street had already turned to wet slush.

"We were just talking about getting Simon's things into the storeroom, Lyddy. So if he comes when I'm upstairs, you'll know what to do. And we'd best find the key for that door so we can keep it locked."

Lydia nodded. "I know just where it is, but maybe I should have a duplicate made, so Simon can have his own."

"Whatever you think." Elizabeth sank back in the chair, and Lydia realized she was tiring. It had been this way ever since she was sick. She'd be talking and working like her old self, and then suddenly she'd be exhausted and need to lie down.

"I'll take care of it." Lydia glanced at Enos to see if he'd noticed, but he seemed oblivious, as did Simon. She paused behind Elizabeth's chair. "Isn't it about time for your rest?"

Elizabeth reached up to pat her hand. "In a minute. Why don't you see if there's something Becky can do? She's tired of listening to our talk."

That was like Elizabeth, ignoring her own difficulties to pay attention to someone else's. And she was right. Becky struck her as too well-behaved to wiggle, but she did look up hopefully at the suggestion.

"Sure thing." She held out her hand to the little girl again. "How about helping me make a poster?"

Becky shot a look at her father, maybe asking permission, and then she slid down and grasped her hand. Lydia took her to the counter where she'd been working on the list of specials and provided her with some colored pencils.

"Suppose you help me put some flowers around the edges so it will look like spring? And then I'll do the lettering in the middle. Okay?"

Becky looked carefully at the tulip Lydia was drawing, and then she nodded. Still without speaking, she started making a blue flower.

Was she always this quiet? With her hair so pale it was nearly white and her very light skin color, she resembled her mother the way Lydia remembered her. Every child was close to her mother, of course, and their resemblance might have made the bond even tighter. Perhaps she had inherited her father's quiet disposition, too, but even so, this seemed extreme.

"I like that flower. It's really pretty—just the color of your eyes."

That brought a startled look to Becky's face. "Really?" she said, as if she'd never thought of it.

"For sure. Your mammi had those bright blue eyes, too, I remember."

Abruptly she was aware of having said the wrong thing. The tiny face closed again. Becky slid down from the stool she was perched on and went silently back to her father. And although Becky didn't speak, she seemed to communicate with her father, because the look Simon shot at Lydia made her feel about six inches high.

If she could explain…

But she suspected that would only make matters worse. Probably she shouldn't have mentioned Becky's mother, but how would she know that? In any event, she didn't see Simon regarding her as anything but trouble. Probably the best thing she could do was to avoid both father and daughter as completely as possible, but that wasn't going to be easy.

Chapter Two

Determined to avoid any further misunderstandings with Simon, Lydia kept her mind on her work. Unfortunately, the café wasn't as busy as normal. The snow had discouraged shoppers, and now the melting slush looked equally messy underfoot. When she found herself starting back to the same table for the fourth time, she decided that pretending to be busy was harder work than actually being busy.

Another glance at Elizabeth left her feeling even more concerned. Elizabeth seemed to be staying upright through sheer force of will, and her gaze had become glassy with fatigue. Couldn't either of the men see it? Perhaps she should try again to persuade her...

A tug at her skirt interrupted Lydia's train of thought. Becky stood next to her, looking from her to the counter where the poster still lay unfinished. The sight of that tiny heart-shaped face struck her heart and melted it even faster than the sun melted the slush.

"Do you think we should finish the poster?" she asked.

Becky's nod was accompanied by a slight smile.

"Let's do it, then." She pulled a chair over so Becky could kneel on it next to the counter. "There, that should make it easier. Which color do you want next?"

Becky studied the colored pencils for a moment. Then her small finger pointed to the yellow one.

"Yellow it is," Lydia said. She put the pencil in the child's hand. "Yellow's a pretty color, isn't it? It reminds me that the daffodils will be coming out soon. Your grossmammi has them planted along the front of the porch, I know."

"She does?"

It was the closest Becky had come to continuing a conversation, and Lydia was delighted. "You ask her to show you where the daffodils are. I think you might find the green spears of the plants out of the ground already. You can check how they're growing, ain't so?"

Becky just nodded, but it was a companionable nod, as if they didn't need words between them.

Maybe Becky resembled her mother in looks, but certainly not in personality. From what she remembered of Rebecca, she had been always poised and in control of herself. Not outgoing, but friendly. Becky clearly took after her father in personality. She had the same grave, questioning attitude that Lydia remembered on Simon's face whenever he was confronted by something new. Funny how clear that image was in her mind.

Picking up a purple pencil, she added a row of the Dutch irises that fringed the creek near the old willow tree. But her mind was still busy with little Becky. How was such a shy, reserved child getting along in the crowded Fisher household? Enos and Mary had four children younger than Simon, and his next brother was married and lived there with his wife and baby. And all of them were cheerful, talkative and a bit overwhelming, she'd think, for Becky.

"I have to see if anyone wants more coffee," she told Becky. "Do you want to stay here until I get back?"

Becky looked from her to the poster, which had sprouted a whole row of what were probably meant to be daffodils. "Stay here," she said firmly.

"Gut." Lydia nodded, satisfied that Becky was feeling more at ease here. Picking up the coffeepot, she moved from table to table, refilling cups.

She paused next to where Elizabeth sat with Simon and his father. She couldn't help it. She'd have to say something, even if she annoyed Elizabeth.

But even as she thought it, she caught Simon's eyes, and a message seemed to pass between them. He glanced toward his aunt and frowned slightly, clearly seeing what Lydia did.

"Becky, come along. And thank Lydia for letting you help her."

The child did so reluctantly, with a longing look at the poster, and gave Lydia a slight nod and a soft denke.

Nudging his daad's elbow, Simon got up.

"Time for us to be moving along," he said. "And time for Aunt Bess to have a rest, ain't so?"

"Ach, all of you fuss over me too much," Elizabeth said, but it was clear that fatigue dragged at her, and she tacitly admitted it, getting up slowly.

"Some people are worth fussing over," he replied, giving her a hug, his face softening so that he resembled the boy he'd been before sorrow had driven those lines of pain into his face. "Lyddy, you make sure she rests, yah?"

The old nickname, coupled with the reminder of the

boy he once was, disoriented Lydia for a moment. Telling herself not to be so foolish, she nodded.

"I'll see to it. And I'll get Becky's coat." She'd hung it in the hallway to dry, so she hurried to take it from the peg and help Becky to put it on. The little girl paused to study the poster for a moment.

"It looks fine," Lydia assured her. "Next time you come, you'll see it right up there on the wall for everyone to look at."

Simon moved next to his daughter, helping her to fasten her coat and wrap a muffler securely around her neck. Meanwhile, Lydia gathered up a handful of colored pencils, making sure to include the yellow one, and put them in a bag.

She knelt next to Becky, very aware of Simon's strong figure standing next to her. "Here are some colored pencils for you to take home."

Becky's eyes grew wide, making her look even more like her mother. "For me?" she whispered.

"For you," Lydia said, touched. "Will you draw some more flowers?"

The child nodded, holding them close. "Yah, I will." Turning, she showed them to her daadi.

Simon cupped his daughter's face with his large hand, his smile very tender. "You'll make lots of them, ain't so?"

He turned the smile on Lydia then, and her heart seemed to grow warm in her chest. "Denke, Lyddy."

Usually the use of the nickname called forth a correction. She was Lydia now. Not a child with a childish name. But it didn't seem to matter at all what Simon called her, not when he looked at her with the lines of pain eased in his face.

She nodded, unable to find any words.

They headed for the door, and Lydia told herself firmly that she wouldn't stand there and watch them go. She put her arm around Elizabeth's waist.

"Rest time for you," she said, in a tone that didn't allow for argument. "Komm."

"You're a gut girl, Lyddy," Elizabeth murmured, patting her arm. "Gut for Simon and Becky, too, I see."

Firmly telling herself that she would not blush, she led Elizabeth toward the stairs.

Despite the slush that lingered, the buggy moved smoothly along the two-lane road as Simon drove home.

"Typical late March snow," Daad commented. "Feel the warmth of the sun. The road will be dry by the time Lyddy heads home."

Simon nodded. Maybe this was a good time to get some questions answered. "I didn't realize Lydia was so close to Aunt Bess."

"Ach, yah, she's been as gut as a granddaughter to her. I don't know what we'd have done without her a couple of months back when Aunt Bess was so sick. She wouldn't listen to anybody, and wouldn't hear of us coming to stay, but Lyddy managed everything."

That was the impression he'd gotten from the conversation, and at one level it still seemed surprising to him. "I guess little Lyddy has grown up and left mischief behind."

Daad chuckled. "I wouldn't say that, exactly. She still likes to laugh, and she'll play with the young ones like she's their age. Well, you saw how she made friends with our little Becky."

"Yah, she did." And it looked as if he'd have to refine

his opinion of Lydia a bit. She might have been flirty with the customers, but she'd been good with Becky as well as taking care of Aunt Bess. It was quite a mixture.

Thinking of Becky, he glanced at the back seat. Becky had the bag open, but with her usual caution, she hadn't taken the pencils out in the buggy. But she'd put her hand in to finger them, smiling and relaxed. Yah, whatever her flaws, Lydia had been good with Becky. Still, that didn't mean he should encourage their relationship. Without Rebecca to help him, he had to be extra careful in raising their daughter.

When he turned into the farm lane, he naturally looked toward the site they'd decided on for his house and shop. Daad followed his gaze, shaking his head.

"All this wet isn't going to help in getting your house done, ain't so? We'll not get the foundation dug until it dries out, that's certain sure."

Simon nodded, fighting the depression that swept over him. His longing to have a place of their own had risen to a point where he could hardly think of anything else. He'd get out there with a shovel by himself if he thought it would do any good.

"Don't fret." Daad seemed to read his thoughts, and he put his hand on Simon's shoulder for a brief moment. "Once it's started, it will go up fast. And you know we love having you and little Becky living with us as long as you want."

"Denke," he murmured. He could hardly say that he and Becky were eager to get out, not when everyone was so happy that they were there.

But it was true. If he couldn't go back to the life he'd had with Rebecca, then he'd settle for just the two of them—him and Becky—in a home of their own.

Rebecca. His heart ached at the thought of going on without her beside him. It had been a great sorrow to both of them that there had been no more babies after Becky, but they had adjusted. The three of them had been contented, happy in their own home. Now he wanted, as best he could, to provide that again for Becky.

Daad meant it when he said they were welcome to live with them, but he knew, and he thought Daad was beginning to realize, that it wouldn't do.

When they walked into the kitchen a few minutes later, he was reminded all over again why it wouldn't do. The rest of the family had started lunch, and everyone seemed to be talking at once. They were hustled to the table with even more laughter and chatter, and Becky seemed to shrink against him.

"Denke." He resisted his brother Thomas's efforts to get Becky to sit between him and Sarah, his twin. "I think Becky wants to stay next to me for now."

"Sure thing." Thomas gave Becky a big smile. "Maybe next time." He was trying to understand, Simon thought, but it was obvious that he didn't. The entire family was outgoing, cheerful and noisy. He had always been the odd one, and he wondered sometimes where it had come from.

Rebecca had understood, and their home had been a haven of peace. Then the accident had robbed them—his mind cringed away from that. He couldn't think about it. He wouldn't.

Mammi leaned over to talk softly to Becky, and Daad began telling the story of finding Lyddy's buggy off the road. The twins, at fourteen eager to find humor in every mishap, promptly started talking about how they'd tease Lydia.

"You'd best be careful," Simon put in. "Or I might just have to tell her about the time you forgot to buckle the harness and the gelding trotted off without you and the buggy."

Thomas flushed, but he was laughing, always ready to take a good joke on himself. "No fair. I wasn't old enough to remember any of your mistakes."

"I am." His brother Adam looked up from the baby daughter he was bouncing on his knee. "Let's see what I can think of."

"If you don't mind how hard you're bouncing, the boppli is going to spit up her lunch all over you." Adam's wife, Anna Mae, swooped down on him and rescued her small daughter. "Komm, now. Get finished and back to work so Simon and Becky can have their lunch in peace."

Peace. That was what Becky needed. He'd grown up in this house, with all his noisy younger siblings, and he'd survived all right. Why not? It had been that way ever since he could remember.

But Becky hadn't. Instead she'd been plunged into it while still in the midst of her grief over losing her mother. Naturally, she was finding it hard to cope.

They meant well. He couldn't doubt that. The twins were old enough to feel responsible for their little niece, and they wanted to love her and help her. It wasn't their fault that Becky was so easily overwhelmed. He couldn't ask them to change their ways in their own home. If only he and Becky had someplace else to stay. Then Becky could get acquainted with them more gradually, learning to join in the fun, he hoped.

But finding another place to stay was impossible. Mammi had taken it hard enough when she'd learned he planned to build a house of his own for himself and Becky. Oh, she'd never dream of saying so, but he knew she longed to have them both right here under her wing. The idea that they'd stay someplace other than the family home until their place was ready—well, she couldn't possibly understand, and she'd be hurt.

Somehow they had to make it through this. His gaze rested on Becky. Somehow.

By the time the coffee shop closed at four, Lydia had already done most of the cleanup. Once the snow had melted from the sidewalks, she was briefly busy again, but that had ebbed as the afternoon wore on. Now she could set off for home.

Elizabeth was coming out of the storeroom Lydia had emptied for Simon's belongings. Lydia glanced inside but saw nothing different. "Is something wrong?"

"Ach, no." Elizabeth patted her cheek. "You go on home now, Lyddy. I'll lock up."

Lydia took a closer look at her elderly employer. The fatigue seemed to be hanging on for a long time. "Are you sure?"

"Positive." Elizabeth made shooing motions. "Go. And thank you for being so sweet with little Becky. That poor child needs all the love and kindness she can get."

Lydia nodded, her eyes stinging at the thought of losing a mother so young. "If I know the Fisher family, she'll be overwhelmed by it."

"Yah." Elizabeth looked thoughtful. "Maybe…well, never mind. I'll see you tomorrow."

As she drove out of town, Lydia was still wonder-

ing what had been on Elizabeth's mind. Perhaps she
was thinking, as Lydia herself was, that a shy child like
Becky needed careful handling. Simon, seeming con-
sumed by his own grief, might not be the best judge of
how exactly to give her that.

It wasn't her business, she told herself firmly. Except
in so far as they were neighbors and part of the church
family, anyway. If she could do something for them,
she would, but Simon hadn't looked as if he would welcome her interference.

The day's unexpected snow had melted from the road
as if it had never been. Only a rut in the side of the road
was left to show where she'd slid off, and already the
sun felt warm. Small patches of bright green showed
here and there—onion grass, she supposed. That was
early spring in central Pennsylvania. Or late winter
Unpredictable, but even under the snow, spring was
waiting.

When she walked into the kitchen a few minutes
later, Mammi looked pleased.

"Just in time. I have some laundry to go over to the
daadi haus for your grossmammi. You can take it."

"Yah, sure." Lydia hung up her bonnet and reached
for the basket, but her brother Josiah got there first.

"Not until we hear all about it," he said, teasing.

"All about what?" She tried to look innocent, knowing she'd have to endure some kidding about her mis-
adventure.

"The accident? You know. Going right off the road
and needing Enos to rescue you?"

"Was ist letz?" Mammi was instantly alert. Apparently, Josiah hadn't blabbed to her.

"Nothing, Mammi. The right-side wheels slid off

the road a little when that snow hit. I'd have persuaded Dolly to pull back on even if Enos hadn't come along."

"So you say." Josiah wasn't done teasing.

Daad frowned, setting down the coffee mug that was always in his hand when he wasn't working. "How did you come to do that, daughter? Dolly is usually sure-footed."

"It wasn't Dolly's fault. A car came up behind us way too fast, shoving us right off the edge."

Mammi shivered a little, touching Lydia's shoulder as if to make sure she was still there. "Those cars go too fast."

"Especially when it's snowing," Josiah added, handing her the basket.

"Give me a horse every time," Daad said. "Animals have instincts. Cars don't." He picked up his coffee mug, apparently feeling he'd said it all.

"Right." Lydia seized the basket and headed toward the daadi haus before anyone could mention Simon and start asking questions.

Of course, when she reached the daadi haus, she'd have to avoid Grossmammi's sharp eyes, and no one ever succeeded in doing that. She and her cousins used to think her grandmother could see right through them, and Lydia still wasn't sure about that.

Sure enough, Grossmammi took one look at her and gestured to a chair at the small round table in her kitchen. "Komm, sit, and we'll have tea. You can tell me about Simon Fisher."

Sighing, Lydia put the basket down. No one ever evaded Grossmammi for long. And there was no one else she'd rather talk to anyway.

"There's not much to tell," she said. "He's back with his little girl, and he's planning to settle here."

Grossmammi put two mugs of tea on the table and sat down next to her. "Poor boy. How does he look?"

She considered, stirring sugar into her tea. "Older. Much older. Losing Rebecca has aged him. I hardly knew what to say."

Grossmammi clucked softly. "Poor boy," she said again. "It's never easy to lose a spouse, no matter the circumstances. And Rebecca was so young."

Lydia could only nod, because her throat choked at the thought. She swallowed hard and found her voice.

"I suppose he never imagined such a thing. Now with the little girl to raise, it will be so hard for both of them." Lydia took a gulp of the hot tea. Mint, this time. Grossmammi grew her own herbs and made her own tea, and she knew mint was Lydia's favorite.

"Tell me about the child. She's called after her mammi, I remember."

"Yah, but he calls her Becky. She seems small for her age, and she's very fair."

"Just like Rebecca," Grossmammi commented. She had an encyclopedic memory when it came to every member of the Leit, as well as their families going back several generations.

"She is the image of Rebecca," Lydia said slowly, remembering the child's reaction. "But she acted very odd when I mentioned that she had eyes like her mammi. She just…" Lydia spread her hands, palms up. "She closed down. That's all I can call it. We had been coloring together, and she put down her pencil and went straight back to her daadi." She didn't add that Simon had given her an angry look. Grossmammi didn't need to know that.

"Poor, poor child," Grossmammi crooned sadly. "She needs lots of loving. Still, I'm sure she'll get that if I know the Fisher family."

Lydia nodded, but she wondered. How was that shy little girl going to react to the rest of the noisy, outgoing Fisher clan, no matter how loving?

She didn't realize how long she'd been silent, musing about it, until her grandmother clasped her hand. "Is it making you sad, then, seeing Simon again like this?"

For a moment she didn't know how to respond. Just as Grossmammi seemed to be able to read her thoughts, so she could tell what her grandmother had in mind.

"For sure. It would make anyone sad, ain't so?" Feeling Grossmammi continue to study her, she had to go on. "If you're thinking that I had a crush on Simon once, forget it. I was nothing but a child then. I'm all grown up, and I don't get crushes any longer."

"You always have a soft spot for the first person you loved, no matter how impossible it was. But it's not impossible now. Simon ought to remarry. Not right away, but soon enough to give his daughter a mammi."

"Don't look at me," Lydia said emphatically, hoping to ward off any matchmaking. "I'm not looking for a husband. And I don't think I ever will be. Somebody has to be the maidal aunt. Why not me?"

Her grandmother shook her head slowly. "Are you still fretting about Thomas Burkhalter? It wasn't your fault."

The name was like a knife in her soul. "Of course not." Lydia kept her voice firm and tried not to show what she felt. "That would be foolish."

But foolish or not, it was true, and she suspected Grossmammi knew it as well as she did. What happened to Thomas— She backed away from the memory and slammed the door on it. She would not start remembering. She wouldn't.

"I just wondered," Grossmammi said, her voice mild. "As for the little girl, it sounds as if you made friends with her, at least, if you were coloring with her."

Lydia nodded, grabbing at the change of subject. "She needs friends, that's certain sure."

"Maybe that's why the gut Lord put her right in your path, Lydia. He may mean for you to help that child, so don't you miss the chance."

"I'll try not to." She knew Grossmammi's teachings about not ignoring the jobs the Lord put in front of you. But she suspected that Simon wouldn't be eager to see her doing anything with his daughter.

Chapter Three

True to the fickle weather, the next day was a delicious taste of spring. The sun shone, the onion grass and dandelion greens looked ready to be plucked, and spring bulbs sent green spears reaching heavenward.

Lydia smiled as she arrived in town. She could look ahead to a busy morning, given how many people were out on the street already. A cluster of children skipped and hopped along the walk to the elementary school, and an elderly woman stepped out of her door and tilted her face toward the sun, looking as if she'd emerged from a long winter's nap.

Sure enough, no sooner had she turned the sign on the door to Open than the bell jingled. Frank and his buddy Albert burst in laughing. "We're first," Frank announced, grinning at Lydia. "Keep the coffee coming."

Albert waved the weekly newspaper in one hand, which meant for sure that they'd have plenty to talk about. The paper might only come out once a week, but it was crammed with the sort of news that they liked best, since it was all about their neighbors.

Lydia exchanged amused glances with Elizabeth and seized the coffeepot. "They've got spring fever, yah?"

"I don't doubt it." Elizabeth shook her head as she pulled out a tray of cream horns. "Naomi hasn't come by with the shoofly pies yet, so they'll have to start on something else."

Nodding, Lydia hurried to take care of her favorite customers. Several of their Amish neighbors supplied the coffee shop with fresh-baked treats, which gave them an extra source of income while also making it unnecessary for Elizabeth to spend so much of her time baking.

She'd pushed Elizabeth into letting her set up the arrangement with the women when Elizabeth had been so ill, and she just hoped it would continue. Elizabeth had enough drive for a woman half her age, but she'd begun to look frail, and Lydia feared for her health.

Scurrying back and forth, keeping customers happy, Lydia was relieved to see Naomi Schutz rush in carrying her usual boxes of shoofly pies. Naomi began unpacking them, and after a quick glance at the crowded room, started cutting and serving without waiting to be asked.

"Denke," Lydia murmured to her in passing, with a cautious glance toward Elizabeth.

"I was late, so I'll stay and help for a bit. It won't hurt James to listen for the baby this morning." With only one child left at home, Naomi seemed to be enjoying her time out, and Lydia nodded her thanks.

In another hour, the rush was over. Lydia had just persuaded Elizabeth to sit down with a cup of coffee when someone banged at the back door.

"I'll get it." She pressed the woman back in her chair. "Must be a delivery."

It was a delivery, all right, but not anything she expected. Instead, a moving van had pulled up by the door, and a burly man in jeans and a T-shirt leaned against the door.

"Furniture for Simon Fisher," he declared, waving a paper in one hand.

"That's right." She stood back, holding the door wide. "Come in and I'll show you where it goes."

He kept shaking his head as she led him through the kitchen. "We thought we were supposed to be stacking it inside the door, not traipsing through a business."

Elizabeth had joined them by that time, and she looked upset. "But you can't do that. How would we get through? The furniture…"

Lydia put her arm around Elizabeth. "It's all right. You go and leave a message at the farm for Simon. I'll show them where to put the things."

Elizabeth fussed for another minute while storm clouds gathered on the man's face, but Lydia finally convinced her. As she trotted off to the phone, Lydia turned to the man.

"Come, now. You know you're supposed to put things where I want them."

"You're not Simon Fisher." He made what she hoped was a final objection.

"I'm acting for him," she said firmly. "You stack everything in the storeroom, and I'll get coffee and shoofly pie ready for you and your crew."

He considered for another moment and then gave in. "All right," he grumbled. "It better be good."

"Freshly baked this morning," she assured him, wondering why some people had to make a fuss before getting on with things.

Once the decision was made, they worked quickly. Boxes, trunks, tables and chairs all began to make their way through the kitchen, while she kept the way clear for them.

As the parade dwindled down, Lydia followed them into the storeroom, hoping everything had made it safely. Things were stacked in a helter-skelter fashion, but at least they were all upright and in one piece. She winced when she saw a hand-painted dower chest dropped on top of an oak table, but a look at the man's face convinced her that further argument wouldn't help.

Besides, since Simon wasn't here, she couldn't very well sort things out. No doubt there were some things he'd want to unpack right away, but she didn't have any idea what. She'd just have to help him rearrange when he got here.

But when a barrel of dishes nearly fell off a dresser, she grabbed for it, letting her annoyance show. "That's breakable. Set it on the floor in the corner."

"Yeah, okay. Sorry." Fortunately, it was a younger man she was addressing now, hardly more than a boy, with a thin face and long hair straggling over his shoulders.

"Finish up now, and I'll fix you something to eat," she said after another look. "Okay?"

"Yes, ma'am." This time she got a smile, and he moved a little more quickly.

In another half hour the job was finished, and the workmen were clustered around one of the larger tables, drinking coffee and eating baked goods so fast it seemed there'd be nothing left for the customers. Before they could eat everything in sight the foreman seemed to recall another job, and he hustled them out.

Lydia exchanged glances with Elizabeth. "Not the best job I've ever seen, but at least everything is in."

"I'll just see if I should rearrange…" Elizabeth began, but Lydia shook her head, diverting her away from the storeroom.

"There's no point until Simon sorts through it himself. I'll take care of it later."

Elizabeth didn't look entirely convinced, but the sound of a buggy pulling into the alley distracted her. In another moment Simon and Becky came in from the side door.

"Our furniture is here?" He looked…torn, Lydia decided. As if he didn't know whether he wanted to see those remnants of his previous life again or not.

She could understand. Probably everything in the room would remind him of the happiness he used to have.

At her nod, Simon stalked toward the storeroom while Elizabeth busied herself with helping Becky and admiring the stuffed doll the child clutched. That left Lydia to deal with Becky's father, so she trailed after him.

They had hardly both gotten into the room before he rounded on her, anger replacing any other feelings. "What's happened in here? Did you let them just throw things in? Couldn't you have taken a little more care than that?"

Lydia tried to remind herself that this was difficult for him and struggled to keep her voice calm. "I thought you'd want to sort things out yourself before stacking them for storage. You weren't here when they came, remember?"

* * *

Simon saw the stricken look on Lydia's face the instant the words were out of his mouth. He barely had time to recognize it before Lydia was responding calmly. Young Lyddy had learned to control her temper, it seemed, while he…well, he'd discovered a temper he hadn't known he had.

From childhood, Lyddy had had the sort of temper that flared up quickly and was as quickly over. He hoped the fact that she could now hold it in check didn't mean she'd hold a grudge.

"I'm sorry," he muttered, feeling small in comparison. "That wasn't fair of me."

"Forget it." Lydia's smile said she had already done so. "I'm sure there are things you'll want to get out right away, and we can put the rest back against the wall. Where shall we start?"

He couldn't very well say that he didn't want help. He'd been rude enough for one morning. The truth was that he shrunk from unpacking boxes filled with memories.

"You have your own work to do. I can handle this."

Lydia smiled as if she'd expected that response. "We're not busy right now. And if I go out, you know that your aunt Bess will come in."

Frowning, Simon glared at her. The look didn't disturb her smile.

"Well?" She lifted her eyebrows in a question.

He forced himself to nod, even if he couldn't manage a smile. "Right. Denke. Becky wants some of her books and the clothes her mother made for her doll. And I'd like to find my tools. They're somewhere in this mess."

Looking around a little helplessly, he realized what

a state he'd been in when he'd packed. Once the decision had been made, he'd been so eager to leave that he hadn't taken much time over packing. Their friends had all pitched in, of course, and he had no idea what they'd put where.

"I guess we'd best start opening boxes, then. I'll get something to cut the tape with."

Her brief absence was enough time for him to give himself a talking-to. He had to stop reacting so stiffly to people who were trying to help. He knew well that folks here would be just as eager to do something as their friends out West. They'd understand and forgive his rudeness, but he'd have trouble forgiving himself.

Lydia came back with a box cutter and a pair of long scissors, and her eyes twinkled with amusement.

"What?" he asked.

"You should see them with their heads together over cups of hot chocolate. Elizabeth is telling Becky a story, and you know what a storyteller she is—she almost acts it out while she talks."

He chuckled. "I remember. It's her gift, ain't so?"

Lydia nodded, laughing a little. "Now she has a new little one to listen to all of them. You've made her very happy."

"I hope." Suddenly whatever strain had been between them was gone, and he was talking to her as if she were the little neighbor he'd known since she was born. "Let's get on with it. I don't want Aunt Bess to have any excuse for trying to work in here."

They started opening boxes. Lydia worked methodically, checking the contents, asking if he wanted them now, and then marking each box before pushing it back against the wall. Simon realized he was grateful for her detached attitude. He tried to follow her lead.

He found he was watching her, liking the way she approached the job and her calm acceptance of the fact that he needed help. She would for anyone, he guessed. Little Lyddy had grown into a very competent young woman.

How was it that she wasn't married? She must be in her midtwenties by now, and she certain sure was appealing. The boys around here must not have any taste if they ignored her.

"I think I've found your tools," she announced.

Simon dropped what he was doing to move to her side, grasped the box and tore it the rest of the way open with an eagerness he hadn't felt in a while. "Right." He lifted out a caddy loaded with tools and then found the box that contained the smallest, finest tools he used on intricate clock repairs. Opening it on the spot, he took them out one at a time, making sure everything was there and none had been damaged.

"You look like a child at Christmas," Lydia observed, and he had to laugh.

"I feel like it, too. There's nothing I'd rather do just now than get back to work."

She looked at him, seeming to consider his words. "Can't you? I mean, I know your house isn't built yet, but clock repair doesn't take a lot of space, does it? Maybe you could get started in a small way."

"Maybe I could." Reality asserted itself. "But not at home. The boys would be trying to borrow my tools, and Mammi would interrupt every five minutes to see if I wanted something to eat."

She chuckled at his words. "Ach, that's how a mother says she loves you, ain't so?"

Nodding, he put all of his repair tools back into a box and set it closer to the door. At least it would be there if he could figure out a way to get started.

"I guess you would need a little peace and quiet to do such detailed work," Lydia commented, replacing some sheets back in a box and labeling it. "I glad I don't have that sort of job. I'd rather have folks around while I'm working."

"Like those old guys who flirt with you?" He couldn't seem to keep a little tartness from his voice.

But Lydia shrugged it off. "It doesn't mean anything, and it makes them happy," she said placidly.

He almost didn't hear her, because he was too intent on the piece of furniture she'd just pulled into the light.

"Don't," he said sharply. But uselessly. Of course it had to come out, bringing the memories with it.

He stood next to her, reaching out to touch it with reluctant fingers, as if it would burn him.

It didn't, of course. It was just a piece of furniture, that was all. No matter what memories were attached to it.

"I'm sorry." Her voice was soft. "It's something special."

"Yah." For a moment he stood there, silent, letting his hands run over the smooth wood of the rocker, as warm as if it were alive.

The momentary rebellion at the sight of it faded away, and he experienced a longing to talk—to say something to a listener who didn't share his grief.

"I made it for Rebecca when she was expecting Becky." With love in every step of it, he told himself.

"She laughed, telling me to make it sturdy enough to last through a big family." His throat tightened. "It wasn't to be."

"It's hard to understand the Lord's will sometimes." Lyddy put her hand lightly on his arm, a featherlike touch that spoke of caring.

"Yah. It is." He put his hand over hers, turning to her to thank her for understanding. But the words didn't get said. They just stood there, inches apart, hands touching. And time seemed suspended. "Lyddy." He murmured her name. This was a new Lyddy, it seemed, with all the laughter and liveliness of the child added to a woman's softness and caring.

He thought…

Whatever it was, it was lost in the opening of the door and Aunt Bess's cheerful voice. He yanked his hand back and sensed Lyddy turn away. She was trying to put space between them, and he couldn't blame her.

Aunt Bess was asking him a question, and Becky was peeping cautiously into a box, her doll held against her. With a fierce effort, he turned to them, forcing himself to listen. Forcing himself not to show the mortification he felt.

He must never do that again. Never. He had found love once, and it had been taken away. He wouldn't look for it again, ever.

Lydia went straight to the kitchen, where she leaned against the sink and tried to catch her breath. Her cheeks felt as if they were on fire. She couldn't let anyone see her until she had control of herself, but she should be serving customers. Elizabeth would think she'd taken leave of her senses.

Come to think of it, maybe that wasn't so far wrong. Sucking in a breath, she bent over the sink and splashed some cold water on her face. There, that was better.

Lydia straightened, running her cold hand across the back of her neck. She had been caught off guard when the unthinkable happened, but she could control herself. But she'd never experienced anything like the feeling that overwhelmed her when she'd been so close and looked into Simon's eyes.

This was foolish. She was a grown woman, not a giddy teenager. She could keep her feelings in check. Still, it might be safer to stay clear of Simon as best she could.

Her grossmammi's voice sounded in her head at that. *God puts people in our path because He expects us to help them.* That was what Grossmammi believed. If that grieving little family had been placed by God in her path, it wasn't right to run away from her responsibility.

Before she could argue with herself, she heard voices, and all three of them came out of the storeroom just as Lydia reached the counter. To be exact, Elizabeth was doing most of the talking. She seemed even more delighted than Simon and Becky over the arrival of their belongings. Maybe that made it more certain in her mind that Simon and Becky were here to stay.

Lydia smiled, watching them. Elizabeth would never admit to having favorites among her many great-nieces and nephews, but Lydia knew from the way she talked that Simon had a special place in her heart—maybe just because he was so different from his siblings.

Becky, clutching something to her chest along with her doll, trotted over to Lydia. "Look." She held out a little bundle of clothes.

She took them, spreading them on the counter and smoothing them out with her hand. Doll clothes, hand-made for a typical Amish faceless doll. Every little girl had one, and although there might be other dolls, this one was usually the much-loved favorite. Lydia still had hers, tucked away in a dower chest her grandfather had made for her.

"They are so pretty." She held up a dress made from a bit of dark green fabric. The stitches were so tiny as to be almost invisible. "I think your doll must love this one."

Becky nodded solemnly. Then she looked through the rest, her face clouding as she looked a second time.

"Was ist letz? What's wrong?" She hated seeing the child's smile vanish.

"Her nightgown isn't here." Becky's eyes filled with tears. "I was certain sure it would be. Daadi said it must be."

She could imagine it without any difficulty—the rush of getting ready to leave, trying to get all their household belongings packed up when they were already stressed and grieving. How easily something could go astray.

Lydia knelt beside her, blotting the tears with a napkin. "You know what? I have my doll and her clothes at home, and I'm sure she has a nightgown you can have. All right?"

Becky's face cleared a little, but not entirely. "But then your dolly wouldn't have a nightgown to sleep in."

"That's all right," Lydia said hastily. "I know she has an extra one, and we'd love to share. I'll get it out and bring it over as soon as I get home."

"For sure?" Her eyes lit up.

"For sure," Lydia echoed, smiling. It wasn't hard to help Becky. Helping her father would be a much more difficult, maybe impossible, task.

Elizabeth hurried over to grasp some coffee cups. "What's for sure? Are you two planning something?"

"The nightgown for Becky's doll is misplaced, so I'm going to get out the one—the extra one—I have. She'll want to have it by bedtime."

"Sehr gut," Elizabeth said approvingly. "Will you bring some doughnuts to the table? Simon wants a snack before he goes back to his sorting."

"You mean you insisted I have a snack," Simon said, looking himself again but avoiding Lydia's gaze. He took the coffee cups from his aunt and carried them to the nearest table, while Lydia brought a plate of doughnuts.

"Hot chocolate for Becky?" she asked, evading his eyes.

"Maybe a glass of milk instead. Denke, Lyddy."

She went for the milk, feeling slightly better at hearing the nickname on his lips again.

When she returned, she caught the end of something Elizabeth was saying. "…don't see why not. It's the best solution."

Simon was shaking his head. "I don't think—"

"Ach, that's just because you think it would be a trouble for us, but it's not." Elizabeth was at her most determined, and when she set her mind on something, most folks just gave in, knowing she wouldn't let up until she was satisfied. Never something for herself, mind. Always something she thought best for others.

Lydia set the milk down in front of Becky and popped a straw in it. Becky's eyes widened, and she gave Lydia a whole-hearted smile, cradling her doll to her chest.

"Denke, Lyddy," she whispered.

Her heart expanding, Lydia nodded. Becky was opening up.

"Don't you agree with me, Lydia?" Elizabeth demanded.

She looked at them, trying to switch mental tracks. "Agree? I might, if I knew what you were talking about."

Elizabeth heaved a sigh. "Simon was showing me his tools. Didn't he show you, as well?"

"Yah," she said cautiously, wondering where this was going.

"It's obvious. Simon wants to get started on his business as fast as possible, and the ground is so wet that who knows when they'll be able to start on his house. So I think he should set up in the storeroom." She switched to Simon abruptly. "You said you had some work already in hand, and no place to do it. The storeroom is perfect—well, not perfect, but there's room, and we can bring in a table and extra lighting."

"I'm sure we could," Simon said, his patience stretching. "But I don't think it's a gut idea. It'll mean extra work for you and Lyddy, and…"

"That's ferhoodled, and you know it. It won't bother us to have you working in the other room. We won't even know you're there."

Lydia didn't know about Elizabeth, but she certain sure would be aware if Simon were in the next room. And she could see he was running out of excuses.

"You're forgetting about Becky." His face softened, and he touched his daughter's head lightly. "She wouldn't be happy at the farm without me all day. Not yet, anyway."

"So you'll bring her along whenever you want," his aunt replied. "She's a quiet child, and she'll be no trouble at all. She can even help, can't you, Becky?"

Becky's eyes, darting from one to another, settled on Elizabeth, and she nodded.

Elizabeth turned to Lydia, as she'd known she would, and her thoughts whirled.

"You agree, don't you, Lyddy?"

If Elizabeth was going to start calling her Lyddy, the battle against the nickname was lost. And as for having them here, with Simon in and out every day, intruding into her thoughts and unsettling her emotions—well, any opposition was lost there, too. She couldn't look at Becky and say she didn't want them there, no matter how much she wanted to retreat.

"Yah, I do. I think it's a fine idea." She managed to look at Simon and smile, hoping her thoughts didn't show. Or her feelings.

Simon gave her a serious, measuring look, as if he were trying to see through her to the contents of her heart. Finally he nodded.

"I guess we may as well try it. Denke."

Were his reasons for reluctance the same as hers? She couldn't believe he felt anything for her. That was impossible, for a reason that anyone could see. He was still in love with his wife.

Chapter Four

A flurry of customers distracted Lydia and kept her busy for the next hour. But she couldn't help being aware of Simon and Becky's presence. Somehow it upset the balance of the shop, and she couldn't quite figure out why. Anyway, she just worked here. The important thing was that Elizabeth seemed happy and satisfied with this turn of events.

Becky stayed in the storeroom for a time, coming out now and then to put things in a box to be taken home with them. Lydia couldn't help smiling when she glanced at the child. Becky was entirely engrossed, and she'd lost the worried look that was too old for her little face.

Eventually, Becky seemed to tire of the activity. She came to Lydia and stood there, looking at her.

"Can I get something for you, Becky?" The earlier rush was over, and she had time now to concentrate on other things.

"Do you have some more paper I can use? Please?"

"For sure," she said, delighted that the child had come to her and asked for what she wanted. "Here's a table right here." She pointed to one near the wall, and Becky climbed onto a chair while Lydia got out paper placemats for coloring and a batch of the colored pencils.

She put one of the placemats in front of Becky and stacked the others. "There. That way you can make a lot of pictures, yah?"

Becky nodded and picked out a red pencil. "I'll make some tulips for you and Aunt Bess."

"Wonderful gut! We'll like that."

She stepped back, her gaze meeting that of her employer. Elizabeth was smiling, and she touched her chest lightly. "She's stealing your heart, ain't so?" she murmured.

Lydia could only nod. "I can't resist her, I guess."

Elizabeth's smiled broadened, and she studied Lydia's face as if she'd been struck by an idea. But whatever it was, she didn't say anything, and Lydia turned away as the bell over the door tinkled.

Pleasure rushed through her when she saw her cousin. Beth was not only a cousin, she was a dear friend, and just the sight of her warmed Lydia's heart. The black dress she wore was a reminder that Beth had lost her husband last fall, but after a time of grief and pain at the revelation of his misdeeds, Beth seemed to have come through that dark night. Glancing at her sweet face, anyone could tell she'd regained her spirit. And if Lydia knew what was going on, Beth was well on the way to a lasting love.

Beth's son, five-year-old Noah, came in her wake, carefully wiping his shoes on the mat. Then he looked toward Lydia and grinned, blue eyes sparkling. "We came to see you," he announced.

"So I see." She gave him a quick hug. "I'm wonderful glad you did."

"We were shopping." Beth announced the obvious, putting a large paper bag on the floor near the coat hooks.

"Don't tell me you needed something you don't carry in your own store," she teased. Beth and Daniel Miller, her late husband's partner, ran a general merchandise store on the edge of town, and Noah was a proud helper there.

"Fabric and yarn," Beth said, showing her the contents of the bag. "I need to do a little sewing."

Lydia wondered if the deep purple fabric was meant for a dress that would mark the end of Beth's mourning clothes but thought it better not to ask. She and Beth and Miriam, their other girl cousin, told each other most everything, but this place was too public for a serious conversation.

"I heard that Simon Fisher is here. He's back to stay, ain't so?" Beth gave her a quick hug once she'd hung up their jackets. "That's gut news."

"Yah, it is." She glanced toward the storeroom, but Simon wasn't in sight. "He's back in the storeroom now, but you'll probably see him before you leave. And this is his daughter, Becky." She led them to the table where Becky was ensconced. "Becky, this is my cousin Beth, and her boy, Noah. He's about the same age as you. That means you'll both start school in September."

"Hi, Becky. What are you doing? Making a picture?" Noah leaned on the chair across from her.

Becky stared at him shyly, and Lydia hoped she'd respond. She didn't speak, but after a moment she shoved a paper placemat and a handful of pencils toward him.

Apparently, Noah recognized that as an invitation, and he climbed on the chair and seized a colored pencil.

"That's fine," Beth said. "You color, and then you can have a treat later. Cousin Lyddy and I want to talk."

"Your timing was perfect." Lydia said, leading her to a nearby table. "We've been busy off and on all day, but it should be fairly quiet now. Coffee?"

"What about some of Grossmammi's herbal tea?" Beth took a packet from her bag and handed it to Lydia. "For you."

"You didn't have to bring it," she protested. "You should know we have a wonderful supply at our house."

"I know, but I thought some spearmint would taste right, and you might not have it here."

"You're getting as bad as Grossmammi," Lydia teased, taking the packet. "A special herb for every season. Spearmint for spring, yah?"

"Yah, and who knows why? It's Grossmammi's secret."

Still smiling, Lydia went to bring the kettle to a boil and warm the teapot. Seeing Beth always made her feel better, not that she'd needed cheering up. They'd been constantly together when they were kinder, but growing up had changed some things. Not their friendship, though, no matter how many times they saw each other.

When she returned with the brewed tea, Beth was smiling in the direction of Becky and Noah. "She's a child of few words, ain't so?"

"Shy, that's all." Lydia grew more serious. "This hasn't been easy. Losing her mammi and now trying to get used to a new place and new people."

"Kinder do adapt," Beth said gently, a touch of wistfulness in her voice. And she should know, having her own fatherless child. But Noah had Daniel, who seemed to be doing a wonderful gut job of being just what they both needed.

Brushing away her momentary sadness, Beth pulled something else from her bag and handed it to Lydia. "A letter from Miriam," she said, referring to their cousin. "She says she's coming home soon, and she sounds excited about it."

"We're be sehr happy to have her back." Lydia seized the letter and tucked it away for later reading and answering. Their round-robin letters had kept the three of them close while they were apart. She was about to say something else about Miriam when Elizabeth, coming down from a short rest, saw Beth and exclaimed happily.

In another moment the two of them were chatting, and Lydia fetched another cup, then moved to the children's table to check on Becky and Noah.

Noah showed her his picture. "I made a really big daisy."

She might not have been positive without his identification, since the daisy seemed to have purple spots. "Very colorful," she said tactfully.

"My picture is big, too." Becky's voice was soft, but she seemed determined not to be outdone, which Lydia considered a good sign.

"I like that one, too."

"Mine's brighter." Noah frowned. As an only child, he wasn't used to competition.

Becky's lip trembled, and Lydia realized a quick intervention was needed. "I'll show you something else you can do with a flower picture." Grabbing an extra sheet, she sketched a quick flower with an orange pencil, and then made two holes in the center.

"You'll ruin it," Noah said.

"No, I won't." She held it up to her face, peering through the small holes. "I made it into a mask, so I can pretend to be a flower."

She made the flower sway from side to side, as if it moved in the breeze.

Noah clapped. "Show Mammi. I want one, too. Look, Mammi." He grabbed her hand, trying to swing her around.

Lydia swung, the mask slipped, and she couldn't see a thing.

"Whoa." She broke up in laughter. "You're going to pull the flower right out of the ground."

"I'll help you." Becky actually said it loud enough to be heard, and she jumped from her chair to catch hold of Lydia's skirt.

Laughing with sheer joy at Becky joining in, Lydia caught hold of her hand and swung her and Noah around until they were all laughing.

Except for one person. Simon had come out of the storeroom, and laughter was the last thing on his face.

For a moment no one spoke, and it must have been as obvious to Elizabeth and Beth that Simon wasn't pleased about her.

"There you are, Simon." Elizabeth sounded deliberately cheerful. "Komm, join the fun. Lyddy is helping Becky get to know a new playmate."

His expression cleared, but not without some effort. "So I see. Who is this young man?"

"That's my boy, Noah." Beth rose to greet him. "You remember me, yah?"

"For sure. It's gut to see you, Beth."

Lydia realized he was trying to sound friendly, but it

was a shame that he had to try so hard. Couldn't he see that everyone here wanted the best for him and Becky?

She handed the improvised mask to Becky. The child smiled, looked through it, and then handed it to Noah, a gesture that warmed Lydia's heart. If Becky could open up, even a little, it was surely the best thing for both father and daughter. Maybe he'd be able to follow her example, and Lydia prayed it might be so.

Simon found it impossible to relax, even when he was well on his way back to the farm. He'd longed to return to Lost Creek, and for the most part he was pleased to be here. But being around people who'd known you all your life had disadvantages, too. They felt only too free to meddle.

He glanced at Becky, snuggled up next to him on the buggy seat. If she hadn't wanted to leave the coffee shop, she hadn't complained, either. Had she really enjoyed the silly playacting that seemed to erupt when Lyddy was around?

Chiding himself for being unfair, he shook his head. He shouldn't criticize Lyddy, even in his own mind. She must have many good qualities, or Aunt Bess wouldn't be so fond of her. Still, he wasn't sure she was the best person to have around his Becky.

Such a good child. He put his arm around her, and she looked up at him with a sweet smile that almost brought tears to his eyes. He was the one who knew his daughter best, he assured himself.

She was very quiet, he admitted. More so than when Rebecca was alive? Maybe so, but that was only natural, wasn't it?

"Did you have fun with Noah?" He asked the question to shut out the memories of Rebecca and Becky together.

Becky considered for a moment, head tilted slightly. "Yah, I guess so." She thought some more. "Boys are a little rough."

The pronouncement, delivered in a serious tone, made him smile. "Yah, I guess they are, sometimes. But that's just how they play." In a few more months she'd be going off to first grade at the Lost Creek school. She'd have to get used to little boys, he supposed.

The mare turned into the farm lane automatically, picking up her pace a little at the sight of the barn and the thought of a bucket of oats, most likely. He drew her back a little and pointed across the field.

"Right over there, by the trees. That's where our new house is going to be."

Becky studied the site seriously, as she did everything. "Will I be able to climb those trees?" she asked at last.

He had to chuckle. "When you're big enough, I imagine you will. Your aunt Sarah was always just as good at that as her twin."

She nodded. "Maybe she can teach me."

This desire to climb trees was certainly new. Was it something Noah had said that put the thought into her mind? He guessed he'd best be prepared for lots of new ideas once she started school.

"I'm sure she'd like to," he responded. "Do you want to go and see the place where our house will be?"

"Yah. Then I can see how big the trees are."

Simon wasn't quite sure how to respond. A wave of longing for Rebecca swept through him. A little girl needed her mammi, that was certain sure.

Daad came to join them as he unharnessed the mare. His first words were for Becky. "Did you find the things you wanted for your dolly?"

How was it Daad knew what she'd wanted to find when he hadn't?

"Yah, except for her nightgown. But Lyddy said her doll has an extra one. She's going to give it to me."

Daad didn't blink an eye at the idea that Lyddy still played with dolls. "That's nice of Lyddy. And I think your grossmammi would like to make a new one for her, too."

Becky's face lit up at the idea, making him wonder why he hadn't thought of that. He seemed to be lagging behind on the whole subject.

Becky slid her hand into Daad's. "We're going to see where our new house will be. Will you come, too?"

Daad glanced at him, and Simon saw that his eyes were bright with tears at the invitation. "I will, for sure."

One step forward, two steps back. Or maybe he was the only one finding problems. Or inventing them where they didn't exist.

They'd reached the spot, and Daad found the peg, almost hidden by the grass that was springing up. "Here's where the corner of your house will be." Holding Becky's hand, he paced off. "And that means your back door will be about right here. What you do think about that?"

She eyed the trees that would shade the backyard, once they had one. "I like it," she announced. Releasing his hand, she skipped off through the wet grass toward the nearest tree.

Seeing the questioning look in Daad's eyes, he shrugged. "She wants to learn how to climb trees all of a sudden. Only thing I can figure out is that she was playing with Beth's little boy at the coffee shop, and he must have put the idea in her head."

"If it wasn't Noah, it would be something else. You can't stop kinder from stretching their wings a little bit."

"That's for sure." He repressed the instinct to say that she was just a baby. She wasn't, and he had to get used to it.

"Noah will be starting school in September, too, yah? Your mamm was talking about having Becky meet some of the other young ones her age." He chuckled. "She's been longing to have a little one around again. The twins are getting too big for her to baby."

"I'll say. I can't believe how they've grown. Maybe I can put Thomas to work when we can finally get started on the house."

Daad studied his face. "Getting impatient, ain't so? And everyone is saying it'll be a wet spring."

"Maybe everyone is wrong," he muttered. If he just saw some sign of progress, he'd feel better. That reminded him that he hadn't mentioned Aunt Bess's idea. "Aunt Bess wants me to use that storeroom of hers as a workshop. There's plenty of space, and I could get started on a few old clocks I want to refurbish and sell."

"Sounds like a fine idea." Daad greeted the plan so fervently that Simon suspected he was tired of his impatience to get the house built. "But you could do it here, if you want." He turned to gaze at the farmhouse. "Maybe—"

Simon shook his head, smiling. "You're full up, Daad. And I'd need a space where I can feel stuff out without somebody deciding to clean or somebody else borrowing my tools."

Daad might have been annoyed, but instead he chuckled. "That sounds like our house, all right. Between your mother and Anna Mae, they'll clean anything that stands still. Well, if you do work at Aunt Bess's place, you know your mamm will be happy to watch Becky."

This topic did require careful handling. "Aunt Bess said I could take her there, too. Becky has taken a liking to Lyddy."

"Couldn't find anyone better to like," Daad said promptly. "Lyddy's a fine girl. Well, you can just take Becky with you or leave her here, whichever seems best any day."

"I wish I thought Mammi would see it that way. I don't want her to feel hurt."

That was another reason he wanted to get into his own house as soon as possible. Living in someone else's home made it hard to do want you wanted without affecting another person.

"She'll understand." Daad clapped him on the shoulder. "You'll see." He paused for a moment. "Anyway, I think so."

Simon chuckled. "Not so sure, are you?"

Daad smiled back. "It comes of having so many females in the house. I have to watch my step between your mammi, and Anna Mae, Sarah and Becky, and even the boppli is a girl. We're outnumbered."

"Yah." He moved restlessly, feeling the earth boggy under his feet. "You see why I'd like to get us into our own place, ain't so? We'll only be a stone's throw away, but it will be best."

"Yah, I know how you're feeling." Daad laid a hand on his shoulder again, just as he'd always done when he wanted one of them to listen carefully. "But there's one thing none of us can control, and that's the weather. They'll not get the heavy equipment in here to dig the foundation while it's this wet." He stamped his foot, and water squished up. Apparently satisfied he'd made his point, he added, "Maybe you'd best ask the bishop to pray about it on Sunday."

Knowing Daad was joking, he smiled. Praying to bend the weather for his own benefit wasn't something any of them were likely to do. Still, there were times when prayers for the weather were suitable, like the times Lost Creek overflowed its banks and the river flooded the lower end of town. Then Amish and Englisch had joined in prayers for relief.

But his need to have a foundation dug didn't come into that category. Maybe what he needed to pray for was patience.

Chapter Five

Lydia slipped the last pin into place in the front of the blue dress she was wearing to worship and double-checked to be sure her hair went smoothly back under her kapp. A call from the kitchen below her room had her scurrying down the stairs.

Mammi, in the kitchen, was shepherding her flock toward the family carriage. "Komm along. We can't make up time with a horse and buggy, remember?"

Mammi said that every church Sunday, so they should remember, but whether it kept her brothers on time, she'd never been sure.

"Lyddy, will you check and see if Grossmammi needs any help?" Her mother turned from putting on the black wool coat she wore on chilly Sunday mornings.

"Yah, Mammi." Grasping her own jacket, she turned toward the door to the daadi haus just as it opened.

"No need," Grossmammi said, hustling into the room while trying to push her arm into the sleeve of her coat. "I'm ready."

Lydia eased the sleeve into place and buttoned the

coat, knowing that Grossmammi's arthritic fingers might have trouble this early in the morning.

"Denke, sweet girl," she murmured, patting Lydia's cheek. "Who is not here?"

"Josiah is bringing the carriage up, and here is Joanna," Mammi said. Joanna, Lyddy's eighteen-year-old sister, turned to her.

"Is the length right on this dress, do you think?" She turned around slowly. "I know Mammi thinks it's too short."

Lydia surveyed it carefully, hiding a smile. Joanna had become very fussy in the past month or so about how she looked. Since Jesse Berger had been bringing her home from singing, in fact.

"It looks fine to me. Don't you think so, Grossmammi?"

"I do, yah." She touched Joanna lightly on the shoulder. "I'm sure Jesse will think so."

"Grossmammi…" Joanna began, but Lydia gave her a gentle push toward the door.

"We know what you're going to say, but save it. It's time to load up."

Outside, the air was crisp but the sun warm, even this early. Lydia helped her grandmother in and slid onto the front side of the buggy next to Josiah.

"Who's last?" he muttered.

Lydia checked a giggle. "James, of course. Who else?" She and Josiah tried not to tease the younger ones, but sometimes they had to share a laugh.

Josiah, the oldest, was only eighteen months older than Lydia, and although he sometimes got bossy, they had always been close. It was Josiah who'd gone with her when she'd gotten that frightening note from Thomas Burkhalter.

Telling herself that was no thought for the Sabbath, she pushed it away. But she'd always be grateful to Josiah.

The past few days had been so calm and normal that she'd begun to think she'd been imagining things with Simon. He had been in and out of the shop, taking some things out to the farm and setting up others. She hadn't had occasion to go in the storeroom, and since he locked the door when he left, there had been no opportunity to get a glimpse.

Still, she had no cause for complaint. If Simon hadn't felt anything in that odd, speechless moment between them, she wouldn't bring it up. She just hoped that her own expression hadn't given anything away to Simon. Even the thought of that made her cheeks grow warm.

They reached the site of worship without too much time to spare, and judging by Daad's expression, her little brother was going to hear about that before the day was over.

The youngest Miller boys took charge of the buggy, and Lydia held Grossmammi's arm for the short walk to the barn where the service was being held. She deposited Grossmammi among the women and found her own spot at the end of the line of unmarried women, while Joanna moved to the girls who were in her rumspringa group. Beth wasn't one of the unmarried, of course, and hadn't been for some time. But she'd missed Miriam during the months the latter had been in Ohio helping out relatives. Miriam's absence had left Lydia feeling odd, stuck as she was between the rumspringa-age girls and the young married women.

Not that she was eager to become one of them, she reminded herself. She had no desire to marry. Inevitably, her thoughts replayed that conversation with Grossmammi, and her mention of Thomas Burkhalter.

That had stunned her. She'd told herself people had forgotten what happened to Thomas, but Grossmammi never forgot anything. She'd remember everything about those days, just as Lydia did.

Poor Thomas. She stared firmly at the barn door and waited for it to open. If she'd been a little older, if he hadn't been her first beau, if she'd realized sooner what was happening in his mind...

If. Grossmammi always said that thinking *if* was a waste of time and better forgotten. But sometimes thoughts couldn't just be dismissed. She could never chase away the strain of those days. She'd never forget Thomas's tears, or his wild talk. And certainly not the note she'd found. The note that said he couldn't live without her, and that by the time she read it, he'd be dead.

She shivered in the warm sun, her gaze seeking out her brother Josiah in the line of young men opposite her. Josiah had seen her face when she'd opened the note. He'd hustled her into the buggy and driven the gelding at a gallop to the Burkhalter farm, driving straight into the barn.

Thank the good Lord he hadn't stopped at the house first. As it was they were just in time—standing on the buggy, trying to hold on to Thomas while Josiah cut the rope he'd put round his neck.

Most folks said it wasn't her fault. Even the bishop had declared that she and Josiah should be thanked for arriving in time so that Thomas could get the help he needed. Thomas's own mother had told her not to blame herself. But none of it was any use. She couldn't possibly keep from blaming herself, and she never had.

The door had been opened and she hadn't even noticed, not until the line began to move. She shivered and walked more quickly, trying to bring her thoughts out of the past and back to today.

It was a relief to get inside. She moved along until she reached her usual place on the backless benches, again wishing Miriam were next to her. Miriam would distract her. But she wasn't here, and Beth was married, and Lydia felt very alone.

The remaining members of the Leit filed into the barn. At the end of the line was a visitor. Someone must have company visiting from out of town, although she hadn't heard.

She was still watching as the woman turned around to sit. Her breath caught in her throat, and her heart pounded so loud it seemed everyone would hear it. It wasn't just any visitor. It was Judith, Thomas Burkhalter's twin sister.

Lydia was aware of the service going on around her. Somehow she was able to sing, to kneel, to respond, even though her thoughts were churning. Her prayers were a wordless plea for…what? Forgiveness? Strength? Courage?

What she wanted at heart was to be mistaken—to glance behind her at the rows of benches and see that it wasn't Judith at all. But that wouldn't happen.

Please, Lord… She reached out for help. Slowly, very slowly, her mind stopped spinning. She could think again.

It had been foolish of her to think that she'd never see any of the Burkhalter family again. They'd only moved to an Amish community in Indiana, not to Alaska. Thomas's parents had felt it best to seek treatment for Thomas away from here, and she'd been grateful—selfishly so.

Now Judith was here, probably to visit the people she'd grown up with. They were the people Lydia had grown up with, as well. Odd that no one had mentioned her visit, but people may not have known what to say.

The last time she'd seen Judith was the day after the paramedics had taken Thomas to the hospital. Judith hadn't been short of words then, and Lydia seemed to feel them again, flung at her like stones.

It's all your fault. My brother might have died, and it's all your fault. I'll never forgive you. Never!

No one else but Josiah had heard her, and Lydia knew he would never repeat the words. Nor would she, but that didn't matter. She'd heard them, and they were engraved on her heart forever.

With immense effort, she brought her thoughts back to the service. The bishop was preaching the long sermon today, and as he often did, he was speaking about forgiveness.

Forgive as you would be forgiven. Forgive your brother seventy times seven. Forgive us our debts as we forgive our debtors.

She had long since forgiven Judith for her harsh words, but she was afraid that Judith had not forgiven her. *Never* was a very long time.

Judith didn't need to worry that her words had been wasted, because Lydia had never pardoned herself.

Poor Thomas. If she had been older...if she had been

wiser…maybe she'd have known how to deal with him. But she'd been sixteen, and what sixteen-year-old was wise?

The service ended, and as soon as people started to move around, Josiah came across to her and clasped her arm. "Are you all right?" he murmured softly.

"Yah, sure." She tried to say it with a smile, but it failed miserably. She tried again. "I should speak to her…"

Josiah squeezed her arm tightly. "Don't even think about it. If she wants to talk, she'll come to you." He lowered his voice. "She should be telling you she's sorry, but I don't suppose she will."

"It's all right." She patted his arm. "She can't eat me, ain't so? I'll be fine, and you'd best start helping with the tables before you get in trouble with Daad."

"I will." He still looked worried. "Promise me you'll stay around other people, all right?"

She nodded, touched by his concern. For all his bossiness, Josiah was the best brother a girl could ever have, and the only reason she didn't say that to him was because she knew how he'd react.

Beth came over to her then, and Josiah moved off to help with the tables. The expression in Beth's soft gaze said she was aware of Judith's presence, but she didn't say anything about it. Instead she linked arms with Lydia.

"Komm and help with the serving. You know how those men are—as soon as they have the tables set up, they expect food to appear on them."

She found a genuine smile that time, knowing well how her brothers always felt about food after the three-hour worship. It couldn't arrive soon enough. Arm in arm, they headed for the kitchen, where no doubt the King family would appreciate some help.

Sure enough, Rebecca King welcomed them with a huge smile and handed each one a heavy bowl. "Denke. I'd do the running myself, but..."

She didn't finish the sentence, but she didn't have to. It wouldn't be talked about in mixed company, but every woman in the community knew that her baby would arrive soon. Very soon, Lydia thought. Rebecca's husband, Daniel, had been working on the tables outside, but his gaze didn't often leave the kitchen door, Lydia had noticed.

Such a blessing, she thought, as she hurried to help. Daniel and Rebecca were so happy together it hurt to watch them, and Rebecca's son by her first marriage would be delighted to be a big brother.

They went back and forth, carrying bowls and trays of food to the wooden tables. The food was typical of after-church lunches, with trays of meat and cheese, bread, and the always popular peanut butter and marshmallow crème spread. In addition, Rebecca and perhaps her sisters-in-law had provided salads and one dessert after another. No one would go away hungry.

Eager to avoid anyone who might want to talk to her about Judith, as well as Judith herself, Lydia appointed herself chief assistant to Rebecca, hanging around the kitchen until Rebecca's sister-in-law chased her out, saying she should relax and get some dessert.

Lydia went outside, enjoying the increasing warmth of the sun. She started toward the long tables where people were still clustered, feeling oddly uncomfortable. After a moment's thought, she recognized what was troubling her. Josiah's words ran right into the bishop's sermon on forgiveness and shattered there. If she had truly forgiven Judith's hasty words, didn't that mean she should do her best to heal the breach between them?

She really would rather not think so, but Grossmammi always said that if the Lord put a duty in front of you, you had to do it. No excuses.

Sighing a little, she pushed the excuses aside and walked steadily toward where Judith, who had stepped back a little from the others, as if to distance herself. Lydia wondered if Judith felt uncomfortable to be back in Lost Creek again.

When she was a step away, she spoke. "Judith?"

Judith swung around to face her, and for a second she looked so like her twin that it was as if Thomas himself stood there.

The words she wanted didn't come, so she stretched out a hand to Judith, palm up, as if to ask for something. Judith stared at her for another second. Then her face twisted, and she struck Lydia's hand away, stalking off across the lawn.

Simon had been watching Lydia. He would have liked to put it some other way, but he couldn't. He had no idea what had just happened, but he could see Lydia standing there, her face white and frozen, pain and embarrassment written there for everyone to see.

Before Simon realized what he'd done, he'd closed the distance between them to stand between her and the rest of the group, his back an effective screen to keep others from staring and reading what he saw there. That instinct to protect had always been there when it came to the younger ones, and it seemed it still was.

Lyddy blinked and seemed to register that he was there. "Simon, I... I can't talk..."

"No." He kept his voice low, leaning toward her a little. "I don't guess you can. But if you don't want everyone here to be watching you and whispering, you'd best pretend."

She seemed to come back from whatever numbed state she'd been in. "You saw that."

"I did, but I don't think a lot of people did." That might not be entirely true, but it was what she needed to hear just now. "Just get yourself together, and then I'll make an excuse and disappear."

"I'm all right."

"You look as if someone threw a bucket of cold water over you. And maybe the bucket, too," he said bluntly.

He expected her to flare up at that, in which case he'd have felt able to walk away. But she didn't. Whatever had happened between her and that other woman had shaken her badly.

"Here comes Becky. We can take a little walk together."

Becky slipped up to him and tucked her hand in his. "Lyddy, what's wrong?"

The question from Becky seemed enough to alert her. "Nothing." She smiled warmly at his child. He saw Becky respond, but she was still troubled.

"Are you sure?" she persisted. "Why doesn't that lady like you?"

Lydia stooped down to her level, her smile becoming genuine. Becky was taking her out of her daze better than he had done.

"It's all right, Becky. She's just in a bad mood today, I think. It'll be better tomorrow."

While Becky considered that, he squeezed his daughter's hand. "Let's take a little walk with Lyddy, okay?"

Becky brightened. She held his hand and reached out to grasp Lydia's. Giving a little hop, she skipped along between them, and much of the strain ebbed out of Lyddy's face.

Simon watched her as they walked, wondering. "Do you want to tell me about it?" He was hesitant, pretty sure he knew the answer.

Sure enough, Lydia shook her head firmly. "I'm fine. Really. Maybe we shouldn't be walking off together."

"Why not?" He raised his eyebrows, wondering what she thought would happen if they took a walk together.

"Because your aunt and my grandmother are watching us."

He glanced toward them. Sure enough, the two older women had their eyes on him and Lydia, and they were talking in low voices.

He shrugged. "So what?"

"Matchmaking," she said darkly.

He couldn't hold back a chuckle. "Come to think of it, I have seen a twinkle in Aunt Bess's eyes when she looks at us. But so what? They won't bother us, even if they chatter."

"You don't know them as well as you think, if you believe that," she said, wrinkling her nose. "Once the two of them get started, they'll drive us crazy."

"All we have to do is ignore it, and they'll stop."

She paused and looked at him, her gaze pitying. "You poor thing. You really believe that."

They looked at each other, laughing a little, and he realized he felt a connection again, just as he had when she was a troublesome little kid. As for what happened between Lydia and the Burkhalter girl, he realized he didn't even need to ask. Either Aunt Bess or Lyddy's grandmother would be bursting to tell him.

They crossed the lawn and fetched up against the paddock fence. "Relax," he said.

"Relax? You don't know what you're talking about." She shook her head, but she was laughing, too.

Simon let himself relax. They were back to where they'd startled, when she was a mischievous kid leading his siblings into trouble and he was the grown-up. Or at least he'd thought he was.

Chapter Six

Sunday's sunshine had disappeared, and soon after Lydia arrived at work, the rain started. Her morning coffee guys came in, shaking rain off their jackets before settling at their usual table. When Lydia reached them with mugs in one hand and the coffeepot in the other, they were already grousing about the wet spring.

"I thought I'd get the garden in early this year. Got out my tools, bought a bag of mulch... I should have saved my time." Frank made a face. "The ground's so wet it'll take until June to dry out."

"Maybe not even then," one of his buddies said, a twinkle in his eye. "Maybe you should start building an ark."

Frank flapped his napkin at him while the others laughed. Lydia reached over his shoulder to pour the coffee.

"You just like to look on the gloomy side, that's all. Cheer up. Who wants cinnamon rolls this morning?"

It turned out they all did, not surprisingly, and Lydia was kept busy for several minutes tending to them. They kept on talking about the weather the whole time, sharing memories of famous floods and trying to top each other's stories. They made her smile, just as they always did.

Elizabeth came down a little late, but Lydia had noticed she always did after church Sundays. Apparently, the long day still tired her, but she was bright enough now.

"Are they still talking about the weather?" She nodded her head toward the coffee group.

"Mostly reminiscing, I think. I believe they're back to the flood of '78 now. Pretty soon they'll get back to 1899." Lydia started cleaning up the counter space to be ready for the next customers. "The rain may keep people home this morning."

"Most likely it has Simon fretting," Elizabeth said. "He's that anxious to get this house started you'd think the rain was on purpose to slow him down."

Lydia's thoughts flickered to Simon. "You can't blame him. I'm sure he wants to get Becky settled well before school starts in the fall."

Elizabeth nodded, but her thoughts seemed to have moved on. "About yesterday…" She lowered her voice, even though there was no one near enough to hear. "Judith Burkhalter had no call to act like that. I was afraid you'd be upset."

Lydia tried not to let her expression change. "She and Thomas are very close, being twins. She still blames me for what happened."

"It was not your fault." Elizabeth was at her tartest. "You'd better not let me hear that you're blaming yourself, because that's just plain ferhoodled."

Turning to the baked goods cabinet, Lydia tried without success to find something that needed rearranged.

Anything would do to divert Elizabeth from the subject. When she didn't respond, Elizabeth clucked disapprovingly.

"At least Simon was quick enough to see you were upset. He always has been a noticing kind of person. It was gut of him to come talk to you so folks were distracted."

"Yah, it was." She couldn't argue with any of that, but she hoped Elizabeth would stop there.

For a few seconds it seemed her wish would be granted. But then Elizabeth's gaze settled speculatively on Lydia.

"You know, Simon needs to start thinking about getting a wife to go along with the new house. Becky certain sure needs a mammi, and he can't go on grieving forever."

"It hasn't been that long," she murmured.

Elizabeth shook her head. "Becky took a shine to you right away. Her grossmammi says she's as shy as can be with strangers, but she clung to you from the first time she saw you."

She might as well face the issue head-on. "Don't start matchmaking, Elizabeth. Simon wouldn't like it, and I don't need it."

"I wouldn't dream of interfering," Elizabeth said, and how she managed to keep a straight face, Lydia didn't know.

Before she could retort, the side door opened to admit Simon and Becky. Simon stopped to shake off his rain jacket, but Becky ran straight to Lydia, as if determined to confirm Elizabeth's opinion.

"See my new boots?" She stuck out one foot, attired in a green plastic boot.

"Very nice." Lydia turned her back on Elizabeth to help the child off with her jacket. "Sit up on this chair, and I'll pull them off. We'll set them on the rubber mat to dry off, yah?"

Becky nodded, sliding onto the chair and sticking her feet out. She was obviously admiring the green boots. "Grossmammi gave them to me."

"That was wonderful nice of her."

Becky grew thoughtful. "Mammi got me some once, but I outgrew them." Her mouth trembled, and Lydia feared she was blaming herself for outgrowing them.

"Mammi would be happy you grew enough to need new ones. Mammis are always happy when their kinder grow."

Becky considered that for a moment, and then she gave a sharp little nod. She slid off the chair and picked up the boots. "I'll put them on the mat to dry." She marched off with them.

Lydia watched her go, and she realized something. Becky was burrowing deeper into her heart with every meeting. And what could that possibly lead to that wouldn't hurt?

The child was so sensitive about every mention or thought of her mother. Surely after all these months, she should be able to talk about her more normally. Or maybe the problem was that Simon never gave her a chance. If he didn't speak about Rebecca, how would Becky know that she could?

Her natural instinct was to plunge right into the problem—to tell Simon what she thought. She was well aware of what her friends said about her—that if she saw a problem, she'd rush in where angels feared to tread. Maybe that was true, but wasn't it better than holding back and seeing things go wrong?

Simon had gone straight into the storeroom with an armload of boxes, and Elizabeth was getting hot chocolate for Becky. Seizing the moment, Lydia slipped into the storeroom after him.

He glanced up at the sound of someone coming in, and his frown made her think twice. But it didn't deter her. "Simon..."

"Yah?" He didn't sound welcoming, but that made her more determined.

"Have you noticed how upset Becky gets whenever her mother is mentioned? I thought—"

She didn't have a chance to finish when his glare withered the rest of the sentence. "Becky is my child. I'll take care of her, and I don't need interference. Or want it."

He turned his back on her, obviously considering the matter finished. The gesture lit a spark in her.

"Really? You didn't hesitate to interfere in my life yesterday, as I recall. I don't think you have room to talk."

"That was different," he snapped, swinging back toward her with a forbidding expression.

"How?"

The single word seemed to infuriate him. "Fine. Have it your way. In future I won't interfere in your life, and you don't interfere in mine. Or my daughter's."

"You can try," she said sweetly. "But I'm right about Becky, and I was right yesterday, when I said people would talk. Your aunt Bess has already started matchmaking."

She walked out and closed the door, satisfied that

she'd had the last word, but feeling helpless when it came to little Becky, who needed someone to help her.

Simon stood for a moment, staring at the closed door, baffled. What did Lydia mean? Nothing good, that was sure.

In the months since Rebecca's death, he'd figured out that virtually every woman, relative or friend, wanted to interfere with Becky. They all acted as if he was incapable of taking care of his own child. It irritated him so much that he went on the offensive each time he encountered it.

Shaking his head, he forced himself to go back to setting up his workspace. Handling the familiar tools started to settle him down gradually. He would focus on this, nothing else. If Lydia didn't like what he said, it was too bad.

But a thought slid into his mind, sneaking through the barriers he'd put up. What if Lydia had a point? Could she have picked up a problem with Becky he hadn't even considered?

He slammed the lid down on that treacherous suggestion. He was Becky's father. He knew her better than anyone. And Lydia—she meant well, but she'd known Becky only a week. She was wrong, that was all, and the sooner she admitted it and left them alone, the better.

Simon found the bracket clock he'd picked up at a yard sale shortly before they'd moved. It was a beautiful old piece with the glass front still intact. Usually that was the first thing that went of these old clocks, especially if no one treasured them. He ran his fingers along the back, feeling the temptation to start work on it now. If he did, he could lose himself entirely in the work, and he wouldn't have to think of anything else.

A knock sounded on the door, and it opened before he had a chance to say anything at all. Aunt Bess appeared, carrying a steaming mug of coffee.

"I'm not disturbing you, am I? I just thought some coffee would be a good idea. It's such a damp day."

"Denke. That does sound fine."

She set the mug down on the workbench. "Gut." She beamed. "I want you to feel at home. You can work here as long as you need to."

The irritation seeped out of him. How could he resent the intrusion when Aunt Bess was so good to him?

"If you're sure, I was thinking maybe I should put a sign up in the front window. Just so folks will know I'm here."

"That's fine. You should ask some of the Leit who have businesses to put up signs for you. They'd be glad to." She was getting excited, and her cheeks flushed with pleasure at the idea of helping him. "And we should get Lyddy to make the posters for you. She's wonderful at it."

She spun, as if to rush out and grab Lydia at this moment, and he grasped her arm. "Don't trouble Lydia. Not just yet, okay? I have to decide what to put on them and pick up some poster paper and markers."

Aunt Bess nodded, but she was eyeing him in a way that said she wasn't going to give up on whatever was in her mind. "I saw what you did yesterday. You jumped right in when Lydia needed someone. That was wonderful kind."

Embarrassed, he shrugged. "I didn't do much. I just saw she looked upset." Curiosity overtook him.

"That business with Judith Burkhalter—what was it all about?"

"Didn't Lydia tell you?"

"No. Listen, if it's a secret…"

Aunt Bess dismissed that and pulled a chair over so she could sit. "Everyone in the community knows about it. I supposed you'd heard from someone."

"I didn't." Was she trying to discourage him from finding out? No, if everyone knew, she couldn't mean that.

Aunt Bess hesitated, but he realized she was trying to decide where to begin. "Lyddy was only sixteen at the time—just getting into rumspringa activities. She was such a lively, pretty girl she had all the boys gathering around her."

"I can imagine." He could. What he couldn't imagine was why she hadn't married one of them by now.

"Yah, well, Thomas Burkhalter just went head over heels for her. You wouldn't remember him, I guess. When I saw Judith yesterday, I had a feeling it wouldn't go well. Judith always blamed Lyddy."

"Blamed her for what?" Aunt Bess had a backward way of telling a story. Maybe she didn't like remembering it.

"Thomas. Her twin. Like I said, he was crazy about Lyddy, and I think she liked him well enough. He seemed as lively and happy as she was, for a time, anyway."

"Something changed?" he asked, alerted by the way she spoke.

She nodded. "Thomas got more and more possessive. He wanted Lyddy to say she'd marry him. The more she pulled away, the worse he got." She paused, studying his face. "You understand, nobody knew all this at the time. Kids that age—they don't confide in their parents much."

He thought back to his own teenage years. He guessed he hadn't, either, wanting to hold his feeling for Rebecca a secret in his heart, half-afraid to share it for fear it would vanish.

"Lyddy struggled with it, I guess. She tried to talk sense to him, but he wouldn't listen. Maybe he couldn't. He kept pushing and pushing, wanting to talk to her daad about them getting married. She got him to abandon that, but when she tried to break away from him, it seems he got…well, I'd say crazy, but that wouldn't be kind. He was sick, they said afterward."

Once again she was skipping around. "What happened when Lyddy said she didn't want to be his girlfriend?" That had to be where this was heading.

"He started telling her that if she didn't love him, he didn't want to go on living. Said he'd kill himself before he'd let her go. Mind, he never threatened her—I'll give him that. But it was just about as bad, making her feel like she held his life in her hands."

"She should have talked to someone." But he knew even as he said it how difficult it would have been. What sixteen-year-old would want to admit that she was out of her depth?

"Yah, well, it's easy to say that but not so easy to do, I guess. Anyway she did tell someone eventually—her brother Josiah. Those two have always been close. Maybe she felt stronger having someone else knowing about it, and it was a gut thing, because Josiah found a note Thomas had left for her—a note saying that by the time she got it, he'd be dead."

"He didn't, did he?" Surely he'd have heard about it if someone in the community had killed himself.

"Not for lack of trying. The way I heard it, Josiah and Lyddy rushed over to the Burkhalter place. Maybe they had some idea what he'd do, because Josiah drove the carriage right into the barn. They found him, already with the rope around his neck, and he jumped just when he saw them."

"Awful." Simon discovered that his hands were clenched into fists, so tight that the nails dug into his palms. "But he didn't succeed."

"No. Between them, Lyddy and Josiah got him down. Saved his life, although it seems like Judith could never give them credit for that."

Simon was silent for a long moment, thinking about the Lyddy he knew—the happy, carefree little girl, always laughing and filled with joy. It had been a harsh entrance to grown-up life for her.

"What happened to him? I take it the family doesn't live here any longer."

"Thomas went into the hospital right away. And then he had to see a doctor. There was a special clinic out in Ohio that was recommended to his parents, and they moved out there, figuring it would be best for him. And for all of them, I suppose." Aunt Bess looked worn down by the story she'd told him, and it was clear that her love for Lyddy had deepened throughout that trouble.

He reached out to squeeze her hand. "But it's all right now. I mean, surely everybody knows Lyddy wasn't to blame."

"You'd think so, wouldn't you? Still, folks will always talk. And that scene Judith made will have them talking even more. Poor Lyddy. I thought maybe she wouldn't come in today, but she's not one to let a person down when she has a job to do."

"I hope she's not going to mind you telling me the story." He figured it would take him some time to come to terms with all of it. And in the meantime he had to be careful of what he said to Lyddy. He'd been hard on her already today, and even if he was in the right, he didn't want to add any more burdens on her.

"Ach, I'm sure she intended me to tell you. It's best that you know, since everyone else does." Aunt Bess stood up slowly and put her hand on his shoulder. "I wouldn't want you to have any bad feelings about Lyddy because of what happened. She's a wonderful girl, and the way Becky attached to her is so sweet to see. Becky needs someone like Lyddy in her life, ain't so?"

And there it was…the matchmaking Lydia had predicted. He opened his mouth to say something and closed it again. If he protested, she'd just think he was interested. And even if he ignored it…well, Aunt Bess wasn't one to give up easily when she'd set her mind on something. Maybe working here wasn't such a good idea after all—not if Aunt Bess was going to spend every day trying to throw him and Lydia together.

Lydia sorted clean silverware into the drawer, amused by Becky's intent expression as she stood next to her, watching.

"Would you like to help me?"

Becky's face lit with pleasure. "Can I?"

"For sure. Just be careful to pick each piece up by the handle, so you don't touch the part you eat with, okay?"

Nodding, Becky took a spoon, holding the handle with care.

"Gut. Now spoons go here and forks there." She demonstrated. "And we just washed our hands, so that's all right. We always put the handles toward the front of the drawer, so we can pick them up quickly."

Becky nodded again and put the spoon neatly into the proper place.

"Just right." She glanced up to see that the tableful of older men was shifting around and getting ready to leave. "Just keep going while I take care of the customers."

Lydia slid around the counter and hurried to help with raincoats and umbrellas. Usually someone left something here unless she kept an eye on them.

"Here, Frank. Don't forget your umbrella." She handed the oversize black umbrella to him, knowing his sister would scold him if he came back without it.

"No chance I'd do that." He zipped his jacket and looked out at the steady rainfall, his usually cheerful face glum. "If it keeps up like this, the creeks will be flooding before you know it."

"Ach, don't be so gloomy." She put the umbrella in his hand and patted his shoulder. "It's just a spring shower, you know."

"Yeah, Frank," one of his buddies added. "They bring spring flowers, remember?"

"Not if they drown the bulbs, they won't," he retorted. "Well, let's get out in it."

Lydia held the door to see all of them out. Neither Frank nor his buddy Albert was as light on his feet as before, and she didn't want them tripping on the doorsill.

As usual, they'd left their tabs and cash scattered across the table, and she scooped them up. Also as usual, they'd been generous with their tips. If she had a few more customers like them, she could retire, she kidded herself.

The coffee shop was quiet after they left, and given how the rain was pelting down, she thought it would probably stay that way. Just as she finished her cleanup, Elizabeth came hustling out of the storeroom.

"Lyddy, I have a job for you. Simon needs some posters made to advertise his clock shop, so I was sure you'd do it for him."

"Of course," she said, hiding a smile at the sight of Simon standing behind his aunt, shaking his head furiously. He thought she'd been wrong about the matchmaking, had he? Well, it was just what she'd expected, and it served him right.

"Don't bother Lyddy now," he said quickly. "I don't even have the materials to make the signs yet. And I don't want to trouble her."

Lydia gave him a sweet smile, knowing he understood exactly what she was teasing him about. "No problem. I have poster paper and markers at home, and I'll start them tonight. Just tell me what you want on them." Aware of Becky watching, she added, "Becky can help me color them tomorrow, ain't so?"

Becky nodded cheerfully. "It will be fun."

"Fine," Elizabeth said, her tone brisk. "You talk to Lyddy about what you want while Becky and I get some cookies out for a snack."

Giving Simon a slight push in Lydia's direction, she went off with Becky by her side.

Lydia picked up a pad and pencil. "So what do you want me to put on the posters?"

Simon scowled at her. "You want me to say you were

right about Aunt Bess and the matchmaking, don't you? Okay, you were right."

"I thought you'd come to see it my way," she said lightly. It was no manner of use for him to get so annoyed. To Elizabeth, it seemed natural to start pairing people off. "It didn't take your aunt long to get started, did it?"

His only answer was a growled one. "You wouldn't understand."

The trouble was that she did understand, only too well. It would be better for Simon if he didn't take it so seriously, but it seemed he couldn't help it.

"Look, I do see what the problem is," she said. "You don't want people to start thinking that you're tied up with me when you have someone else in mind."

"I don't have anyone in mind." Simon sounded as if he'd reached the end of his limited patience. "I'm not going to marry again—not you, not anyone. I found love once, and I don't suppose anyone has a second chance at a love like that."

His bleak expression wrenched her heart, and she couldn't find any response.

Simon blew out a breath. "Never mind me. I just don't want Aunt Bess to start pushing you. You're bound to be upset."

Lydia suspected he was the one who was upset. She shrugged. "Not upset, exactly. It's a little aggravating, but it's kind of funny in a way."

Diverted by her reaction, he raised an eyebrow. "You've got a strange sense of humor if you think that's funny."

At least he wasn't looking pained any longer.

"You'll have to work on it. By the time she's thrown us together three or four times in an afternoon—"

"I'd rather not."

"Well, then, I don't see what you're going to do about it. I've never been able to distract your aunt when she's set on something."

He frowned, staring at the table as if he were thinking of something. "What do you suppose would happen if I hinted to Aunt Bess that I was thinking that way, but that I really needed to get to know you without scaring you off?"

"You think that would keep her from pushing?" She turned it over in her mind. "I don't know. She might be even worse. Still, I guess you could try it."

"Not just me," he said. "You'd have to at least act as if you were willing to be friends."

Somehow she had the feeling that she'd end up regretting this. But on the other hand, he could hardly discourage her from trying to help Becky, in that case.

"Just one thing. If we're supposed to be becoming friends, then you won't be angry if I take an interest in Becky, now, will you?"

Simon stiffened, but she was right, and he had to know it. Finally he nodded. "All right. But..." He seemed to grow more serious. "If this makes you uncomfortable for any reason, we stop."

She tried to chase away the little voice in her mind that said she'd get hurt if she got too close to him. "No problem," she said firmly, and slammed the door on her doubts.

Chapter Seven

The next morning it was raining again, and as Lydia drove past the area where Lost Creek ran close to the road, she frowned at the muddy, swirling waters. She didn't like the way it was rising, but she tried to shake off the apprehension. Maybe she'd been listening to Frank and his buddies too much, with their talk of flooding.

Still, the cheerful lights of town were a welcome sight on such a gloomy day. With innate wisdom, the mare headed straight for the stable, and Lydia was soon ducking through the rain, holding the plastic in place over the posters she'd worked on last night.

"Goodness," she exclaimed, shedding her wet jacket the minute she got in the door. "I feel like I've been ducked in a pond."

"Ach, you don't look that bad," Elizabeth said. She held up the coffeepot. "No one's in yet, so relax and have some coffee to warm up."

"That sounds good." She unwrapped the posters carefully, discovering that they'd come through the drive without a touch of dampness. Elizabeth, carrying a thick white mug of coffee, came to look at them.

"Very nice." She patted Lydia's cheek affectionately. "I knew you'd do a wonderful gut job. What are you going to have Becky do?"

"I thought she could color in the border I put round the lettering." She glanced out at the gray rain. "But Simon might not bring her today."

Elizabeth followed the direction of her gaze. "Maybe better that way, but I hear she still doesn't like to stay all day without him." She shook her head. "Poor little thing. It's like he's the only security she has left, and she doesn't want him out of her sight for long. What she needs is a mother."

She suspected that hint meant that Simon hadn't put his plan into action yet. "She's probably not ready for that yet, but I hope she'll let us be her friends."

Before Elizabeth could respond, the door rattled, and a second later Simon came in, holding an oversize jacket around Becky. He set her down and pulled the jacket away. "There, now. I told you it would be wet."

He sounded a little exasperated, making Lydia sure he'd tried to talk her out of coming today.

She hurried to help Becky off with the rest of her outdoor clothes. "That's not a problem, is it, Becky? We won't melt in the rain, ain't so?"

Becky considered it a moment before nodding with a slight smile.

Lydia took her hand. "Komm. I'll show you the posters I worked on. Do you want to help color them?"

She got a bigger smile in return as Becky seized her hand, and they scurried over to the table. Lydia caught a glimpse of Simon's frown and hoped she didn't have to remind him that he'd agreed to this.

Once Becky was settled and understood what she was to do, she set to work happily enough. Lydia stood looking at the child, wondering whether she'd talk if Lydia sat down with her. But at that moment the bell on the door jingled, and she hurried to welcome the first customer of the day... It was the truck driver who delivered snacks to various stores around town. He always stopped by for coffee and a doughnut when he'd finished his rounds.

"Here you are, Mike. Hope you didn't get the potato chips wet while you were delivering them."

"Not a chance," he said, grinning. He shoved his ball cap back on graying hair. "I keep the deliveries dry, even if I get wet myself. Sure is determined to keep raining."

She nodded. "A wet spring, that's certain sure."

"Nobody's getting a garden in. And the equipment out at that construction project in Fisherdale is just sitting in the mud."

With a word of sympathy, she turned to prepare the usual tables for Frank and his buddies. She noticed Becky had stopped coloring for a moment while Mike was talking and wondered what about it had interested a child.

But Frank and two of his comrades hustled through the door, and she was too busy to do anything else for the next few minutes.

When she finally had time to catch her breath, she returned to the table to find that Becky had finished two of the posters and started on a third. Simon was nowhere in sight, but the storeroom door was closed, so she supposed he was working.

"What gut coloring, Becky. Why don't we put one up on the bulletin board, and another one in the front window?"

Becky nodded, but not with the enthusiasm Lydia had expected. When they reached the bulletin board, Lydia stooped to help her push in the thumbtacks to hold the poster in place. "That looks wonderful gut. You're helping with Daadi's business, ain't so?"

But Becky seemed to be thinking of something else. She glanced toward Mike, who lingered over his coffee, probably not wanting to go back out in the wet. "That man..." she whispered. "Did he mean nobody could go on building because of the rain?"

Lydia tried to remember what she and Mike had talked about. She was so used to chatting with customers that she could do it without thinking. "You mean about the building project and the mud? I guess it depends on what the builders are doing. If they had a roof on the project, they could work inside. But if they need to dig a foundation, I guess it's too wet."

Becky's blue eyes filled slowly with tears. Shocked, Lydia put her arms around the small figure. "What is it, sweetheart? Why are you crying?" She whispered the words in Becky's ears, not wanting to draw attention to the child.

"Daadi is going to build a new house for us to live in. It'll be our home. He said so. But if they can't work on it..."

She stroked Becky's back gently. "Just right now they can't. It doesn't mean forever. Soon the weather will change, and then they'll start on your new house."

"Home," Becky corrected softly, and Lydia's heart clenched. "Home," she murmured. "It won't be long. All right?"

Becky wiped her eyes with her fingers and nodded, looking at Lydia with trust in her face. As for Lydia, the look made her feel guilty—almost as if she were responsible for the delay.

"Let's put the other poster in the window." She tried for a cheerful smile, but it wasn't easy. Poor Becky. All she wanted was to have a home of her own again.

Ironic, Lydia told herself. She had a home, but the longing in her wasn't satisfied. She'd always felt it— that yearning for something different, something out of her normal life. She didn't know what it was. She just knew that when she found it, she would be happy.

He wasn't exactly avoiding Lyddy, Simon told himself as he set to work on the old clock. He couldn't, not if he wanted Aunt Bess to think he might be interested in her. But he also didn't want to talk to Lyddy until he'd figured out how to do so in view of what Aunt Bess had told him.

Poor Lyddy, that had been his first reaction. But what about poor Thomas? It seemed he was to be pitied, as well. He vaguely remembered the boy, as he remembered most of the young ones in the church district. Who would have guessed that boy would try to take his own life?

Surely Lydia could have found a way to turn him down that wouldn't have led to such a terrible thing. Aunt Bess seemed to think she'd been too young to cope with it, but…

He stopped, tool in hand. Was he actually presuming to judge her? Or the boy, for that matter? With a shock, he realized that Lyddy would have been only a little older than his sister, Sarah. At the thought of Sarah facing something like that, he cringed.

No, Aunt Bess was right. A young girl that age should be enjoying volleyball games and singings and giggling with her rumspringa gang. Not coping with a friend threatening to kill himself.

Should he let her know that Aunt Bess had told him or ignore the subject? He knew perfectly well what he wanted to do, and that was bury the subject so deep it would never surface again. But Lyddy—the grown-up Lyddy he knew now—probably couldn't do that ever.

A tap on the door was followed so quickly by the door opening that he didn't have a chance of calling out. He'd been so intent on Lyddy that for a moment he thought she was the one coming in, but it was Aunt Bess, closing the door behind her.

"I know you want to work and not be bothered," she said, her cheeks wrinkling in a smile. "But I'm going to bother you anyway."

He got up and gave her a quick hug with one arm. "You know I'm happy to see you anytime. And besides, this whole space belongs to you, ain't so? I can't shut you out, and I don't want to."

"Ach, I promise not to be a pest. This is your work, and I don't want folks interrupting me when I'm in the middle of making pastries. Still, I thought I'd let you know that Becky finished a couple of posters, so she and Lyddy put one in the window and one on the bulletin board. So you have to notice them when you come in and tell Becky what a gut job she did."

"You already did that, I'd guess." He smiled at her

with affection. Aunt Bess delivered hugs and cookies and compliments to her many great-nieces and nephews lavishly, leaving it to their parents to provide the discipline.

"I did," she admitted, proving him right. "But it's more important for you to notice. Seems like she treasures everything you tell her. I've seen her sitting there smiling to herself when you've spoken to her."

"Yah, I guess." He felt guilty all in a moment. "You know I've never been much of a talker. Rebecca chattered to her all the time, and I'd best remind myself she's missing it."

"What she needs is a mammi," Aunt Bess said predictably. "It's high time you thought about it, especially now that you're back in Lost Creek."

He wondered for a moment if Lyddy's grandmother was as determined as Aunt Bess was. Probably.

Well, this was his chance to do what he'd told Lyddy he's do, but he'd have to be careful, or he'd cause more harm than good.

"Maybe so," he said at last, not looking at her. "But if I were interested in someone—"

"It's Lyddy, isn't it?" She jumped on that in a second. "I knew it."

"You're not going to turn into a blabbermaul, telling everything to everyone, are you?"

"You know me better than that!" Indignation brought a flush to her face.

"Yah, I guess I do," he admitted. Aunt Bess was interested in everything, but she didn't go passing stories around. "Anyway, if I were interested in someone—" He paused to be sure she wasn't going to jump in with Lyddy's name again. "Well, I certain sure can't rush it.

Not with Becky to think of. I wouldn't want her to get any ideas and then maybe be disappointed."

"She already loves Lyddy," Aunt Bess hurried to point that out.

Sighing, he started again. "Maybe she feels that way as a friend, but a new mammi is something different." His stomach twisted, and he wanted to throw away the whole thing and tell her bluntly not to interfere in his life. But he couldn't. She had loved him all his life, and he couldn't respond by shoving her away.

At least that point seemed to have made her think. She nodded. "I can see you'd have to move slowly."

"As for Lyddy," he went on, mentally apologizing for involving her, "I don't know what she feels, any more than I'm sure what I feel. And I'm certain sure this would go better if nobody said anything to her about it."

"Yah, I guess you're right. I'll keep my lips closed." She put a withered hand over his. "You know it's just that I want the best for you. I always have."

"I know." His throat tightened. He hadn't shown her how much he appreciated what she did for him, and it was time he started. "Denke."

She patted him. "That's all right. Komm soon and tell your Becky what a fine hand she has for coloring."

"I will. I'll come in just a couple of minutes," he promised, and he watched as she went out, moving a little more slowly than she'd done earlier.

A pang touched his heart. Aunt Bess was getting older. His whole family had changed in the years he'd been gone, and if he and Becky were to be happy here, he had to bridge any gap between them.

Becky worked steadily at coloring the remainder of the signs, and Lydia didn't think she'd ever seen a child that age who could stay at a task that long. At least none of her siblings had. As she remembered, they always had to be active.

"Looks as if you're almost done." She paused with the tray of cups she was holding to watch Becky put the last poster on the pile.

"I am." Becky's rare smile came again. "I liked it."

"Gut. And I know it helped Daadi, too."

Becky's reaction to that innocent comment surprised her. Instead of the eagerness she expected, Becky seemed a little hesitant, as if not sure how to react.

She toyed with the colored pens, putting the caps on and off. "Mammi helped Daadi a lot," she said, and her voice dropped to a whisper. "I can't help that much."

What was the right thing to say to that? She'd never encountered a child quite like Becky, and she felt at a loss. But she had to say something.

"It's not important whether it's a lot or a little," she ventured. "We just do the best we can, ain't so?"

Becky's lips closed tightly. She nodded, but Lydia had the uncomfortable feeling that she'd disappointed the child. Murmuring a silent prayer for guidance, Lydia patted her shoulder. "Want to help me get some cookies out?"

At that question, Becky reverted to being any five-year-old, and she hopped off the chair and followed Lydia to the kitchen.

When they came back with a fresh tray of cookies, Simon stood in front of the bulletin board, admiring the poster that was placed among signs offering babysitting services, announcing a concert at the middle school and advertising a harrow for sale. He turned to smile at his daughter.

"That's a wonderful gut sign, Becky. Especially the coloring." He shot an apologetic glance toward Lydia, as if hoping she wouldn't be offended that he hadn't mentioned her lettering.

"It does draw attention, doesn't it?" She took the tray behind the counter and started arranging cookies in the display window. "I'm sure it will bring you some customers."

Becky's serious face lightened, as if she finally believed she'd helped. "I liked it. We have more." Grabbing her father's hand, she showed him the stack of posters, carefully colored, on the table.

Once Simon had exclaimed over the posters, Elizabeth collected Becky, suggesting they make some hot chocolate for a snack and leaving Lydia alone with Simon.

"Denke." Simon moved next to her, looking a bit awkward. "I didn't want to put you to so much work."

She smiled, knowing how reluctant he was to accept help from her—or anyone else, for that matter. "You didn't. Your aunt Bess volunteered me, and it's much easier to just do what she says."

His face relaxed. "Thank you, anyway." He cleared his throat. "I talked to Aunt Bess about…you know. I said that if I were interested, I'd have to take it slow because of Becky, so it was best if no one said anything. Seemed like she understood."

"It sounds very convincing." She couldn't help but be amused by how uncomfortable he found it. Was it because he persisted in thinking of her as a little girl? Or because he really had no intention of ever marrying again? She longed to ask him, but that was out-of-bounds. All she could do was wonder.

Simon nodded shortly, obviously ready to change the subject. "I talked to Aunt Bess about something else, too," he said abruptly.

"Yah?"

"Actually, she talked to me. She said…well, she explained about the situation with the Burkhalter woman at worship." His gaze scanned her face and as quickly skipped away again. "I hope you don't mind."

She'd already regretted what she'd said to him after worship. He'd wanted to help, and she hadn't exactly been appreciative. Now was her chance to set that right.

"No, I don't care if you know. Everyone else does." She found, to her surprise, that she meant it. The situation had been hurtful, but it was best that Simon wasn't left wondering. "I'd hoped Judith didn't hold a grudge against me, but…"

"She can't forgive." His voice had lowered to a bass rumble. "I'm sorry for her."

Lydia couldn't help reacting to that, and Simon nodded at her expression. "Yah, I know you were her target. But she had to be hurting a lot to act that way."

"She and Thomas are twins. They were always close."

"I guess. My brother and sister certain sure are." He frowned slightly, seeming to search for words. "I know what it is to feel as if you can't forgive. But you only hurt yourself."

She studied his face…the deep lines seemed even deeper right now, as if just talking about such a thing was hard. Was he thinking about his wife's death? She'd heard it had been a buggy accident—had he blamed someone for it?

"You sound like you've felt that way yourself." She held her breath, hoping she wasn't intruding too much.

"If you live long enough, I guess we all do."

It wasn't an answer, but at least he wasn't angry. And maybe she was starting to understand the riddle he'd become.

Becky and Elizabeth came out of the kitchen just then, settling at a table with mugs of hot chocolate in front of them. Becky's was topped with a tower of whipped cream that looked in danger of collapse. Had Elizabeth turned her loose with the whipped cream?

Simon caught her eye, and they exchanged smiles. It wasn't any use trying to keep Elizabeth from indulging her little great-niece, she guessed.

"Becky looks better today." He sounded as if he were talking to himself. "Seems like it's a step forward and a step back sometimes."

"Maybe that's part of getting used to being here." She wanted to comfort him while at the same time she longed to express her own concern about Becky.

"Do you think so?" His gaze darted to hers. "Does she seem more at home to you?"

"Usually she does." She hesitated. "When we were working on the posters, she said something I didn't understand."

Simon's eyes darkened, and she thought it was a warning. "What?" he snapped the word in an undertone.

"I had said she was helping you by coloring the posters," she said carefully. "She said her mammi used to help you a lot. Then she said she couldn't help that much."

For an instant she thought Simon was actually going

to open up to her. Then he clamped down on his emotions with an almost visible effort.

"I already told you. Don't talk to my daughter about her mother." He ground out the words. "It's not your business."

"I didn't… I mean, I didn't bring it up. I just thought—"

He wheeled away from her. "Don't. Don't think about it and don't say anything. I'll do all the talking about her mother that my daughter needs." Somehow having to keep his voice low when he'd rather shout at her seemed to make him even more angry.

That certain sure told her where she stood. He was so defensive he couldn't listen to anyone on that subject. She ought to accept it, but the stubborn determination to do what she'd set out to do wouldn't let her.

"Maybe so, if you're doing it. Are you?"

Simon sent her a glare that would have wilted someone less hardy than she was. "Leave it, Lyddy. I can't say it any more plainly than that."

With a final glare, he marched off to his improvised shop and closed the door behind him with a sharp crack.

Chapter Eight

Lydia turned, hoping her face wasn't red. And hoping, too, that they hadn't been overheard. A glance around the room showed her that no one was looking her way. No one, that is, but Elizabeth, who caught her eye from where she was sitting with Becky. Clearly, if no one else had noticed, she had.

They couldn't talk in front of Becky, and even if they could, she wasn't sure she wanted to. Fortunately, several people came in just then, and she was busy enough to have a good reason for not chatting. They often had a small rush of folks for coffee in the afternoon, mostly Englisch. The Amish were more likely to show up for coffee and a bite of something in the morning after finishing whatever had brought them to town.

Refilling coffee cups and exchanging chatter with some members of the library committee, she noticed someone standing at the counter and hurried over.

"Sorry if I kept you waiting." She smiled at Jim Jacobs, who ran Lost Creek's water treatment plant. "What brings you in today? No problems at the water plant, I hope?"

Jim grimaced. "Don't say that, even as a joke. No, I just had a yearning for some of your shoofly pie and a coffee. To go, please."

"For sure." While she was filling a paper bag with his food, he gestured toward the bulletin board. "I saw that sign in the window when I came in. That's a new business, isn't it?"

Thinking how pleased Becky would be, she smiled. "Yah, it is. It's just here temporarily until the shop is built. Do you remember Simon Fisher? He just recently moved back from Ohio, so he's getting his business settled here. If you have a clock to repair, you couldn't do any better, that's certain sure."

"You're a good salesperson, Lydia." He smiled, probably at her enthusiasm. "I do have an old mantel clock that belonged to my grandfather. Hasn't worked in a lot of years. You think he might do that?"

"I'm sure. He's actually rebuilding an old clock similar to that right now. Just drop yours off anytime."

"I'll do that." He collected his coffee and shoofly pie. "Thanks."

As soon as he'd left, she turned to Becky, who had lingered behind the counter with Elizabeth. "Did you hear understand what he said, Becky?" She had switched to Pennsylvania Dutch. Since Becky wasn't in school yet, she probably didn't have much mastery of Englisch. "He saw the poster you colored, and it made him decide to bring a clock in for Daadi to repair. So you really were a big help, ain't so?"

A slow smile crept over Becky's face. "For sure?"

At Lydia's nod, the smile turned into a grin. "I'll tell Daadi right now." She whirled and dashed toward the workshop.

Elizabeth was smiling as she looked after her. "Ach, it's gut to see that child happy for once, ain't so?"

"Yah, it is." Lydia's throat grew tight. It shouldn't be that unusual to see a child her age happy, should it?

Elizabeth nodded, and she suspected they were thinking the same thing. "Poor little thing," the older woman murmured. "I couldn't help but notice—did you and Simon have a tussle?"

"It was nothing, just a little disagreement." She tried to dismiss it lightly but didn't think she was convincing Elizabeth.

"Something about Becky, was it?"

Lydia tried to evade her eyes, but it was no good. And did it matter? Elizabeth was as concerned for the child as she was.

"Becky had said something about her mammi that troubled me." She frowned, shaking her head. "Maybe I'm wrong. But it seems as if she needs to talk about her mother."

"And Simon won't." Elizabeth provided the answer.

"You noticed," she said, relieved. It wasn't just her, then.

Elizabeth nodded. "I went out there, you know. After Rebecca died. It seemed like he was all locked up inside himself. He couldn't even talk about Rebecca. I had hoped by now it would be different."

"It's not just me, then?"

"His mamm is concerned, too, I know. But what can we do?" She opened her hands in a gesture of helplessness.

"I guess, if that's how he copes with it, there isn't anything. But Becky..." Lydia gave in to the need to talk about her worry. "Simon was angry because he thought

I'd talked to her about her mother. Said he'd tell Becky anything she needed to know."

"That would be fine if he did," Elizabeth said tartly. "But as far as I can see, he won't. Short of using a hammer on him, I don't guess we can make him open up."

"Better not tempt me." She was glad to know that Elizabeth felt as she did. Maybe between them, they could be of some help.

Elizabeth chuckled. "You're a gut girl, Lyddy. I guess we have to be patient with him." She hesitated. "You're not taking a dislike to him, are you?"

"No, not at all." She remembered Simon's idea for stopping matchmaking. "I'm sorry for him, and I'm trying to understand."

She should be able to understand him, seeing that she'd known Simon well as long as she could remember. But a child's view of him wasn't much use to her now.

One thing did strike her, looking back on it. Simon had always liked to be in control, whether it was with the younger children or with his work. Maybe with Rebecca's unexpected death, he'd run into something he couldn't control, no matter how he tried.

We aren't in control. The Lord is. Turn to Him.

Grossmammi had comforted her with that thought in the aftermath of Thomas's suicide attempt. Lydia clung to it now, lifting her heart in wordless prayer.

Simon's thoughts were so tangled that it was difficult to focus on what Becky was saying, but he forced himself to respond cheerfully.

"A customer already! That's wonderful gut. Thank you for making the posters so colorful."

"I helped you, ain't so?"

His heart twisted at the expression on her little face. She wanted so much to know she was helping him.

"You were a wonderful help." He touched her cheek lightly. What was in her mind? For an instant he wondered whether Lydia had a point, but he dismissed the idea at once.

"Lyddy did most of it," Becky pointed out. "I just did the coloring. You should thank her, ain't so?"

For a moment he had no words, and his mind went blank. He had thanked Lyddy, hadn't he? He pulled himself together.

"I think I did, but I certain sure will thank her again. Let's go and do that now, and then we should be getting along home."

Standing, he put his tools back in their proper places while Becky handed him each one. Then he clasped her hand and together they walked back to the coffee shop.

A final customer was paying his bill at the counter and commenting about the weather at the same time. "Wettest spring I can remember." He pocketed his change. "And the television weather says there's a storm moving up from the south that might bring us a bunch more rain."

Lydia smiled, handing him a paper bag. "Be sure and keep those doughnuts dry until you get home, yah?"

He chuckled. "I could always eat them before I go, but my wife wouldn't like that idea." He lifted a hand in a wave as he headed out the door. "See you tomorrow."

"Another of your regulars?" As soon as he asked the question he was aware of the edge to his voice, and he saw her eyes flash. He had to stop that. He wasn't responsible for Lyddy, and if she had admirers, it didn't matter to him.

Aunt Bess replied before he could get himself in deeper. "Yah, George is as predictable as the rest of them. Always has a coffee and every couple of days he takes something home to his wife. That's so she won't get mad at him for wasting time."

In the meantime, Lydia had seized a tray and begun clearing tables, dishes clattering. He had to speak over the noise to make her hear him, but he'd told Becky he would.

"Thanks again for those posters. That was wonderful kind of you." He glanced toward the front windows. "Once this rain stops, I'll take them around town and get them put up."

Lyddy nodded pleasantly, but she didn't say anything. He'd guess she hadn't forgiven him yet for speaking so harshly earlier. Well, she had been interfering, hadn't she?

Aunt Bess spoke quickly again, maybe thinking he needed a little help. "If George is right about that storm, we're not getting rid of the rain very quick."

"My mamm will be fretting. She wants the garden harrowed so she can do some more planting." Lydia took the loaded tray to the kitchen, coming back through the swinging door almost at once for a few more things.

"Everybody's getting tired of it," Aunt Bess said. She looked at him. "You're wanting to get started on your house, ain't so?"

He saw Becky watching him anxiously and shrugged, trying to look as if it didn't trouble him all that much. "I talked to Daniel King, and he's going to do the construction. He says as soon as the ground is dry enough, he has someone lined up to dig the foundation. Guess we just have to put up with the delay."

Becky tugged at his hand. "That's what Lyddy said. She said it wouldn't be long, and they'd get to work so we'll have our own house soon."

He gritted his teeth. If anyone should be reassuring his daughter about their future home, it was him. But it seemed Lyddy had beaten him to it.

"We'd best get on the road," he said abruptly. "Grossmammi will be looking for us."

With a few more prolonged goodbyes, he and Becky got on their way home. A light shower continued, but it encouraged him to think maybe the weather was clearing. He got the occasional spray of water in his face, but Becky was tucked into the back and curled up comfortably.

He frowned at a spritz of water in his face. Time to get himself under control when it came to Lyddy. Just because she'd always been like a little sister to him, that didn't mean he had a right to censure her behavior now. Why had he lost his temper when she tried to talk to him about Becky? He should have explained it to her quietly. That would have been a lot more effective than snarling at her.

The truth was that he had never been very good at talking, especially about his feelings. He'd always dealt with things that way. Becky was like him, not a talker. Lyddy shouldn't feel she knew what his daughter needed more than he did.

And he shouldn't be going over and over it. Was it possible there might be something in what she said?

He rejected that suggestion promptly and turned into the lane at the farmhouse just as the rain turned into a downpour. Stopping by the kitchen door, he turned to Becky.

"Jump down quick and get into the house so you don't get soaked." As she obeyed, Mamm appeared in the doorway and hustled her inside, closing the door quickly against the rain.

His mother must have been watching for them… and probably fretting that he hadn't gotten Becky home sooner. She'd wanted him to leave Becky with her that morning, but he'd felt uncomfortable doing so. Still, he'd have to do it sometime.

By the time he got back to the house, the whole family seemed to be collected in the kitchen, anticipating supper, he guessed. Mamm looked as if she could do with their space rather than their presence, so he stood back against the door and watched Becky helping Sarah to set the table.

"So after supper we'll have a game, yah? What will it be?" Sarah asked.

"Happy Farm," she said, naming her favorite board game, one that Sarah had taught her since she'd been here. She smiled up at his sister, and some of his tension relaxed.

Becky was starting to settle into the family. His little sister had done a good job of understanding what things Becky liked and what upset her. Sarah had done a lot of growing up in the past few years.

"How high was the creek when you came home just now?" Daad asked, interrupting his thoughts.

"Not too bad," he said, though the truth was he'd hardly noticed, being intent on his own thoughts. "Someone said the weather prediction is for a big storm headed our way, though."

"Yah, I heard that, too," Adam put in. "They were talking about it at the hardware store this morning."

Daad nodded. "We'd best not put the cows in the pasture nearest the creek tomorrow, then. No sense looking for trouble." He turned back to Simon. "Are you going to town tomorrow?"

"I'd like to spend a couple of hours at the shop in the morning. Someone was talking about bringing in a clock for repair. But I'll come back early to give you a hand if there's any trouble."

Not that there was much they could do if the creek rose, he knew. A person couldn't contain nature, no matter how he tried.

Daad was nodding, but before he could speak, Mamm turned from the potatoes she was dishing up.

"In that case, Becky can stay here tomorrow," she said, as if daring him to argue. "There's no sense in her getting soaked."

It seemed he'd made Mamm annoyed by his failure to leave Becky with her. He should have realized that, he guessed. He had, in fact, but he hadn't wanted to admit it. One thing he hadn't reckoned on about coming home—everyone here seemed sure they had a say in how his daughter was raised.

He couldn't argue with his mother about it, so he just nodded. But he thought again that the sooner they were in their own house, the better.

The steady drum of rain on the roof created an undertone to sleep that night. When Lydia woke, the rain still splattered against the window, but it seemed to be slacking off a bit. As she rose and dressed, her mood lifted. Perhaps it would have stopped entirely by the time she had to leave for work.

The sun rose on a sodden world, but at least it was

clearing. When she took down the black waterproof jacket she'd hung on the wall to dry, only a slight dampness around the bottom reminded her of the wet drive home she'd had.

Mamm caught her arm as she started to put the jacket on. "Do you really have to go in today? I don't like the look on the weather."

"Now, Mammi." Josiah put his arm around her shoulders. "Lyddy knows enough to stop if the creek is too high. You can trust her." He dropped the slightest wink toward Lydia.

"That's right." She picked up on his words at once. "I won't do anything risky. Anyway, Elizabeth is counting on me. I can't let her down."

"You'll call us when you get there." Daad never suggested the use of the telephone, but it was a measure of his concern that he did now.

"She'll be fine," Josiah said again.

But when she reached the buggy, she found he'd put a tarp and a length of rope in the back.

"Just in case," he said, giving her a hand up. "You won't make me sorry I stood up for you, ain't so?"

She squeezed his hand, thankful for him. "I'll either come back or call to let you know I'm there. I just hope it doesn't get worse during the day."

Josiah nodded agreement and stood back while she clicked to Dolly and headed out the lane.

The rain pelted down as the buggy turned onto the blacktop road, and Dolly shook her mane irritably.

"I know you don't like the wet. But soon you'll be nice and dry in the stable. Just a few miles."

Just a few, she repeated to herself. The ditches on either side of the road were nearly bank-full and the fields across the road were waterlogged. Still, the road was clear, and if it stayed like this, there'd be no problem getting back and forth to town.

They passed the flat area and rounded the bend where the trees pushed close to the road. No problems there, but what lay ahead?

When she came out of the wooded space to where the road lay along Lost Creek, she knew her apprehension had been correct. Lost Creek ran high and tumultuous, ever closer to the road. She pulled on the lines, slowing Dolly. She'd said she'd turn and come back if it were bad, but it was already too late. With the creek on the very edge of the road and the ditch full on the other side, there was no space to turn ahead.

For a moment she hesitated, murmuring a silent prayer. If she couldn't turn around she'd have to go on. She clicked to Dolly. The mare lay back her ears, the whites of her eyes showing, and hesitated. Lydia held her breath. Josiah would have something to say if she ended up in the creek, to say nothing of Daad.

"Just a little farther," she said. "A few more yards and we'll be past the worst. Step up, Dolly." She shook the reins.

Dolly took a tentative step and then another. It was all right…they were going to make it.

And then she saw it—a huge log surging down the creek, pushed by the raging water. Caught by the current, it struck the edge of the road and veered off, but the damage was done. Lydia slapped the lines, urging Dolly on. Too late. The blacktop began to crumble, the road fell away under the buggy, and in an instant they were in the water.

The shock of it blanked out whatever might be in

Lydia's mind, and for an instant she couldn't think at all. Then, gripping the lines with one hand and the buggy rail with the other, she forced herself to think.

Thank the gut Lord they weren't out into the foaming current. She was all right and so was Dolly, as far as she could tell. But the mare was nearly up to her belly in water, and while it hadn't gotten into the buggy yet, the whole thing shook with the force of the water. They were several feet from land already, and at any moment Dolly could lose her footing.

She had to get them out. It was already too far for her to jump. *Think, Lyddy, think.* She'd heard once of someone climbing atop the buggy and waiting for help, but if she did that, they were just as likely to be swept away down the creek.

One thing was certain sure. She couldn't let Dolly drown. If the mare could get them a little closer to solid ground...

"Step up, Dolly. Come on, girl."

She couldn't see Dolly's legs, but the movement of muscles under the skin told her the mare was trying. She managed to move one step before stumbling, lurching, and nearly falling before she recovered herself. She stood there trembling, and Lydia felt herself shaking, too.

The only possible way out was to unhitch the mare and cling to her headstall. Without the weight of the buggy, they might be able to make it to shore.

Lydia moved closer to the landward side of the buggy. The water was turbulent, but not nearly as bad as on the other side. Remembering the rope Josiah had put in the buggy, she reached back to retrieve it, murmured a fervent prayer for help, and slid over the side.

The water was colder than she'd expected, taking her breath away. But her feet found a stable spot on the rocky bottom, and before she could lose her nerve, Lydia pulled herself along the side of the buggy to reach the mare.

Dolly turned her head at a touch, and if a horse's gaze could express relief, hers did. Scolding herself for being fanciful at a time like this, Lydia felt her way along the harness, looking for the first buckle. Her fingers, numb in the cold water, brushed it, but before she could grasp it, the mare stumbled in a fresh onslaught as an uprooted bush hit the buggy.

"Easy, girl." She clutched the harness, trying to shake away the water that splashed in her face. She would not let herself think of Mammi and Daad, of Josiah and the rest of the family. Nor of Simon, who shouldn't be in her thoughts anyway. She had to move, and fast.

Clutching the buckle, she forced her fingers to obey her, struggling to stay upright against the force of the water. Finally the buckle opened. Praising the Lord, she moved forward. One more buckle, and she thought she'd be able to pull the mare free.

Fighting the current, she edged to the forward strap, her hand closing on it, but her numb fingers refused to do her bidding. She struggled, pulling at it. No breath to speak, none to cry out. In another minute—

"Lyddy!" The sound shot through her with a surge of hope. Pulling herself around, she saw Simon on the bank, his buggy behind him, nearer town. "Are you all right?"

"So far." Silly question, she managed to think.

"I don't have a rope. I'll have to come in without—"

She managed to hold up the rope she'd slung over her shoulder.

"Gut girl. Tie one end to Dolly's headstall and throw me the other. Can you do that?" He sounded perfectly calm, as if this happened every day. But that was always how Simon reacted in a crisis.

The realization that she was not alone sent a wave of energy through her. She threaded the rope through the headstall after a couple of tries before she looked back at Simon.

He'd turned his buggy so that it faced toward town, and now he came to the edge of the water, reaching out. "Throw me the rope now, Lyddy. You can do it."

Could she? Her brief spurt of energy was nearly spent. She forced herself to lift her hand with the rope. It fell short, but in an instant Simon had lunged into the water and grabbed it. Moving fast, he fastened it to his buggy.

It was going to work. He'd be able to pull Dolly out, and she could cling to the mare and go with her.

And then she remembered that last buckle.

Her face was wet already. He wouldn't notice the tears.

"It's no good. I couldn't get the harness free. She'll never be able to get out with it dragging us down."

Almost before she saw what he was doing, Simon charged into the water. Hanging on to the rope, he made short work of the distance between them, clasping her arm as he reached her. In his hand was a knife.

Not wasting words, she guided his hand to the right strap. A few moments' work, and the strap was free.

"Hang on," he muttered. Grabbing the headstall, he forced Dolly toward land.

The mare stumbled, shook and refused to move.

Simon looked at Lydia, and she knew what he was going to say—that they'd have to leave Dolly and use the rope to save themselves. Anguished, she grabbed the loose strap and swung it at Dolly's headquarters. "Step up!"

She readied the strap for another strike, but with a convulsive movement Dolly lunged forward. Simon tugged, encouraged, urged her on, and all Lydia could do was drag herself along.

Every step seemed to take an hour, but finally she felt the road surface under her feet. Stumbling forward, she pulled herself on, falling headfirst on the road.

Dolly scrambled to safety, and Lyddy felt Simon's arms around her, half carrying, half dragging her toward his buggy. He held her so close that she could feel the pounding of his heart and hear his ragged breathing in her ears.

And then she knew the truth—so clear and simple she should have seen it before. She loved Simon. In that moment it didn't really matter that he felt nothing for her. She loved him.

Chapter Nine

Lydia struggled to gain control of herself as Simon lifted her into the buggy. Her teeth were chattering and her whole body shaking, but she was safe, thanks to Simon. Whatever else she did, she had to control her emotions. Anything else was unfair to him.

She huddled on the buggy seat, trying to force her brain to work. Were they really safe?

"Dolly…" she began.

Simon was quick to reassure her. "I'll get her. You grab the lines and move ahead. We have to get clear before any more of the road washes out."

They weren't out of danger yet, then. Simon thrust the lines in her hands. She tried to grasp them, but she was shaking so badly she didn't think she could.

Simon didn't give her time to think. He slapped the gelding's rump, clicking to him. The horse moved on, obviously eager to get away. Simon, now holding Dolly's headstall, walked beside them. After a few yards he halted.

"We should be all right here. Let me tie Dolly properly and then we'll go."

Lydia gestured back the way she'd come. "My family...the buggy..."

Simon clasped her hand firmly as if to steady her. "We can't get back. We'll have to go on to town. There's no way to save the buggy."

She wanted to protest, but he was right. A look back told her there was no way to reach the buggy, not now. She watched as Simon secured Dolly to the back. He came quickly around to the front, pausing a moment to look up at her.

"All right?"

She managed to nod. She was alive, thanks to him. She couldn't seem to find the words to say that, but he didn't seem to expect it. The rain, still streaming down, flattened his clothing against him, and his face seemed stripped down to the bones, lean and strong.

He swung up to the buggy next to her, reaching into the back to pull out a blanket. "Put that around you. We'd best get to Aunt Bess's and try to call our folks to let them know we're unharmed." He had to raise his voice to be heard over the thunder of rain on the buggy roof and the roar of the creek.

She nodded, grateful when he took the lines from her hands. Even as he clicked to the horse, they heard a crashing sound behind them and turned to see that another sizable portion of the road had collapsed. The rush of stones and broken concrete hit her buggy, and the next instant it had crumpled into itself and washed away.

A shudder went through her, and Simon drew the blanket around her, snuggling her against his side. She knew he was only doing it because she was shaking with cold, but she couldn't deny the pleasure and comfort it gave her to feel him close to her—warm and solid in the midst of terror.

"We'll not get back and forth that way very soon." He pushed the gelding into a faster trot. "There'll be a lot of damage in the valley. I'm just thankful I left Becky at home."

"She'll be safe there with your mamm." She forced her voice to be steady, thinking of how upset her family would be, as well as Simon's. "How did you come along at the right moment?"

Lydia realized she had to be feeling better if she could ask the question.

"I went in early and saw how bad it was, so Aunt Bess called your folks. Josiah was out near the phone shanty, so she told him you shouldn't come. But you'd already left."

So of course he'd set out to find her. Simon's sense of responsibility wouldn't let him do anything else.

"They'll be worried," she said, thinking of Josiah and his insistence that she turn back if it was bad. "Josiah will be angry that I didn't turn back sooner."

She felt him turn to look at her face.

"Don't be ferhoodled. He'll be too happy that you're safe to think of that."

"You don't know Josiah," she said, making him chuckle.

As the houses of town began to appear ahead of them, Simon pointed off to the right. Lost Creek came raging down the valley, ready to pour into the river. The lower end of town was perilously near to the stream, and as they drew closer, she saw water creeping across lawns toward the houses.

"It's going to be bad, isn't it?" Without thinking about what she was doing, Lydia clasped Simon's arm, finding the strong muscles and warm skin under his sleeve reassuring.

"I'm afraid so. If it doesn't stop soon, they'll have to evacuate."

She had time to murmur a fervent prayer for those in the path of the water, and then they were in town. Simon stopped by the side door of the coffee shop. "You go in. I'll take care of the animals."

Almost before he'd finished, a figure in a bright yellow slicker emerged and grabbed the gelding's headstall. "I'll take care of them. Go get dry."

To her astonishment, Lydia saw that it was Frank Pierce. One of his coffee buddies was right behind him.

"You shouldn't—" she began.

"We're not so old as that yet," he said, helping her down. "Get inside, the both of you."

Simon hesitated, as if about to argue, but she shook her head slightly. Frank was right. This was looking like one of those times when everyone in town would have to pitch in, young or old.

Simon grasped her arm and hustled her inside, wet blanket and all.

Inside, the coffee shop was busy, but she didn't have time to notice much more before Elizabeth was wrapping her arms around her. "Ach, thank the gut Lord you're safe. Call your family right away. They'll be frantic. Then we'll find you something to change into."

While she turned her attention to Simon, Lydia hurried into the kitchen and the telephone. Most Amish businesses in the area had either cell phones or landlines. Elizabeth declared that a cell phone was too complicated for her, and she was reluctant even to use the regular phone.

Mammi answered on the first ring—she must have been camped out in the phone shanty. "You're all right?" she said immediately.

"I'm fine. Just wet. Simon had come looking for me. He got me and Dolly out, but the buggy…"

"Ach, don't worry about the buggy, not so long as you're safe." Daad must have been crammed into the shanty with Mammi. "Is Josiah with you?"

"Josiah? No. Why would he…"

"He set off to find you when we heard you hadn't made it to town. He hasn't come back."

That set up a whole new stream of worry that she knew her parents shared. "He'll come back soon." She tried to sound positive. "Or he'll show up here. But the road is washed out, so he'll not get a buggy through it."

"Yah. We'll call when he shows up. Or you call." Her daad sounded as if he were trying just as hard as she was. "You'll have to stay there."

"Yah." There was no question of that, and her teeth were beginning to chatter again. "I have to get these wet clothes off…"

"You do that." Mammi had grabbed the phone again. "So long as you're safe, praise God."

They said goodbye without any last-minute additions, and she knew why. Neither of them wanted to talk until they knew that Josiah was safe.

Praying constantly, she took off her wet things, hanging them up to dry, and hurried into the clothes Elizabeth had laid out for her. A glance at the way the dress hung on her told her that she looked ridiculous, but that couldn't be helped now. She tied an apron as snugly around her waist as she could and rushed back downstairs.

Now that she had time to look, she realized that the coffee shop was crowded not with customers but with people trying to help. They were making coffee and pouring it into thermoses as quickly as possible, while Elizabeth directed several women who were making sandwiches just as fast.

"What do you want me to do?" She touched Elizabeth's arm, fearing she'd see strain on the elderly woman's face, but Elizabeth seemed charged with the energy provided by an emergency.

"Start heating water on the gas stove," Elizabeth said with an approving look at her. "If the electric goes off…" She stopped, looking at Lydia intently. "What's wrong?"

She couldn't hide it—she was too worried for that. "Josiah went out to look for me, but he hasn't come back yet."

"Josiah will be all right." She hadn't seen Simon come in, but there he was, like her, changed into dry clothes. "Josiah's too wily to get himself into trouble."

"Unlike me," she muttered, wishing she'd turned back before she couldn't. Still, if she had she'd be trapped at home, and this was where people needed help.

"Don't worry," he said, and clasped her hand briefly.

Pressing her lips together, she nodded. "I'd best get busy."

She turned away, and as she did so, the back door opened. The figure that stamped in was as soaked as she had been, but he had a grin that split his face at the sight of her.

"Josiah!" She rushed to throw her arms around him. *Thank You, Lord. Thank You.*

Things started to move quickly after that. Thankful that some of his clothing was still in the storeroom, Simon found something for Josiah to wear, while Lydia called home with word that he'd arrived. Word started filtering in about flooding threatening the houses that stood with their backs to the creek on the edge of town.

Simon glanced at Josiah and saw that he was thinking the same thing he was. "They'll need some help."

Josiah grabbed his soaked rain jacket. "We'd better go."

Lyddy caught him as he followed Josiah toward the door. "Where are you two going? You're barely dry yet."

"Don't worry." He couldn't help but smile. "You look like a little girl dressing up in her mammi's clothes."

"Never mind that," she said, her cheeks flushing. "What's happening?"

"We're going to help people in those houses down on the lower end of town." He realized her gaze was following Josiah. "I'll make sure he stays safe, and you look after Aunt Bess. Okay?"

She managed a smile, but her eyes were dark with concern. "I will. You'll be careful, ain't so?"

He nodded, and then escaped before he could consider whether any of her concern was for him. Foolish, he scolded himself. She'll worry about anyone caught in the flooding.

The rain still drummed down fiercely as he hurried to catch up with Josiah, soaking into his jacket again. Josiah glanced at him, but if he was curious as to what his sister had to say, he didn't ask.

"Hope they've got sandbags down there," he said instead. "Not that I think it'll do that much good."

"Yah. Best thing we can do is probably get furniture moved up to the upper stories." He'd always wondered why those folks in the flood-prone houses didn't move, but he supposed it wasn't as easy as that. Who would want to buy them?

Anyway, it was human nature to think it wouldn't happen again. Until the next time.

They rounded the corner leading down to the lower street, and Simon caught his breath. "It's worse than I thought."

Josiah nodded. "The heaviest rain has been upstream of all those little runs that flow into Lost Creek. If it doesn't slack off soon, it could be the worst we've ever seen."

"What we saw was bad enough." He relived those moments when he'd seen Lyddy out in the creek, battered by the water, hanging on to the mare.

"Yah." Josiah's face looked grim. "You want to tell me what happened?"

"When we get time. And you can tell me how you—"

"Look!" Josiah started to run, and he raced after him, realizing what he'd seen. An elderly man was struggling up the bank beside his house, pulling a trunk about as big as he was.

They reached him at the same time. "Here, we'll take that. Can you make it up the bank yourself?"

White hair plastered in strands across his face, the man nodded. "Couldn't leave it behind—pictures of our whole life in there. Don't leave it." He added anxiously as Josiah gave him a hand up the bank.

"We won't," Simon said quickly. He hefted one end and Josiah took the other. When they felt the weight, they exchanged looks.

"How did he get it that far?" Josiah said quietly. "He doesn't look like he could get himself out."

"Guess it's a lifetime of memories. We'd best check the house."

A police car pulled up in front of the house, and a young patrolman came scrambling to help, while an older man rushed inside. By the time they'd reached the sidewalk, he'd brought an equally elderly woman out, sheltering her under a rain poncho.

After a quick assessment of the situation, the older officer opened the back door of the patrol car. "I'll run them up to the Presbyterian Church. They're starting a shelter there. Porter, you get folks organized to move furniture and start sandbagging."

"Yessir." The young man looked gratified but a little scared.

As the police car pulled out, a town truck loaded with sandbags drew up. There was no way of driving any closer—they'd have to carry sandbags down the hill.

Other folks arrived to help—he saw Daniel King leading a group of Amish teenagers and a bunch of men coming from the lumberyard down the road. It seemed natural to team up with Josiah, and together they lugged sandbags and stacked them.

"Getting worse fast," Simon muttered as he hefted sandbags and handed them to Josiah, who piled them up along the bank. "Worse than where the road went out from under Lyddy."

"Yah." Josiah gasped a breath. "I shouldn't have let her go. I should have stopped her."

Simon grunted, lugging the bags that seemed heavier every second. "You think you could stop her?"

Josiah grinned at that. "No, probably not. My little sister has a mind of her own."

An hour passed with everyone working at top speed,

but Simon grew increasingly aware that they were losing. As fast as they added sandbags, the creek took them. There was no fighting the water. You could fight a fire, but not a flood. All you could do was save what you could.

The patrol car pulled up again, siren wailing. The patrolman hailed them. "Get out." He swung his arm in a gesture. "It's no use."

"A few more..." Josiah said reaching for another sandbag, and then a rush of water hit, biting into the sandbags and nearly taking Josiah with them.

He teetered on the edge for a moment, trying to get his balance. Simon threw himself forward, grabbing his hand, and yanked him back to safety.

"Whew." Josiah pounded his shoulder. "Gut thing you're around to get the Stoltzfus family out of trouble."

"Komm," he ordered. "That cop is gesturing to us."

They stumbled up the bank to where the young patrolman was gathering men together. "School bus stuck in the run out on Fisherdale Road. We're needed."

They piled into the car as fast as they could, one on top of the other, as the cop roared out into the street, siren wailing.

"Kinder," someone murmured, and he knew they were all thinking the same thing. The Englisch school buses would be loaded with young ones trying to get home. *Stuck in the run* didn't sound good.

The few minutes it took to get there were the longest Simon had spent in months. All he could manage was a silent, incoherent plea for the Lord's help.

When they pulled up, they saw that others had made it there before them—neighbors, maybe, or passersby who'd rushed to help. Simon scrambled from the car, following the others to where the yellow school bus had skidded into the run. The water was coming up fast here, too.

They formed a line, holding on to each other. The water wasn't deep, but it was fast—too fast even for adults to keep their footing easily. Once they had enough to reach the bus, the driver handed out one child at a time. The first man passed the child to the next. Stumbling for footing in the rocky bottom, he passed the child along, and by then more neighbors were waiting with blankets.

Simon took the little girl Josiah passed to him. The child couldn't be much older than his Becky, and she was crying quietly, her little face wet with tears and rain. "No need to cry," he said quietly. "You'll soon be home and safe."

She sniffled and nodded as he handed her to the next man, turning again to Josiah for another child. The water was getting higher, making it harder to maintain his balance, but the line of helpers never faltered.

Josiah worked steadily next to him, holding on to him as the current battered them. Simon had time to realize how many people he knew there. Amish and Englisch, he had grown up with them. He thought of the elderly man risking his life to save his family pictures. He understood. A lifetime was made up of memories, and Lost Creek was where all his memories had been formed.

For a second he wondered about Aunt Bess and Lyddy, but he knew what they'd be doing. They'd be helping their neighbors, doing their duty, just as everyone else was.

Lydia discovered that there was no time to think about Simon and what had happened to her feelings—

and no time to worry about Simon and Josiah, either. She was far too busy for that. The bakeshop quickly became a center for folks to share information and to stop for a quick cup of coffee before rushing off to help someone else.

Elizabeth set Lydia to making urn after urn of coffee, sending some of it in insulated jugs by volunteers to people working in the hardest-hit areas. Frank appointed himself her helper, and he brought in a small radio that he tuned to the local radio station.

In other circumstances Elizabeth might have objected, but now she didn't even seem to notice. Instead of music, the station switched to a continuous broadcast of news bulletins on the state of the flooding, fielding calls from people reporting on different areas, announcing road and bridge closings, warning people who had to evacuate, and broadcasting appeals for volunteers at the food bank and at the shelter that was rapidly being set up.

Frank, listening to a report of floodwaters going over a dam on Fishers Run, furrowed his brow. "That hasn't happened as long as I can remember. And that's a long time."

"Maybe the rain will let up soon." Lydia tried to find the most encouraging thing she could think of to say, but Frank just shook his head.

"All those streams and runs that empty into Lost Creek will still be pouring into the creek for a couple of days, even if it stops now. We're in for worse before it gets better."

As if to punctuate his words, the electricity flickered and went off. Lydia looked toward Elizabeth, noting the lines of tiredness drawing down her face. But it would do no good to tell her to rest. She'd never stop as long as she saw her duty in front of her.

"Get the water heating on the gas range," Elizabeth said. "One of Frank's friends has been drawing water, so we should be good for a time. And we may as well get everything out of the freezer. Whatever we can't use we'll send to the shelter."

Lydia nodded and headed for the kitchen with Frank on her heels. He grabbed the kettles from her hands. "I'll fill these. Maybe you should start on the freezer."

"Denke. Get someone to help you with the kettles, though."

There were plenty of willing hands now that there was something they could do, and in a few minutes the kitchen had filled with women making sandwiches to take to the shelter and thawing cakes and cookies for use.

Lydia moved quickly back and forth, helping and supervising. The day was so dark that without electricity it was hard to see what they were doing.

"We'll soon be putting ham on the peanut butter sandwiches if we're not careful," she declared. "I'll bring out some lights."

Elizabeth would have several lamps in her apartment upstairs, and there were a few more in the pantry. She put them out on the counter and gave Frank and his friends a crash course in operating the gas lamps.

"Just like at my grandmother's cottage when I was a little boy," Frank declared after pumping one and seeing it start. "It's a good thing you folks still have such things."

Lydia smiled. People who depended on electricity sometimes didn't know what they'd do without it. Elizabeth had electricity in the shop, because otherwise she couldn't serve food, but once the shop was closed, she went back to the customary batteries and propane. Plenty of Amish businesspeople did the same balancing act every day, treading the line between modern convenience and living separately.

Lydia turned at the sound of a clatter at the back door, hoping it might be Josiah or Simon. Instead, it was Daniel Miller, who was now married to Lydia's cousin Beth and owned a general store a little way from town.

"Daniel, what brings you here?"

Carrying an armful of boxes, Daniel was looking for a place to put them down, so she hurried to help him. The boxes were laden with groceries from canned food to coffee.

"When we heard how bad it's getting, we loaded up what we could from the store." Daniel straightened from putting a box on the floor, looking cheerful as usual despite the water dripping from him. "I have more in the wagon to take to the shelter, but I brought what I thought you could use here."

"Wonderful *gut*." The words hardly expressed the gratitude she felt. "You're okay out your way?"

"Fine. The field across the road is flooded, but that won't get to us."

"What about Beth and Noah?" Noah was her cousin's five-year-old son.

He grinned. "Beth is baking up a storm. Emergencies affect her that way. Noah wanted to come with me, but I thought not this time, not knowing how bad the roads might be."

"Give them my love." To her surprise, her eyes welled with tears. "*Denke*."

He shook his head, maybe a little embarrassed. "I brought you a couple of jugs of water from the spring, too. I'll set them inside the back door. And I'll try to bring more tomorrow."

She was running out of words to thank him, but he didn't wait for them, just hurried out to his buggy.

A couple of teenage girls who'd shown up to help started unloading the boxes, and Elizabeth came into the kitchen to see what was going on.

"Ach, people are sehr gut."

"Yah." She turned to the two girls, realizing how quickly time was passing. "Shouldn't you two go home? Won't your mothers be worried?"

The older one, brushing shoulder-length curls back from a pert face, shook her head. "When they dismissed school early, we thought we'd look for somebody to help. They chased us away from the creek, so we came here. I called my mom, and she'll call Gina's mom. We are helping, aren't we?" She was suddenly anxious.

"You're both a wonderful blessing," Lydia said, touched, and they beamed.

The girls moved off to take cans of coffee to Frank and his helpers. Lydia exchanged smiles with Elizabeth. "A flood brings out the good in people," she said.

Elizabeth nodded, but Lydia could see the signs of fatigue in her face and in the way her body drooped. Compassion gripped her. "Please, Elizabeth, go up and rest for a bit."

She knew the answer even before Elizabeth shook her head. "Not now. There's too much to do."

"We have plenty of helpers," she pointed out. "At least sit down here at the table and have some coffee and something to eat. It's a long time since breakfast, and you'll work better if you have some food in you."

It was the only argument that would have worked, and Elizabeth pulled out a chair and slumped down heavily. "Guess that's right."

Once she'd put coffee and a sandwich in front of Elizabeth, Lydia walked out through the front to see if everything was all right. They had set up a separate stand with free coffee and food for volunteers, and she discovered that someone had put another cup out into which a man in a wet slicker and muddy boots was stuffing bills.

"You don't need to—" she began.

He managed a smile, though his face was drawn with worry. "Cash I've got. It's a house I'm worried about now."

"I'm sorry." She couldn't find anything else to say.

"They're trying to save it. I'd better get back."

"Wait a minute." She grabbed a paper bag and stuffed baked goods into it. "Take this for the workers."

"Hey, thanks." This time his smile looked more genuine. "Thanks." He tilted his head. "Listen."

"I don't hear anything." She didn't know what he meant.

"Right. The rain is stopping." He grinned, elated. "Maybe we'll beat the water after all."

Others had realized now, and people streamed out onto the front porch. Sure enough, the sky was starting to lighten a bit, and over the ridge she could see a patch of blue.

"Not over it yet," a voice said in Lydia's ear, and she smiled at Frank.

"No, but it's encouraging, ain't so?"

He was looking at the sky, not at her, and a smile spread across his face. "You think that's encouraging? Look there."

She followed the direction he was pointing, and her breath caught. There, over the ridge, the faintest of colors began to etch themselves on the sky. A rainbow arched across the valley, getting stronger by the moment. A hush seemed to grip those who were watching, and Lydia knew they were as moved as she was.

A rainbow—God's promise that all would be right with the world. Just as it had been for Noah in the Scripture, it was a promise for them, too.

Chapter Ten

Sunlight streaming in the windows of Elizabeth's apartment woke Lydia early, making her wonder where she was. Then yesterday's events swept over her, and she swung herself out of bed. According to the clock, she'd had about three hours of sleep, but she was sure that was more than many people had on that frightening night.

The sound of coughing from Elizabeth's bedroom made her pause and listen, but the sound was not repeated. It would not be surprising if Elizabeth had a relapse after the day she'd put in. With Simon's assistance, she'd finally been able to persuade Elizabeth to get a few hours' sleep.

Simon. For a second she relived the relief that had overwhelmed her when Simon and her brother had returned from their rescue work—grimy, soaked and exhausted, but going on some sort of adrenaline that had them talking and laughing at two in the morning.

Hurrying to dress in the clothes her cousin Beth had kindly sent in by way of Daniel on one of his trips, Lydia tried to arrange her thoughts to meet the challenges of the upcoming day. Without electricity and clean water, the town had seemed paralyzed yesterday, but folks would be bouncing back today. At least those who hadn't suffered damage would.

But the water had continued to rise, and the last she'd heard before tumbling into bed was that they couldn't expect a crest before early tomorrow morning. That meant another full day of losses and misery.

Well, as long as they had gas and water, they'd continue feeding people. And she'd better get started. Tiptoeing down the stairs, she looked around, trying to think of what to do first. Get some coffee started on the stove, she decided, and then see if she could sweep out some of the mud that had been tracked in.

Sweeping her way to the door, she stepped out into a sunlit early morning. It was surprisingly warm for the early hour, and the combination of sunlight and warmth couldn't help lifting her spirits. Main Street looked much as usual, though there were few people out this early. She took a few steps to the corner and looked down the hill toward Lost Creek.

She gasped at the sight that met her eyes. The water had come up dramatically overnight, with several houses inundated up to the second floor. The area used last night to launch boats to take people out of the hazard zone was now under water, as well. But they'd gotten everyone out. That was the important thing.

She and Frank had trundled a wagon loaded with insulated jugs and sandwiches down the hill at some time during the night. They'd provided food and drink to anyone who needed it, rescued and rescuers alike. She'd still been there when the last couple of boats had come in, with Simon and Josiah helping bring them ashore.

"All clear," the fire chief had called when he'd finished his sweep. "We even got the dogs and cats and canaries." Like the others, he was somehow both exhausted and exhilarated.

A ragged cheer had broken out from those waiting as they hurried to help unload the last boats. Finally, when all was finished, they'd straggled back up the hill again.

Lydia stood there lost in memories until she heard a step and Simon moved next to her. He stood with her, looking down at what had once been a peaceful residential area overlooking the creek.

"Could be worse, I guess," he said at last. "We got everyone out."

She wanted to speak, to tell him how she admired his courage and dedication, the sense of responsibility that wouldn't let him quit. But if she brought up so emotional a subject, she'd fall apart, and she couldn't let herself do that. Simon was beginning to see her as a friend. She couldn't ruin it by letting him see that she longed for more.

She cleared her throat. "Did you get some sleep? And Josiah?"

Simon chuckled. "He'll be along in a minute. The guys we were working with insisted on putting us up last night, and the last I saw Josiah, he was stowing away a huge breakfast."

"Gut."

"Yah. There'll be more to do today. I heard they're hoping for help from the county or state, but I doubt they'll get trucks through today. Too many bridges down for that. Maybe tomorrow."

"So we'll get along the best we can, then," she said. "Komm. The coffee should be ready by now."

As he fell into step with her, she realized she hadn't thought to ask an important question. "Have you heard from your Mamm? How is Becky?"

He frowned. "The phone lines are down in a couple of places. I couldn't get through on a regular phone, but one of the guys had a cell phone he let me try. Mamm says they're fine. They'll try to bring water and food in today."

"But the road…"

"The road will be closed awhile yet, but Daad says he and your daad think they can clear enough on the old railroad bed to get a pony cart through, if nothing bigger."

Lydia couldn't believe how encouraging it was to think that they wouldn't be isolated from their families. "I hope Daad thinks to bring some of my clothes," she said lightly. "Everything I have on is borrowed from my cousin Beth."

He glanced at her. "Looks gut on you. Good thing Beth and Daniel are close enough to get back and forth."

As they went inside, she realized he hadn't really answered her question about Becky. Was that on purpose? She wasn't sure, and she waited until they were both supplied with coffee to press the subject.

"How is Becky doing?" She tried to keep her voice casual, not wanting to earn one of his sharp rebukes for intruding into his private affairs.

Simon frowned, staring down into his cup as if looking for an answer there. "Mamm says she keeps asking about me. Last night she couldn't go to sleep until Sarah took her into her bed. Mamm said Sarah told her stories until she fell asleep."

"Sarah is growing up to be a wonderful kind young woman," she said, hoping he'd continue talking.

"She is that," he agreed, but the worry in his face hurt her. "I wish I knew what to do. Becky...since her mammi died, she doesn't want to let me out of her sight. But I'm needed here, not out at the farm. Seems like whatever I do, I'm letting someone down."

She'd hoped he would confide in her, but now that he had, she couldn't seem to find anything to say that would help.

"I'm sorry," she murmured, struggling for words. "I think...well, maybe it's a gut thing. Becky is a smart girl. She'll understand that this is an emergency. And it sounds as if she is getting attached to Sarah and your mamm."

With what seemed a deliberate effort, he wiped away the frown. "You forgot someone."

She blinked, not understanding him. "What..."

"Becky's getting attached to Aunt Bess, too," he said. "And you."

It didn't mean anything, she told herself. "I'm attached to her, too," she said lightly.

Treat it lightly. Don't let him guess your feelings.

It was ironic, she thought. She'd been convinced, after Thomas, that love was too dangerous to be risked. Now that she knew what it was to love, she knew true love was worth the risk. But Simon—Simon didn't think so, and he probably never would.

Simon was still nursing his coffee when Aunt Bess came down from upstairs. A quick look at her face told him two things—she was tired, and she was determined not to give in to it.

Lyddy hurried over to her, putting her arm around his aunt's waist. "What are you doing up so early? I hoped that you would sleep in today after a day like yesterday."

"Nonsense. I'm not old and done yet."

"Of course not. You're just like Frank and his friends, ain't so? Why don't you join Simon? I'll bring you a cup of tea, and you can keep him company."

Aunt Bess looked as if she'd insist on getting right to work, so he rose and pulled out a chair for her.

"Komm, sit. We were so busy yesterday we didn't have time to talk. Looked like you were feeding the multitudes."

That made her smile, and she joined him, slumping down heavily as if exhausted already this morning. Over her head, Lyddy gave him a look of thanks and hurried off to return a few minutes later with the promised tea.

"Yah, we surely did feed a lot of people, what with those who came here and the food we sent over to the shelter." Aunt Bess coughed and took a deep drink of the hot tea. That seemed to remind her of something. "Lyddy, do we have much left from the freezer? It won't keep if it's not cooked."

"Don't worry." Lyddy paused to pat her shoulder. "We got everything into the refrigerator, and I thought I'd start cooking the meat today. And I hear the church where the shelter is has gas ranges, too, so we'll use it all up."

"Gut, gut." She paused again, looking at him. "Will you try to get home today?" She studied his face. "You're worried about Becky." She made it a statement, not a question.

"I think, later. I'll see what's to be done in town, first. With the water going up until sometime tonight, they'll need help." Even as he said the words, he saw Josiah come in, probably looking for him.

Lyddy saw him, too, and rushed to offer him coffee and shoofly pie.

Simon had to laugh at his expression. "Josiah's already stuffed like a turkey, ain't so?"

Josiah grinned. "Just about. I'll come back later for the coffee. Right now we're needed. They're going to evacuate another street, just to be on the safe side."

"Right." He rose, handing the coffee mug to Lyddy. "We'll see you both later."

To his surprise, Lyddy walked to the door with them. "I don't like the way your aunt is coughing," she said, her voice low. "Did you notice?"

He nodded. "Was she all right during the night?"

"I heard her coughing a few times, but she didn't get up, at least." He could see the concern in her eyes.

"You'll try to get her to rest?" He frowned, wishing he knew how sick she'd been during the winter, and whether he ought to be getting a message to his parents.

"I'll do my best, but you know your aunt."

"Only too well." He grimaced, knowing Lyddy was right. Aunt Bess wouldn't allow herself to rest when there was work to be done. "I'll stop back later to see how she is." At least Lyddy was there with her. He was beginning to see just how responsible a woman she'd become.

He and Josiah headed down to the area where they're been working yesterday, pausing for a moment to watch the foaming, whirling water pound its way through the very place where they'd stood to carry things out.

"Bad," he muttered, knowing it was an understatement.

"Look at the size of that tree coming down," Josiah exclaimed. "And that looks like a china closet." He shook his head. "If we'd been here yesterday, we might have seen Lyddy's buggy go by."

"Don't even joke about that. I wish—"

"Now don't say you wish you could have saved it." Josiah gave him a light punch on the arm. "You saved Lyddy and the mare. Nobody could ask for better than that."

But even as he nodded, he was considering what he might have done. He didn't have much time for it, as they were quickly rounded up to carry furniture out of a house. The elderly couple who lived there stood watching.

"No point to that," the man protested, catching Simon by the sleeve. "We've been here fifty years, and the water never has reached us. Besides, if the house is going to go, I'd just as soon go with it."

Simon longed to pull his arm away and get on with the task, but he couldn't. "If it's not needed, so much the better," he said. He glanced at the man's wife, who was tugging at her husband's arm, trying to get him to leave. "I promise, we'll bring it all back. And I think your wife doesn't want you to go down the creek with the house."

"That's right," she declared, pulling him away. "Come along, you old fool. Let the boys do their work."

Simon exchanged a grin with Josiah over being called boys, knowing the scolding tone was a cover for love. He watched them being guided into a car by a volunteer. He understood. Nobody would want to risk losing a lifetime of memories.

They'd finished that house and moved on to the next when Simon heard someone calling his name. Stepping out into the street, he saw Frank waving at him and hurried to him.

"What is it? My aunt?" His heart thudded in his chest.

"Lyddy called the ambulance. She's on her way to the hospital. I've got my car up on Main Street. I'll drive you."

Simon started up the hill at a run and then had to stop, realizing it would do no good to reach the car before Frank. Impatience surged through him. Couldn't Lyddy have found someone else to send?

They were soon on the way to the hospital, though, but Frank couldn't answer any of the questions Simon bombarded him with. He'd gone to take some things to the shelter, and when he came back, Elizabeth was in the ambulance and Lydia climbing in to accompany her. She'd just had time to shout to him to get Simon, so he had.

So Simon, hands clasped into fists, had to wait, his stomach churning. Aunt Bess was as close to him as his grandmother, maybe even closer, because his grandmother had moved to another community. But Aunt Bess was always there.

Frank swung to a stop by the emergency entrance. "They won't let me stay here, so just go straight in. They should be able to tell you where she is. And tell Lyddy not to worry about the shop. We'll take care of it."

Giving a quick nod, Simon jumped out and ran toward the door, then had to stop and identify himself to the nurse who sat behind a glass panel and controlled the door. Once he did, she pressed a buzzer and the door opened.

"The woman who came in with the patient is in the waiting room. She'll be able to tell you what the doctor is saying."

Nodding, he hurried in the direction she indicated. Sure enough, Lyddy sat in a crowded waiting room, hands folded as if she were praying. He strode across to her.

"What has happened? Tell me," he demanded.

"Shh." She frowned at his tone. "Sit down and I'll tell you."

The man next to her, covered in mud and holding his arm against his chest, obligingly slid over a chair so Simon could sit next to Lyddy.

"She got worse after you left," she said quietly. "She didn't want to lie down, but she finally got so dizzy she couldn't argue. She tried to sit down, and then she passed out for a few minutes. So I called 911, and..."

"What has the doctor said?"

"He hasn't come out yet." Her look was full of sympathy. "I'm sure it won't be much longer."

How could he just sit and wait, when Aunt Bess might be dying, for all he knew? "Why didn't you call sooner?" He growled the question, knowing it was unfair, but couldn't help himself.

"Please, Simon." She put her hand on his arm. "Just wait. It's all we can do. All anyone can do." She gestured at the other waiters in the room—people in dirty and sometimes wet clothing, some of them wearing anxious expressions while others seemed numb.

He subsided, telling himself he wasn't the only one. The man next to him gave him a nod. "They're moving pretty fast," he said, as if hoping to console him.

Simon nodded, a little ashamed. "How did you get hurt?"

He grimaced. "Tried to pull a cabinet out the door. Didn't know my dad was pushing from behind and got caught between the cabinet and the doorframe."

"Sorry," he muttered, feeling small. He'd acted as if he were the only one with problems. And he'd blamed Lyddy, when he knew quite well she'd have done everything she could.

A man walked out of the emergency area. Wearing a suit and tie, carrying a briefcase, he looked as if he were in the wrong place at the wrong time.

Everyone in the room stared at him as he walked past them and out the opposite door. Simon's neighbor gave a noise halfway between a snort and a laugh.

"Clean, ain't he?"

As if the words had released a spring, people smiled and started talking to each other. Maybe it didn't solve their problems, but it eased the tension in the room. Including Simon's. He smiled at his neighbor and turned back to Lyddy.

"Sorry," he said, touching her hand lightly. "I didn't mean—"

"I know." She smiled, but her blue eyes were still watchful. "I know."

Relief washed over Lydia when she spotted the doctor heading for them. Simon clearly wasn't very good at waiting in hospitals. Then she realized that it probably made him flash back to Rebecca's death, and she chided herself for being unfeeling.

"The doctor," she murmured to Simon, rising to meet the man.

"Ms. Stoltzfus?" he asked, fumbling a little over the name. She suspected he wasn't from around here, or he'd have known how to pronounce it.

She nodded. "This is the patient's great-nephew, Simon Fisher."

"Ah, good. We always prefer to have a relative. Is there anyone else…?"

"My parents," Simon responded. "But they can't get into town yet. You can talk to me, and I'll tell them."

"Good, good." He led them a little away from the waiting area. "Your aunt is running a fever and coughing, and I understand from her records that she had pneumonia a few months ago. We'll be doing X-rays to have a look at her lungs, but I can't hear anything, so that's good."

Lydia nodded, familiar with the rasping sound in Elizabeth's chest during her last illness. "Will she have to stay here?"

"We'll want to keep her overnight, at least, until all the test results come back. If all is well, then she can leave." He looked harassed. "She'll need care, and I'd like to see her out of the flood zone. If the family can't do it, there are nursing homes—"

"No," Simon said quickly, before Lydia could protest. "The family will take care of her as soon as she's able to be moved. I'm sure of that."

Lydia was equally sure, but like everything else in the middle of a flood, it proved to be difficult to arrange. By the time Simon got through to his parents and they contacted the rest of the family, it was several hours later.

Eventually, it came down to Simon's parents, who took up the responsibility of Elizabeth's care. Enos and Mary Fisher, along with Simon's sister, Sarah, and Becky were all gathered around the table in the kitchen of Elizabeth's apartment. Mary Fisher had arrived with a basket full of baked goods to supplement their supplies in the shop. With a freshly baked cherry pie in the middle of the table, Lydia couldn't help but smile. Like virtually every Amish woman, Mary met emergencies with food.

"We've talked to the others," Enos was saying, "and they're all agreed that we take Elizabeth to our house, at least for the time being. Now that we've opened the old track through the woods, we can get back and forth."

Lydia had suspected that was what would happen. Elizabeth had always been especially close to Enos's family, and the farmhouse was her old home.

"Jim Foster says he'll bring her to the house once the hospital lets her go," Mary said. "She'll be more comfortable in his truck than in a buggy. About the shop—"

"Ach, you don't need to worry about the shop," Lydia said quickly. "I'll keep things going here until Elizabeth is well. And until things get back to normal, we'll just have to carry on the way we are."

"You'll need help." Mary looked concerned. "You can't handle it all alone."

"I'll help," Sarah said promptly. "I can do it." She glanced from Lydia to her mother. "Honest I can."

"I'm thinking Lyddy could handle anything she wanted to," Simon said, and he seemed to surprise himself as much as he did her. "But it would perhaps be best for Becky and me to move into this apartment for the time being. And Sarah, too, if you'll let her."

"I don't think..." Lydia spoke before she could think. All her instincts told her that having Simon here full time was far too dangerous for her peace of mind.

"Lyddy, please." Sarah reached across the table to catch her hand. "You know how much I'd love to help."

"And having Becky here will make her much more comfortable," Simon added. "She'd just be in the way when you're nursing Aunt Bess, Mamm, and I don't like her to deal with any more upheaval. Not that you wouldn't take wonderful gut care of her," he added hastily.

Simon was concentrating on swaying his parents to his way of thinking, Lydia told herself. He wasn't thinking of her at all. Of course he wasn't. He had no idea she'd been so foolish as to fall in love with him.

Mary nodded reluctantly. "I suppose so. But it's really up to Lyddy, isn't it?"

"For sure," Simon said, turning his gaze on her. "Please, Lyddy?" he said, repeating his sister's words with a slight smile.

Her heart seemed to tremble at that smile, and she knew she didn't have a choice. No matter what it did to her, she had to agree.

"Yah," she said. "That will be fine."

Chapter Eleven

When Lydia got home that night, driving Dolly along the railroad bed with the pony cart Daad had brought in for her, she decided she could handle the challenging days as long as she could get home and sleep in her own bed at night. In fact, when she reached her bedroom to clean up for supper, the bed was so appealing it was all she could do not to slip under her quilt and escape into sleep.

Selfish, she chided herself. There were still people in town who wouldn't be able to sleep in their own beds for a number of nights to come. So she splashed some cold water on her face and hurried downstairs to help get supper on.

Once the whole family was gathered around the table, Daad bowed his head in the sign to begin their silent prayer. It struck her that Daad held the silence longer, and she knew why. They were all praying for whatever would come when Lost Creek crested sometime in the night.

Food started to circulate around the table. Josiah, heaping a mound of mashed potatoes on his plate, glanced at Daad. "Did you hear that the highway department is talking about running a new road alongside the old one, but farther from the creek?"

"I heard." Daad grimaced. "Whatever they do, it'll take time. We'll have to get used to using the railroad bed until then. Lyddy, how was it when you drove home?"

Her mind was several miles away, but she managed to collect herself. "Not bad. It was boggy in one spot, but Dolly got through. She gave me a look about being hitched to the pony cart, though."

Josiah laughed. "She's spoiled, that's what. If she'd gotten the buggy out of the creek—"

"Don't," Mammi said sharply. "That is nothing to joke about. Just thank the gut Lord for preserving our Lyddy. And Dolly."

"Yah, I do." Josiah looked abashed, and Lyddy gave him an understanding look. They'd both seen so much sorrow in the past days that it was better to joke than to weep.

"I know the spot you mean," Daad said, firmly changing the subject. "If I can get a load of gravel, we'll be able to make that better. We can take it up in the old spring wagon."

Josiah nodded. "I'll help. We could do it in no time. It'd be gut to have it done before they try to bring Elizabeth out to the Fishers' place."

"So Simon and Becky will be moving into Elizabeth's apartment, I hear." Grossmammi's gaze grew thoughtful, and Lydia hoped that wasn't matchmaking she had in her eyes. "I'm not sure how much help he'll be in the coffee shop, but it's better than having the place empty. Or you being there alone, Lyddy."

"I'm sure he'll find something to do." She was determined to put a good face on the situation. "Elizabeth wants me to keep on offering free coffee and drinks to all the volunteers, and another pair of hands will help. And his sister is coming in, as well. She'll watch Becky along with helping in the kitchen."

"I'll bake tomorrow," Mammi said, eyes glowing at the thought of cooking for more people. "And Dorie said to tell you she'll be bringing some things to the bake shop, as well."

Dorie, Lydia's older sister, lived with her family on the other side of town, so she shouldn't have trouble coming in. She just hoped Dorie wouldn't bring her three-year-old twins along. Much as Lydia loved her little nephews, she hated the thought of having those two active boys run free through the coffee shop.

"That will be a big help," she said, her words interrupted by an enormous yawn.

"Ach, you've had such a couple of days." Mammi began gathering up plates. "After dessert you'll go straight to bed."

She hated to admit how wonderful that sounded. "I'll help with the dishes—" she began, but Mammi interrupted her.

"You'll do no such thing. As if I can't manage them by myself. Sleep is the best thing for you right now."

Josiah grinned. "You might as well give in. I'd guess no one will tell me or Simon to go to bed early, and we put in a long day, too."

"You go up early, as well," Mammi scolded. "And I'd tell Simon the same if I had him under my wing."

Lydia began serving the cherry pie Mammi had cut,

and she managed to elbow her brother while she did it. "You mind Mammi too, you hear?"

He gave her a mock glare. "I'll say this, I found out hauling furniture isn't so easy, especially on stairs. And when folks are following you around, all upset, it's even worse."

Mamm clucked in sympathy, looking as if she'd take all those folks in, if she could. Of course she would. Everyone would do what they could in a crisis like this. But it would still be a long road back for some of those people.

Half an hour later, Lydia was twisting her hair into a long, loose braid, ready to slip into bed, when someone rapped softly.

"Komm." Maybe Mammi, wanting to fuss a little more.

But it was Grossmammi. "Let's talk a few minutes before you sleep," she said, closing the door.

Lydia sat down and patted the bed beside her. "I can always stay awake for you."

"Ach, that's ferhoodled, for sure." Grossmammi settled herself and clasped her hand. "Now tell me the things you didn't say. About Simon."

Lydia could only stare at her for a long moment. Denying it would be useless. Grossmammi would always know the truth. "I love him," she whispered. "I never thought, after what happened with Thomas, that I could love someone."

"That was even more ferhoodled," Grossmammi said. "What happened to Thomas was not your fault, and he's alive to make a new start because of you and Josiah. It has nothing to do with what you feel for Simon."

"No. It doesn't." And she was able to believe that was true. "But Simon doesn't think of me that way. Even if he did," she hesitated, "I know he hasn't accepted losing Rebecca."

"Let me tell you a secret," Grossmammi said. "Most times men don't notice what's right in front of them until they're pushed into it."

She couldn't help smiling at her grandmother's philosophy. "I don't think I'd be very good at pushing him. And Rebecca..." Her throat tightened at the thought of his loss and Becky's.

Grossmammi's fingers tightened on hers. "Are you sure? It's been nearly a year, and he did come back."

Her eyes filled with tears. "He won't talk about her. Can't talk about her, even to Becky. And that child needs to know what to think about her mammi. She's all tied up inside with it."

"Have you talked to her?"

That was a sore spot. "I would, but any mention of her mother to Becky makes Simon so angry. He says he'll tell her anything she needs to know. But he doesn't."

"Sounds like he needs something to force him into it." Grossmammi gave a short nod. "I'll pray on it."

Lydia blinked away tears. "Denke," she murmured, although she couldn't imagine what that something would be. She was silent for a moment, trying to recover herself. "But even so, I don't think he'll ever love someone else the way he loved Rebecca."

Her grandmother studied her face for a long moment, her eyes filled with the wisdom of years. "Maybe not," she said finally. "She was his first love. But that doesn't mean she has to be his only love. There is always room in the heart for more."

Lydia wanted, so much, to believe that. But she didn't know if she could.

Lydia had just finished making the first pot of coffee at the shop the next morning when she heard noises at the kitchen door. She turned to greet Becky, who came running to give her such a big hug it seemed she hadn't seen Lydia for a week.

"Lyddy, I'm back," she said, and the happiness in her face melted Lydia's heart. How could she object to having Simon and Becky living here when it obviously meant so much to the child?

"I'm wonderful glad to see you." She glanced over Becky's head to smile at Simon and Sarah.

Simon just nodded in greeting, but Sarah looked almost as happy as Becky. Tying an apron around her waist, she hurried to Lydia. "I'm ready to help. Just tell me what I should do."

Deciding to take her at her word, Lydia sent her off to the storeroom to bring in a fresh supply of paper cups. The coffee shop normally served its coffee in the thick white mugs most people preferred, but until they had water coming out the spigot, it would be impossible to keep enough of them washed.

"What can I do?" Becky tugged at her hand, but Simon grasped the child's shoulder for a moment.

"Just let me have a word with Lyddy, and then you can talk," he said.

Becky nodded, agreeable as always to anything her father suggested. It occurred to Lydia that she'd never even seen Becky pout a little at an unpopular suggestion. Lyddy appreciated cooperative children, but somehow a little dissatisfaction would seem more normal.

But Simon was claiming her attention. "I'll bring in the jugs of spring water I brought with me, and then I think I'd best see what happened when the water crested. I'll probably be needed there again today."

"We'll be fine here. Won't we, Becky?" She got the expected nod. "Come back and tell us about it when you have time. And tell any of the volunteers you see that there's free coffee and snacks again today."

He nodded and bent to give Becky a hug. "Don't forget to help and be sure to tell Sarah or Lyddy if you need anything."

Without waiting for a response, he turned and was gone in a few long strides.

She would not stand here staring after him. There was work to be done.

Sarah returned with the cups, and together they began to get the shop ready to open. Becky trailed behind them, helping everywhere she could, and Lyddy soon realized she'd have to find something to occupy the child, especially when they were carrying pots of hot water around the kitchen.

Luckily she had just the project at hand. "Becky, we need to put up a couple of new signs, so that people who are helping in the flood area know they can have free coffee. Do you want to help with those?"

That was a project after Becky's heart, as she knew, and in a few minutes the little girl was settled at a small table ready to color in and decorate the wording Lydia had done.

Sarah smiled when Lydia returned to the kitchen.

"Becky sure loves to color and draw. That will keep her busy."

"And doing something helpful." She glanced back in Becky's direction, loving the total concentration on her face. "That seems really important to her…that she's helping, especially her daadi."

"Yah, I noticed that, too." Sarah bent over the oven, pulling out the pan of cinnamon rolls she'd been warming. She hadn't waited to be asked. She'd just done it. Clearly, she was another person who wanted to be helpful.

With her dark brown hair and eyes, Sarah looked very much like her older brother. Fortunately, Lydia thought, she didn't have his square, stubborn jaw.

"I'll open the door. We're as ready as we can be."

When she reached the door, she found that Frank and his buddies had already arrived. "Come in. You're early today."

"We've all got jobs for the day," he said, obviously relishing having something important to do. "Some at the shelter and some at the food bank. But we have to have our coffee, first."

"Coming right up," she said. "You know it's free to you in return for all your volunteering."

She could hear them teasing each other about who deserved free coffee, and then the shop started to get busy. She didn't get back to their table until they were leaving and wasn't surprised at all to find that someone had left money on the table, despite her offer. But that was the sort of people they were, she knew. She put the money in the box they were using for a cash register until the electricity came back on.

The morning seemed to fly past, almost as fast as the

rumors that were flying about what was going to happen when. Apparently, assistance hadn't arrived from the state yet, but the Salvation Army was already busy finding housing for those who were displaced.

"It must be awful not to even know what you can save from your house," Sarah commented, loading a tray. "I feel so bad for them."

"I'm sure your brother will have some stories to tell about it when he gets back. At least folks are doing everything possible to help them." She paused for a moment while Sarah carried the tray of doughnuts to the front, thinking how useful the girl was being.

"What next?" Sarah said, coming back.

"Next I think you should sit down and have something to eat for yourself." Lydia gestured toward the table. "I'll take care of the front, but it looks as if we'll have a lull for a bit."

"I'm fine," Sarah protested. "This is the most fun I've had in a long time."

It occurred to Lydia that the girl was probably doing the very things that she'd consider chores at home. But being here was different, and that was important at Sarah's age.

"You like getting out of the house, I guess," she ventured.

"For sure." Sarah poured a cup of coffee for each of them. "Did you know that my twin is going to start as an apprentice at the machine shop this summer? He's not a bit older than me, but when I told Mammi I wanted a job like him, she wouldn't listen."

"Working in a machine shop?" Lydia asked, smiling.

Sarah giggled. "That would be fun, wouldn't it? But I'd like to work in a restaurant or here, in the coffee shop. I don't see why I shouldn't learn to do something useful."

Lydia couldn't agree more, but she decided it wouldn't be right to say so. Not unless she wanted to get into trouble with Sarah's parents.

"Everyone has a job but me," Sarah said, a trace of rebellion in her voice.

"You know, when Simon sees how capable you are here, he might be willing to talk to your parents about it," she suggested. Simon wouldn't appreciate her interference, she guessed, but Sarah deserved some encouragement.

"You feel he might?" Her face lit up at the thought.

"It's worth a try," she said. "Since we're not so busy right now, I'm going to run upstairs and see what needs to be done for tonight."

"All right," Sarah called after her. "But I'll do it."

Smiling, she went lightly up the stairs. Sarah was really mature for her fourteen years. Maybe, like everyone else, she was rising to the occasion.

One of the bedroom doors stood open, so she headed for it first, making a mental note that the beds would have to be changed. When Lydia stepped inside, everything she was thinking flew out of her head.

Becky sat on the edge of the bed. She had taken her braid down from under her kapp, and as Lydia watched, she picked up a red marker and started to color a strand of corn silk blond hair.

"Becky, stop." She hurried over to the child, reminding herself that she must be careful. Simon wouldn't want her to interfere, but he also wouldn't want his daughter to color her hair red.

Becky looked up at the sound of her voice, clutching the marker, and her face set stubbornly. "I want to color my hair."

Gently, she reminded herself. "You do? I don't think markers are very good for that." She took the marker from the child's hand, relieved that Becky didn't resist.

"I want to," she repeated.

"I see that you do." There was something almost desperate in the set look of the child's face, and she prayed silently for guidance, her heart aching. "But why? I think you have pretty hair."

For a moment she thought Becky wouldn't answer, and she wished Simon was here to deal with his daughter. But then Becky looked up at her, blue eyes filling with tears.

"People keep saying I'm like my mammi. But I'm not. I'm not! Mammi could do everything. I can't do anything."

Dropping the marker, Lydia gathered Becky's hands in hers. Her throat was so tight she struggled to speak, and she had to. She had to assure this precious child that she was unique and loved.

"Becky, you have it all wrong. Really. Mammi was a grown-up woman, and you're such a little girl. I think by the time you grow up, you'll be able to do all the things Mammi did, and maybe even more."

Becky's expression didn't change. She was failing to get through to her.

"People say it. All the time."

"People say silly things sometimes." Herself included. But who could guess the child would interpret the innocent words that way? "They're just trying to start talking to you. They mean that you look like your Mammi did when she was a little girl. That's all."

Some of the tension drained from her face. "Are you sure?"

"Yah. I'm positive. I said it to you, and that's what I meant."

Becky considered the words, her face serious. "But…if I'm not like Mammi, will Daadi love me just as much?"

"Ach, Becky, of course he will." Her grandmother's words slipped into her mind, and she clung to them. "There's always room in the heart for more love."

Hope dawned slowly on Becky's face. Then she threw herself into Lydia's arms. Tears spilling over, Lydia held her close. A faint sound made her glance toward the door. Simon stood there. Watching. Listening. And she couldn't tell what he was thinking.

Simon froze, immobile with shock from the power of that conversation. He shook it off, trying to be angry with Lyddy for talking to Becky about her mother after he'd made his feelings clear. But he couldn't. He couldn't, because however it had happened, Becky had turned to Lyddy, not to him. Lyddy had brought out the things that he needed to know about his daughter.

This wasn't a time for recriminations. Lyddy had already seen him, and in a moment, Becky might turn and spot him, too. Praying for the right words to say, he walked quietly into the room.

Lyddy moved, as if she'd get up and leave the room, but he gestured her to stay. She was in this now, like it or not. Becky looked up, saw him and huddled against Lyddy, the gesture hurting his heart.

"Lyddy is right, ain't so?" He sat down next to them, touching his daughter gently. "There's always room for love in your heart. Your mammi taught me that, and I know she wants you to know it, too."

Becky looked up at him, blue eyes wide and wondering. "You...you're sure?"

"I'm sure."

"You see?" Lyddy said. "You don't need to color your hair or try to be perfect. Daadi loves you just the way you are."

He spotted the markers scattered on the quilt as Lyddy touched Becky's braid lightly. Why would she think...? But that didn't matter right now. What mattered was that his daughter know he loved her more than anything.

Stroking her hair, he smiled at her, hoping she couldn't see the tears in his eyes. "I would love you just the same if your hair was purple with green stripes. Okay?"

Becky giggled, and the tension seemed to vanish as if it had never been. "Mammi wouldn't like purple and green, would she?"

"Probably not. You know, when you were a tiny baby, you had a little wisp of blond hair right on top of your head. And Mammi said it was the prettiest curls she'd ever seen."

"She did?"

But even as he nodded, her little face clouded up again.

"Sometimes...sometimes I can't remember things about Mammi," she whispered. "I don't want to forget."

Simon felt as if he'd been stabbed in the heart. How could he have been so thoughtless? How could he have understood so little?

"You know, I think that's because we haven't talked enough about her." And it was his fault. "Suppose we make an agreement between us. Whenever you want to talk about Mammi, I'll help you remember. And you'll do the same for me. All right?"

Her smile blossomed. To his surprise, his daughter reached out and patted his cheek as if to comfort him. "I promise, Daadi."

His throat closed completely, and he couldn't possibly speak. He looked at Lyddy in a wordless appeal for help.

"I think we'd better go back and help Sarah, don't you think? She probably needs us."

"Okay." Becky hopped off the bed as if none of this had happened. "I'll help."

As Lydia moved to follow her, Simon touched her arm. "Denke, Lyddy. Denke."

He should say more, but he couldn't. He'd have to hope she understood. But as they walked down the steps together, he realized he didn't need to worry about that. Lyddy was probably the most understanding person he knew.

Chapter Twelve

By the next morning, Lydia had come to terms with her feelings. As she drove up the trail to the woods and then turned onto the makeshift road, the sunlight filtering through the trees seemed a promise of better things to come. If not for her, then at least for Simon and his daughter. She had to rejoice over that, and she did.

She had feared, in those first moments after she'd seen Simon standing at the door listening to his daughter, that his reaction would be an explosion of wrath against her. But Simon had finally listened instead of closing his heart, and the results could only be good. He'd opened up to his daughter at last, and Becky's response was lovely. Her heart warmed again at the memory of that small child patting her father's cheek to comfort him.

If only she could comfort him, but she knew she couldn't. Not unless he opened up to her the way he had to his daughter, and she'd seen no signs that he'd even thought of doing that.

Lost Creek looked better this morning, she decided. Not back to normal yet, but with the sun shining and the streets dry again, the few people she saw looked more cheerful than they had for the past two days.

Stabling Dolly, she hurried inside, to be met by the fragrance of brewing coffee. Clearly, Sarah had remembered what Lydia had told her. With all their dependence now on the gas stove, it was a juggling act to get everything done.

Sarah turned from the stove at the sound of her footsteps and gave her a beaming smile. "The coffee is ready. Can I pour a cup for you?"

Instinct told her the girl would be disappointed if she refused. "Smells wonderful gut. Yah, I'd love one. It was still a little chilly when I left home."

Hanging up her heavy sweater, she scrubbed her hands and did a quick check of the kitchen. Sarah had gone above and beyond, with a pan of breakfast cake just coming out of the oven, and several trays of rolls ready to go out front.

"Everything looks fine." She checked the clock. "We'll open in fifteen minutes, so if you haven't eaten, now's the time."

Sarah giggled. "My bruder fixed breakfast for us this morning. I never knew that Simon could cook eggs. Or anything else." She poured coffee for both of them and brought the cups to the table. "I wish we could use the regular mugs. I think the paper cups give a different taste."

"Don't say that to any of the customers." The voice came from above them as Simon came down the steps, with Becky skipping alongside him. Becky darted ahead of her father to give Lydia a hug.

Lydia hugged her back, marveling at the change a few hours had made in Becky. Now she looked like a normal, happy little girl instead of the anxious, fearful little mouse she'd been.

"Have you had breakfast already?" she asked.

Becky nodded vehemently. "My daadi made breakfast. He makes wonderful gut dippy eggs." She smiled up at Lydia. "He'll make some for you, ain't so, Daadi?"

If that had caused Simon any embarrassment, she'd have found it encouraging, but he just smiled and turned to check the front of the shop.

She was thankful to God for what had happened between Simon and Becky, she told herself fiercely. She didn't expect anything else. But her unruly heart denied the words even as she thought them. All this time that she'd been uninterested in marriage—now she knew it hadn't been just wariness. It had been because she was waiting for Simon. But she couldn't say the same about him.

"Time to open," she said cheerfully. "Do you think we're ready, Sarah?"

Pleased at being consulted, Sarah nodded, then was attacked by a sense of caution. "I think. If I missed anything, you'll tell me, won't you?"

Lydia smiled, nodding. Sarah had learned a great deal in just a day. "I promise. Let's do it."

In a few minutes they were busy with the usual morning rush. Lydia threw herself into work, relieved for the distraction from her own thoughts.

As the rush was abating, Frank and his friends came in, and she hurried to get their table ready. Responding to their usual greetings and joking felt like getting back to normal for about a minute. Then they started updating her on all the news, and Simon came over to listen.

"The crest came through about one a.m., near as I

could tell," Frank said. "The rumor is there's considerable damage to the water treatment plant, so no water in the pipes for a week or more."

"You should hear my wife on the subject," somebody else complained. "She'll have me hauling water all day if she has her way."

"So that's why you're here." Frank grinned at him. "Anyway, they're going to let people on Tenth Street back into their houses today. Water didn't reach the first floor, thank goodness."

Simon noticeably relaxed, and she remembered he'd been moving furniture from those houses the previous day. "They'll have a lot to do," he pointed out.

Frank nodded. "They're asking for help, but not before ten o'clock. Guess the emergency management people have to okay it first."

Simon glanced at the clock. "I'll go down then if you can spare me here." He looked at Lydia as if she were in charge.

"Whatever you want," she said. "We'll manage."

Frank started talking about their plans to run food and beverages down to the workers later, and by the time she looked up again, Simon was gone.

Forcing herself to focus on what they could supply, she went back to the kitchen. She and Sarah were quickly immersed in work, with Becky running back and forth being helpful.

It was nearly ten when Simon reappeared in the kitchen. "Can you come out for a minute, Lyddy?" he asked. "I want to show you where I'm putting the water jugs that Daniel King brought in."

With a quick glance to be sure everything was running properly, Lydia followed him.

Simon led her to the shed attached to the stable, but once there, he seemed to forget why they'd come.

"The water storage?" she reminded him, sensing tension and not knowing how to account for it.

"Ach, I didn't need to haul you out here just for that." He gestured at a row of water jugs. "You can see for yourself. I just…" He seemed to run out of words.

Lydia studied his face, trying not to think about how dear it had become to her. "Is something wrong?"

"No, no." Prompted, he seemed to find he could go on. "I hardly had a chance to thank you yesterday. And you have to know how much I appreciate what you did. Even when I told you not to." He gave her a rueful grin.

"That's all right. I was butting in and trying to take charge, like always. My cousin Miriam says I'm like a tornado sweeping up everything in my path once I get started."

It would be easier for both of them to turn it off lightly than to talk about it seriously.

But from the way Simon was shaking his head, it seemed he wouldn't let her get away with that. "When I put Becky to bed last night, we sat for a long time talking about her mammi." He grimaced. "I'm her father. I should have seen how much she needed to talk. You did."

"Ach, don't think that." She could hardly get the words out fast enough. "You were trying to handle your own grief." She saw his face tighten at that and slipped away from such dangerous territory. "It's often easier for an outsider to see a problem than the person who's involved."

That made it sound as if she weren't involved. She

was, with her whole heart, but she couldn't say that to him.

"Even so…"

She understood his reluctance to let go of the blame, and she wasn't sure anyone could help him with that. But she had to try.

"You couldn't help it, Simon. Nobody could. I know you feel responsible…"

"I am responsible." His voice was filled with passion. "I was responsible for taking care of Rebecca, and I failed her. And then I failed her daughter."

Somehow she knew soft words wouldn't help now. "Don't be so ferhoodled," she said sharply. "You couldn't have predicted the accident. Or prevented it."

"If I'd been driving the buggy—"

"If you had been driving the buggy, maybe you'd both be gone, and Becky would be left alone. How would that help anyone?" Afraid to say too much and afraid to say too little, she stopped.

"I know what I know." His stubbornness had never been more pronounced. He pushed the door open and held it for her. "I'll always be thankful you helped Becky, Lydia. But don't try to help me. No one can do that."

Obeying his gesture, she walked out of the shed. He was right. As long as he felt the way he did, no one could help him.

Simon walked down the slight hill toward the creek, but his thoughts were still on Lyddy. It was as natural as breathing for her to want to help, but in this case she couldn't, and it was best she realized it.

He didn't want to hurt her. That was uppermost in his

mind at the moment. It had become crucial that Lyddy not be hurt, by him or by anyone else.

He reminded himself that he had no responsibility to Lyddy except as a friend, but that didn't seem to make a difference to his feelings. He'd known her since childhood, and he owed her a debt he could never repay.

Forcing himself away from thoughts of Lydia, he tried to focus on the scene in front of him. The creek was fast, roiled and muddy, but it had gone down visibly, leaving behind it a sea of mud with a rank smell. The houses on Eleventh Street still had water lapping at their doorsteps, but the ones they'd emptied yesterday were safe. They'd have to have water pumped out of the cellars, but at least it hadn't reached the first floor. As soon as they could get the trucks in, volunteer firefighters would begin the pumping process. It'd be a long job.

"You did come back."

Simon turned at the voice to find the elderly couple he'd met the day before. They were looking tired but considerably more cheerful than they previously had.

"I said I'd come back," he reminded the man. "How are you? Did you have a place to sleep?"

"Goodness, yes. Our friends have been so nice, and they said they'd come to help so we can get back to normal." The wife seemed so happy that Simon didn't have the heart to point out that the basement was most likely full of mud and water that it would begin to stink if it hadn't already.

"I told you my house hadn't flooded in fifty years," her husband said, interrupting. "Now don't forget your promise when the truck brings our furniture."

His wife hushed him disapprovingly, but Simon just

smiled. "I'll be here. But just now I'd best see what they want me to do first."

His spirits lifting irrationally that they, at least, had been spared the worst, he went over to where the police were organizing volunteers.

With a job in hand, Simon helped remove the sand-bags that had done their job. This spring had for sure been different than he'd expected. Different, but not really disappointing. There was work to be done, and he could do it.

More volunteers arrived as the morning went on. Josiah showed up, along with Simon's daad and brothers. With all those willing hands, the work went quickly, and they were soon diverted to unloading the furniture for the Tenth Street houses.

It seemed inevitable that he'd be carrying back in the furniture he'd carried out yesterday, with the same elderly man hovering over them to make sure he did it right.

He must have seen a resemblance between Simon and his father, because he stopped Simon to ask and be introduced.

"We're mighty thankful," he said, shaking Daad's hand vigorously. "We didn't get any water in the house, like I said, though."

"Better safe than sorry," his wife added. She lowered her voice as her husband moved out of range. "He doesn't like to admit he needs help," she whispered. "Thank you. Thank you," she repeated, tears glistening in faded blue eyes. "God bless you."

Daad clapped him on the back as they moved on to the next job. "That's better than any pay," he said. "You did a gut thing for them."

"Lots of folks are," he protested. "Including you."

"And Lyddy," Daad said, glancing past him.

Simon turned to find Lyddy and her elderly admirers handing out sandwiches and drinks to both volunteers and victims.

"Yah." He watched her talking with people, expressing caring in every word and gesture. Everyone seemed to know her, or else they could respond to her warmth even without knowing her. He could only marvel at the woman she'd become.

"Lyddy's a fine girl," his father said, too casually. "I don't know what Aunt Bess would do without her. Or a lot of other people. Ain't so?" His raised his eyebrows, and Simon thought he recognized the look in his eyes.

"Don't tell me Aunt Bess has got you matchmaking, too," he groaned. "Yah, Lyddy's a wonderful gut person, but I'm not looking for a wife." He hoped that would end it.

Daad nodded, but he hadn't lost the twinkle in his eyes.

"Maybe you should be," he said, tossing the words back over his shoulder as he headed for the sandwiches and coffee.

Lydia went back to the coffee shop, feeling oddly flat. She'd seen Simon, but he'd made no effort to come over and speak to her.

Well, why should he? Seeing him every day was already having an effect if she expected attention from him in a situation like this. Sarah came back from the phone, looking pleased. "That was Mamm. She says Aunt Bess is coming home. She wants you to pack up some things for her. I wrote them down." Sarah handed her a list. "They'll stop and get them on the way home."

"Wonderful." She scanned the list. "How soon are they coming? Maybe I should get them ready before I start anything else."

"Mammi said she was going to the hospital now. Someone is driving and will take them back home."

Lydia nodded. "I'll do it now, if you can manage here."

No need to ask—Sarah was delighted to be left in charge. Holding the list, Lydia hurried up the stairs.

Hearing someone behind her, she turned to find Becky scrambling after her.

"I'll help," she said.

Smiling, Lydia took her hand. "Those must be your favorite words," she teased gently.

Becky dimpled. "I like to help better than anything." She stopped to consider with that grave look of hers. "Except maybe coloring."

Her careful honesty made Lydia feel small. How many adults could be as honest about themselves? She didn't think she could.

It wasn't hard to find the things on the list, since Elizabeth's bedroom and bathroom were as well-organized as every other aspect of her life. Lydia handed each item to Becky, who put it carefully in the small suitcase Elizabeth used for her rare trips.

Lydia found herself wondering, as they worked, if this illness spelled the end of Elizabeth's life here over her shop. Goodness knew that most of her kin had been trying for years to convince her to make her home with them. It might be the best thing she could so. But what would happen to the shop then?

"Lyddy?" Becky's voice interrupted her thoughts. "Yah?"

"I heard someone talking," she said carefully, as if not wanting to say who, "and she said that Daadi should get married again so I would have a mammi. But I already have a mammi, even if she's in heaven."

Lydia had to clench her teeth to keep from saying what she thought about supposed adults who'd be so careless as to say that in front of a child. Several Amish women who baked for the shop had been in that morning, and she could guess which of them it had been. For Becky's sake, she had to move carefully now.

Becky tugged at her sleeve. "What did they mean?"

She was committed to being Becky's friend, and she had to be as honest as the child was.

"People sometimes say silly things," she began. "I'm sure they know that no one could replace your mammi. I expect they thought that if Daadi got married, it would be to someone who would love you and take care of you like a mammi would. Not replace her but try hard to do what she would do."

She looked for signs of understanding in the small face. Becky nodded slowly.

"Do you think Daadi will?" she asked.

Another difficult question that required an honest answer. "I don't think so," she said. "At least, not right now. But you could talk to him about it."

Becky considered that. "Maybe not right now," she said, echoing Lydia's phrase.

That seemed to finish their conversation, so Lydia checked the list one last time and snapped the suitcase closed. "Okay, we're finished," she said. "Denke."

Together they walked out of the room, only to find

Simon looking into one of the kitchen cabinets. Lydia's stomach clenched. Was she never to have a conversation with Becky that he didn't overhear? She braced herself for a lecture on the subject of minding her own business.

But none came. Simon seemed occupied by something else. "I just came in when Mammi called again. She's up at the hospital getting Aunt Bess ready to leave, and she says Bess wants some of her special tea. Do you know what that is? I don't see it."

Relieved, she reached into the cabinet he had opened. The tin was right in front of him.

"It's this one. An herbal blend that she makes with mint and ginger. Was there anything else?"

"Not now," he said, relaxing. "But I imagine there will be something else about every day for a while."

Lydia almost asked him if he thought his aunt would be giving up the shop, but stopped herself, first because he might consider it interfering but also because she felt sure he wouldn't know, any more than she did. She headed down the stairs, very aware of him behind her and knowing she'd be waiting the rest of the day for him to tackle her about what he'd overheard.

Chapter Thirteen

Lydia stood outside the shop with Becky, waving as Elizabeth rode off looking like a queen, ensconced in the back seat with blankets and pillows around her. Becky waved energetically, but she was easily distracted when Lydia suggested they bake some cookies.

"I'm going to help make cookies," she announced when she entered the kitchen, heading straight for the oven.

"Yah, but we wash our hands first before touching food. Ain't so?"

Becky nodded, hurrying to the sink and standing on tiptoe to reach the faucet. Lydia watched her affectionately. What a wonderful thing it was to see Becky so happy and sure of herself. It was too bad that Elizabeth wasn't here to see it.

Her mind immediately switched gear to what would happen to the shop if Elizabeth didn't feel able to come back. She could always get another job, of course, but it wouldn't be the same. She'd always felt part of the business here with Elizabeth. No one else was likely to treat her so.

She shook the thought away irritably and set out to make a big batch of snickerdoodle cookies with Becky. As they stirred and rolled the cookies into balls, Becky kept up a steady stream of chatter. It was as if she were making up for all the silent days at one time. Once they got a couple of trays in the oven she waited, watching the oven doors anxiously.

"They're fine," Lydia assured her. "We have to give them time to bake."

"You're sure they'll be crinkly on top?"

"You know, I always used to wonder how they got that way," she said, smiling at Becky's surprise that Lydia should have worried about that, too. "I still don't know, but I know they always do."

That seemed to be good enough for Becky. She stepped back immediately when Lydia asked her to, holding her breath until the first tray of cookies was on the rack. She stood on tiptoe to check them out.

"They are crinkly," she crowed. "We did it."

"We certainly did." Grabbing a spatula, Lydia lifted the first cookie out, putting it on a small plate for Becky. "Mind you let it cool until I tell you it's okay. We don't want a burned tongue, now, do we."

Becky nodded solemnly, trying to look down at her tongue, and making Lydia laugh at the resulting expression. For a moment she wished Simon hadn't gone back to the work site so that he could enjoy the fun. But if he were, it would be hard to stop…

The bell on the front door jingled, and not sure where Sarah was, Lydia settled Becky at the table with her cookie and hurried through the swinging door.

Ella Burkhalter came through, carrying a large basket carefully. "Ach, Lyddy, I hope these rolls aren't down to crumbs by now. I wanted to bring something along to help, but the road is still torn up out our way."

"That's so kind of you, Ella. Everyone has helped so much—" She lost her voice at that point, because the person behind Ella was not her daughter but her niece, Judith Burkhalter.

"I'll put some of these in the kitchen," Ella said. "The rest can go in the display case if there's room."

"Yah, for sure." Lydia gathered together her straying wits. "Go ahead."

Ella hustled into the kitchen, leaving her alone with Judith. Intentionally? She didn't suppose she'd ever know.

Judith didn't speak for a few minutes. Then she walked closer. "I see you're taking care of everyone, like always."

Lydia felt as if she'd been hit in the face. "I don't know what you mean..." she began, but stopped when Judith began shaking her head, her lips trembling.

"I'm sorry." Judith sucked in a breath and seemed to steady herself. "I didn't mean to do that. That's not why I came."

Lydia put her hand on the counter, thankful the shop was empty at the moment. "Why did you come?" She didn't mean to sound curt, but she wasn't going to put herself through another nasty scene with Judith.

Judith pressed her fingers against her lips for a moment before she spoke. "Since I saw you at worship..." she stopped, then started again. "My aunt was ashamed of me. And I don't blame her. I never meant to be that way, but being back here and seeing you just made me relive that awful time. Seeing Thomas lying there—"

Her voice stumbled, and she stopped. Lydia found

she couldn't hold on to her defenses for another moment. She moved quickly to put her arm around the girl, feeling the sobs she was trying to choke back.

"Komm. We'll sit down here. You don't have to tell me anything if you don't want to."

Judith sat where she indicated, and in a little while the sobs died away. "I do," she whispered. "Want to, I mean."

Nodding with as much encouragement as she could manage, Lydia sat down, glad to hear Becky's voice chattering about the snickerdoodle cookies.

"Thomas is doing much better," Judith finally said. "He got a very good doctor, and he's on some medicine that helps him a lot. I never thought… I mean, I believed he did that because of you. I thought you hurt him. None of us understood that he had something wrong with him. My mother and father felt so guilty once they understood."

Guilt and sorrow could be a powerful combination. Like Simon, still feeling responsible for Rebecca's death even though he wasn't to blame.

"I'm sorry," she said. "But he's better now?"

Judith nodded, dabbing her eyes with a tissue. "He works with Daad on the farm, and he got Daad to plant an orchard that's doing wonderful good. He's even talking about maybe getting married to a woman who lives just down the road."

"I'm glad," she said, wondering how much her brother's marriage plans had upset his devoted sister. "If I'd been wiser, I might have been able to handle the situation better."

Judith sniffed into her tissue. "Yah. I guess we all have something to be sorry about."

She decided against responding to those words. She didn't want to say anything that might make Judith flare up again.

"I just hope he's not making a mistake again." Judith seemed to be talking to herself.

Lydia leaned back in her chair, hoping this had done Judith some good. It hadn't felt very pleasant to her, but it seemed the least she could do.

"I suppose you think I'm being silly." Judith darted a look at her, sounding sulky.

"No, not a bit. He's your bruder, and you love him."

Apparently, that was the right thing to say, because Judith gave a sudden nod and stood up. "I'll find my aunt," she muttered and turned away.

She seemed so incredibly young to Lydia, even younger than she was. It was as if her brother's troubles had become hers, and Judith had gotten stuck back in the past.

Poor girl. If Lydia had harbored any resentment against her for the scene at worship, it was completely gone now. All she could feel was pity.

With Aunt Bess in his mother's capable hands and Sarah and Lyddy in charge at the shop, Simon found himself at loose ends. He'd go back to the work he'd started in the shop, but it seemed wrong to enjoy himself with the old clock he'd rescued when other people were in such trouble. So, with a quick goodbye, he went back down to the flood zone to see if he could find something useful to do.

He reached the corner where he could see down to the creek, and as he did, his father joined him.

"Aunt Bess is settled at home already," he said, before Simon could ask the question. "It went okay, so I got dropped back here."

Simon grinned. "You mean you want to get out of the way of Mammi fussing over Aunt Bess."

"That's about it," he admitted. "Not that Aunt Bess doesn't deserve some fussing over. She's always doing for other folks, but she doesn't want anyone doing for her."

He nodded, knowing how true that was, and they both turned to survey the scene in front of them. The creek was still muddy, but it had gone down visibly since earlier in the day, allowing people to see the row of houses that had been flooded. Stained and muddy, some with porches swept away, they were still standing.

Nearby, an older couple stood, obviously looking down at the houses that had just emerged from the water. Even as Simon watched, the woman's tears began to flow.

"How will we ever get it back to the way it was?" She began to weep, seeming too distraught to care who heard her, and Simon's throat tightened with sympathy.

He turned away, not wanting to stare. "Those poor people," he murmured.

"Yah." Daad nodded to where the other volunteers were gathering. "Best thing we can do for them is put in a couple of hours' work, ain't so?"

Daad was right, of course, but it was frustrating to see neighbors in such distress and not be able to do more.

They joined a group that was sweeping water and mud from one of the houses where the basement had been flooded. It was muddy, smelly work, but at least it was something.

After a half hour, the fireman in charge of the crew called a halt. "Everybody outside and breathe some fresh air for a few minutes. We need it."

They all trooped outside, and most of them sat down on a convenient log fence. Muddy and wet, it was still better than standing.

There was a little flurry of movement down by the lower houses, with a small group advancing on one of them. Simon looked a question at the firefighter.

"They're starting to let folks in for a look at the damage," he said. "Not that they can do anything about it now." He shrugged. "Still, they want to see the worst."

Judging by the way people looked as they came away, there'd been nothing good to see.

"Wish I could do more," the firefighter muttered.

"Guess we all wish that. Still, there's been no loss of life. We have to be thankful of that."

Daad nodded. "There's always something to be thankful for. But they're grieving the life they knew and most likely the memories they lost."

"I guess I was just thinking about the physical loss," Simon admitted. "But I know what you mean about the life they lost. That's what it's been for me and Becky. Not just Rebecca, but the whole life we built together."

He regretted saying it at once. Daad had never been one to talk about his feelings. He'd probably be embarrassed...

But his father put a comforting hand on his shoulder. "You and Becky still have each other. You'll build a home, maybe marry again. Not forget but move on."

"I don't think so." Simon stared absently at the scene in front of them. "I can't love anyone else the way I loved Rebecca."

His father's hand tightened on his shoulder, and Simon sensed that he was struggling to speak. He actually hoped he wouldn't. There was nothing anyone could say that would change how he felt.

But Daad wasn't done with him. "Not the same way, maybe." His voice was husky. "But you can still love someone. Marriage isn't just for the young, remember. Folks get married for companionship, or for family, or just to have someone to take care of. God still blesses them."

Simon sat silently until they were called to return to work. He'd never heard Daad speak that way before and probably never would again. He'd retire back into his taciturn manner and stay there.

Maybe that was why it had made such a strong impression. He didn't agree—didn't think it was possible. But if it could…that was something to ponder, wasn't it?

To Lydia's relief, the next few days saw a return to something like normal, although the people who'd lost the most likely didn't see it that way. She and Sarah were still providing coffee and treats to the volunteers and the emergency shelter, and Simon, like a lot of others, worked several hours a day in the flood zone.

It was a measure of how much the conditions had improved that Jim Jacobs, the water treatment plant manager, was actually there ordering his usual coffee and cruller.

"Nice to be able to come out in public without worrying someone will punch me." He grinned as he handed her the cash.

"It wasn't so bad as that, surely. Still, when you're used to turning the spigot and having water come out…"

"I know, I know. We worked twenty-four hours a day, but the pumps had to be rebuilt." He grimaced. "Not easy, and how the town's budget is going to hold up, I don't know."

"You should have heard how folks cheered when the water came back on," she told him. "That would encourage you."

When he wasn't smiling, Jim looked drawn and tired. "I kept thinking there should be more I could do."

"Probably we all felt that." She thought about Simon's frustration at not being able to do more. And her own, feeling much the same. "We can each only do our part and trust God for the rest, ain't so?"

Jim nodded, picking up the bag with his coffee and cruller. "I'll try to remember that."

Lydia stood musing for a moment on how strange it was. She'd heard the same thing from so many of the volunteers, working twelve hours a day but wanting to do more and feeling helpless against the flood. But on the other side were the complainers, who did nothing. An emergency seemed to bring out the best in some folks and the worst in others.

She automatically checked on Becky and found her drying teaspoons and arranging them neatly in the drawer. Her heart warmed. Becky had the ability, rare in a five-year-old, of concentrating fully on a task until it was finished. It had taken her younger siblings another ten years to manage that, as she remembered.

Finishing, Becky closed the drawer and hung her towel up neatly. As she looked up, she caught Lydia's eyes on her and smiled. Skipping over to her, she caught Lydia's hand.

"Could you help me with my sewing? Please?"

Lydia had started her off on a sewing project a few days earlier, and Becky was an apt pupil. Her neat fingers took to handling a needle quickly.

"Yah, let's do that." A glance told her that Sarah had everything under control. She reached for the sewing basket she'd put on a shelf, and Becky led the way to her usual small table near the kitchen door.

"Do you think you can finish your heart pillow today?" They'd been working on a small pink heart shape which would become a pillow when stuffed with foam.

Checking the stitches to be sure they were lined up, she put it on the table and smoothed it out. "Just keep on stitching until you get right here." She put a straight pin in to mark the spot. "Remember how to make a knot at the end?"

"I remember," Becky said, her face scrunching up. "I think. But maybe you'd better do it."

"I will." Lydia touched her cheek lightly, thinking how much she'd miss the child when she wasn't seeing Becky every day—to say nothing of not seeing Simon.

He'd gone out to see Aunt Bess after lunch, and he hadn't returned yet. There should be nothing to make her tense in his visit, but she couldn't seem to help herself. She kept waiting to hear that his great-aunt was giving up the shop. And in the process giving up Lyddy's job.

It didn't necessarily mean that, she knew. Even if she sold or turned the shop over to someone else in the family, Lydia might be able to keep working. Might, but might not. Whoever took over the shop could have family of their own to help run it.

For a moment she toyed with the idea that she might

be able to buy it herself, but what would she use for money? She'd saved some, but not enough. Daad would help her if she asked, but she wasn't going to ask. He had the others to establish, and she could take care of herself.

"Ready," Becky said, taking her mind off herself. She held out the fleece heart, its bright pink a cheerful contrast to her dark green dress.

"Okay." She took the fabric, making a small knot at the end of Becky's sewing. "Now you get to stuff it."

Becky clapped her hands. "I want to do it."

Pulling out the plastic bag filled with foam, Lydia showed her how to poke each piece through the hole she'd left, pushing it into the farthest part of the pillow first. Giggling a little, Becky pulled out a handful of foam and began pressing it in.

"And then we sew the hole closed and it's done, ain't so?" Becky said eagerly. "I want to give it to Aunt Bess. Do you think she'll like it?"

Lydia blinked back a tear at the child's thoughtfulness. "I know she'll love it. That's a wonderful gut idea."

She was kneeling next to Becky's chair, helping her, when she glanced up to see Simon standing a few feet away, watching them with the strangest expression on his face.

Standing up quickly, Lydia took a step toward him. "What is it? Is something wrong with your aunt?"

"No, no, there's nothing wrong." Whatever had been troubling him, Simon seemed to wipe it away quickly. "Aunt Bess is a little stronger every day. Today she even asked if we've started filling up the freezer again." He hesitated. "I told her yes, but are we?"

Lydia laughed at his expression. "Yah, we have." She

tried to take her mind off her own worries. "Look what Becky is making."

Becky held it up with a smile of satisfaction. "See? It's almost finished. I'm going to give it to Aunt Bess. Lyddy says she'll like it."

"Lyddy's right," he said, smiling at his daughter with a tenderness that melted Lydia's heart. "She'll love it. You're doing a wonderful gut job."

He sat down next to Becky, and Lydia murmured an excuse and headed for the kitchen. She treasured seeing him each day, but sitting there with him and his daughter suddenly overwhelmed her with emotion. That was too intimate for her control.

The rest of the afternoon she managed to keep too busy to have any time to spare thinking about either Simon or the possibility of losing her job. Gradually her emotions returned to normal, and she was able to take her usual interest in her customers. Everyone had a story to tell about how they'd weathered the flood, and in some ways they almost took pride in the fact of having survived.

Also, the bond that had formed when the people of Lost Creek struggled with the flood seemed to make them a more tightly knit community. She was reminded of the Israelites fleeing Egypt, growing stronger as a people from the hardships they faced.

Closing time came soon enough, and she was pleased to see Sarah moving through the routine with the efficiency of an expert. She remembered the conversation they'd had earlier and decided that Sarah was certainly proving that she was growing up.

When Lydia said her goodbyes and headed for the stable, she was surprised to find Simon walking along beside her. When she glanced at him questioningly, he shrugged, his face serious.

"I'll help you harness up." That was all he said, but she felt as if something troubling lurked beneath the surface.

She unhooked the stall door and paused for a moment before leading Dolly out. "If there's something wrong, I wish you'd tell me." She managed to say it without looking at him.

"There's nothing wrong." He bit off the words and then took a deep breath. "I have something to ask you."

Lydia looked up, startled. "What is it?"

Simon sucked in another breath. "Lydia, will you marry me?"

Chapter Fourteen

Lydia could only stand there, shocked and stunned beyond belief. Simon had spoken the words she thought she'd never hear. Asked her the question she'd imagined but hadn't expected. Why was she standing there speechless when he was offering her the gift she'd always dreamed of?

Because there was something wrong. Shouldn't Simon be looking at her with love in his eyes when he said those words? Instead, he stood holding Dolly's halter with one hand and patting her with the other. She could almost convince herself she'd imagined it.

He cleared his throat, sent a flickering glance her way, and then concentrated on the mare again. "I guess I shouldn't have sprung it on you that way. But I've been thinking it over. I mean, we're so well suited to each other. We've known each other since we were children…know everything there is to know, I guess." He stopped to take a breath after getting that much out. "You'll think this is sudden, but I know some of what folks say is true—I do need a wife. There's Becky, and

I shouldn't keep her from having a normal life because of what I feel."

Lydia's sense that this was all wrong increased. She managed to make her lips form the words. "What do you feel?"

Again that quick, sidelong glance that flickered away almost before it landed. "Guess you know as well as anyone what my feelings were about Rebecca. I can't love anyone else the way I loved her. But Daad pointed out to me that folks get married for a lot of reasons other than falling in love. There's friendship, and family, and…well, just having somebody."

Anybody. Her numbed mind formed the word. Anybody would do…well, any mature Amish woman with a gift for making a home and the heart to love another woman's child.

He'd seen her so often with Becky. He must have realized how close they were getting, and from that it was a simple step to finding a way to make it permanent. That is, as long as he could keep love out of the equation.

Her heart had been growing heavier and heavier, and now it felt as if it would sink to her toes. Simon had said they knew each other. Maybe that was true for her, but he didn't know her all that well, not when he didn't understand what he meant to her.

And he must never know. If he even guessed, it would be the ultimate humiliation. She felt as if he'd put a beautiful, fragile gift in her outstretched hands and then dashed it to the floor, breaking it into a thousand pieces.

Somehow, she had to prevent him from knowing

the truth. Summoning all her strength, she forced her voice to stay calm.

"No." After she got that out, the rest was easier, and like him, she found it better to stare at Dolly. "Denke, Simon, but I can't."

He didn't visibly react, although she thought he grew a little more rigid. His hand fell from the halter, and he took a step back, giving a short nod.

"Denke. I'm sorry if I embarrassed you."

She ought to say something in reply, but she knew she couldn't. She couldn't even watch as he walked away.

Forcing herself to hold back the sobs that threatened to rip her apart, she harnessed the mare with shaking fingers. She had to get somewhere to break down in decent privacy. Not the house, that was certain sure. But the daadi haus—Grossmammi wouldn't badger her with questions and comments and sympathy that didn't help. Grossmammi would allow her to be alone to let out all her grief and pain. That was all anyone could do for her right now.

Well, that was that. Simon muttered an excuse to Sarah and shut himself in his workroom. The old clock was still waiting on his table, and involving himself in its workings would be guaranteed to keep his mind occupied.

But for once, that didn't help. What was wrong with him? He'd tried, and he'd lost. He wasn't even especially surprised. After all, what did he have to offer a woman like Lyddy? She was still hardly more than a girl, probably still hoping for a prince to carry her off to her happily-ever-after.

All he had to offer was a life of cooking and cleaning and looking after children. She'd probably rather continue the job she already had and hold on to her life of freedom. And what right did he have to deprive her of the chance at that wonderful head-over-heels, walking-on-air feeling of first love. He'd already had it, but she hadn't.

Annoyed with himself, he picked up the tiny screwdriver he used to loosen the parts inside the clock. But his fingers seemed to have lost their cunning, and all he succeeded in doing was breaking off the first screw. He slammed the screwdriver down on the table, and the end of it snapped off.

He shoved his chair back and surged to his feet. He'd best find something else to do before he ruined the clock and his tools. Striding to the door, Simon hesitated before turning the knob.

Lyddy would be gone by now. He could go and help Sarah with the cleanup and not worry about seeing Lyddy. Maybe by tomorrow she'd have forgotten the whole stupid thing, and they'd be able to go on as they had been. But he doubted it.

Still, the next day it seemed he was right. Lyddy appeared to be as calm and pleasant as if the previous day hadn't happened. He should be glad. He was glad, he assured himself.

The only problem was that Lyddy seemed to be… well, evading him, he guessed. When he came into the kitchen, she found a reason to hurry out front. If he walked behind the counter, she picked up her pad and dashed off to check on her tables.

The third time it happened, Simon realized it wasn't his imagination. That must mean that despite her cheerful expression, his untimely proposal had made things awkward between them. He'd apologize again, but he didn't have a chance. Lyddy was very skilled at making sure they were never alone together.

By late morning it had become so evident that he decided he'd be better off going down to the flood zone, even though he wasn't scheduled to work until two in the afternoon. He caught Sarah on her way through the kitchen.

"I'm going to head down to work now unless you need me for anything. You'll look after Becky, ain't so?"

"For sure, but what about the shed? You said you'd clean it out for us today."

"I'll do it tomorrow," he said shortly, eager to go now that he'd made his decision. If Lyddy didn't want to be alone with him, he'd remove himself.

Sarah frowned. "Don't you remember? We have a big shipment of paper products due this afternoon, now that the trucks can get through. You'll have to make space for them."

"Stop nagging," he snapped. "I'll get to it before tomorrow."

"What's wrong? Why are you so short-tempered today?"

"I'm not." He practically snarled the words, halfway out the door.

"Then I'd hate to see you when you are."

Simon frowned at her. His little sister had grown disagreeably outspoken, it seemed to him.

"Later," he said, keeping his voice calm with an effort. He was out the door before she could say another thing.

The trouble was, sassy or not, Sarah was right. So he

trudged into the shed and made quick work of clearing up so the delivery guy could get at the shelves. The jugs that had been used for carrying water in would have to be returned to their owners, but that, at least, could wait.

He was welcomed with open arms at the flood zone, since one of the other volunteers had had to switch his time to afternoon. Relieved, Simon set to work. Shoveling mud out of someone's basement seemed a lot better than trying to stay out of Lyddy's way, and by the time he'd put in a few hours of hard labor, he'd worked off most of his ill humor.

Sarah had been right, of course. He'd been taking his feelings out on anyone who was handy, and that wasn't fair. And now he owed her an apology, as well. He'd certain sure done a fine job of making things worse.

It didn't make any sense to be so put out about Lyddy's answer. So she had turned him down. He'd known that was a possibility. It wasn't as if his heart was involved, so why was he so distressed?

By the time Simon returned to the shop, he was determined to be pleasant to everyone if it killed him. His resolution was tested immediately by his sister's approach.

"There you are at last," Sarah said, looking at him as if he'd missed something crucial. "Aunt Bess called twice while you were gone, asking for you."

"Is something wrong?" But if her illness were worse, someone else would surely have called.

Sarah shrugged. "She didn't say. She just said to tell you to get out there this afternoon. She has to see you."

He opened his mouth to object, but a glance at Sarah told him she wasn't going to be sympathetic. "All right."

He glanced down at his clothes, splattered with mud and worse. "I'll clean up and go. All right?"

Sarah shrugged again. "Fine with me," she said, and hustled off with a tray of cups.

Stopping only to greet his daughter and admire the picture she was making, he tramped upstairs to shower and change, just managing to catch a glimpse of Lyddy at a table in the very front of the shop.

By the time he came back down, it was closing time, and Sarah was locking the front door. "Lyddy just left," she said, even though he hadn't asked.

Mindful of how testy he'd been earlier, he managed to smile. "Can I help you clean up?"

Becky answered. "I'm helping," she pointed out.

Sarah smiled. "That's right. Becky and I can do it. You get along before Aunt Bess calls again."

With a quick wave, he headed out to the stable, revolving in his mind the possible things that might have upset his aunt. He reached the double doors and realized that Lyddy hadn't left yet. She was still harnessing Dolly.

He stopped, unsure what to say. "Sorry. I mean, I'm heading out your way, too. Aunt Bess wants to see me." Lifting the harness from its peg, he approached the gelding.

"Yah, I heard," she said, not looking at him. "I'll be out of your way in two shakes."

"No need to hurry. In fact, if you'll wait a minute, I'll follow you home, just in case." In case of what, he didn't know.

"You can't," she said quickly. "I mean, I'm not going your way. I'm heading out to see my cousin Beth."

Simon took a deep breath, trying to find the words that would make things normal again. "Lyddy—"

But she'd already swung up to the buggy seat. "I'll see you tomorrow." She snapped the lines and rushed off as if she were being chased. Obviously she didn't want to talk to him—now or later.

Lydia hadn't intended to go to Beth's until she said the words, and then she realized that seeing Beth was exactly what she needed right now. She and Beth had gone through so much together, from childhood mischief to teenage crushes to the death of Beth's husband and the discovery of his betrayal. She had been with Beth through that trying time, and she knew instinctively that Beth would want to walk through this desolate valley with her.

When she tugged the line to turn away from home, Dolly shook her head, making the harness jingle. In Dolly's opinion, it was time they went home.

"Not today," she said firmly. "We have another call to make first." Confiding in the mare might be foolish, but there were times when she needed to speak without being careful of what she said—the way she had to be with Simon.

Lydia's throat grew tight at the thought of his name, but she shook it off much as Dolly had tried to shake off her directions. She didn't want to have herself so upset that she burst into tears at the sight of her cousin. So she forced herself to concentrate on mundane things like how many doughnuts they'd need the next day.

It wasn't far to Beth's place. Lydia turned in the lane next to the country store that Beth and Daniel owned, hoping Beth was at the house rather than busy in the store.

A moment's thought reassured her. At this hour, Beth was likely to be in the kitchen getting supper started. Sure enough, when she pulled up at the house, Beth came hurrying out with a welcoming smile. But the smile faded as soon as she got a look at Lydia's face. She put her arm around Lydia's waist and led her into the house.

"It's all right. We're all alone, and you can tell me. Was ist letz? What's wrong? Is it Simon?"

The tears started to flow as soon as she saw Beth's caring face, and she wiped them away impatiently. She'd cried enough.

"Yah, it was Simon." She sank into a chair, feeling the need of something to hold her up. "He asked me to marry him."

Beth took the chair next to her and took Lydia's hand in hers. "That's usually a happy thing. Are you going to tell me you don't love him?"

She shook her head. "That's the problem. I do love him. But Simon was very honest. He's not looking for love. He's looking for a good Amish woman who'll be his helpmate and a mother to Becky." She stopped, pressing her fingers to her temples. Holding back tears guaranteed a headache, it seemed.

"He never said that to you." The indignation in her cousin's voice warmed Lydia's heart. "He wouldn't."

"Oh, yes, he would. He did."

"You should have hit him with something."

Clearly, gentle, sweet Beth was angry enough for both of them. Too bad Lydia didn't feel anger. It would probably be easier than the desolation in her heart.

"I couldn't," she murmured. "It hurt too much."

"My dear." Beth put her arms around Lydia, patting her back as she might a small child who'd skinned his knee and required comforting. "I'm so sorry. The first time you fall in love, and it has to be with someone who's so wrapped up in the past that he can't see what's right in front of him. You'd be perfect for him."

Beth's anger for her pain and her comforting touch were doing their work. Lydia began to feel that she'd live through this.

"That's exactly what he thinks. That I'd be the perfect stepmother and the perfect housekeeper. Nothing more."

"Ach, that's so foolish. Does he think you'll sit around waiting until he comes to his senses?"

Lyddy leaned back in the chair, feeling spent. "I don't think he ever will. He's still in love with Rebecca." Another tear escaped, and she dashed it away. "Anyway, I can't stay where I'm going to see him every day. I'll have to get another job." She hadn't really thought that out, but she knew it was true. She didn't want to go through any more days like this one.

Beth squeezed her hands tightly. "But I thought this was just temporary. Simon having his workshop at the store, I mean. I'd hate to see you give up a job you love."

What Beth said was true. This was never intended to be long-term on Simon's part. But then again, his aunt might decide to give up the store, and she'd have to find another job anyway.

"I don't know," she said, uncertain of the way forward. "I guess I can't walk away while Elizabeth is sick, can I?"

"That's certain sure." Beth's hands gentled, patting

hers. "Why don't you try to hang in there a little longer, anyway? Just until you see what everyone's plans are. After all, you can make a point of avoiding him, can't you?"

"I guess so." With Simon off several hours each day volunteering, it shouldn't be that difficult. And she could be training Sarah to take her place in the event she did decide to move on.

"I wouldn't think it that difficult. After all, he must be feeling embarrassed and awkward around you anyway. Ain't so?"

She nodded. Beth was right, and just talking it over with her had made Lydia feel better. Stronger, and more able to cope with whatever came. She couldn't possibly walk out on Elizabeth when she was ill.

"You're right," she said, coming to a decision. "I'll have to do it. I don't have any other choice."

"Maybe…well, maybe Simon will realize what he's missing. It could happen, couldn't it?"

She hated to dash Beth's dreams of happily-ever-after for her, but she knew they were futile. "Perhaps," she said. "But as far as I can see, Simon is still in love with Rebecca. And I don't think that will ever change."

It was a hard thing to accept, but she had to do it and move on. If she didn't she'd be like Simon, stuck in the past in an endless loop of grief and guilt. And that wasn't how she wanted to live. No, she would heal from this. But it was going to take a long, long time.

Chapter Fifteen

Since Becky was very occupied in helping Sarah to close the coffee shop, Simon didn't suggest she go with him to see Aunt Bess. Instead, he drove out the road alone, stopping for a moment at the point where the old lane led off to the right. The barricade ahead of him sealed the spot where the road had collapsed. Looking at the creek now as it tumbled gently over rocks in the stream bed, he had a vivid image in his mind of Lyddy's buggy rocking perilously in the raging current, while Lyddy struggled to get the mare to safety.

His heart gave an uncomfortable thud at the picture. Would she have gotten out if he hadn't come along just then? Maybe, but thank the gut Lord he had. It was a wonderful example of how the Lord cared for each one.

With a silent prayer of thanksgiving, he turned onto the lane and made his way over the rutted surface toward the farm. It got a little worse each day, and another load of gravel might not be enough. The highway department probably hadn't even considered this small area in the midst of the damage the flood had done.

Arriving at the house, he greeted everyone and then

hurried to the bedroom where Aunt Bess was waiting. Waiting impatiently, he realized as soon as he saw her face.

"It took you long enough," she snapped.

He didn't find it hard to see that her forced confinement was hard on Aunt Bess's nerves. She was always one to be up and doing, not taking it easy as the doctor had said she must.

"The way through the woods is in pretty bad shape. There's no way to take it at a trot, that's certain sure."

She nodded, but she didn't look mollified. Frowning, she pointed to a straight chair that was across from the rocker she occupied. "Sit down there and account for yourself. What did you say to get Lyddy so upset?"

At first he could only gape at her. He'd never thought Lyddy would talk about it. "How did you find out?"

"Lyddy's grossmammi got it out of her after she came home weeping her eyes out."

Lyddy, weeping because of what he had said to her? The words felt like a punch in the heart.

"I… I don't understand. She seemed to be all right when she left the shop. I'd never have guessed she'd be upset." He remembered the calm with which she'd turned him down.

"You were wrong. What exactly did you say?"

He suspected he wasn't going to be forgiven very quickly for this misstep. And he guessed he didn't deserve to be forgiven, but how could he have known it would perturb her that much?

"I asked her to marry me. I said we'd known each other from childhood, and we got along well, and I knew how much she cared about Becky. And I told her what Daad said—"

He stopped, because Aunt Bess's expression said he shouldn't quote Daad.

"Go on," she snapped. "What did your daad say?"

"He…he said that…well, that there were lots of reasons for getting married besides falling in love." Under her critical gaze, he stumbled to a stop.

"First of all, don't ever follow another man's advice about women. Your father meant well, I guess." She made it sound like a bad thing. "Never mind what he said. What do you feel about Lydia?"

Thoughts tumbled around in his head. "I admire her. She's a wonderful good person—loving and sympathetic and always helping others. But as for love, I don't feel for Lyddy what I felt for Rebecca, and—"

"You're ferhoodled, that's what you are!" She smacked her hand on the arm of the rocker, looking like she'd like to smack something else. "For sure you don't feel what you felt for Rebecca. You're not seventeen now. You're not a boy, waiting to tumble head over heels in love."

She started to cough, alarming him. "Aunt Bess, don't upset yourself. I'd better leave. We can talk later."

"Yah, you go away." She glared at him, and he winced. "Go away and think about how you feel when you're with Lyddy. And then ask yourself how you'd feel if you never saw Lyddy again."

The words snatched his breath away for a moment. Before he could speak, she went on.

"If you ever figure out what you want, then tell her what that is, starting with your feelings."

"I couldn't, even if I wanted to," he said, unwilling to say another word about his feelings and searching for an excuse. "She hasn't let me get anywhere near her, and I don't think she will."

Aunt Bess looked at him, shaking her head as if he'd given a foolish answer. "That's something you'll have to figure out for yourself. There's always a way if you want something badly enough. Now go away and do some thinking."

Chastened, Simon headed back toward town, carefully avoiding the worst of the ruts and holes. He appreciated Aunt Bess's caring. He did. And he was sorry he'd made Lyddy cry. But he couldn't...

He'd made Lyddy cry. The words surrounded his heart, squeezing it without mercy. He'd made her cry.

What was it Aunt Bess had said? *Think about how you feel when you're with Lyddy.* That was easy enough to answer, wasn't it? He felt warm, safe, understood, happy. And he wanted to be with her more and more.

But that wasn't love—at least, it wasn't what he had felt when he'd fallen in love with Rebecca. Aunt Bess had made short work of that reasoning, hadn't she?

He'd reached the blacktop road. Once again he stopped, staring at the creek, remembering. And hearing Aunt Bess's words again. *Ask yourself how you'd feel if you never saw Lyddy again.*

Eyes fixed on the swirling water, he found his thoughts swirling as if they were being tumbled in the creek the way Lyddy's buggy had been. He seemed to see Lyddy back in the raging waters, being swept away and out of his sight while he stood helpless, unable to save her.

And then the truth overwhelmed him until he felt as if he were drowning in it.

He knew now what he wanted. He wanted Lyddy, not

because she'd be a good mother to Becky but because she was as important to him as breathing. But after the mistake he'd made, how could he ever convince Lyddy?

By the next morning, Lydia still wasn't sure how many of her family members knew what had happened. She hadn't thought to urge Grossmammi to keep it quiet, but she'd know it wasn't the sort of thing Lyddy would want drifting around the community.

Judging by the sympathetic glances Mammi was sending her way as she ate breakfast, Mammi must know. But at least she wasn't talking about it. That was the last thing Lyddy wanted right now. She was still too close to the edge of tears for anything like that.

Josiah started to ask her something, but Daad caught his attention and sent his mind off in another direction. Thank the good Lord. One day this would fade from her memory, and she'd be able to talk about Simon, and to Simon, in a normal way. But that day seemed very, very far away.

As soon as possible, Lyddy set out for town. She wasn't looking forward to seeing Simon, but she was responsible for keeping the coffee shop running, and she lived up to her responsibilities. Given how embarrassed he'd seemed the previous day, she could hope that Simon would find things to do that kept him out of her vicinity.

Beth had been right to urge patience. Simon wasn't going to be at the shop forever, and once he'd moved, she'd see very little of him. She shouldn't have to give up a job she enjoyed just because he had spoken out of turn.

Fortified by her thoughts, she followed the lane down

toward the spot where it joined the road. The surface was worse here, probably because excess rainfall was flowing down the hill toward the stream. Daad had been talking about getting together with the neighbors to put another load of gravel on it, tamping it down firmly. He seemed to think very little of the chances the state would get at the job soon. Simon's daad would be wanting to help, no doubt.

Her thoughts occupied, Lydia rounded a stand of dense pines and found the blacktop road in sight. Just where the lane joined the road, a buggy stood, half-on, half-off the lane. A buggy she recognized—Simon's buggy. And Simon was on the ground next to the front wheel.

Lydia didn't think. She just ran, jumping from the buggy even before the mare came to a halt, and raced toward him. If Simon was hurt…

As she neared him, he rose, and in another moment she felt his arms close around her, holding her as if he'd never let go. She felt his heart beating with hers—his breath moving in rhythm with hers. She couldn't think; she could only feel.

"Are you all right? You weren't hurt?" She managed to gasp out the words.

A rumble sounded in his chest as he chuckled. "Not hurt just sliding off the seat, that's certain sure. I cut the corner too sharp and slid right into the ditch." He pressed his cheek against hers. "Serves me right for teasing you about your driving." His arms tightened convulsively. "Lyddy," he murmured, his voice roughening. "Forgive me."

She leaned back just enough to look into his face, and what she saw there silenced all her doubts.

"I will always forgive you." She knew she was making a promise to last a lifetime. "I love you." It was such a relief to say the words, to express the feeling that surged through her at his touch and his nearness.

"I love you." He moved, cupping her face in his hands and looking into her eyes. "I love you, and I was so foolish. I didn't even recognize love when I saw it."

She could smile now, any smidgen of doubt chased away for good. "What made you see?"

"Aunt Bess." He made a rueful grimace. "She always knows everything. She asked me how I would feel if I never saw you again." His palms pressed against her cheeks. "I couldn't bear it. I knew in an instant. If you went away, I couldn't..." His eyes filled with tears. She reached up to pull his face to hers.

"I won't," she said. "You have me for keeps."

His lips touched hers, and joy filled her heart. Simon had given her the most precious gift he could. He'd given her his love. On that gift they would build a family with Becky and whatever other children the Lord should send them. And every day she would thank God, the giver of all good gifts, for bringing them together.

* * * * *

THE AMISH TEACHER'S WISH

Tracey J. Lyons

This book is dedicated to the loving memory of my dad;
Theodore J. Pinkowski—gone but never forgotten.

Cheers, Dad!

But I will hope continually,
and will yet praise thee more and more.
—*Psalms* 71:14

Chapter One

❦

Miller's Crossing
Chautauqua County, New York

Sadie Fischer should have known better. After the rains they'd had this past week, the hillsides were muddy. She probably should have stayed on the main road. But, *nee*, she was in a hurry to see her friend Lizzie Burkholder and to deliver the latest supply of quilted pot holders she had made for the store Lizzie ran with her husband, Paul. A schoolteacher here in Miller's Crossing, Sadie helped her *mamm* with small quilting projects during the summer months when school was not in session.

As she hurried along the old cow path shortcut through the field at the bottom of the hill below the *Englischer*'s church, Sadie was glad her students couldn't see their teacher now. It hadn't taken long for her haste to catch up with her. A few steps onto the path, and her feet started sinking into the soggy earth. She always chided her students for trying to take shortcuts in their schoolwork. She couldn't help but smile, thinking how they'd be the ones wagging their fingers at her now.

Looking down, she grimaced. Her feet were almost ankle-deep in the murky water. The soles of her shoes were caked with mud. Her *mamm* would have her doing the dishes for months if she caught her in this predicament. Oh, Sadie could almost hear her *mamm* scolding her now, reminding Sadie to pay attention to where she was going.

Of all her siblings, Sadie was the most talkative and the most distracted. In her *mamm*'s words, she was a *blabbermaul*. She couldn't help being chatty. As the youngest, she'd learned at an early age to speak up in order to be heard over the din of her sisters and brothers. She had three of each. When the others were busy with chores, she'd also learned how to fend for herself and to take shortcuts.

Clinging tightly to the bag filled with the pot holders, Sadie attempted to lift one leg and then the other out of the sloppy mess. She hoped she could make her way out of this quagmire and back to the main road.

"Oh, dear," she murmured, looking down to where the mud now bubbled around her feet. Her movements only caused her to sink farther into the soft ground.

Blowing out a breath, she looked around for something to grab hold of. Spotting a low-hanging tree branch a few feet away, she thought she might be able to grab hold of that and pull herself out. Although, she'd need to find a safe place to put her bag. Lifting her arm, she flung the bag high into the air, watching it land on a dry spot in the field a few feet away from the cow path.

Next, she stretched her right arm as far as she could for the branch, her muscles straining against the effort. The leaves tickled her fingers, and her heartbeat kicked up. She was so close to getting out of this mess. She had the first bit of the branch in her hand when suddenly it snapped free, sending her backward. Sadie let out a yelp as she fell with a splash into the mud.

"Nee! Nee!"

She sat there looking down at her blue dress now covered in mud, the cool wetness seeping through the fabric. A honeybee buzzed around her head. Without thinking, she swatted at it, splashing more mud up onto her prayer *kapp*. She wanted to cry. But crying wasn't in her nature. However, getting out of the many messes she always seemed to end up in was.

Once again, she looked around for something she could grab hold of to pull herself out of this muck. When she couldn't find anything, it seemed like the only thing to do might be to give up what remained of her pride and crawl out onto the drier part of the field. She made a face at the idea of getting even dirtier. Still, she was just about to give it a try when she heard the sound of a wagon.

Craning her neck, she spotted a long work wagon coming up over the rise in front of the church.

She waved her arms in the air and shouted, "Help! Help!"

At first, she wasn't sure the driver could hear her, so she yelled louder. "Help! I need help!"

She sent up a prayer of thanksgiving as the wagon pulled to a stop in the church parking lot. A man jumped down from the wagon. He was too far away for her to tell if she knew him. He stood with a hand shielding his eyes from the sunlight, looking out over the field. Maybe he couldn't see her.

Sadie waved her arms over her head, hoping to catch his attention. "I'm over here! Over here!"

She breathed a sigh of relief when he began to run toward her. By the time he got to her, she had only managed to dig herself even deeper into the mud. That's what she got for trying to get up on her own.

"Miss, are you all right?"

"*Ja.* I'm just stuck in this mud pit." She tried to laugh but couldn't quite manage it.

"That you are. Here, let me help you up."

When he moved closer, Sadie realized she'd never seen him before. The depth of his hazel-colored eyes struck her—hues of blues, greens and browns all mixed together. His fine cheekbones were cut high on his face, and his hair was a touch lighter brown than most of the men's around here. She also noticed he wore his suspenders fastened on the outside and not on the inside of his pants like the men in her community.

A million questions flew through her mind. Where had he come from? Why was he here? Was he just passing through Miller's Crossing? And if so, where was he headed?

He raised an eyebrow, his mouth pressing into a thin line. "Miss, I don't have all day to stand here while you make up your mind about staying or letting me help you out of your predicament."

Surprised by the abruptness in his voice, Sadie replied in her best schoolteacher voice, "There's no need to use that tone with me."

He drew back his shoulders. *"Es dutt mir leed."*

Sadie narrowed her eyes, wondering if his apology was sincere. His gaze softened a bit. "I accept your apology."

The wetness was seeping into her skin, and she looked down at the mess she'd made of herself. When she looked back up, she found the stranger extending his hand to her.

She hesitated, then took hold of it, surprised as his large hand swallowed hers in a firm grip. She let out a yelp as he tugged her up to stand beside him on the dry grass.

Sadie felt his warmth against her side and took an acceptable step backward. It wouldn't be proper for her to be seen out in a field, alone, with any man, especially with someone she didn't even know. She imagined the scolding she'd get from the elders who ran the school if they could see her now. No doubt not unlike the one she would get from her *mamm* when she saw the mess Sadie had made.

Due to her reputation within the community for being, what some would consider, too outgoing, Sadie had struggled to convince the board to let her teach the students in the first place. With no one else available for the last year, they'd reluctantly agreed to let her take over on a temporary basis. But with summer and harvest time nearing an end and still no permanent teacher found, Sadie had been given another chance to prepare for the upcoming semester.

She hadn't seen teaching as a lifelong endeavor, more as something to hold her over until she met the man who would become her husband. However, while all her friends had married off to eligible men in Miller's Crossing, Sadie had been left with suitors who were either too old or too young. So, for now, she was content to focus on *her* students. Though she knew it was wrong to think of them as hers, it was hard not to feel that way when she had no husband or *kinder* of her own yet.

Although if her parents had their way, Sadie would

be forced into a courtship with Isaiah Troyer. The man was older than her, a widower with no children. She had no desire to be involved with him even if her *vader* thought they could be a *gut* match.

She knew the right man was out there. She just had to be patient in finding him.

Pushing those thoughts aside, she rubbed her hands together and thanked the tall, lanky man at her side. "*Danke.* If not for you, I might have had to crawl my way out."

His eyes took on a deeper brown hue as he folded his arms across his chest and looked down at her. "Then it's a *gut* thing for you I came along when I did."

"*Ja.*"

"I've got to be in town for an appointment. I can drop you someplace if you'd like." He studied her for a moment. When she hesitated, he shrugged and turned away.

"*Ja*, a ride would be nice. If you wouldn't mind," Sadie said. Hurrying to pick up the bag of pot holders, she followed him.

Halfway to the wagon, he paused so she could catch up. "Dare I ask why you were stuck in the mud?"

She blinked up at him. "I...um...I was taking a shortcut to my friend's house. And as you can see, that didn't end well."

"Am I taking you there?"

Sadie knew she needed to change out of her wet clothes before she did anything else. The pot holders would have to wait. "*Nee.* You can take me home."

They walked the rest of the way to the wagon in silence. Pausing alongside it, she put her hand on the seat to hoist herself up.

"Do you need help getting up?"

"*Nee.* I can do it," she assured him.

But when she put her wet foot up on the step, it slipped off, throwing her backward. If not for the grace of God, she might have landed on her backside again. She managed to right herself just in time.

The stranger rushed to her side, but Sadie waved him off. While she may have needed help getting out of the mudhole, she could handle getting into a wagon on her own.

"I'm fine."

Nodding, he walked around to the other side of the wagon and climbed up.

Sadie scraped her shoe across the dirt in the parking lot to give the sole a little grit, then managed to get up onto the seat without any more mishaps. Settling a respectable distance away from him, she pulled her skirt in close, hoping to keep the seat free from the mud.

Blowing out a breath, she looked over the vista spreading out below the church. The view always filled her with hope and happiness. In her mind, this was the prettiest place in all of Miller's Crossing, even all of Chautauqua County, New York. Her family's Amish community had settled here back in the middle of the last century. Her ancestors had come from Ohio, leaving scarce farmland to make a living here.

Sadie wiggled around on the seat, trying to ignore the fact that the mud was beginning to dry. She looked down at the floorboard where drips of mud were falling off her shoes.

"I'm afraid I'm making a mess of your wagon."

The man didn't respond. He nudged the single workhorse along with a flick of the leather reins. He appeared to be focused on the roadway and not her. Only now did she notice the way his eyes were narrowed as if he were in deep concentration, and there were grim lines around his mouth.

A smile could make those disappear.

"I'm Sadie Fischer."

Keeping his hand steady on the reins, he said, "I'm Levi Byler."

In all his days, Levi had never seen a young lady looking such a sight. Mud covered most of her, and streaks of dirt ran through the loosened strands of her blond hair. A smudge of mud was drying on her chin. He had to hand it to her. Most women he knew would be crying right about now. But Miss Fischer sat there smiling at him like nothing had happened.

Her light blue eyes seemed to take in the sight of him. Levi swallowed. He knew better than to be sucked in by a woman's ostensibly innocent smile. He struggled to ignore the ache in his chest. The hurt of his recent breakup was still too fresh. On most days since that horrible time, he managed to go about his business quietly, but then there were days like today. He'd taken a wrong turn on his way to Miller's Crossing and ended up on this road.

He was coming to help his cousin Jacob Herschberger with his shed business and to heal his broken heart. Levi hoped that lending his expertise as a craftsman would not only be useful to Jacob but also aid in his own healing. He figured if he kept his hands busy, then his mind wouldn't wander to the past.

Pushing those thoughts aside, he stole a glance out of the corner of his eye at the woman sitting next to him.

He supposed it was a good thing he'd come along when he did, otherwise there was no telling what would have happened to Miss Fischer.

"Where are you headed?" she asked.

Concentrating on the unfamiliar road ahead, Levi did his best to ignore the soft, friendly lilt of her voice. Her tone reminded him of the woman who'd broken his heart.

Keeping his answer simple, he replied, "I'm going to help out a family member."

"Does this person have a name? I know all of the Amish families around here."

His emotional situation was not her fault, so Levi answered, "Jacob Herschberger."

"Oh, his wife, Rachel, is a cousin to my best friend, Lizzie Burkholder. Lizzie is from the Miller family, the same ones who first settled this area. She and her husband, Paul, have a furniture and art store in Clymer," Miss Fischer went on. "Lizzie does beautiful watercolor landscapes. I wish I had half her talent. The only thing I can make are quilted pot holders from my *mamm*'s fabric scrap pile. I sell them at Lizzie's store. That's where I was heading when I got sucked into the mud."

She paused and Levi thought she might be taking a break, but in the next breath she asked, "So, you'll be working on Jacob's sheds?"

"*Ja.*"

"That's a *gut* thing. I know he's been looking for help. He and Rachel have a small house on the other side of the village, close to his shop. Where are you traveling from?"

Levi gave her a sideways glance, wondering if she

ever stopped talking. "A district near Fort Ann," he said, keeping his answer short hoping to satisfy her curiosity.

"Oh. That's a long trip for a horse and wagon. I haven't been anyplace other than Miller's Crossing, and of course the village of Clymer."

"I came in on the bus." He didn't feel it necessary to tell her that he'd picked the horse and wagon up in the village. Levi wasn't interested in anything beyond getting her to where she needed to be in one piece.

"That was smart of you."

"Miss Fischer, you still haven't told me where you'd like to be dropped off."

"I'm afraid my *mamm* is going to be upset when she sees me looking a mess and returning home with the bag of pot holders. You can leave me at the end of my road if you'd like. That way you won't have to hear her scolding me."

"In order for me to do that, you'll need to tell me where the end of your road is. I do need to be somewhere," he said in a soft tone, hoping to coax directions out of her.

"It's not that late in the day." She gave him a small smile. "But you are right. I'm the one troubling you, not the other way around."

He waited for a second, raised an eyebrow and asked again. "Miss Fischer, the directions to your house?"

"Ja." She pointed straight ahead. "Just over that rise, right on the other side of that cow fence, you will find my driveway."

Levi's patience was wearing thin. Perhaps it was the long trip he'd taken added to meeting this woman and wondering about his new job. With the pain of his past still fresh in his mind, he just wanted to be left alone.

He didn't want to worry about Sadie Fischer. He wanted to selfishly drown in the sorrow of his heartbreak for a bit longer.

But his past had nothing to do with Sadie. She had needed help and he'd come along at the right time. He wasn't sure if he wanted to leave her alone on the road. Levi didn't feel like being friendly, but he wouldn't leave someone in distress either.

He pulled up to her drive and looked over at her. The spark seemed to have left her. Her shoulders sagged as she turned to hop down from the wagon seat.

He started to apologize, and then suddenly it wasn't her face he was seeing. *Nee*, it was the face of the woman who had shunned him.

Levi blinked. The pain of betrayal welled up inside him again. No matter how sweet Sadie Fischer appeared to be, no matter how much she might need someone to be a buffer between her and her *mamm*, he had to protect his heart. He simply could not allow himself to be drawn in again.

Over her shoulder, he saw a long tree-lined drive leading to her family's property and in the distance the roofline of a house. The better side of him—the old Levi—was starting to feel a bit of remorse for his short temper.

"Please, let me drive you the rest of the way."

Chapter Two

"*Nee*. I told you I'd be fine and I will be. I know you've someplace to be," Sadie replied as she stood on the side of the road, making a sad attempt to straighten her soggy skirts.

She paused to look up at the man. She'd kept him long enough.

"I wish you a good day, Mr. Byler," she said in a soft voice. And she meant that. Crankiness never got one anywhere in life, which is why she always tried to find the bright spot.

"*Gut* day to you," he said, giving her a courteous nod before heading on his way.

Lizzie waited for the wagon to be out of sight. She shook her head, thinking that he hadn't had such a good start to his first day in Miller's Crossing. Deciding to pay him no more attention, she turned and began to walk to the house.

She passed the complex of white barns with black trim where her *daed* had the farm equipment lined up nearby. The hay baler was missing. No doubt he was out in the field working on the recent cutting.

Sadie smiled as a small flock of white hens skittered over to her, pecking around the toes of her shoes. Seeing them reminded her she'd yet to collect today's eggs.

Letting out a sigh, she hurried along, hoping to skirt around the backside of the house and enter through the mudroom before anyone saw her. She glanced back at her muddy shoe prints. Sadie hoped her *mamm* was in a *gut* mood, otherwise she'd be in for it. Her dirty skirts slapped against her stockings as she ran behind the house.

A movement in the shadows behind the screen door caught Sadie's eye as she stepped onto the cement stoop. It appeared she wasn't going to best her *mamm* after all. The screen door flew open, slapping against the clapboard siding. A tall dark-haired woman came out onto the porch, her face flushed. Sadie sucked in a breath.

Wagging a finger at her, *Mamm*'s voice rose. "Sadie Fischer! What mess have you gotten yourself into this time?"

"*Mamm.* I'm sorry. I tried to take the shortcut into the village and got stuck in a big mudhole down behind the *Englisch* church on Clymer Hill Road."

"And who dropped you off? I didn't recognize the wagon."

"How did you know I was dropped off?"

"I was coming in from the barn and saw you up at the top of the driveway. I'd have waited for you, but I had my hands full carrying a basket of eggs."

"I was going to gather those as soon as I cleaned up," Sadie told her.

"The day was wasting and your sister needed them for her cake mix." In a gentler voice, her *mamm* added,

"You know better than to be alone with someone you don't know."

Sadie knew *Mamm* was right about that. She did her best to explain what had happened. "Levi Byler helped me out and then he kindly offered to bring me home. He's a cousin of Jacob Herschberger, so he's not really a stranger. He will be working at Jacob's shed company."

Her *mamm* gave her a sideways glance. "You are the schoolteacher, and you are held to a higher standard in the community."

"I do understand that, *Mamm*. But if not for Levi Byler coming by when he did, I'm afraid I'd still be stuck in the mud."

"Well, then you should have brought him down here so I could have thanked him properly."

Sadie nodded. She saw no need to tell her *mamm* that the stranger had been distracted and in a hurry to be on his way.

Looking her up and down, *Mamm* scolded her again. "Sadie, today of all days, you decide to take that shortcut! And you didn't get the pot holders delivered like you promised. Furthermore, you know we have your special dinner guest coming over."

Sadie made a face. She felt bad about the pot holders but didn't care much about Isaiah. She knew he was a man of means. He had his own farm, after all. But when it came to matters of the heart, a man's stature in the community shouldn't matter. Even so, her parents were set on making this match.

Sadie thought the man would be more appropriate for her sister Sara. She'd always acted years older than her age.

"I know what you're thinking, Sadie." Her *mamm*'s

voice softened. "You think we should be more concerned with marrying off Sara. But worrying over you is what keeps your *vader* and me awake most nights. You've a way about you. And this traipsing off into the mud is yet another reason why we want you to have your future secured. You can't keep doing things on impulse."

Sadie met her *mamm*'s gaze, seeing both concern and love reflected in her eyes. She almost gave in. Sometimes she thought it might be easier to let her parents choose her spouse for her. But then she remembered that this was her life, and she was determined to live it her way. Even if it went against what her parents considered to be right. Sadie wasn't doing harm to anyone. She lived a good faithful life led by her church's teachings. She worked tirelessly to bring her beliefs into her classroom and to teach her students about acts of kindness and love.

"Think about what I've said," her *mamm* said.

The last thing Sadie wanted was to disappoint her parents, but on this one topic she would remain steadfast.

Sitting down on the stoop, she pulled off her shoes. "Yuck." She set them on the edge of the cement step. Then, standing, she rolled down her stockings and placed them with the shoes. She wiggled her toes, feeling the coolness of the air touch her skin.

"You might as well come inside the mudroom and leave your skirt here," her *mamm* said from behind her. "And anything else that has mud on it."

"*Ja.*"

"Get inside before someone else sees you." Her *mamm* held the door open for her.

Sadie walked past her into the small coatroom off the back of the kitchen and stepped out of her skirt, now heavy with the dried mud. She unpinned her prayer *kapp* and caught her *mamm* narrowing her eyes and giving her another stern once-over. Perhaps she'd really gone too far this time.

"*Mamm*, I'm sorry for making such a mess. May I go wash up?"

She nodded. "When you are finished, you come right back to the kitchen. Your sister and I have been working to get the food ready for *your* dinner. You can wash the dishes."

Washing dishes had always been her least favorite chore. Sadie expected nothing less as her punishment. Holding her prayer *kapp* in one hand, she headed upstairs to the bathroom just past the bedroom she shared with her sister Sara. She turned on the cold water in the sink and carefully rinsed the mud off the *kapp*. Hanging it on the rack to dry, she turned her attention to peeling off the rest of her garments.

She made quick work of washing up and then went across the hall to her bedroom to change into another light blue dress and apron. Once she had pinned a fresh *kapp* on her head, Sadie took in a deep breath, blew it out and prepared to meet her *mamm* in the kitchen.

Mamm greeted her in the doorway. "Ah. Here you are, all cleaned up. *Gut*. Now let's get you to work on those dishes."

"I'll get my clothes washed up after I've done the dishes," Sadie told her *mamm*, knowing that would be her next concern. *Cleanliness is next to godliness.* The old phrase popped into her thoughts.

Walking over to the double sink, Sadie made quick

work of the first batch of dishes and then listened as her *mamm* and sister discussed the upcoming meal.

"We'll make mashed potatoes to go with the roast beef," Sara said. "We want to be sure to impress Isaiah. For Sadie's sake, of course."

Sadie's head snapped up. She heard something in the tone of Sara's voice that made her think that perhaps her sister might be excited about their dinner guest.

"Sadie," her *mamm* said, "when you've finished with the dishes, you can get out the tablecloth."

The tablecloth to which her *mamm* referred was only used on very special occasions. The last time it came out of the drawer was for her *bruder* John's wedding dinner. He and his wife, Rebecca, had had a small family ceremony here on the property two years ago.

Sadie began to worry.

She didn't want to be married off to just anyone. *Ja*, like every girl she dreamed of one day falling in love, but in Amish communities, courtships and marriages weren't always about love. A lot of times *vaders* picked the match for their *dochders*.

But she didn't need to be watched over by someone older than her nineteen years. Isaiah Troyer's first wife had died soon after their marriage. She shook her head. She didn't want to be married to an older widower.

She found the tablecloth her *mamm* wanted. Spreading it out on the table, she inhaled the delicious aromas coming from the kitchen. The roast smelled like onions and garlic. A pot of potatoes sat on the back of the stove, ready for mashing. Again, she thought all of this effort a terrible waste of everyone's precious time. But there was little to be done about this situation without causing a whole bunch of trouble.

The living room clock chimed four times. And then came the sound of a low rumble of thunder.

Her *mamm* let out a gasp and spun around from the counter where she'd been gathering the milk and butter for the potatoes. "Oh my! Sounds like there's a storm brewing."

Sadie ran to the front door and, sure enough, the sky to the north had taken on a very ominous appearance. Dark clouds swirled about. This time of year, with the high humidity and hot days, pop-up thunderstorms were common. But she had a feeling this one might turn into more than your run-of-the-mill storm. A flock of birds flew from the large oak tree in the side yard, their noise startling her. Even the hens seemed to be running for the cover of the henhouse.

"Do you see your *vader* out there?" her *mamm* asked.

Sadie looked up the drive. Trees swayed as a hard wind blew through them. Off in the distance, lightning flickered against the dark sky, followed by another roll of thunder. It looked like the strike was right near the schoolhouse. Sadie began to worry, not only for the school but for her *vader*. There was no sign of his wagon. He should be coming in from the field by now.

Relief flooded through her when she saw the barn door being rolled open and her *vader*'s form stepping outside. He struggled to push the door closed and then ran across the yard just as fat, round raindrops pelted the hard earth.

"We're in for it with this one," he said to Sadie as she held the door for him. "I saw Isaiah when I was coming in from the back field. He sends his apologies but he had to go home to his farm. He has animals outside in the pen. He needs to get them to safety. He said his knee pain was kicking up, telling him this storm could be a bad one."

Sadie held back her relief and managed to say, "*Es dutt mir leed* to hear that."

"*Dochder.*" Her *vader* raised one of his bushy eyebrows, giving her a knowing look. Leaning in, he whispered to her, "I'm not sure you are all that sorry."

"I'm sorry there's a bad storm coming," she said with a tiny smile.

Patting her on the shoulder, he said, "There will be another time for our special dinner."

Sadie turned her attention back to the storm. A shiver ran down her spine. The clouds blackened as the air churned. She let out a yelp when a branch broke off the maple tree in the front yard, landing on the porch steps.

"Come away from that door this instant, Sadie!" her *mamm* shouted as another crack of lightning hit close by the house.

Doing as she was told, she slammed the front door closed. And in that moment, she found herself praying that Levi Byler had safely found his way to Jacob's house.

Levi pulled into the parking area near Jacob's shed company just as the first wave of thunder rolled through Miller's Crossing. A man came running out of the large steel structure, and Levi immediately recognized his cousin.

It had been a few years since they'd seen each other at a construction safety symposium in Saratoga Springs. At the time, Jacob had hinted that his company was growing at a fast pace, while Levi had been preparing his own future, one that included marriage.

It amazed him how quickly things had changed. One day he was happy and the next he'd found himself alone, uncertain where his life should be heading next. When Jacob had called and offered him the work, Levi's parents insisted he move to Miller's Crossing.

While Levi was happy for his cousin's success, he still wished his own future had gone the way he'd planned.

"Pull the horse and wagon into the barn over there!" Jacob shouted, pointing to the structure on the far side of the driveway.

The leather strap tugged in Levi's hands when the horse shied away from a sudden gust of wind. Carefully, he led the beast and the wagon to the safety of the barn. Jacob followed him in and rolled the barn door halfway closed behind them.

Wiping the rain from his face, Jacob said, "You've picked a fine time to arrive."

Jumping down from the wagon, Levi started to unhitch the horse. "*Ja*, this storm came up pretty fast."

"I was hoping you'd be here earlier," Jacob said. Taking the reins, he led the horse to a free stall.

"I had to stop and help out a young woman. She was stuck in the mud way down in a field behind the church at the top of the hill."

Jacob paused, looked over his shoulder at Levi and raised an eyebrow. "A young woman stuck in the mud?"

"Sadie Fischer. Do you know her? She tells me she knows you and your wife."

"We know her. That one is fiery."

Levi pondered the comment. He supposed that was one way to describe her, though *chatty* came to mind.

"You'd do best to steer clear of her. Last I heard, her *vader* has been trying to get her married off."

Even hearing the word *marriage* made his stomach muscles tighten. A union such as that was now the furthest thing from his mind. It didn't matter what the young woman was like. Levi wasn't looking for a courtship anymore. The pain that his ex-fiancée, Anne Yoder, had put him through was still fresh in his mind and in his heart. Levi didn't think he would ever be able to bear the pain of a broken heart again.

He and Anne had seemed like the perfect match. Both of their families had agreed the marriage would be a good thing. But then Anne had abruptly changed her mind, leaving him for an *Englisch* man. No amount of talking to her had changed her mind. He felt badly for her *mudder* and *vader*. It was hard enough having a relationship end, but then to have their *dochder* leave the community... Well, he imagined that must have crushed their hearts.

As for Levi, he'd come to Miller's Crossing to work and to heal. Absently, he rubbed his hand over his belly as his stomach rumbled. He hadn't eaten much in the way of a meal since he'd left Fort Ann in the predawn hours this morning.

"You must be hungry after your day of travel. My wife, Rachel, is a *gut* cook. She'll have a hearty meal ready for us."

Levi had never met Rachel, although Jacob had talked about her at length the last time they'd been together.

Bright streaks of lightning slashed through the dark sky.

"Come, let's get to the house," Jacob shouted over the thunder.

Levi grabbed his travel bag from the back of the wagon, and the two men dodged mud puddles as they ran to the safety of Jacob's house. Once on the porch, they shook the rain from their hats.

Jacob and Rachel's home looked good and sturdy. Built on a slight knoll overlooking the shed company, the house had dark wooden slat siding, and a grapevine wreath hung from the front door. Through the side windows, Levi could see soft light coming from the lamps hanging on the wall near the doors.

Jacob held the door open for him, and Levi stepped over the threshold into a great room that served as the kitchen, dining and living room. Off to one side was a large stove where a young woman wearing a white apron over a blue dress stood putting the finishing touches on their meal.

Jacob followed him into the house, saying, "Rachel, Levi is here."

Jacob's wife turned from the stove. Her smile was warm and kind. "*Willkomm* to our home. You made it to the house just in time. I fear this storm isn't going to let up anytime soon. You must be tired. After dinner, Jacob can show you to your room. We've a small bedroom you can use for as long as you need it."

"Levi, this is my wife, Rachel."

"*Sehr gut* to meet you." Levi nodded to her. "I've heard so much about you."

"Pleased to meet you, too. All of Jacob's family is *willkomm* in our home. Nodding her head in the direction of the table, she said, "Come, come, dinner is ready."

Rachel carried the steaming pot of stew to the table, then they took their seats.

Levi dug into the meal as Rachel and Jacob caught up on their day. It was obvious the couple loved one another. It occurred to him then that he might never get to experience this in his own life. He chided himself that this wasn't the time to worry about his future. He should concentrate on getting through the present. The exhaustion of the long day of travel had caught up with him, jumbling his thoughts.

Stifling a yawn, he thanked his hosts. "Rachel, *danke* for this meal. Jacob, if you don't mind, could you direct me to my room?"

"Ja. Ja," Jacob said, jumping up from his seat. "Right this way."

Levi picked up his travel bag from where he'd left it by the door and followed his friend down a long hallway toward the back of the house.

"Here is the room. I hope you find the bed to your liking."

"I'm sure I will." Levi was so tired he would be comfortable sleeping on a straw mat.

After Jacob left, Levi settled onto the single bed. He bent one arm under his head and lay there, listening to the storm. The thunder rumbled all around the house, sometimes so loud the windows rattled. He blinked into the darkness, holding his breath as he waited for the next strike of lightning. One hit close to the house, the flash illuminating the bedroom.

The storm rumbled away over the countryside. Then, just as it seemed that the storm had lost its fuel, it gathered energy once more and circled back around again. He hoped and prayed that the village wouldn't rise in the morning to find too much damage. After lying awake for a bit longer, he finally drifted off to sleep.

The sound of a voice calling his name jolted him awake, and thinking he was home, Levi shot out of the bed. By the time his feet hit the floor, he remembered where he was. The voice was not his *vader*'s but Jacob's.

Quickly, Levi got dressed and ran down the hall.

"Levi, come! We must hurry!"

Chapter Three

He met Jacob in the kitchen.

"I was out in the shop, and my workers came in and told me about storm damage throughout the area. We are going to head over to the schoolhouse. There's been a lot of damage there."

"Oh my! Sadie will be beside herself if something has happened to the school," Rachel said as she came up behind them.

Levi wondered what Sadie had to do with the schoolhouse. But there wasn't time to ask questions as they hurried outside into the early-morning light and hitched up one of Jacob's wagons, then joined the line of others on the main road heading toward Miller's Crossing.

Looking out from the wagon, Levi could see where the storm had cut a path. Trees were felled in single rows along one of the hedgerows, and sirens were going off. They had to pull off onto the shoulder of the road to wait as an ambulance and fire truck sped past.

"I fear there's been a lot of damage, Levi."

"Me, too." He hung on tight as Jacob took the next

corner at a good clip. "You were lucky your property was spared," Levi said.

"The storm circled around my house. I'm praying most of my neighbors have escaped any serious damage." Jacob pulled in the reins, slowing the horse's pace, and said, "The schoolhouse is up ahead."

Levi sat up taller, trying to catch a glimpse over the three wagons that had stopped on the side of the road just ahead of them. He let out a low whistle at the sight of what, by his best estimate, had to be a one-hundred-year-old oak tree split right down the middle. Half of it lay on the lawn in front of the long white schoolhouse. The other half was twisted in large sections. Large limbs had landed on an outbuilding and on top of the roof on a section of the one-story schoolhouse.

Hopping down, Jacob attached the reins to a hitching post on the side of the graveled driveway. Levi followed him.

"Come on. Let's go see what we can do to help." Jacob led them over to the downed tree where a group of men had gathered. A few of them moved to the side to allow Jacob and Levi room to step in.

"I think we should break into groups," a tall man was saying. "One can start cutting the tree off the roof of the school and the others can see if the shed can be salvaged."

Out of the corner of his eye, Levi saw movement toward the back of the school building. Quietly he left the group to go investigate. There was no telling how safe the structures were under the weight of the trees, and he would hate to see someone get hurt. Pushing aside branches and stepping over twigs, he picked his way through the debris, coming to a stop around the backside of the schoolhouse.

He saw a flash of black. Was that a prayer *kapp*? A young woman raised her head, and there was no mistaking who she was.

Sadie Fischer.

Placing his hands on his hips, Levi looked at her. There were branches and twigs stuck all around her. He wondered how she even got in the spot to begin with. Even though she had tiny brown twigs sticking out from her hair, she looked a darn sight better than she had when he'd first met her yesterday. She lifted her head to look up at him, one hand holding a branch, the other shielding her face from the morning sun.

She narrowed her eyes. "Levi Byler, is that you?"

"Ja."

She frowned. "I don't need your rescuing today. As you can see, there's plenty of help to be had."

"I know that." Folding his arms, he widened his stance, trying to decide if he should help her out from the tangle of branches or go find someone else to help her.

She gave him a cross look, sucking in her lower lip as she wiggled around trying to find a way out of the brush pile.

"Ugh!"

"Geb acht!" Levi yelled.

Letting out a sigh, he dropped his arms and stepped toward her. If she wasn't careful, she would fall and get hurt. Levi was a stranger in these parts and there was no way he'd be accused of letting this woman get injured his first full day in town.

"Let me take hold of that branch and then you can slide out."

To his surprise, she did as told, letting the branch slip from her grasp into his hands. Once he felt certain it wouldn't spring back and hit her in the face, he let go and then reached for her. Of course, she pushed his hand away, stepping out of the branches on her own.

"Danke," she offered, brushing some leaves from her apron and pulling the twigs from her hair. "I can't believe the damage the storm brought. I came here with my *vader* to check on the building, and we were shocked to see all the trees that are down. And our *Englisch* neighbors had a tree come down on their car. I think they've lost power, too."

"It was a big storm."

"Some are saying it might have been a tornado. I'm not sure. What do you think?"

He shrugged, once again amazed at how quickly she could talk. "I think it's too soon to tell. Straight-line winds for sure." He tipped his head, looking her over. It was dangerous being out and about in the middle of broken tree limbs. "What are you doing back here by yourself?"

"I came to check on the flowers." Her mouth dipping downward, she shuffled her feet along a brown patch of grass. "I think they are a total loss."

"Why would you be worrying about the flowers at a time like this?" He was more concerned about the building coming down around her.

"The *kinder* and I planted them at the end of the school year. The flowers were a special project." In the next breath, she asked, "Are you here to help out with the cleanup?"

"I came over with Jacob. Some of his workers were talking about this damage."

"Probably Abram Schmidt. I have two of his *kinder* in my class."

Levi tried to put this all together. Obviously, she cared about the school a great deal, otherwise she wouldn't be here worrying about the plants. Was she some sort of assistant? "You help out here at the school?"

Sadie pulled back her shoulders. "I do more than that, Mr. Byler. I'm the teacher here."

Levi's jaw dropped. He gave his head a shake in disbelief. But she had no reason to tell him otherwise. He frowned, trying to imagine her in a classroom as anything other than a student.

"You seem surprised."

Remembering his own teacher, who had been much older than Sadie and a lot more stern-looking, he offered, "Well, you just don't seem the type."

He didn't think it possible that she could narrow her eyes any more, but she managed. In a firm voice, she asked, "There's a type?"

Seeing he'd upset her, Levi held up his hands, gave her what he thought was a friendly grin and said, "You know what I mean."

Putting her hands on her hips, she glared up at him, her blue eyes filled with indignation.

"I don't know what you mean," she snapped.

Sadie had better things to do than stand here talking to this man. Why did he have to be the one to find her out here? She hadn't been all that stuck. Not like yesterday, anyway.

"Levi! There you are. We were wondering where you'd gotten off to," Jacob said as he came around the back of the building. And then he noticed Sadie. "Sadie! What are you doing back here?"

"Checking on the flower garden."

He wagged a finger at her. "You shouldn't be worrying over that."

She knew that, not when the school was in such a state. But her first thought had been for the children and how they'd worked so hard on this project. They'd been looking forward to seeing the fruits of their labor. If the garden could be saved, then they would have some hope.

Jacob said to Levi, "We were just dividing up the workload for the cleanup."

Sadie looked at Jacob, was thankful he'd saved her from any further chatting with Levi. To think he'd been surprised that she could be the schoolteacher. Sadie was well aware that pride goeth before the fall, but she was a *gut* teacher. She took her time smoothing down the folds of her dress, waiting for her temper to settle. It wouldn't do a bit of good to show her annoyance. Today was a day when everyone needed to work together, even if part of that everyone included Levi Byler.

She focused on Jacob. "*Gut*. The sooner we get this cleaned up, the sooner I can get on with preparing for the upcoming school year. We've only a few weeks until the first day," she reminded him.

"*Ja*, I know." Patting Levi on the back, Jacob added, "Come on around to the front. We need to get you your assignment."

Sadie stayed a few steps behind as the three of them walked around to where Abram Schmidt was speaking.

"We're going to have the older boys remove the brush

and smaller tree branches, while the men can cut the tree up into manageable lengths. The good news is the cleanup here will give us enough wood for next year's winter heating. The Lord does provide. And this will surely help with our next school budget.

"I think it best if we break up into three groups. One will work on getting the shed area cleared, one will work on the front and the other will see about damage to the school building," Abram went on.

Sadie looked around the lawn and noticed a few more buggies had pulled up in front. Some were loaded with saws and young men who'd come to help. Others carried women with baskets of food and thermoses. Confident the cleanup would be handled in a timely manner and knowing she wouldn't be needed there, Sadie headed off to join the women.

Rachel ran toward her. "Sadie!"

Sadie gave her a wave. "Rachel. *Gute mariye.*"

"*Ach*, I'm not sure how *gut* the morning is, what with all the damage in our community." Rachel wrinkled her nose.

"It is a *gute mariye* because no one was injured," Sadie reminded her.

Rachel gave her a thoughtful smile. "This is true. What do you think the damage is to the school?"

"I can't say for certain. I was out in the back hoping the flowers the *kinder* and I planted in the spring had survived. But I'm afraid all I saw were broken stems, and some of the plants were smushed underneath the tree limb that fell across the back."

"Those can be replanted," Rachel assured her.

"They can." Still, Sadie knew the *kinder* would be disappointed.

She linked her arm through Rachel's as they walked over to their friends. She said hello to a few of her students' *mamms* and was happy to see Lizzie Burkholder in the circle. Sadie broke away from Rachel to give Lizzie a hug.

"*Es dutt mir leed* my pot holders never made it to the store. I got myself into a bit of a mess while walking over."

Lizzie laughed. "You will have to tell me all about it."

"Well, let's just say it wasn't my finest moment."

Rachel came up to them. "Let's talk while we set up the food table. I see there are a few picnic tables we can use. You know how our men are. They will be hungry before you know it."

Sadie and Lizzie walked to where the tables had been set up in the side yard. They put out red-and-white-checked tablecloths as Sadie filled her friend in on yesterday's mess. Telling her how she'd taken the path behind the church and ended up stuck in the mud. By the time she'd finished recounting her day and how she'd been rescued by a stranger, the table was laden with sandwiches, salads and a big basket of apples.

Sadie kept her hands busy, but her mind was elsewhere. She was anxious to hear what the damage to the school might be and prayed they'd be able to open it in time for the new school year.

"Who is that man standing by Jacob?" Lizzie asked. "He keeps looking over this way."

Sadie glanced over her shoulder. Pulling her mouth into a thin line, she answered, "That is Levi Byler."

"Your rescuer," Lizzie said, her eyes widening in curiosity. Nudging Sadie in the side with her elbow, she added, "He's headed this way."

Turning around to face him, Sadie figured he was coming for some food. She guessed he might not have had time for breakfast. His strides were long and purposeful as he crossed the lawn.

Levi stopped in front of her, and the gaggle of women behind her grew quiet. Sadie knew they were going to listen in. She had no desire to be fodder for their gossip. Squaring her shoulders, she tipped her head back to look up at him. He did not look happy at all. Of course, there was a lot of work to be done, and perhaps he was still tired from his long day yesterday. Either way, Sadie was beginning to think one of Rachel's egg salad sandwiches was not going to help his mood.

Sadie pasted her best smile on her face, the same one she used when a student became unruly. Folding her hands in front of her apron, she asked in a cheery voice, "Is there something I can help you with?"

Levi wasted no time with his answer. "It appears that the work assignments have been given out."

A bad feeling wiggled along Sadie's spine. "I'm afraid I don't understand what that has to do with me."

"I am to work with the schoolteacher to get the schoolhouse ready for the new semester. And once that's done, I'll be overseeing the shed repair. Since you are the teacher, I guess this means you and I will be working together."

Sadie's jaw went slack.

Chapter Four

Behind her she heard an "oh" escape Rachel's mouth. Sadie didn't dare turn around. She knew Rachel and a few of the others must be grinning in delight over this turn of events. Her friends knew she was independent and enjoyed being in charge of her classroom. While she did have older students who helped with the lessons of the younger *kinder*, the setting up and running of the schoolroom fell to her.

Having to work side by side with this stranger would be a challenge for sure, even if he was a relative of Jacob's. She decided it was best to remain professional. After all, she was the teacher and she wanted the best for her students. Her discomfort over the matter shouldn't be of any concern.

Except that feeling didn't seem like it would be going away anytime soon.

Sadie blew out a breath, then said, "Well, why don't you grab something to eat, and after that, we'll take a look at the damage and make a list of what needs to be done in order to get the school fixed."

She followed him to the food table and did the neighborly thing by introducing him to the women who'd cooked the food. They piled his plate high with an egg salad sandwich and spoonfuls of two kinds of potato salad, along with a generous helping of her own *mamm*'s locally famous macaroni salad. A smile tugged at her mouth when she saw Rachel add a large chocolate chip cookie. She wasn't sure Levi would be able to eat everything.

But he managed. After he finished, he tossed his empty paper plate and utensils in a nearby trash can and gave her a half smile. "Shall we go take stock of what needs to be fixed?"

Nodding, Sadie couldn't help thinking again that Levi Byler needed to smile more. Smiles had a way of warming one's soul. From his stiff demeanor, she had a feeling Levi's soul was in need of some warmth. She walked ahead of him, leading the way to the front door of the schoolhouse, which was ajar.

As she stepped over the threshold, her breath caught in her throat, and her hand covered her heart. "Oh my," she breathed at the sight before them.

Shards of glass littered the floor where a window on the left side had been broken by a tree limb. The wood floor had puddles of water clear to the center of the room. Some of the educational posters on the wall had blown off and were lying in the water. One of the green blackout shades flapped in the breeze against the broken window.

Sadie paused to send up a fervent prayer of thanks that all her students had been safe in their homes when the disaster hit. This damage could be fixed.

Still, a sadness filled her. It was difficult to see the classroom that she'd grown to love and take comfort in looking such a mess. The storm had been ferocious. Sadie knew in her heart this all could have been so much more devastating.

Bending down, she picked up a paperback book that had fallen off a shelf. Setting the soggy mess on a desk she was standing next to, she turned to look at Levi. He, too, stood taking in the storm damage. Her gaze followed his up to a basketball-size hole in the roof. She could see clear out to the sky, now blue. They'd need to get a tarp on that right away.

Looking down at her, he said, "It could have been worse."

"Ja," she agreed, as he gave voice to her thoughts. "At least it's not a total loss like the shed appears to be."

When she'd gone out earlier to check on the garden, she'd carefully avoided what was left of the shed. They'd kept the garden supplies and some of the playground equipment out there, but all of that could be replaced.

She picked her way through the debris. Walking over to her desk, she found a notebook and a pen. Picking them up, she started making a list of what needed to be done. First off, *clean up.* Then *fix the window.* She was about to add *replace torn posters and damaged books* when Levi approached her.

"I'm going to see if anyone has a tarp stored in their wagon. At least we can get that hole covered up until we get the supplies needed to fix it."

"That sounds like a *gut* idea," Sadie replied. "Then we can work on the rest of the list."

He raised an eyebrow.

"Is there something the matter?"

He shook his head.

Twirling the pen between her fingers, she kept her

tone even as she said, "Please don't tell me you have a problem with making lists."

Sadie, for one, liked lists. They kept her on track. Maybe Levi was the type of person who kept everything in his head.

"I don't. You give me what you come up with and I'll see that whatever is on there gets taken care of."

"Mr. Byler, I'm perfectly capable of helping out here. I know the students and what needs to be in place before they return in a few weeks for the start of the fall semester. It makes sense that I handle getting the ruined classroom supplies replaced. Besides, you're going to be very busy working on the building." Softening her tone, she added, "Unless you think you'll have time to go to the King's Office Supply and Bookstore to pick up what I'll need."

While she waited for his reply, Sadie looked beyond him, once again surveying the mess caused by the storm, only now seeing the torn strip of paper hanging from the wall. One of her most loved quotes:

Be Kind, Be Thoughtful, Be Genuine, But Most Of All, Be Thankful

Reading that reminded her she should be thankful for all of the help here today, including Levi Byler's.

It also reminded her that she loved this building and what it represented. Here was where the *kinder* came to learn not only their numbers and letters but how to be kind. She taught them about their faith, forgiveness and how to work together. They also practiced the Golden Rule, to treat others as you would want to be treated.

It pained her to see even one thing out of place. The

kinder she taught were part of her community. Many were a part of her family. They deserved to come back to a building that had been repaired to its fullest potential. She owed it to them to see that that happened.

Besides, she didn't want to disappoint the school board either. It had been hard enough convincing them she was the right person for the job. It wouldn't do to have some storm come through and prove otherwise.

She knew full well the men of this community were strong, but the women could be counted on, too. Sadie could find a way for her and Levi to work together.

Levi watched various emotions play out on Sadie's face. Her expression had gone from determination to sadness and finally to acceptance. He didn't want to waste time arguing with her, but this project was the first one for him as Jacob's helper and he wanted it to go well. He had to make this work. It shouldn't be too bad. Obviously, this teacher wanted what was best for her students, as did he.

Of course, his way of tackling a project wasn't necessarily making lists. He liked to get a feel for a job before stepping into it. He got the idea that Sadie wanted to get her lists made and then dole out the tasks.

Being a stranger to this community didn't make his job any easier. He didn't mind helping where help was needed, even if repairing the school hadn't been the reason he'd come to Miller's Crossing. But you never knew what life was going to hand you.

Levi came close to letting out a snort at that last thought. Life certainly hadn't gone the way he'd planned. He should have been married by now, setting up a home with the woman he loved. But the Lord had other plans. Levi knew better than to try to interpret what those might be. He had to trust in the Lord.

Letting those thoughts tumble from his mind, he looked at Sadie.

She had gone back to writing on her notepad. From the way her hand had moved three quarters of the way down the page, he surmised the list had grown a bit longer.

He realized that she would know better than he what needed to be replaced. Looking around, he took in the larger damage. The broken window, the hole in the roof. That roof damage in and of itself could lead to more work. He wouldn't know until he got up there how many shingles were damaged. And he had no idea about the books and other things that needed to be replaced.

Putting his hands on his hips, he said, "I think you are right. It would be best if you took care of going to the office supply and bookstore."

"Danke."

He noticed a wisp of her blond hair had fallen from underneath her prayer *kapp*. She caught his gaze on her. Lifting her hand, she tucked the strand back in place. A light blush rose high on her cheekbones.

Levi looked down at the desktop. "Tell me what else you have on your list."

"Cleaning up the storm debris will be first because we won't know the full extent of the damage until we can see underneath everything. Then we'll need to clear out this room so we can scrub and paint." Letting out an exasperated sigh, she added, "There's so much to see to. I'm not sure this can all be done in a few weeks."

"There is a lot of help waiting right outside those

doors," he said, pointing over his shoulder at the group of men, both old and young, who had come out to assist.

"Yes. You are right. I'm overreacting."

He shook his head. "*Nee*. This mess is hard to look at. But we'll all work to get everything fixed, and it will be better than before."

The schoolteacher gave him a smile.

Levi simply nodded in return. "All right then. It seems like we're making headway."

"We are. Do you think you could call some of those helpers inside to start moving things?"

Levi left her at her desk and walked outside to find Jacob. On his way over to the men, he noticed that more tables had been added to the area where he'd eaten earlier, forming a long row of communal seating. Someone had erected a blue pop-up canopy to cover the food, and it ruffled in the warm breeze.

He met Jacob in the front yard. "Sadie and I have come up with a plan for the schoolhouse."

"I'm glad to hear that," Jacob replied. "We've given our groups their tasks. We're lucky enough that some of the older students have come by to assist. I think they should work with you and Sadie."

Levi nodded. It would be *gut* for the boys to help rebuild their own school. "I think the first order of business is to get a tarp up on the roof," Levi advised.

"*Ja*. I looked in the wagons that are here and didn't find any. You should go into the village and pick one up at the hardware store. I've an account there for my business. You can tell him you're my cousin and you have my permission to add the purchases to my account. And let Herb, the owner, know that I'll be in at the end of the week to settle as usual."

"I can do that. Is the tarp all we'll be needing?"

"Why don't you pick up extra tarps? We can use them to cover up the school desks and other items that Sadie wants protected. I have some boxes over at my shop that we can put the books and supplies in. And I think among the men who came today, we have enough supplies to begin the cleanup."

Jacob and Levi agreed to have the crews start removing the tree limbs from around the school first, and then they would take the portion of the trunk off the roof. Jacob took his tools out of his wagon and then told Levi to use that to go into town.

"If you think of anything else we might need, don't hesitate to buy it," Jacob told him as Levi climbed up onto the seat.

"Would you mind telling me the best way to get to the village?"

"Sure! Turn left at the first intersection and then go two more intersections. You'll see the sign pointing the way to Clymer. Go through the stoplight and you'll find the hardware store in the next block."

"Danke."

Levi set off the way Jacob instructed. Here and there along the way were signs of storm damage. A tree had fallen into a portion of the road, causing him to maneuver the horse onto the opposite side. When he came to the first intersection, he waited for a pickup truck and two cars to go through before proceeding.

Eventually he made it into the village and parked the wagon next to a small hitching post. Hopping down from his seat, he took a look around. Clymer was a quaint village. He noticed the hardware store and bank, and down the road he spotted a three-story, redbrick schoolhouse. This one was for the *Englisch kinder*. At the main intersection, he noticed the grocery store. Good to remember in case he needed any sundry items. He also saw the storefront for Burkholder's Amish Furniture and Art store. A really nice dining table and bench set were displayed in the window.

The door opened and a couple came out. The man was tall and carried some sort of canvas. At first Levi wasn't sure why the couple held his attention, and then it dawned on him that the woman looked very familiar. Her dark hair and her height, the angle of her jaw. She looked just like his former fiancée.

Levi didn't think it could be possible for her to be so close to Miller's Crossing. This woman wasn't wearing dark skirts and a prayer *kapp*. She was dressed in blue jeans with a sleeveless white top tucked into the waistband.

Shock rolled through him as he stared at the woman he'd once thought he loved. *What is she doing here?*

Chapter Five

"Anne?" he whispered.

The woman looked across the street, their gazes colliding, and he realized it wasn't her. Upon seeing him, an Amish man, the woman quickly reached into her pocketbook. She pulled out her cell phone and held it at arm's length, pointing it at him, and quickly tapped her finger on the screen. He ducked his head, hoping to avoid having his picture taken. Though he felt certain she'd managed to capture his image.

Levi's knees went weak with relief as he realized this woman was nothing more than just another *Englisch* tourist. Still, his breathing was quick and shallow. He kept his head bowed as he tried to absorb the pain that tore through his heart. He'd been trying for weeks to shut that part of his life off. And today, in this very minute, like the ripples of water lapping against a shoreline, the sadness washed over him. He kept his head downturned and swallowed against the tightness gripping his throat like a vise.

Taking in a breath, he waited for the tightness to ease. He exhaled, concentrating on the ache in his chest.

Levi knew a few deep breaths wouldn't fix what ailed him. He wanted this feeling of hurt and betrayal to be gone. There was no place in his life or in his heart now for it, and yet for the moment the unbearable pain crippled him.

He stood on the side of the road with life's noises in the background. Car horns and kids playing in their backyards filtered through the fogginess of his brain. He knew deep in his soul that Anne had made her choice. He'd accepted that. She had moved on and he'd chosen to come to Miller's Crossing to help his cousin, with the possibility of maybe starting fresh.

He heard a car door close, then an engine start, and he lifted his head, looking up as the two tourists drove off. Squaring his shoulders, Levi pushed his pain back down and entered the hardware store.

Within seconds, an *Englisch* man came over to ask if he needed assistance. Levi asked for a tarp large enough to cover the hole in the roof at the Amish school in Miller's Crossing. The man, whose nametag read Herb, led him to the back of the store.

"Wow, this shelf is almost empty. I guess with the storm we've had a lot of people come in needing these," the man observed. Pulling a large blue tarp off the top shelf, he handed it to Levi.

Levi noticed right away that it was the last one. "I don't need to take this if there's a chance someone else might come in with a hole in the roof of their home."

"Thanks for the offer, but we have an order coming in tomorrow morning. The storm damage in some sections of Clymer is pretty intense," Herb said. "Can I get you anything else?"

"*Ja*, I'll add a couple cases of roofing shingles and

nails." It wouldn't hurt to have them in case they were able to get started on the repair today.

He followed the man down another aisle, where they picked up the supplies. Back at the checkout counter, Levi told Herb this would go on his cousin Jacob's account. Herb seemed fine with that, looked up the information and then rang up the items. He printed out two receipts, handed one to Levi and put the other inside a ledger.

"If you need us to deliver any more supplies, just let me know."

"*Danke.* I'll tell Jacob."

"Do you have a wagon outside?"

"I do."

"Well, let me help you get this stuff loaded up."

Hefting one of the boxes of shingles onto his shoulder, Herb followed Levi outside and set it in the back of the wagon. Once everything was loaded, Levi headed back to the schoolyard. He imagined the crew would be about ready to get the tarp in place.

He was amazed at the amount of work that had been done in the two hours he'd been gone. The tree had been removed from the schoolhouse, and the older students had already started cutting the wood into smaller sections. Even from the driveway he could see a decent-size hole in the midsection of the roof. The tarp would cover that nicely until they could get back up there tomorrow. He parked the wagon with the others.

Jacob saw him drive in and came over to help unload.

"Looks like you've been busy," Levi commented.

"It's nice the older schoolboys are helping out. I think being a part of working on something that's for the good of the community keeps them grounded."

Levi agreed. When he was a young lad, he'd enjoyed working on community projects. It made him feel like he belonged to a larger family.

Hefting the heavy shingles onto one shoulder, he headed off toward the front of the schoolhouse, where he dropped the heavy shingles to the ground. Looking up, he noticed Sadie standing in the doorway speaking to a man he hadn't met. He appeared to be much older than her. With a gray beard and gray hair, the man stood with a slight hunch in his shoulders.

Sadie had her arms folded in front of her, and she wasn't smiling. As a matter of fact, he thought there might even be a scowl on her face. He wondered if the man was someone she didn't like.

Taking a handkerchief out of his pants pocket, Levi brushed the brim of his straw hat back and wiped the sweat from his forehead. The storm that had plowed through last night had left behind air thick with heat and humidity. The sweat seeped through his work shirt. Tucking the cloth back into his pocket, he walked over to the entrance. He was anxious to see what the interior looked like now that some of the debris had been cleared.

Sadie stood on the top step watching Levi's approach over the top of the man's head. Levi couldn't decide if the man was a relative or a neighbor. He overheard a portion of what the man was saying.

"I'm sorry I didn't come last night. The storm came in so fast."

"*Ja.* That it did."

Levi thought Sadie sounded agitated. He wondered why.

"Your *daed* was kind enough to invite me back to

dinner on another night," the man spoke softly, shifting his weight from one foot to the other.

"Then I'll see you on that night," Sadie replied in a dismissive tone.

Levi took that moment to step up to them. "Hello," he said to the man.

With a half smile, the man met Levi's gaze and stuck his hand out to shake. "I'm Isaiah Troyer."

"Levi Byler."

"New to the area?"

"I'm here to help my cousin Jacob Hershberger with his shed company." Looking around, Levi added, "And to help with these repairs."

"I imagine the storm caught you a bit off guard."

"It was a rough night."

"And now you are helping out here. *Gut* sturdy men can be hard to find. The community is fortunate you came to visit when you did," Isaiah said with a tip of his hat. "There seems to be enough help here and I've got work to do at home." Turning his attention back to Sadie, he said, "I hope to see you again soon."

Sadie nodded, spun on her heel and went inside. Again, Levi couldn't be certain, but it seemed that she really didn't like that man. Following her inside, he paused and looked around in surprise. The desks had all been moved to one side of the room and the bookcases were nearly emptied out, with the books stacked in cardboard boxes. The exposed hole in the roof brought in a lot of sunlight. That would be covered shortly.

The green blackout shades had been removed from all but one window in the back of the classroom. Sadie was working at getting the rest of the posters down and rolled up to be stored away. The side walls were bare, and there were still three left behind her desk on either side of the chalkboard.

He let out a short whistle. "You've been busy!"

Sadie shook her head. "I didn't do this alone. I had plenty of help."

"This is a *gut* start."

"It is. I'm thankful for all the students who've come by. And the *mudders* have restocked the food table twice now," Sadie said with a laugh. "If you're hungry, you can go out and grab something."

"I'm *gut*," Levi told her.

She noticed the sweat on his brow and seeping through his shirt. Even she was feeling the heaviness of the humidity and had gone out a few minutes ago to get herself something cold to drink.

"How about a lemonade?" she asked.

"I can get one if I'm thirsty."

"Okay," she said. *Suit yourself.* She turned around to look at what was left of the posters on the wall. She reached up to take the one with the alphabet down from behind her desk. Except the tack on the top right side held firm. Her first instinct was to give it a tug, but she didn't want to tear it. Instead she grabbed for the back of her desk chair, planning to stand on it, but jumped when she felt a warm hand on hers.

She hadn't heard Levi come over. She spun around and looked up, ready to offer him a thankful smile. Except he stood scowling down at her. She bit her lower lip and wondered why he acted as though he didn't like her. Maybe she was being too judgmental. She did her best to be kind to everyone, including Isaiah Troyer. Of course, if she were honest, she did not want to do anything to make that man think there would be a union between the two of them.

His arrival here today indicated that he genuinely wanted to help out. This school was a part of his community. But the last thing she needed right now was a distraction. She wanted to concentrate on restoring her school.

"I can get this down," Levi said. "No need for you to climb up on the chair."

Stepping aside, she let Levi remove the last three posters. After rolling and wrapping a rubber band around each one, she gathered them up and placed them in the last open box. With that done, she only had to get the desks moved to the basement and the last green shade down. Then she could think about cleaning the room so they could repair, repaint and reopen in time for her to teach the three R's. Sadie let out a laugh.

Levi looked at her. "What's so funny?"

"Nothing. A silly thought I had, that's all. *Danke* for helping me get those posters down. Now I can move the desks downstairs, and we can begin the hard work."

"You know the menfolk can handle this."

"I do, but it's still my classroom. I'm able to use a paint roller and wipe a window clean."

"I'm sure you are. But you can't do any of those things until we have the repairs finished. By my best estimation, that will be sometime next week."

Sadie did her own calculation, determining they had exactly three weeks to get everything done. Two weeks to do the repairs would leave her with a week to get the classroom set up and ready for the new school semester. "That should work."

"Keep in mind, Sadie, that we still don't know the extent of the roof damage."

"Speaking of the roof," Jacob said as he strode into the classroom, "we've got a ladder so we can get up there, take a closer look and get the tarp on before nightfall."

Coming around from behind the desk, Levi joined Jacob, saying, "All right then, let's go."

The three of them went outside. Sadie stood off to one side. Raising her hand to shield her eyes from the brightness of the sun, she watched while the men took turns climbing up the ladder. Jacob yelled down for someone to bring up the tarp. Once that was done, they covered the hole. She ran her hand along her forehead to wipe the beads of perspiration away.

Someone bumped into her elbow, and Sadie smiled when she turned and saw Lizzie.

"Lizzie!" Sadie gave her friend a big hug.

"This heat is getting to me. Why don't you come over to the tent and have something cold to drink? I made my pink lemonade."

Sadie loved seeing her dear friend so happy. Lizzie's transformation had been nothing short of a miracle. Ever since marrying Paul Burkholder, she'd been beaming. Right now, she was smiling from ear to ear. Even the scar that had marred her dear friend's face since the childhood accident that took her *bruder*'s life had faded into nothing more than a barely noticeable thin line.

"Let's go get that drink," Sadie said, sliding her arm through Lizzie's. She wouldn't tell her that she'd just had one. On a day like this, a person couldn't get enough to drink.

"This storm left behind a lot of humidity."

"That it did. Maybe tomorrow will be better for working outside."

"I know we shouldn't be complaining." Lizzie laughed.

They walked across the schoolyard to the shady area where the tents and tables were set up. The women were busy doling out the last of the salads and sandwiches from the coolers. Sadie knew they'd be refilled and brought back tomorrow. She let Lizzie lead her to the drink table, where Lizzie handed her a glass of the cold lemonade. Bringing the paper cup to her lips, she drank in the mixture of tart sweetness. Always a perfect fix to the heat.

Sadie turned and looked out over the yard. She could see the area where the *kinder* played kickball. Beyond that were the swing set and slide. Branches and twigs littered the area. But that would all be gone in a few days.

"Tell me how things are going." Lizzie picked up a drink and stood beside Sadie.

"We accomplished a lot today. And I feel that tomorrow, with the desks cleared and the books packed away, the men can get in and fix the window. There are a few spots in the one wall that need to be patched."

"I saw Isaiah Troyer earlier."

Sadie swallowed a mouthful of lemonade. She concentrated on watching the men put away their tools for the day. She wasn't sure how much Lizzie knew about the situation. But she had to talk to someone about her feelings.

"*Ja.* He came by to check on me."

"That was nice of him, don't you think?" Lizzie asked, keeping her voice low so the other women couldn't hear them.

"What I think is that he is too old for me."

"He's the man your *vader* has chosen."

"He is, but my *vader* understands my feelings on this matter."

Lizzie looked at her sympathetically. "He can understand, but do you think it will make any difference?"

Sadie shrugged. "You know how I feel about finding the right man."

Lizzie's face softened with laughter. Her eyes lit up as she chuckled, recited Sadie's very thoughts on the matter. "He can't be too old or too young. He has to be your perfect Amish man."

They burst out laughing. Someone cleared their throat. Sadie swung her head around and came face-to-face with Levi Byler.

Chapter Six

She heard Lizzie's surprised intake of breath. Her own seemed caught in her throat.

Oh my goodness!

Sadie could only imagine what Levi must be thinking of her now. Although if the deep frown he wore was any indication, she might think he didn't approve of her requirements for a husband.

At that moment, Sadie couldn't help wondering if perhaps she was turning into one of those women who simply couldn't make up their minds about things like this. *Nee.* She knew what she wanted. Lizzie's words were Sadie's truth.

She coughed, then asked, "Are the men done for the day?"

"They are. Everyone is packing up and heading home. Most of them have evening chores that need tending to," he answered, avoiding making eye contact with her.

Sadie felt bad that he'd overheard a conversation between two lifelong friends. Friends who very rarely kept things from one another.

"Well, Lizzie and I are going to help pack up here and then we'll be heading to our homes, too."

"Okay. Will you need a ride?"

She shook her head. "My *vader* is right over there." She pointed behind Levi to the place in the yard where her *vader* had pulled the family wagon in line with the others a few minutes ago.

"I'll see you tomorrow."

"I'll be here bright and early," Sadie quipped, giving Levi her best smile.

She watched him walk off, then turned to help with the last of the packing up. Lizzie was bent over a large red cooler, putting away empty plastic containers. Sadie joined her, handing her the last three left on the picnic table.

"I take it he heard what I said?" Lizzie wanted to know.

"I'm afraid so."

"You don't seem too upset by that."

"I'm not. He didn't mention our conversation, but I could tell by the look on his face that he'd heard us. I don't know Levi all that well. But from what I've seen so far, he tries to keep to himself."

Lizzie shrugged. "Maybe that will change as he gets to know us all better. He is Jacob's cousin, so he does have some family here. I'm sure once he settles in, he'll get more comfortable."

"Maybe." But even as she agreed, Sadie had a feeling Levi just might not be the outgoing type.

After saying her goodbyes to Lizzie and the other women who'd been helping out under the food tent, Sadie went to meet her *vader*. He was waiting for her in the shade of a stand of maple trees. She waved at him. When he saw her coming toward him, he smiled at her.

"Good afternoon, *dochder*."

"Good afternoon, *vader*."

Nodding in the direction of their wagon, he walked with her over to where he'd parked it. "Did the day go well?"

"*Ja*. The men came out in full force. Tomorrow we can start repairing the inside of the schoolhouse."

Sadie caught him looking beyond her to where Levi and Jacob were getting into Jacob's wagon. Both men looked flushed from the heat and tired.

Sadie rubbed a hand along her face, feeling the warmth of her skin beneath her fingertips. The humidity had spiked. She prayed there wouldn't be another storm tonight. Unfortunately, this was the time of the year for them. She'd long gotten over her childhood fear of late-night storms and the thunder and lightning that came with them. The crops needed the rain.

"This cousin of Jacob's, did he help out today?"

Sadie gave a start at his question. It was interesting that her *vader* wanted to know about Levi. "*Ja*." She thought it best to leave her answer at that.

Her *vader* wanted a union between her and Isaiah Troyer. Sadie knew that wasn't going to happen. She feared her *vader* might be upset if he knew she was working with Levi Byler. Being the schoolteacher, her life required a different set of proprieties. She had a reputation to keep. Even though they were working among a lot of other community members, her *vader* might frown upon their partnership.

However, the only thing that concerned her was get-

ting the school up and running in time for the new semester. She didn't care how that came about.

Settling herself onto the seat of the wagon, Sadie adjusted her blue skirt. The toll of putting in a long day's
work was catching up with her. Her shoulders ached
from moving the desks, and her feet felt as if they might
explode out of her shoes. She couldn't wait to get her
shoes and stockings off. She wiggled her toes in antic-
ipation. As they rode past the white schoolhouse, she
saw the blue tarp flattened against the roof covering the
hole. She sent up a prayer of thanksgiving that today
had gone well and that the Lord had sent an extra pair
of hands in the form of Levi Byler.

"Did you happen to see Isaiah?" her *vader* asked.

"He came by to check on me," Sadie admitted.

"Gut."

"Vader—" she started, wanting to tell him to stop
wasting his time and effort on something that would
not happen.

His stern voice interrupted her. "*Dochder*, you have
no idea how I wish you would abide by my decision
concerning you and Isaiah."

"I understand."

He slapped the leather reins against the backside of
the large mare pulling the wagon. "I'm not sure you do."

"Can't you please give me a little more time?" Sadie
asked softly.

A breeze blew in from the north, bringing with it a
hint of coolness. Sadie lifted her face, letting the air
wash over her. She waited for an answer from her *vader*,
hoping he would continue to allow her lenience in this
matter.

"I know you're going to be busy at the school, and

that's where your attention should be. The community needs you there. But that doesn't mean I'll be forgetting about my wishes where your future is concerned."

Sadie looked over at her *vader*. His jaw was set in that stubborn way he had when he was mad.

She didn't want him to be angry with her over this. There was too much at stake. Her future, for one. And her heart. She couldn't waste either on a man she would never love. She knew there were plenty of marriages built on love. Jacob and Rachel, and Lizzie and Paul came to mind. They'd all overcome obstacles, but in the end, they'd found their true love. That was all she wanted.

Blowing out a breath, she wondered if that kind of love was even in the Lord's plans for her.

A week later Levi stood in the schoolyard, the early dawn light casting soft shadows from the trees onto the lawn. The air was still and quiet. He liked working in solitude, without distraction. On his way here, he'd seen deer drinking out of a stream and red-winged blackbirds perched on the fence that ran along Jacob's property. The early-morning hours were the perfect time to reflect and meditate on the good word.

Unfortunately, some of today's thoughts were filled with words he'd overheard Sadie and her friend saying last week.

He found it interesting that she was so set on knowing what she wanted for every part of her life. Like how she wanted the classroom to look when it was finished and what she wanted in a husband. Mind you, none of the latter was any of his business, but he'd heard her words and there was no forgetting them.

Levi wanted to tell her, based on his life experience thus far, that there was no such thing as a "perfect" person, be they Amish or otherwise. Every last one of them had been born with flaws. It didn't take much to remind him the reason he was here had nothing to do with finding a proper wife and everything to do with putting his hands to work. Busy hands kept one's mind from wandering back to the past.

Of course, he could have stayed in his community. If not for Jacob's offer of employment, he might have done just that. Levi was a strong person. But he hadn't expected the turn his life took a few months ago to leave him feeling so unsettled. His *mamm* had been the one to encourage him to make a change. She'd seen the pain Anne's betrayal had caused and had told Levi a new start could be what he needed. Coming here to Miller's Crossing had seemed like the right thing to do.

Bringing his mind back to the task at hand, he rubbed his hands together, feeling a blister on the inside of his right thumb. It was his own fault. The preceding days had been filled with many tasks, and he hadn't been wearing the work gloves Jacob had given him. He'd been hammering away on the shingles, replacing some of the wood siding and even helping chop a bit of wood.

Levi rolled the ache out of his shoulders, aware of the heat. Not even nine o'clock and the August day was growing hot. He'd been in the schoolyard since sunup, hoping to get ahead of the workload. Swiping his sleeve across his brow, he walked around the back of the schoolhouse to take a look at where the shed once stood. He knew it would be at least two more days before he could get started out here, but he wanted to get an idea of the size of the original foundation.

He did a quick pace of the area. Walking heel-to-toe along the remaining slab, he estimated the structure had been sixteen by twelve feet. A decent size for storage.

Jacob had told him this morning that he didn't have a shed of this size in stock. They would have to build it from scratch. He also suggested that rather than constructing it at the shed company, they should work here, on-site. This would save them in shipping costs since Jacob contracted with a local transport company to deliver the sheds.

Levi wanted to get this project done. Then he could begin working with Jacob on his business. The shed company was doing really well, and he knew Jacob was anxious to expand. Levi wanted to support him.

Meanwhile, it was time to start repainting the walls inside the school. He said hello to one of the women who still came by to help with the food tent, which had decreased in size as fewer workers were needed. But the food and drinks were still welcomed by the remaining crew.

He walked along the side of the school, noticing how the new clapboards blended in with the old. The windows were open, letting in the summer breeze, and he caught a glimpse of Sadie inside talking to some of her students. He recognized an older boy from earlier this week.

"Miss Sadie, my *vader* said I should work with you today," the tall, lanky boy was saying.

"Thank you so much, Jeremiah. It's very kind of him to allow you to be here. We're going to start painting!"

Levi heard the excitement in her voice. He walked through the tall blades of grass and made his way around to the front door. Entering the room, he noticed that Sadie was indeed ready for painting. She had on a light blue skirt and matching blouse covered by a canvas work apron. Her hair was neatly tucked up under her prayer *kapp*. Three five-gallon pails of flat-white paint sat near the door, along with four rolls of blue painter's tape, paint pans, rollers and paintbrushes.

Surveying the room, he thought it might take the three of them the better part of a day to get this job done. He was pleased when a few others in the community straggled in. That meant he would be freed up to begin work on the shed.

"Mica! Josh! *Danke* for coming today," Sadie greeted the newcomers. Then turning to Levi, she explained, "I asked Josh Troyer and his friend Mica King to help us out, too. I hope you don't mind."

Seeing her delight in getting extra help made him realize that Sadie could be extremely resourceful.

"More hands make less work for us," he commented.

"That's what I was thinking. We should start by taping off all of the windows. Then we can get the paint on the walls. Once that is done, I can have the men help bring the desks up from the basement. Then we can get everything back in place. The room is going to look the nicest it's ever been when we are finished. The students deserve a clean, safe place for their learning. Don't you agree, Levi?"

His head was spinning over all the words she managed to get out in a few seconds. He started to answer her, but she began talking again.

"As soon as the paint dries, we can bring the posters back out and get them hung up and get the shades back up on the windows. And then I can start hauling in the boxes of books. I still have to get over to the stationery store to pick up the replacements for the books that were damaged. I'm so excited, Levi—it's looking like we'll be done on time."

"That it does. You're a good worker."

He didn't know why he said that. She was a *good worker*. That sounded so impersonal, like he was speaking to one of the men. But his compliment brought a light blush to her cheekbones, and Levi found himself wanting to smile.

"*Danke.* I just want everything to be perfect for the students."

"With your enthusiasm, I'm certain that it will be."

Mesmerized by the sparkle of hope reflected in her blue eyes, Levi found it hard to look away. But it appeared that she had her mind set on getting today's work started, and her attention quickly shifted from him to the young man standing next to her.

"The first thing we need to do is get the blue tape around the door and window frames," she said to Jeremiah. "Why don't you help me get that started?"

Eager to please, the young man's head bobbed up and down so hard, his hat nearly tumbled from his head. He managed to catch it in time as he followed his teacher over to the pile of supplies stacked near the door. Sadie pulled the protective plastic wrap off the rolls of tape and handed one to Jeremiah.

"Since you're one of the tallest, let's have you start with the entry door."

Jeremiah's reach went almost to the top of the door-frame.

Levi stopped him.

"Wait. Don't overreach or you'll end up hurting your back. Let me go find a ladder for you, Jeremiah."

Levi went outside and brought back in a five-step ladder. Setting it up, he said, "Watch your step, and don't go above the fourth rung."

Words from the instructor at the Ladders Last safety seminar he and Jacob had attended together in Saratoga last year came back to him. He never imagined he'd be using the lesson at a school. But, he supposed, *gut* advice could be put to use in just about any situation.

Confident that Jeremiah could handle the job, Levi grabbed a roll and began taping around the windows. Sadie worked along the floor and walls.

It took the better part of the morning to get all the tape up. Even though it was a pain to do, it would save them the time scraping the windowpanes and floor-boards afterward.

Eventually, he heard a soft groan coming from the other side of the room and turned to see Sadie getting up from her hands and knees. Rushing over, he offered her his hand.

At first, he thought she was going to push him away, but then she took hold of his hand, saying, "*Danke.* I was down here far too long without a break."

He helped her into a standing position.

Sadie blew out a breath. "*Phew!* I'm glad that's done. Now we can get the canvas cloths on the floor and start this project."

Letting go of her hand, Levi followed her to the other side of the room. Together they unfurled the heavy canvas and laid the cloth out on the floor. Grabbing a steel tool that looked a lot like a can opener, he ran the tip of it around the rim of the first five-gallon bucket of paint. Setting the opener on the canvas, he carefully lifted the lid. The color was a simple off-white.

Peering over his shoulder, Sadie observed, "I really wanted a yellow for the new color. But they didn't have any and I didn't want to make the cost go higher by mixing a custom color."

Sitting back on his haunches, he looked up at her curiously. "Is yellow a favorite color of yours?"

She gave him a soft smile, nodding. "*Ja.* It reminds me of sunshine. But it's frivolous to have that here when most of the walls are covered with posters and bookshelves. Do you have a favorite color, Levi?"

Grabbing the handle of the paint bucket, he carefully tipped some into a heavy metal tray. He'd never really given color much thought. Most of his life had been surrounded by the simple colors of their clothing.

Concentrating on getting the paint into the tray and not onto the floor covering, he answered, "I suppose I favor blue."

"There are so many shades of blue."

He paused and said, "I like the color of the sky." *And your eyes.* He thought Sadie's eyes were about the prettiest blue he'd ever seen.

"*Ja.* The sky is pretty most days. Unless it's storming. But even then, it can be beautiful." Sadie's voice took on a wistful tone.

"We'd best concentrate on our work."

He stood, picked up the package of rollers and pulled them out. Placing one on a handle, he showed the boys how to glide the paint roller along the bottom of the flat metal pan.

"You don't want to get too much or else you'll have drips running down the walls," he advised.

Sadie nodded, adding, "And if you don't get enough,

then you'll have dry patches. We can't have that. Here, let me show you."

Reaching down, she took hold of one of the rollers and gently slid it into the pan. Once she had enough white paint, she moved the roller up and down on the wall.

"See how I'm making a W shape and how you're getting a lesson at the same time!" Sadie let out a laugh. "After you make that letter, you go back and fill in the space. Like this."

"This way you'll get a nice even coat," Levi finished, impressed with her painting skills.

"That's it exactly," Sadie agreed, smiling at him.

He felt the corners of his mouth turn upward and quickly busied himself with gathering a brush and container to pour some paint into. He didn't want to be drawn to Sadie, and yet he was finding it harder and harder to resist her charm. Turning away from everyone else, Levi began applying paint to the baseboard trim along the floor.

It wasn't long before he heard the light, sweet sound of someone humming. Sadie. Her voice sounded so lyrical. Levi listened to her hum one of the songs he remembered from his own school days. A little bit of light broke through the heaviness he'd been carrying around. He wanted to ignore the feeling, because he didn't want to attribute it to being around Sadie.

Levi didn't want another woman to work her way into his life. But the lightheartedness stayed with him as he dipped the paintbrush into the half-empty can. There was no denying the power of Sadie's positive attitude.

They worked until lunchtime.

"Come on, everyone. I believe you've more than

earned a lunch break." Looking at Levi, Sadie said, "You, too, Levi. I know I've worked up an appetite, and I don't care if that doesn't sound ladylike. I'm starving!"

He saw the flush of her cheeks that came with working hard in the summertime heat. With a laugh, Sadie spun on her heel and hurried out the door, stopping at the water pump to the right of the building to wash her hands.

"Boys, don't forget, cleanliness is next to godliness," she called out as Jeremiah, Mica and Josh plowed by her.

They turned around and rushed back to splash their hands in the water after she finished. Levi waited his turn, then putting his hands together, he splashed the water up on his face. The coolness refreshed him.

They formed a short line behind Sadie to get a hamburger hot off the grill that Jeremiah's *mudder* had set up.

"I thought you might be getting tired of the sandwiches. So, I had my husband bring over our gas grill."

"*Danke*, Susan." Sadie patted the woman on the forearm. "Your thoughtfulness is much appreciated."

"*Danke,*" Levi added. The delicious scent of the burgers caused his stomach to rumble loud enough for Sadie to hear.

"We'd best get you fed, Levi. I don't need you collapsing. And when you're ready, I want to talk to you about the new shed."

Levi blinked. They'd agreed to work together on the schoolhouse repair, and then he would be free to continue with the shed. The rebuild would be straightforward. A simple shed. Yes, he knew it was the school's shed, but they were on a tight schedule.

What could she possibly have to say about the shed project?

Chapter Seven

Sadie could tell by the look on Levi's face that he wasn't thrilled with her request. His mouth had taken on the same determined line she remembered from the day she'd first met him.

She pasted a smile on her face. Taking her paper plate with the hamburger and macaroni salad over to the picnic table, she joined the boys. After a few minutes, Levi sat at the opposite end of the bench.

It was clear he did not want to discuss the shed project over lunch. That was fine by her. She was content to enjoy every last bite of her hamburger. The boys sat across from them, inhaling their food.

"Boys. Slow down when you eat. I don't want you choking."

All three of them looked up at her, as if they'd forgotten their manners and that she and Levi were at the table with them.

"*Es dutt mir leed*, Miss Sadie," Jeremiah said. Nudging Josh with his right elbow, he added, "We're all sorry."

The other two boys put what was left of their burgers on the plate and nodded.

Leaning across the table, Jeremiah said, "My *mudder* makes the best burgers."

"*Danke*, son." Susan accepted the compliment as she joined them with her own plate. "Sadie, I cannot believe how much work you've gotten done in such a short time."

Sadie watched as the boys went back to eating at a much slower pace, then turned to Susan. "I've had a lot of help."

Susan glanced over to where Levi sat. "It was *gut* that you came along to our village when you did, Levi Byler. You've certainly been a great help to our Sadie and our school community. Though, I imagine your own community must miss you."

A look Sadie couldn't identify slid across Levi's face. Was it sadness or longing, maybe regret? She imagined he must be a bit homesick. Maybe not, though. It was hard to say, because she hadn't had any conversations with him about his life. She only knew the little that she'd learned the day he rescued her from the mudhole. And, of course, that blue was his favorite color.

They finished eating their lunch and returned to work. Levi got the boys set up painting the wall behind Sadie's desk while she continued to work on the trim around the windows. She was painting the lower half of the one by the entryway when Levi came up behind her with a brush in hand.

"I'll do the tops so you don't have to worry about standing on the ladder."

"That's very kind of you." Sadie grew pensive. Their

close proximity brought her the perfect opportunity to learn more about him.

As she dipped her brush into their shared paint can, she formulated her questions. She enjoyed learning about people. One of her favorite classes to teach was history. For a few days she and the *kinder* got lost in learning about the people who had come and gone before them. She wondered again what Levi's people might be like.

"Tell me, Levi, what is your community like?"

His movements stilled. Sadie thought the question was innocent enough. She continued moving the brush up and down the trim in short strokes. Waiting.

"I live closer to the city than you do. But we have farmland and ten church districts," he said. "Some are smaller than others."

"And your family?"

"My family?"

"Do you have a large family? I know you're part of Jacob's family, but what is your immediate family like? Most of us around here have large families, and some live near their elders or in the same house if it's big enough. My friend Lizzie's sister lives in the house they grew up in, with her husband and *kinder*. Lizzie and her husband, Paul, moved into the village to be closer to their shop."

"I see. I have two older *bruders* and a younger sister. They are all married off."

"But you're not." Sadie drew in a breath, surprised when she voiced her thought. "*Es dutt mir leed.* That is none of my business."

Levi turned away from her, appearing to concentrate on touching up the paint on the windows. Then he said,

"I understand. We're at a time in our lives when court-ships are all our families want to talk about."

"Perhaps I spend too much time ruminating about the subject." Softly she added, "I know you overheard my conversation with Lizzie."

"Ah. *Ja.* I might have heard some of what you were saying." He raised an eyebrow, studying her.

A shiver ran along her spine. It wasn't an unwanted feeling. Still, Sadie found herself wondering at her re-action to Levi. She was about to tell him she'd no inter-est in the man her *vader* wanted for her, then changed her mind. She didn't think Levi would care to hear her thoughts on the matter.

Eventually she turned away from him, focusing on her work. The only sound in the room came from the movement of the brushes and rollers. Even the boys had settled into a rhythm. Sweat trickled down Sadie's back, and she longed for a wisp of a breeze to come through the open windows. All the while she wished she could take back her words about Levi's marital state. His family and his life before coming here were none of her business.

They continued working in silence until she looked up and realized the room was finished.

Sadie sent the boys home, leaving her and Levi to finish the cleanup. She was helping him fold the drop cloth when he finally started talking to her again.

"What are your thoughts on the shed?" he asked, tak-ing her side of the folded cloth out of her hands.

Clearing her throat, she knew her idea might sound like extra work. "I want to add in two windows in the front so we can use them to start our seedlings for the garden. And I think some window boxes would be nice, too. This way the students can try out different types of plants."

"You have windows here." He pointed to the ones they'd just painted.

"We do, but they don't get the right light to grow seedlings in."

"It seems to be bright enough now."

"Yes, but this is the summer sunlight. The early-spring light comes in from that direction." Sadie nodded toward the east side of the room.

"And you can't use those windows?"

"*Nee.* The sills are not wide enough." She saw the stubborn set of his jaw and put her hands on her hips.

She would fight to the end for her students, and even though this might seem unimportant to him, for her this little thing was worth the effort.

Levi stared at her. She waited for his gaze to waver, and when it didn't, she broke the stare down by casting her gaze to the toes of her shoes. That was when she saw the paint spatters and knew her *mamm* would not be happy with her for making a mess of them yet again.

"Doesn't Jacob have a shed that we can use here?" she finally asked. "One with windows?"

"*Nee.* We're going to build this one on-site. He's swamped with business. Even before the storm, his orders were backed up, and now with people needing theirs replaced, he's running out of stock."

She nibbled on her lip, trying to come up with a way to convince Levi to add the windows to the new shed. "Is it the cost?"

"Nope."

"So, it's you not wanting to change your plans?"

"I guess it's been a long day and I don't have the energy left to think about changing any existing plans," he admitted to her.

Stubbing her toe along the floorboard, she grumbled, "I understand. But don't you think my idea is a *gut* one?"

"I do. However, it's not really up to us to make these changes."

She pondered his words, knowing the school board had put Jacob in charge of this project. He was a trusted member of the community. Surely, he would do this for her.

"What I want is to have an area for my students to work on their gardening skills."

Levi took the drop cloth over to the pile of leftover supplies. He fumbled around for a few minutes, tapping a hammer on top of the loosened paint can lid. Then he picked up the can and the drop cloth, brushing past her, and carried them out the front door.

Sadie hurried after him. Her patience thinning, and knowing the fatigue might be fueling her, she called out to him, "Levi! We're not finished with this."

He set the supplies in the back of his wagon. She saw the sweat breaking through the back of his shirt and knew he had to be as tired and worn out by the heat as she was. But that didn't stop her from wanting to know if he might at least consider her suggestions for the windows.

Resting an elbow on the side of the wagon, Levi pushed the brim of his straw hat off his forehead. Sadie tipped her head back a bit, looking up into his eyes. The blue-green color was striking in the afternoon light.

She ignored that thought, even though she knew many of her friends would consider him to be a handsome man. And she wouldn't be able to contradict them on that observation.

Her nerves became a jangle, a feeling she wasn't familiar with. Normally, she would plow through to make her point. But standing here, at the end of a long day spent working side by side, Sadie felt her conviction about the windows waver.

Nee. She must stop thinking like a schoolgirl and remember the interests of her students.

Using a soft, relenting tone, she asked, "Levi, will you please help me out here?"

He knew what she was doing, and while he might not trust her cajoling tone, he understood why she wanted him to make the changes. He supposed there wasn't any harm in bringing her idea to Jacob. She was right about one thing: the students' needs should come first.

Finally, he said, "I'll talk to Jacob."

He went back inside and brought out the rest of the cans, brushes and rollers. Sadie helped him clean up, until the exhaustion of the day caught up with her. Levi noticed her steps slowing on the last trip to the wagon. In two easy strides, he came alongside her, taking the can.

"Danke," she said, releasing the metal handle.

He squinted down at her, "Sadie, you've done a good day's work here. Let me drive you home."

"That won't be necessary. I rode my bike over this morning."

"Come on, it's too hot to ride it back home. The wagon will take half the time. I can put the bike in the back."

He saw her indecision, as well as her flushed cheeks. She had to be feeling the heat as much as he was.

She narrowed her eyes, as if she had a choice in the matter. "I don't want you to get any ideas about my needing rescuing, like the first time we met."

Biting back a half smile, he replied, "Nope. Think of it as a neighbor helping out a neighbor."

"All right. I left my bike near the pop-up canopy. Would you mind getting it for me?"

"I can do that."

After finding her bike, he wheeled it back and loaded it on the wagon. Then he offered her his hand, which surprisingly she took hold of. If he'd learned one thing about Sadie Fischer in his short time here, it was that she had an independent streak. Levi waited for her to settle in the seat, and then going around to the other side, he climbed in, as well. The wagon shifted under his weight and caused Sadie to bump into him.

She pulled away from him with a soft "I'm sorry."

Once back on her side of the seat, Sadie continued, "I guess I am more tired than I thought I was. You know how you go and go and go and then when you stop, you realize how much energy you've spent? That's how I'm feeling."

Urging the horse forward, Levi nodded. He did know. Right now, his shoulders and arms ached from all the painting. Sadie had to be feeling the same discomfort and yet she sat with her back tall and her hands folded neatly on her lap, looking out over the passing hills. Meanwhile, the blister on his right hand was still bothering him. He'd have to be sure to clean and bandage it when he got back to Jacob and Rachel's place.

"Levi, before I forget. We have our annual Miller's Crossing picnic coming up. You must be sure to come. You'll be able to meet more of our community. A lot of the older folks don't come out except for our gatherings, and of course the weekly church services. There will be lots of food and games," she went on. "I might even find time to make my blue-ribbon snickerdoodles! My *mamm* will, of course, make her potato salad, and there will be coleslaw and moon pies. I'm sure there will be a roasted chicken and bratwurst."

She groaned in delight. "My *grossmudder,* on my *vader*'s side, made the best bratwurst. She passed over a decade ago, but we still use her recipe at large gatherings." She rubbed a hand over her stomach. "All of this talk about food is making me hungry. Trust me, the day of the picnic will be filled with fun, and it's a *gut* time to catch up. Which reminds me, you never finished telling me about your people." She gave him a smile.

He knew she was trying to find out what brought him here. And he wasn't willing to share his personal life with her. Sadie didn't need to know about his past. He certainly didn't want her to get any ideas about adding him to her list of what she wanted for her perfect Amish man. He was anything but perfect.

He thought back on this time last year when his life had seemed cemented in place.

He'd been working with his *vader* on the family farm. Because Levi had always been good with the craftsman side of things, he'd been in charge of all the building upkeep. And he'd been in love with a young woman he'd known all his life. Levi thought Anne had been a perfect match. She was kind and gentle. When their families proposed the idea of their courtship, it had seemed like the most natural path for them.

They'd made plans for their wedding day, after which they were going to live in a small house near the back of Levi's family farm. He'd spent weeks cleaning and painting, inside and out. Because he knew how much Anne liked to work on her quilting, he'd set up a separate space off to one side of the living room for her to work in. He'd built a shelf along one wall with cubbies for all her fabric.

Levi had intended those white shelves to be her wedding gift. The only problem was Anne had had other plans. While Levi had been planning a life with the woman he loved, she'd been plotting to leave their community. Absently, he rubbed his hand over his chest, knowing nothing could remove the remnants of the dull ache that still lay inside his heart.

The day he realized Anne had gone still stood out in his memories. His plan on the beautiful sunny fall day had been to put the finishing touches on the house. But when he'd gotten there, he'd found a note taped to the front door. Her words seared into his soul. She was in love with someone else: an *Englischer*. Under the cover of darkness, Anne had left the community.

And in the blink of an eye his life changed.

For days afterward he found himself falling into a well of sadness he didn't think would ever end. Then came the anger. Anger at himself for believing in something that would never be. Anger at Anne for her deception.

Questioning his every move since the day they'd agreed to the courtship, he let his work on the farm go. He spent hours in prayer seeking an answer from the Lord and realizing there might not be one. Until one day his *mudder* came to him with the letter from his cousin. She was the one who convinced him to come here, telling him he needed a new outlook on life. And reminding him that the Lord never gave anyone more than they could handle.

Pausing in his thoughts, he brought his attention back to Sadie. He pushed down all those memories, all those thoughts and feelings, and gave a shrug. "There's not much more to tell."

"Do you miss them?"

He'd have to add *tenacious* to the list of words that described the schoolteacher.

"I've sent them off a letter or two. My *mamm* is *gut* about responding with news. Besides, I'm not sure if this will be a permanent move for me." Levi paused. He had no idea why he'd voiced that thought.

"Right, because you're here to help out your cousin. Who knows, Levi. Miller's Crossing might grow on you and maybe you'll never want to leave."

Her voice drifted off, leaving only the sound of nature and the occasional car zipping by them. Sadie seemed satisfied with their conversation, for now. This young woman was a force to be reckoned with. He'd seen how patient and kind she was with the lads helping them out. And she always, always had a smile for everyone. Levi could tell from the way she took care of the things in her classroom that she was a devoted teacher.

Though he had to admit, he couldn't imagine her scolding anyone, let alone a *kinder*. And her stubbornness? Even that had a soft side.

He knew he shouldn't be thinking this way. He'd learned a hard lesson this past year about trusting his feelings when it came to love. But even in this short amount of time, Sadie Fischer had worked her way into his thoughts. He would be better served focusing his attention on his work with Jacob.

Levi looked out over the landscape unfolding before them. Rolling hills and trees filled with lush green leaves lay on the tapestry the Lord had created. The air, though heavy with the summer humidity, was pure and clean. The rhythmic sound of the horse's hooves tapping along the road settled over him. Levi's mind wandered.

He imagined life here in Miller's Crossing, though tough at times, could in turn be filled with grace and beauty. The people he'd met so far were kind and caring. The nearby village of Clymer had buildings that were obviously cared for with pride. Levi didn't know where life was going to take him. He only knew to trust in the path laid out before him…the path that had brought him here. Still, he couldn't help battling with the changes in his life. He knew for certain he would use caution when it came to making decisions that would last a lifetime.

He suspected that the others, like Sadie, didn't know what to make of him, but like all Amish communities, they were welcoming. And the fact that he had family here helped. He felt he was doing good work at the school, which led him to an idea. One that might make Sadie's workload easier. And even as he had the thought, Levi knew he was going down an emotional path that he shouldn't be taking.

He still believed his life was meant to be lived alone. But that didn't mean he couldn't do something helpful for Sadie. After he dropped her off at her house, he'd take advantage of the lingering summer daylight and head back to the school.

Glancing to his right, he realized Sadie hadn't spoken in quite a few minutes. Her chin was tipped down, and he could see the even rise and fall of her chest. Her hands, though still together, lay limp in her lap.

"Well, I'll be," he muttered in amusement. She'd fallen asleep.

Laying a light hand against her forcarm, he gave her the tiniest of shakes. "Sadie. Sadie. Wake up."

Chapter Eight

Sadie sat up with a start, blinking. She'd fallen asleep. How had she let that happen? She must have been more tired than she thought. Embarrassment flooded through her. How could she let herself be caught in such a compromising position? She worked at brushing the wrinkles out of her apron.

"I wasn't sleeping. I was simply resting my eyes." She couldn't believe she'd resorted to using one of her *grossmudder* Fischer's responses when caught napping.

"If you say so."

Sitting up taller, she quipped, "I do."

By now, Levi was guiding the horse and wagon around the last bend before her home. She could tell by the slant of the sun that it was nearly past suppertime.

"Oh, dear."

"What's the matter?" Levi asked.

"I'm late for dinner."

"We should have left the school sooner."

"But we were busy with painting. My *mamm* will understand my tardiness."

Her *vader*, on the other hand, might not be as accommodating. He liked to have everyone at the table at the same time each evening. Sadie often wondered how he could be so strict with his routine, while she liked to see how the day would unfold. She liked to think that was what made her a better schoolteacher. While she did use a lesson planner that the committee approved each semester, she also set aside time just in case an educational opportunity arose that needed further exploration.

Take last spring when the girls had wanted to know more about the painting Lizzie Burkholder did. Lizzie was getting quite the reputation for her watercolor landscapes. Sadie had spent a week on art, giving a little time each day to let the students dabble in the paints. Indeed, schooling should be used to teach the fundamentals, but Sadie would never subdue her students' natural curiosity. They were young for such a short time, and the adult world would be upon them soon enough.

And that thought brought her full circle to her *vader*'s concerns that she needed to concentrate more on her future beyond the classroom. Her gaze slid to Levi. He seemed intent on steering the wagon around the corner and down her driveway.

She wondered again why he hadn't brought a wife with him to Miller's Crossing. He seemed reluctant to discuss his family when she'd asked. While some might think a man like Levi wasn't the marrying kind, Sadie could tell he cared. Even though he was quiet and pensive, he'd been helpful to her these past days. When they were working at the school, she'd caught him watching over the boys, teaching them how to do things the right way. And he'd worked tirelessly alongside her.

The wagon came to a stop near the hitching post at the front of the house. Sadie hopped down. The first thing she noticed was that the barn had been closed up for the night. And the picnic table in the side yard had been set with the plastic red-and-white-checkered tablecloth. Her *mamm* and sister were busy setting out the food.

Sara looked up when she saw Sadie and Levi. Giving them a wave, she beckoned them over.

"Come. You're just in time. *Mamm* and I were just putting dinner out," Sara said. Taking the lid off of the beef stew, she added, "Our *bruder* William and Kara are coming over with their *kinder*. They should be here any minute."

As if on cue, Sadie heard the laughter of her niece and nephew. She turned to watch as William parked the buggy next to Levi's wagon. William and his family lived about a mile up the road at his wife's family home. Sadie was happy to see them.

"Kara! William! *Guten owed*." Sadie greeted them, giving the *kinder* a big hug.

"*Guten owed* to you, Sadie," her *bruder* said with a nod. He looked to where Levi was getting her bike out of the back of the wagon. "And who might this be?" he asked.

"This is Levi Byler. He's been helping out with the school repairs."

"*Ach*. That was a fierce storm." William held out his hand and Levi shook it.

Sadie looked back and forth between the two men. Her *bruder* was a clever one. Acting nice and neighborly when she knew he was, in fact, taking stock of the man.

"*Ja*, it was indeed," she agreed. "But we're moving along. Tomorrow I have to go to King's Stationery to replace the school supplies that were ruined."

She walked with Kara and the *kinder* while William stayed back to chat with Levi.

"I'm not sure your *bruder* is too happy to see you with that man," Kara commented.

Sadie made a face. Though she loved him dearly, and he was the eldest, William was not in charge of her life. "Levi offered to bring me home. We had a long day's work. I have to admit I was too tired to pedal all the way here. I appreciated the ride."

Sara met them halfway to the picnic table. "*Mamm* wants to know if Levi might like to join us for supper."

The suggestion caught Sadie off guard. It hadn't occurred to her to ask Levi to stay. She knew he had to get back to Jacob's, and that was at least a twenty-minute drive from here. She imagined he would say no. However, she didn't get the chance to invite him. William came over a few minutes later as Levi was driving off.

"He seems nice enough," was all William said.

Sadie nodded, thinking that Levi was indeed nice enough. Her gaze lingered on the roadway as she watched the wagon disappear over the horizon.

"Sadie, come, dinner is waiting to be served."

Sadie smiled at her *mamm* and approached the table. A large maple tree spread shade over the area, and she took a moment to drink in the scene. Her parents, two of her siblings, and the *kinder* all took their places on the wooden benches. She sat between her *mamm* and sister and joined in the thanksgiving for the food set before them.

The breeze floated around them, offering the first bit of coolness she'd felt all day. She wanted to tip her head back and take in the moment, but she tamped down the urge, instead spooning some of the stew onto her plate.

"How far have you gotten at the school?" Sara asked, handing Sadie the bread basket.

"I have a few more days before I can begin to bring in the desks and bookshelves. Tomorrow I'm going to the stationery store to get some supplies."

"William can take you. He has to run there himself," Kara offered. William and Kara ran a small quilt shop out of their home.

From the far end of the table, William said, "I'll pick you up at eight."

Sadie agreed, then finished the meal and helped with the evening chores.

The next morning, she was ready when William pulled into the driveway at eight on the dot. She settled into the buggy and bade him a *guder mariye*.

"I hope your morning is a *gut* one, too, Sadie," he returned.

She'd say it was. The humidity that had been plaguing them for the past week had finally broken overnight, leaving in its wake a clear blue sky and easy breathing. She glanced at her *bruder*—from this side, he reminded her a lot of their *vader*. Both men had the same long nose and graying beards, though her *vader*'s was almost all white now. William had the same shape to his eyes, although the color resembled their *mudder*'s.

He gave the reins a shake and the horse trotted off. Sadie sat back under the cover of the buggy.

"Sadie, I'm not going to waste any time. I need to speak with you about your situation."

She felt the tiny hairs on the back of her neck rise. This couldn't be good. "And what situation might that be?"

"This one between you and Isaiah."

She tried to keep her frustration in check. "As I've told our *vader*, there is no situation there."

"You know there should be."

"I know no such thing, William." She felt her anger rising.

Annoyance didn't do anyone any good. But now she had a feeling that William bringing her into the village hadn't been a kind offer. He'd been wanting to find a way to speak to her about her future, and a ride into the village was a good excuse. Sadie looked out the small window of the buggy. The horse moved along at such a speed that the trees and hillside whizzed by them.

"William, slow down!" She felt the buggy slowing. *"Danke."*

He mumbled, *"Es dutt mir leed."* A mere second passed and then he continued, "Sadie, you are the schoolteacher and as such you have to live up to a certain standard."

"William! Are you saying you think that I'm not good enough for the job?" Sadie felt flushed. She couldn't accept that her *bruder* would think such a thing of his own sister. She worked night and day during the school year planning and preparing for her students to get the best education they could under her tutelage.

"Nee. Nee. Of course not. But you have been ignoring *Vader*'s choice for you, and people are beginning to take notice."

"I don't care."

"You should care!"

"Don't raise your voice to me."

William let out an exasperated sigh. "Oh, Sadie. We, and by we, I mean our family, only want what is best for you."

"Maybe what's best for me would be for you to let me make my own choice in this matter."

"I don't want to see this cause you any trouble."

"See what causing me trouble, William?"

"Your being with Levi Byler. He's driven you home, not once but twice. And you are spending time working with him at the schoolhouse."

"For goodness' sake. Neither of those times count for anything. The first time he rescued me from that mudhole, and yesterday he was doing nothing more than being a good neighbor." Sucking in a breath, she breathed out, "As for being alone at the school, there are others there most of the time."

"*Most* of the time, but not all of the time," William pointed out.

By now they had traveled to the outskirts of Miller's Crossing. The stationery store was over the next rise and then a turn down a narrow, winding road. Sadie grabbed onto the handrail as William allowed the buggy to sail around the corner. Taking his anger out on the poor horse wouldn't help the matter.

"Slow down," she said once more. "Did *Vader* ask you to speak to me?"

"*Nee.* He did not. I'm the one who is concerned." William's voice softened as he slowed the horse coming into the parking lot for King's Stationery. He pulled into a space, tugging the brake back and setting it. Then he turned to look at her.

"Levi Byler seems like a nice person. And yes, helping you with the repairs is a *gut* thing. But you are the teacher. You know you have to be careful with your time and you shouldn't be unchaperoned. Just be careful. Okay?"

Sadie could see that concern softening the edges around his eyes and knew he only had her best interest at heart. She didn't like arguing and hated that they were starting this glorious day sparring over her future.

"Sadie, please consider my words."

"I will."

They entered the store. William headed off to the office supply section, and Sadie went to the aisle that had the classroom materials. It didn't take her long to find the two posters she needed, then she made a beeline to the books. She hoped they had a replacement for a title that had been destroyed by the rain.

She slowed her pace, enjoying the covers on display. An entire row was filled with Christian books with such beautiful art that Sadie paused to admire them. Then she saw a few gardening magazines and the *Farmers' Almanac*. Finally, she found the children's section and was delighted to see the book she'd been looking for. She added it to her basket, then she went up to the front counter to pay for everything.

Her *bruder* had gotten there ahead of her and was chatting with Amos King, the owner of the store and one of the school board members.

"*Gute mariye*, Miss Sadie."

"It's a fine morning, Amos. I think we're in for the best day of the week so far."

"I would agree." He smiled at her and then slid the book into a paper bag. "Should I add these to the school account?"

"Yes, please."

"My *kinder* are anxious to start the new school year. They were very upset to see the storm damage. But I assured them it would be taken care of in plenty of time."

"I've had a lot of *gut* people helping. Some of the older boys have been working inside with me on the painting."

"So I've heard." And as if to prove William's point, Amos added, "Jacob's cousin Levi has done *gut* work there. But please be sure to work in groups."

Sadie turned her back ever so slightly so she didn't have to see the look on her *bruder*'s face. She hated to admit when he was right. It was clear that the community members were indeed talking about her. Sadie didn't want to create any problems for the school board when it came to her personal life.

Sadie chastised herself. She knew better. She needed to give more thought to her actions.

Nodding at Amos, she gathered her things and headed out to the buggy. William came right on her heels. Thankfully he had the wherewithal to keep his comments to himself regarding what Amos had said.

William dropped her at the school, and Sadie thanked him for taking her to the store. "I appreciate the ride, William."

"It's no trouble. You'll think about what I said?"

"Ja."

Sadie waved him off, knowing that where Isaiah Troyer was concerned her mind was made up.

She walked along the pathway to the front door. She swung it open, fully expecting to find the blue tape surrounding the windows and floor trim. But that wasn't what she found at all.

Sadie stood in the middle of the room with her mouth agape.

"I don't understand," she whispered in amazement at the sight before her.

Chapter Nine

Sadie set the posters and book down on the desk. The desk right in front of her. The room was full of them! She spun around with her arms spread wide in happiness.

All the desks were in orderly rows, and the bookcases were set up against the wall near the door. Her teacher's desk was still absent, but that didn't matter. She wondered who she should thank for this gift.

The sound of voices came from behind the building. Sadie hurried out the door and ran around to the back, anxious to see who was there.

Levi stood with Jacob and two of the boys who'd been helping her out.

"Danke!" she blurted out. *"Danke! Danke!"*

"Miss Sadie, were you surprised?" Mica asked.

"I was very pleasantly surprised. *Danke* so much."

"It was Levi's idea. He'd already gotten the cleanup done. All the desks were set out. Josh and I helped bring up the bookshelves this morning."

"Well, that was very kind of all of you." Sadie nodded to each of the boys and then raised her eyes to meet Levi's gaze.

His expression was unreadable She wondered when he'd found the time to do all of this work. It had been quite late in the day when he'd left her house yesterday and it was only midmorning now.

"Levi, I can't believe you found the time to do all of this!"

He was half turned away from her, as if he didn't want to meet her gaze. "I came back last night."

"You didn't have to do this," she said. His generosity touched her.

"I thought getting the desks back up here would push us along. Now you can concentrate on getting the classroom ready for opening day."

There seemed to be a different mood about him this morning. She couldn't quite put her finger on the change. But it was as if he didn't want to be near her. Sadie didn't understand. Maybe Levi was distracted thinking about the tasks for today. Either way, she was grateful for his effort.

"*Danke* again for your thoughtfulness."

While she'd been offering her thanks, two wagon-loads of lumber arrived, one with two-by-fours and the other with roof trusses. Sadie watched as the drivers pulled to a stop next to the old shed foundation.

Levi still hadn't agreed to add in windows. Deciding she could catch more bees with honey, Sadie flashed him her most radiant smile. She needed him to fix the shed the way it should be done. *For the children, of course.*

Not wanting to be in the way, Sadie left the men to carry on.

* * *

After seeing the look on Sadie's face when she'd come around back, he thought his late night, working by the light of one of the most brilliant moons he'd seen in a long time, had been worth it. After he'd dropped her at home, he'd come back to the school and finished taking down the tape, swept the floor, cleaned up a few cobwebs and hauled thirty desks up the flight of basement stairs.

Ja, he'd been exhausted, but it was *gut* exhaustion, the kind that came when you knew you'd done something that would make someone else happy. Sadie had been so tired at the end of yesterday, and while he knew she would work without complaint, he wanted to do something that would make today easier.

He hadn't meant to sound terse with his response just now, but Levi knew from hard experience that Sadie's feelings were softening toward him. The tells were there. The way she spoke to him with a lighter tone, the way her gaze grew steady when she looked at him. He knew the signs because those were the exact emotions he'd experienced with Anne.

Levi wasn't about to be taken in again. He had to be careful where Sadie was concerned, because she was beginning to grow on him.

"Levi!"

He turned to see Jacob coming toward him.

"I'm going to unload these wagons and then we'll be back with the rest of the lumber you'll need to get started on the shed."

"Okay. What were your thoughts on adding in the windows that Sadie asked for?"

"I still have to see if we have any in stock. I might

have two older ones we could use. But go ahead and start with the framework as we originally planned. I don't want to have to redo the walls if we don't have those windows."

"That sounds like a *gut* plan."

Jacob gave him a wink, joking, "Do you want me to tell Sadie?"

"*Nee.* We won't say anything until we know for certain."

"All right then. On second thought, I'm going to send one of my workers back with the next load. I still have a month's backlog to deal with. I'm thankful you came out to Miller's Crossing when you did. I'm not sure how I could have been in all these places at once."

"I'm happy to help."

"You're more than helping, Levi. We'll talk more about the business when things settle down. Have a good day."

"You, too," Levi replied.

Watching his friend leave, he wondered what Jacob had meant. He heard the boys laughing behind him. Turning around, he found Mica and Josh horsing around on the pile of two-by-fours. They were pushing and shoving each other on and off the pile.

"Boys! Get down from there before you get hurt!" Levi didn't like to raise his voice, but he didn't have time to tend to an injury. "Come here."

Doing as they were told, the two of them scrambled over to him.

Folding his arms, Levi stared down at them.

Mica fidgeted in front of him. "We didn't mean no harm, Levi," he said.

"I understand. But we've got a lot of work to do

today. Do either of you boys know anything about putting up a shed?"

"Nope," Josh said.

"How old are you?"

"I'm twelve and Mica is eleven," Josh answered.

Raising an eyebrow, Levi asked, "Do you know how to swing a hammer?"

Both boys nodded.

"*Gut.* Then let's get to work." Of course, Levi had no intention of letting the boys work with hammers and nails. He just wanted them to concentrate on helping him and not roughhousing.

They'd done well enough with the painting, but working with lumber required focus.

"I'm going to tell you what I need help with, and you let me know if you think you can handle it." Levi took an authoritative stance with his feet spread apart and his arms folded across his chest while he let his words sink in.

After a few seconds, both boys stilled.

"I'll need help carrying the wood over to the foundation, then I'll need someone to hold the pieces in place while I nail them in position. You think you can do that?"

Both boys nodded so hard their hats tumbled off their blond heads.

Clapping his hands together, Levi said, "Okay then, put your hats back on and let's get a move on."

For the next few hours, Levi had to delve deep for patience. Mica and Josh took turns holding the two-by-fours while he pounded the nails in place. Though they were good helpers, they would wander off when he wasn't watching them like a hawk.

He didn't understand their behavior. Yesterday they'd been diligent while working with Sadie. Today they were acting like little *kinder*. Listening to them horsing around reminded him of his own childhood with his *bruders*. They'd managed to get into their fair share of trouble during chore time.

Putting the hammer back into the leather work belt he wore around his waist, Levi tilted his hat and wiped his brow with his sleeve. Blowing out a breath, he surveyed the work they'd done. It might be a good idea to nail the frame of the walls together on the ground and then push them up into place. For that he'd need the strength of a few men. Not as many as a barn raising required; just two would suffice.

He thought the boys might be happy to hear they wouldn't be needed for that part.

"Mica, Josh!" he called to them. "Come on over here. You've earned a break."

"Are you pleased with our work today, Levi?" Josh wanted to know.

"I am. You've done a fine job. Now, here's the thing, and I know you'll be disappointed, but I'm not going to need you for a few days. I'm bringing some men in to help me with the wall frames. It's a big job."

The boys did their best to look solemn, but then their faces broke out in grins. Saying their goodbyes, they bounded off across the schoolyard.

"Well, I'll be." Levi shook his head and laughed.

Some days he missed the freedom of being a young boy. The long summers spent fishing and playing in the hayloft. The time before the responsibilities of life intruded.

As Levi laughed to himself, he noticed Sadie coming around the back, picking her way through the construction debris.

"It looks like they were itching to leave you." Her comment came out in a chuckle.

He liked her laugh.

"They hung on longer than I thought they would. Let's face it, working with you inside is nothing like being out here helping lift heavy lumber. But they are *gut* boys."

"*Ja.* They are." Walking over to the pile of two-by-fours, she looked down at them. "I don't see any windows."

"Now, Sadie, before you go getting all in a huff, Jacob is going to look around to see what he has in stock."

Though she tried to hide it, Levi saw the satisfied smile cross her face. "That's very nice of him, and of you, to take my request seriously."

It was more that he didn't want to get bogged down arguing with her over the matter when there was so much work yet to be done.

She stood there with a look he couldn't quite figure out. Her eyes were scrunched up a bit as if she were deep in thought. He fiddled with the hammer stuck in his tool belt.

Finally, she said, "You're good with the *kinder*, Levi."

A jolt of surprise ran through him. He hadn't expected her compliment. With a shrug, he said, "I like them well enough."

"I can tell. It's hard to be patient when all they want to do is be allowed to run free. But you took your time with Mica and Josh today. That was nice of you."

"*Danke.*"

She grinned up at him. "Like it or not, Levi, you are becoming a part of this community."

He didn't say anything. He still wasn't sure he'd be staying on here. But he did like the people, and they were friendly toward him. He was aware of how Sadie's *vader* and oldest *bruder* felt about him. Not that it mattered. Levi was not in the market to find a wife.

"Do you work on projects like this with the *kinder* in your family?"

"If the need arises."

He knew this young woman well enough to know she was trying to bait him into sharing more of his past with her. No matter how sweet she tried to be, Levi couldn't let himself fall into her trap.

"Sadie, I really need to get back to work."

"I'll let you go, but promise me you'll come to the picnic."

Chapter Ten

A week later, Sadie stood in the kitchen putting the finishing touches on the final batch of her blue-ribbon snickerdoodles and thinking about her last exchange with Levi. While she rolled the dough into one-inch balls and dropped them into a bowl of cinnamon and sugar, she realized he'd never given her an answer about whether or not he would be attending today's picnic.

Using a spoon, she coated the unbaked dough with the mixture. She'd gotten out of bed right before sunrise to avoid running the oven in the heat of the day. The entire house smelled like vanilla, cinnamon and warm sugar. Oh, how she loved the scent. Inhaling, she let the smells flood her senses with homey goodness and comfort.

It had been a busy month, but she was looking forward to the annual Miller's Crossing picnic. The day was much like a wedding celebration, but in her mind even better, because you didn't have to wear your Sunday clothes. Today was a day to celebrate life, community and friendships. And Sadie couldn't wait to catch up with her friends.

Setting the balls of dough on the tray, being careful to leave two inches between each one for spreading, she put them in the oven to bake.

She grabbed the chicken-shaped timer off the Formica countertop, setting it for eight minutes. While the cookies were baking, she had two other sheet pans cooling with a few dozen snickerdoodles. The sight of their crackled tops brought a smile to her face.

Sliding a flat spatula under each cookie, she carefully transferred them to a wire rack where they would finish hardening. Later, she would put them in a big red cookie tin. If anyone asked her what her favorite thing to do was other than teaching, she'd have to say baking these cookies. How could you not love a good old-fashioned cookie?

She wondered what Levi's favorite cookie might be. She remembered mentioning her snickerdoodles to him the day he'd brought her home from school. The same day her *bruder* had spoken to him.

Sadie didn't understand why her family couldn't leave her to make her own decision when it came to finding the right person to spend the rest of her life with.

Isaiah hadn't been around much at all. Come to think of it, she hadn't seen him since that day he'd stopped by to see the storm damage at the school. The day Levi had interrupted their conversation. She'd known he wanted to know who Isaiah was. But they didn't discuss those matters. Instead their conversations stayed focused on the school or the little bits when she could get him to talk about his family.

Sadie had tried on more than one occasion to get Levi to open up about his life. In her opinion, he was very good at keeping his life closed. She didn't know why this bothered her so much. His behavior toward her had continued to be polite, but still she found herself wanting to get to know him better.

The spatula fell from her hand, landing on the floor with a clatter.

She liked Levi Byler.

"Oh, dear."

"Sadie, what on earth is all the noise about?" her *mamm* asked, rushing into the kitchen to shut off the timer.

Sadie had been so lost in her thoughts that she hadn't even heard the timer buzzing.

"And who are you talking to?"

"No one." Giving her head a shake, she admitted, "Myself." She picked up the spatula, walked to the sink and rinsed it off.

"Well, your distraction almost caused your cookies to burn." Her *mamm* grabbed a pot holder off a nearby hook, opened the oven and slid the tray out, setting it on top of the stove. "Your *vader* should be in from the barn soon. He wants to get over to the picnic early. Remember last year when one of his prized cows had all that trouble with her twisted stomach?"

She sure did remember. They were two hours late to the fun because they had to help chase the cow around in hopes of getting the poor beast's insides to right. The entire family was out running around in the pasture behind the barn. Eventually the cow settled down. This year the day looked brighter and worry-free.

While she waited for the cookies to cool, Sadie cleaned up her work area. She put the ingredients back in their place, wiped the countertop clean and then washed up the bowls and utensils. Meanwhile, her *mamm* put the finishing touches on her potato salad.

Sara came into the kitchen carrying the wicker picnic basket. She looked extra pretty today. Sadie wondered who her sister had in mind when she'd chosen to wear her best skirts.

"It's looking like we'll have perfect weather for the picnic," her sister observed.

"*Ja.* The sky is blue with only fair-weather clouds. Did you find the bread I set out in the pantry last night?" *Mamm* asked.

"I did. I already put the loaf in the basket along with a pound of butter."

"*Gut.* I think that will be plenty. And did you get out the sacks like I asked?"

"I did," Sara replied, wrinkling her nose. "I'm not going to participate in the sack race this year, so don't sign me up."

"*Ach*, me neither," Sadie agreed with her sister.

"Your school *kinder* will be disappointed if you don't join them, Sadie. You know that's a favorite at the picnic."

Taking the lid off the cookie tin, Sadie started layering the snickerdoodles inside. "My *kinder* will be happy with me cheering them on from the sidelines, *Mamm*."

"If you say so."

"I'm bringing kites for them to fly."

"I guess they'll like that, too." Her *mamm* made a silly face at her.

Sadie laughed.

The potato salad and cookies, along with ice packs, were put inside the picnic basket. The bread was carefully placed on top, so as not to be crushed. Added to the mix were their paper plates and eating utensils. They didn't need to worry about the drinks because the Schrader family had a special wagon they loaned out for weddings that held half a dozen five-gallon containers of lemonade, iced tea and water. Perfect for an event such as this.

Sadie could feel the excitement building. This day was so much fun and she looked forward to it every year. It was a time for the farmers to take a much-needed break. And it was the last hurrah for the *kinder* before the start of the new school year. Maybe Levi had decided to join in the festivities.

"Come, come! Your *vader* is outside with the buggy." *Mamm* thrust the picnic hamper into Sadie's arms, ushering both her and Sara out the door.

"You sure are in a hurry, *Mamm*," Sara observed.

"I don't want to waste a minute of this day."

They all piled into the buggy, and by the time they reached the glade where the picnic had been set up, Sadie could see they were not the only ones with the idea of arriving early. The edge of the field had filled with wagons and buggies. There were *kinder* running about, and *mamms* and *vaders* hauling baskets and blankets over to where a long row of tables and benches had been set up.

Sadie saw Lizzie and Paul, with Rachel and Jacob behind them. Sadie waved. Then her heart thudded inside her chest as she spotted Levi carrying several tins in his hands.

He'd decided to join them.

Trying not to appear excited by his presence, Sadie meandered over to the table where her parents were unpacking. She helped her *mamm* set their places and then took her tin over to the dessert table, three lengths long and already filled with cobblers, pies and cakes. *What a sight to behold.* Their community was blessed with so many wonderful bakers and cooks. The neighboring tables held a variety of salads. Sadie's mouth watered.

She felt the breeze ruffle her blouse, and then something light brushed against her back. She turned around to find Rachel standing behind her. Levi stood next to her, carrying the tins she'd seen him with a few minutes ago.

"Rachel. Levi. *Gute mariye.*" Sadie didn't know why it was happening, but she couldn't stop the heated flush of her cheeks. Her reaction to seeing Levi today was so schoolgirl. Quickly she busied herself taking the tin from his hands and setting it next to hers on the table.

"I recognize that tin." Rachel's voice penetrated the haze of Sadie's mind. "Did you make those blue-ribbon cookies?"

"I did."

"You are in for a real treat, Levi." Rachel nodded to him.

Levi stood there, shifting from one foot to the other, his gaze not quite meeting hers.

She wondered why, after all the time they'd just spent working on the school, that he suddenly seemed shy around her.

"Are you signing up for any of the events?" Rachel asked.

Sadie turned her attention to Rachel. "*Nee*, this year I'm doing kite flying with the *kinder.*"

The trio made their way out from under the shade of the large oak tree and wandered over to the tables where Sadie's family was gathering. It was nice to see everyone. With her siblings getting married off and having *kinder*, her family was expanding. Her *bruder* William stood among the men chatting. He waved while Sadie joined the women. This was how it always was at these events, with everyone breaking off into groups.

Sadie joined Lizzie, Rachel and Sara under a shade tree. The four of them chatted for a bit about the weather and the school. Lizzie told them how good the store was doing and that her paintings were selling faster than she could paint them.

"The one of the fields where Paul and I had our first outing together is the most popular. We are looking into getting prints made. The *Englischers* like to have originals. But I have to charge so much for them. I'd really like to be able to price them so they are affordable for everyone who would like to buy my art."

"Lizzie, that is wonderful!" Rachel gave her a hug. "It's *gut* to hear of your success. My Jacob is so busy with the shed building that he's up at the crack of dawn and works by the light of the kerosene lamps at night. He's thinking of asking Levi to stay on full-time as a partner."

Sadie's heartbeat kicked up a notch. The thought of Levi being a permanent part of the community meant that he liked being here. And maybe he wasn't going to be running off anytime soon.

"Levi has mentioned that the shop is busy," she said.

All heads swung in Sadie's direction.

She waved them off. "Stop looking at me like that. He told me because I asked for windows in the replacement shed they are building at the school," she explained, fighting back another blush.

What on earth has gotten into me today?

"He said he'd have to wait and see what Jacob had lying around. That's all." She tried to talk her way out of the conversation.

"Oh my." Sara looked at her intently. "You are smitten with Levi Byler."

"I am not," Sadie denied, even though she knew her sister's words had some merit. But there was no way she would admit the truth in front of them.

Out of the corner of her eye she caught a glimpse of Isaiah joining the group of men where her *vader* and *bruders* stood talking.

She glanced back to her sister and saw Sara's gaze following the man and knew then and there that Isaiah Troyer had the wrong Fischer *dochder* in his sights.

Sadie knew that, in time, everything would work out for all of them. They just had to be patient. Not one of her finer virtues. She had no intention of marrying Isaiah, and there was no reason why Sara shouldn't be with the one who would make him happy. Sadie only had to convince their *vader* of this. She had faith that everything would work out as it should. It had to.

The bell rang, and they followed the crowd over to the picnic tables.

Their family had managed to crowd in one place at the table. Sadie elbowed her way in between Sara and her sister-in-law Kara.

"It seems that the entire community has come out for this," Kara commented.

"Ja."

Across from them sat Rachel, Jacob and Levi, with Lizzie and Paul lining the bench next to Paul's family. Levi chatted with Paul. Sadie heard him ask a question about furniture making. And then her attention was pulled away as Sara told her it was their turn to go to the food line.

Sadie tried not to pile her plate high, but there were so many delectable choices. She was so busy walking through the line that she didn't realize Levi stood across from her until she recognized the sound of his voice speaking to one of the school board members.

Glancing up from her plate, she watched him, thinking what a good fit he'd be for their community.

"If you don't stop your gawking, people are going to start talking about you."

Sadie jumped and turned to Lizzie, who had come up behind her. Out of the side of her mouth, she whispered, "I wasn't gawking."

Lizzie leaned in close, talking low so only Sadie could hear. "*Ja*, I think you were. He's not too old, heaven forbid, not too young, and as far as I can tell, he doesn't appear to be in a relationship. He could be your perfect…"

Sadie nudged Lizzie with her elbow, cutting her off. "Stop. This isn't the time or the place for this discussion. There are too many *blabbermauls*."

Lizzie cocked her head to one side, the corner of her mouth lifting in a knowing way. And then she moved ahead of Sadie in the line. Feeling an unexpected flutter of nerves in her stomach and her appetite diminish, Sadie left her spot in the line and went back to the picnic table. Some of her students came up to her along the way, telling her of their summer.

Little Mary Stolfus jumped up and down in front of Sadie, nearly knocking her plate out of her hand in her excitement to tell how she had gone fishing with her *bruders* for the first time.

"Mary, you could write a report on that for the class.

I'm sure everyone would love to hear about your experience."

"Homework already!"

Sadie grinned down at the stricken look on the child's face. "Only if you wish to share. I'll tell you what. You can think about what you want to write and then when I give out the assignment, you'll be halfway done. How does that sound?"

"Like a *gut* idea." Mary clapped her hands together. "I've been practicing my letters with my *mamm*."

"You have?" Sadie's heart swelled. It was so wonderful to hear when her students took their learning seriously.

"Yup." Mary's blond head bobbed up and down.

"I'm very proud of you, Mary. I'll be flying kites after our meal. Come find me out in the lower field."

"I will, Miss Sadie!" With that, Mary ran off to join her friends.

Settling back in with her family, Sadie picked at her food.

Lizzie's words had left her with an odd feeling. She never wanted anyone, most of all Levi, to ever think that she was chasing after him, or any other man for that matter. Sadie wasn't like that. But she did know what she wanted, and she knew in her heart she would never settle for anything less. Shouldn't it be everyone's goal to find true happiness?

The minute the thought entered her head, she found herself face-to-face with Levi.

Chapter Eleven

Levi didn't think he'd ever tasted anything quite as delicious as Sadie's snickerdoodle cookies. He took a second bite, savoring the sweet, vanilla taste, and the sprinkle of sugar and cinnamon over the entire cookie was almost too much to bear.

"I see you're enjoying my cookies," Sadie observed from her side of the table.

"I am. And you know what I think?"

"I don't."

"I think there's a reason these won the blue ribbon."

"They've won the award on more than one occasion. I don't enter them in the bake-off anymore. It was time to give someone else a turn at the ribbon."

"Can you give me the recipe for my *mudder*?"

"I'll write it out for you and you can send it to her in your next letter."

"I'm sure she'll like that."

He noticed her plate sitting half-eaten off to one side and wondered if she was feeling okay.

Seeing his look, she commented, "My eyes were bigger than my stomach. There was so much good food on the tables that I wanted to try it all."

"The women in Miller's Crossing sure know how to cook. My stomach is full." He gave his belly a pat.

Sadie gave him one of her pretty smiles, saying, "But there's always room for dessert."

"Always," he agreed. He gave her a half smile.

"I've heard that Jacob is serious about wanting you to stay on."

The bluntness of her statement caught him off guard and wiped the smile off his face. One thing Levi knew for sure was that news in small communities traveled fast, and Miller's Crossing was no exception. Sadie had been after him for days to talk more about his life and what brought him here. He wasn't ready to discuss those parts of his life. Even though the pain of his breakup was easing, Levi didn't want to be caught up in another relationship that would leave him broken. He still wasn't able to trust enough to be sure about Sadie.

He still hadn't been able to figure out if Sadie was looking to settle down or simply looking to settle.

People were beginning to clear away their plates. Some wandered off to the creek, others gathered under the shade tree and some were getting ready to play a game of softball.

"Levi." She spoke his name so softly he almost didn't hear her.

"Ja."

"Will you be staying on?"

They were interrupted by a small girl whose exuberance brought a smile to his face.

"Miss Sadie, we're ready to fly the kites! Are you coming?"

Her gaze lingered on him. Levi wanted to tell her what she needed to hear. But he couldn't. He didn't trust himself to open his heart. Still, he found himself wishing the outcome could be different. Maybe they were meant to be only friends.

While he pondered that thought, Sadie accepted the outstretched hand of the girl. Standing up, she gave him a look that told him she wasn't finished with this conversation.

"Levi! Do you want to play in the softball game?" William called out to him from the field. "We need an outfielder."

"Go," Sadie said. "Have fun with the men."

"All right. You have fun with your kite flying."

"Come on, Miss Sadie!" the little girl clamored, tugging Sadie away from him.

He walked with them partway to the field, then broke off and headed to the ball field. He watched her disappear over the rise, wondering what would have happened if he'd met her sooner.

"Miss Sadie! Look how high my kite is!" Mary exclaimed, jumping up and down next to her.

Raising her hand to shield her eyes from the sun, Sadie looked heavenward, watching the kite dip and flutter in the wind. The tail with the pink-and-orange strips trailed out behind it, spinning in the breeze.

"I'm not having much luck with mine," said another girl. Beth Miller frowned at the tangled mess at her feet.

"Come, let me see if we can get yours going." Sadie walked through the blades of grass. Picking up Beth's kite and handing it to her, she instructed, "You need to hold it here at the crosspieces."

She took hold of Beth's little fingers, placing them where the cross pieces met and once she was certain the girl had a good hold on the kite, she added, "Now you run into the wind until the breeze captures your kite."

Beth looked up at her with wide, brown, doubt-filled eyes.

"Let's give it a try, shall we?"

Beth nodded and then, doing as she was told, ran like the wind. Her little legs pumped hard on the soft earth, and to her delight the paper kite got off the ground, sailing up into the blue sky. The other *kinder* who'd been watching and playing with their own kites let out a cheer.

Beth turned to Sadie, shouting, "I did it! I did it!"

And then without warning the kite lost its lift and fell out of the sky, landing halfway up an oak tree.

Sadie ran over to where Beth stood under the tree, crying.

"Oh. There, there, *liebling*." Sadie patted her on the back. "Wipe away those tears. I'll get your kite for you."

Without a thought, she hoisted herself up onto a low branch where the tail of the kite was just out of her reach. The fabric bows swayed in front of her, flirting with her. Sadie stretched her body tall and extended her arm as far as she could. The kite tail danced against her fingertips. She just started to grasp the string when her foot slipped on the branch.

"Get down from that tree!"

The familiar voice startled her, and she gave a shout as she tumbled backward out of the tree.

Her breath whooshed out of her as she fell hard against Levi. She spun around to face him. What on earth was he doing down here? She'd thought he was playing ball.

Oh my... Her heart skipped a beat as she looked up into his blue-green eyes. He looked frightened for a moment, and then she saw something else as he stared down at her. His gaze softened, taking in her face. His eyes lingered on hers and then his gaze dropped to her mouth. Sadie's breath caught.

Then he blinked and quick as a breeze the look was gone.

In the next instant she jumped out of his arms. She put her hand against the tree trunk to steady herself. Her heartbeat fluttered in her chest, and that fluttering had nothing to do with fear.

"Sadie! What were you doing up there?" he demanded.

"I was helping Beth get her kite out of the tree."

"You should have had one of the boys go up."

"I'll have you know, Levi, that I'm perfectly capable of climbing a tree."

"I don't doubt that, but when you have help nearby, you should ask."

She closed her eyes to keep her frustration from showing. How could he make her want to be near him one minute and then in the next make her so mad? Sadie swallowed, realizing she wasn't really mad at him, just unsettled by these feelings that popped up inside her whenever they were close to each other.

It would do no good to be flustered in front of the *kinder*. And in front of their parents who had made their way down the hill to see what all the commotion was about. Sadie's heart raced as she glanced at the faces of her neighbors, many of whom had known her for her entire life. And many of whom would like nothing more than to have something to gossip about during the next quilting bee.

It wouldn't do to have the schoolteacher be the fodder for their chatter. Sadie knew she should put her reputation first. But how did she do that while keeping her growing feelings toward Levi at bay?

Pushing away from the tree, she squared her shoulders. "You are absolutely correct." Putting on her sweetest smile, she asked, "Would you mind going up the tree and getting Beth's kite for her? Please."

"I'd be happy to."

He was up and back in less than three minutes, handing the kite to a very happy Beth, who took it from him.

"What do you say to Mr. Byler, Beth?"

"*Danke* for getting my kite out of the tree."

"*Du bischt willkomm.*" Levi smiled at the little girl.

The smile brought out the fine lines at the corners of his eyes and a dimple on the left side of his mouth. The look suited him. And Sadie wondered, as she had since the first day she'd met him, why those smiles were so rare.

He brushed the dust off of his dark pants and adjusted his straw hat.

"*Danke*, Levi, for coming along when you did," Sadie finally offered.

The smile disappeared.

Feeling the need to state her case once more, she said, "I didn't mean to scare anyone."

"I know you didn't." His tone softened. "Let's get back to the picnic."

She didn't understand his behavior toward her. One minute he was nice as pie and the next he was acting like he didn't want to be around her and then he was back to being nice again. There was something going on between them, and she felt Levi was battling with these same feelings. She didn't know how to reach out to him, how to deal with this new tension developing between them.

But Sadie was a firm believer in the Lord working in mysterious ways. Levi had been sent here for a reason.

She needed to find out why he was so driven to keep his distance from her. She had to know if there was something between them other than their shared desire to complete the repairs on the school property in time for the upcoming semester. Determination drove Sadie in her work, and her personal life was no different. One way or another, she would get to the bottom of this.

Levi walked ahead of her, leaving Sadie to accompany the *kinder* back up to the picnic tables. Lizzie came up to her, linking her arm through hers, and gave Sadie a reassuring pat on the hand.

"It seems Levi's rescue is drawing a bit of attention."

Sadie looked at her friend. "I saw the women watching us."

"Not just them, Sadie."

She followed Lizzie's pointed gaze, seeing where her concern came from. Sadie's *mamm* and *vader* stood on the knoll watching her walk up the hill. This would only make her *vader*'s case stronger for a match between her and Isaiah. Sadie had to find a way to head this off, and the sooner, the better.

Her parents met her at the top of the hill.

Her *mamm* rushed over to her. "Are you all right?"

"I'm fine. Levi was right there to break my fall. And

even if he wasn't, I would have been perfectly capable of not getting hurt."

"You don't know that, Sadie," her *mamm* scolded. "You are always so impetuous."

"*Dochder*, it's time we packed up to head home."

She nodded at her *vader* and helped her *mamm* pick up their remaining leftovers. This day had left her a bundle of nerves. To hide the feeling, she busied her hands packing up the picnic basket and carrying it over to their buggy. Levi was helping Rachel and Jacob put their basket and softball equipment in the back of their buggy.

Spotting her, he waved.

Sadie waved back.

Off to her left stood her *vader*. She felt his gaze on them.

He came up behind her. "Come, let's get our things loaded up. We have evening chores to tend to." His voice sounded gruff.

A sinking feeling hit Sadie. Her time to be a part of deciding her future was running short.

Chapter Twelve

A week later Levi found himself face-to-face with Sadie's *vader*. The man had been waiting for him at the school.

"Levi, I'd like a word with you."

Drawing in a breath, Levi jumped down from the wagon seat. Pushing his hat back off his forehead, he walked over to Saul Fischer. The man straightened his shoulders. Levi stood a good head taller than him.

"What can I do for you, Saul?"

"I'm not going to beat around the bush. I'm here to talk to you about my *dochder* Sadie."

"I see," Levi said, knowing full well where this conversation would be heading.

"I'm not sure what she's told you about her future. But my Sadie wants things she can't have. Right now, her job is to teach the *kinder* of our community. And she's of the marrying age."

Narrowing his eyes, Levi looked at Sadie's *vader*, trying to figure out where he was going with his thoughts. Levi didn't want to make a decision he might later regret.

"When you are married with *kinder* of your own,

you will understand that a *vader* knows what's right for his *dochders* and *sohns*. I've chosen someone for Sadie. He's a *gut*, solid man with a home that's ready for a wife."

Levi folded his arms across his chest, thinking he must look as though he had none of those traits. He thought he was a *gut* person, but he didn't really know what his future held. He supposed to Saul Fischer, he could look like something of a drifter. A man that wouldn't be a *gut* fit for his *dochder*.

He knew arranged marriages were not uncommon in their culture. But he doubted the Sadie he knew would ever settle for something like that. He couldn't imagine her living with a man she didn't love for the rest of her life.

Levi thought about him and Anne. He'd been so in love with her, and yet he'd come to find out she'd not returned those feelings…leastwise not for him. Now that time had passed, he knew they never would have been happy together. He wanted Sadie to be happy. Still, at this time he didn't think he'd be the right match for her.

But he'd seen Isaiah Troyer. He didn't think the man was a fit for Sadie either. He couldn't imagine her spending the rest of her life with him, bearing his children.

And those thoughts would do him no *gut*. "I understand what you are saying, Saul."

"Do you? I know how Sadie can turn things to her liking. But in this matter, I need her to abide by my wishes. I'm asking you to tread carefully where she is concerned. You would do well to remember her standing as the teacher in our community. She has a reputation to uphold. You two have been working here these past weeks, many times alone. If nothing else, I want you to steer clear of her."

With that, the man turned and boarded his wagon, leaving Levi to his work and his thoughts.

He should have told Saul that he needn't worry. Levi had no plans to rush into any kind of a relationship. He and Sadie were friends, nothing more. At least that was what he kept telling himself.

He'd barely had time to unpack his work tools when another wagon came into the schoolyard. This one carrying Sadie's *bruders* William and John. William jumped down from the wagon and came over to him.

"Levi! *Gut* to see you again."

"You, too."

"John and I were going fishing today on Lake Erie. We were wondering if you'd want to join us."

He declined the invitation and sent them on their way. There was no time to take a day off, not if he hoped to get everything completed on schedule. And he suspected that William and John were trying to learn more about him.

He expected nothing less of them. He'd have done the same for his sisters when they were getting ready to be married off. The difference here was Levi had no intention of asking for Sadie's hand in marriage.

Picking up the hammer, he pounded the nail into the piece of siding he'd been putting up on the back of the shed. The wood was stubborn and he had to strike the nail three times before the head settled snuggly against the hearty oak slab siding. He slid the next piece of wood into place, continuing to pound the nails. Maybe if he worked hard enough and long enough, he could ease the thoughts of Sadie Fischer out of his mind.

But that was becoming harder to do. As each day passed, he wondered how the classroom was coming along. Levi knew better than to approach Sadie if she was working alone. Jacob had warned him off, and Levi suspected the elders were concerned that he and Sadie were spending too much time alone, even if it were for the *gut* of the *kinder*. And now with the visits from her *vader* and her *bruders*, he took these warnings to heart. Sadie was a respected member of her community and she didn't need any trouble coming from him.

Still, he found himself missing the sound of her voice and the way she laughed at the simple things. He envied the way she could be so carefree even when he'd seen the hard days she'd had. Sadie was well liked by her students and their families. These were all *gut* qualities. He smiled, thinking about how patient she'd been with the little girl at the picnic. Sadie could easily have flown that kite herself and then handed the string to the girl. Instead she'd taught the girl how to fly the kite.

The phrase *give a man a fish and you feed him for a day; teach a man to fish and you feed him for a lifetime* came to mind.

Nothing seemed to get Sadie down. She clearly loved her job and all of the *kinder* she taught. They adored her. That had been clear when they'd all come around her during the picnic.

She was a kind, decent person. Not what he expected to find when he'd come here. Sadie was nothing like his former fiancée. Though Anne had seemed committed to their relationship, it turned out she'd had other plans all along. He knew Sadie's life was firmly grounded here in Miller's Crossing. But that didn't mean he wasn't going to keep exercising caution where she was concerned.

There would be no more impulsive decisions when it came to finding love. Perhaps he needed to be forceful with his intentions where Sadie was concerned. If he told her there could be nothing between them other than friendship, maybe that would take some of this pressure off of them. He didn't want to be the cause of her losing her job. In his mind, it was too soon to have feelings for her, even though, no matter how hard he tried to deny it, his heart had begun to open up to her.

The one sure thing in his life was his faith in the Lord. Time and time again the Lord had provided for him in his moments of need. Pausing, he turned his attention to the Lord, asking for guidance and giving thanks for what he already had

As he carried on with his duties, Levi worked in silence, stuck within his own thoughts, until he heard Sadie calling out to him.

"Levi? I know you're out here. I've heard your hammering all morning."

"I'm around back," he called out.

Putting his hammer into his leather tool belt, he walked around to meet Sadie.

All of his thoughts about using caution flew out of his mind the minute he saw her. She looked even prettier today than the last time he'd seen her. Her face had a healthy glow from being outside in the summer sunshine. She wore one of her famous smiles. She held a white envelope.

Narrowing his eyes, he focused on that, rather than on how lovely her blue eyes appeared today. "What do you have there?"

"My blue-ribbon snickerdoodle recipe, just like I promised."

"*Danke*. I know my *mamm* will enjoy making them. I'll send it along with my next letter."

He stood there, gazing into her eyes. His thoughts swirled around in his mind once again. Sadie deserved better than what he could offer. His heart had been broken and was barely mended. Maybe the breakup had been because of something he'd done…something he may be doomed to repeat. The last thing he wanted was to hurt Sadie. They'd already breached propriety by working without others around them. Levi recognized the fact that Sadie's job was important to her. Neither one of them should be putting her future in jeopardy.

Perhaps if she could see his flaws when it came to love, she would go back to focusing on her teaching.

"Levi?"

"*Ja?*"

"Are you going to take the envelope?"

"Sure, sure." In two strides, he closed the gap between them. Careful to keep his distance at arm's length, he accepted the recipe.

"This is coming along," Sadie observed as she took her time meandering to the other side of the building. Stopping in front of the shed, she turned to him. "*Danke* for the windows."

"Jacob found some extras."

"Admit it, Levi, this project is much better with the windows. Just think of all the plants my *kinder* and I can start out here. The light is perfect!"

"You were right in your thinking."

"I'm glad we can agree on that." She let out a laugh, clapping her hands together in triumph. "I can picture all those seedlings tilting toward the sunlight. This year I'm planning on doing more flowers. We need to replace the plants that were damaged in the storm anyway. We can start with the pansies and Johnny-jump-ups. Then we can move on to the marigolds and mums. I can just see their yellow and orange blooms lining the bushes around the front of the building."

"You're planning way ahead of the next spring season," he commented, realizing he'd grown used to hearing her talk in long segments.

"It doesn't hurt to plan or to use your imagination and dream about what something could look like."

They grew quiet. Off in the distance, a tractor engine started up. A few cars drove by the schoolyard. Sadie stilled. She looked up at him, her gaze taking in every inch of his face. By now he recognized that look. Sadie wanted more from him.

Levi swallowed. He needed to tell her there could be nothing more between them. "You got something on your mind, Sadie?"

Rolling her shoulders back, Sadie took her time forming her words. She'd been thinking about this moment ever since the picnic. Now the time had arrived, and she found herself feeling the unthinkable: tongue-tied.

Levi looked at her with one dark eyebrow cocked, his mouth in a firm line. She wondered if he thought she might be about to scold him for something.

Nee, this wasn't the case. She needed to talk to him about their relationship. Sadie knew she wasn't alone in sensing the undercurrent running between them. Her friends and her family had mentioned their observations to her. If others saw it, then there had to be more to it than just her wishful thinking.

"Levi, I..." She hesitated. This was going to be harder than she'd thought. Then she reminded herself how long she'd been fighting her *vader* over the Isaiah issue. If she wanted to have any hope of finding happiness in her future, then she needed to be brave.

"Levi, why are you here?"

A surprised look crossed his face. Then he asked, "Here? As in here at the school?"

"*Nee*, Levi. I think you know what I meant by my question."

She saw realization dawn on him.

"Ah. Here as in Miller's Crossing."

"*Ja.*"

He toyed with the handle on the hammer in his tool belt. Sadie watched as he grew still again, his hands dropping to his sides. His eyes took on a deeper shade of green as he pondered her request. She wanted to grab hold of him and shake the words out. Why was he so stubborn when it came to talking about his past? What was he afraid of? Sadie wasn't some monster who wanted to hurt him. She did, however, long to know if he had been feeling the same way she had.

"I don't have time for whatever this is, Sadie. There's a lot of work yet to be done if my job is to be completed on time."

She stood even taller. "Levi, I'll ask you again. Why are you here? Surely you have a family who misses you and would like you to return to their community."

"Sadie."

There was a plea in his voice. She heard it, and her heart broke for whatever pain he was suffering. Whether or not he wanted to believe it, he had become a part of Miller's Crossing. Levi wasn't just some worker passing through. The *kinder* liked him. Her *bruders* had even begun to change their idea about the man. Otherwise they never would have invited him to go along on their fishing trip.

"Every time I think we're about to grow closer, you shut me off. Why is that, Levi?"

"Sadie!"

He looked shocked at her forwardness, but she didn't have time to waste wondering if whatever was happening between them was simply a figment of her imagination. Desperation was creeping in.

"Please, Levi. Tell me."

"Sadie…" He extended a hand to her. "Don't. Move."

"Why?"

Levi seemed to be focused on something behind her. Suddenly afraid, Sadie started to turn her head.

"Levi, what is going on?"

He brought his finger to his lips. Very carefully, he mouthed, "Skunk."

Sadie's mouth formed an O. She heard the animal rustling around behind her. Levi's hand grabbed her forearm as they both held their breath. Sadie tried not to notice how warm his fingertips felt or the way his steady pulse thrummed beside her.

She didn't know how much time passed. Seconds turned into minutes.

And then he released her.

He gave his head a shake and grinned down at her. "That was a close call."

Her hand flew up to cover her heart. "You can say that again! *Danke* for saving me. Oh, my goodness, I can't even think about how bad that would have been if the skunk had sprayed us."

Blinking up at him, she went on, "Last year one of our dogs got into it with a skunk in the back field. We went through a case of canned tomato juice trying to get that smell off him. *Gut* thing the grocery store had them on sale or else we would have had to empty out the pantry!"

Levi turned away from her. "Perhaps we should get back to work."

"Levi, can't we at least finish our conversation?" Sadie sucked in her lower lip, waiting on his answer, holding out hope.

"I'm not sure that's a *gut* idea."

"Why?"

"Because."

She put her hands on her hips and glared up at him. "As I tell my students, *because* is not an answer.

"All right. How about because I can't tell you what you want to hear? The last thing I want to do is hurt you, Sadie. You've no idea how hard a relationship can be."

Sadie let his words sink in. "I know you would never hurt me." And then it dawned on her. "But you... You've been hurt by someone."

It was not a question. The soul-crushing look on his face told part of his story.

He shook his head as if to clear away the pain. "Please, don't push me on this."

She bit down on her lip, her heart breaking for him. She couldn't imagine anyone hurting a man so kind and giving. "I'm not pushing you."

"*Ja*, you are." His voice rose in anger. "It's like you're on some sort of self-imposed timeline." He paused, clenching his teeth together. Then his look softened. "I know your *vader* has someone in mind for you. Maybe you should consider his choice. Sadie, I'm not sure I'm the man who can be your 'not too old or not too young.'"

Her mouth fell open. He'd overheard the conversation she and Lizzie had had weeks ago, and those words had stayed with him. Sadie was ashamed at their silliness. She and Lizzie had been joking. But deep down, Sadie knew the words carried some certainty. She didn't want to settle. She wanted her own happily-ever-after. Even if he thought differently right now, Sadie knew she could have that with the man who stood before her.

"The day is getting on," he said. "We'd best be getting back to work."

She knew when to let something go, but this time she just couldn't leave it be. While Levi had built up a wall around his emotions that might seem impenetrable, she knew better. Her faith and her instincts were stronger than ever. This wasn't over yet.

"I don't understand why you are being so stubborn."

"Because you could lose your job over this," he said, waving his hand back and forth between them.

"Why do you say that?"

"Because we both know you're under scrutiny right now. Your position has not been made permanent."

"You don't need to remind me of that, Levi."

"Sadie, there is so much about me that you don't know."

"Then tell me," she pleaded.

He shook his head, making her angry and sad at the same time. "This isn't the time for us to begin anything other than a friendship."

His words stung. "You can't mean that." Sadie felt her lower lip tremble.

"Your *vader* has someone picked out for you. Perhaps it would be best if you went with his choice."

"That's a terrible thing to say to me," Sadie said, trying not to cry in front of him.

"I only want what is best for you. First off, your job here is part of who you are. I can't be the reason that would be taken from you. Second, we've only known each other a short amount of time."

"You don't always need a lot of time to know when something feels right."

"Sadie, please don't make this any harder than it needs to be."

She put her hand over her heart, trying to hold back the pain. She wasn't ready to give up. She wouldn't give in this easily. Deep in her heart, she knew they were right together. Isaiah Troyer wasn't the Amish man for her. Levi was.

Sadie tried one more tactic before letting him leave. "Levi, promise me one thing."

He stopped walking and looked over one shoulder at her. "What?"

"Promise me you'll think about this. The Lord brought you here for a reason."

His eyes clouded with emotion. Sadie could almost see the tiny break in the shell he'd put around his heart.

"I'll consider your words." With a shrug, he added, "I can offer you nothing more."

Brushing a tear from her eye, she watched him go. "Hope," she whispered. "You've offered me hope."

Chapter Thirteen

He felt like the worst of the worst, and burying himself in his work did little to alleviate that feeling. Ever since the conversation with Sadie, Levi had been taking on every extra hour of work he could get from Jacob and then some. He figured by keeping his hands and his mind busy, he wouldn't have time to think about Sadie. But just the opposite had happened. By cutting himself off from the community, he'd only had time to think.

Time to think about him and this woman who'd come into his life like a tornado. Her enthusiasm for life couldn't be missed. He envied her patience with her students and the way she'd thrown herself into getting her classroom ready for the new school year. She could be so carefree even when he knew she'd had a hard day.

Sadie was a force to be reckoned with, and the problem was Levi didn't know what to do with his feelings for her. He'd taken the coward's way out when she'd been brave enough to broach the subject of their relationship. He'd been nothing but honest with her, even though he didn't think he'd ever be able to share with her what Anne had done to him. The pain she'd caused, the way she'd ruined his trust and taken away his faith in finding true love.

He walked down the drive to the shed company from Jacob's house. Levi wasn't certain where his life was headed. One thing he knew for sure, he didn't like being in limbo.

Grabbing the doorknob, he pulled the side door open. The scent of fresh-cut lumber wafted by him. Some workers were busy doing finishing work, while others were on the assembly line putting together the framing for the walls.

No doubt about it, Jacob's business was booming.

"Levi! Just the person I've been looking for." Jacob headed toward him, removing his safety glasses and hearing protection. He clapped Levi on the shoulder. "Come on into my office."

Levi followed him and took the seat Jacob offered.

"How's all of this going for you?" his friend asked.

"*Gut.* Except for a few paint touch-ups, I'm finished at the school." Levi didn't feel the relief he'd expected over completing the job. It meant he'd no longer have a reason to see Sadie every day. The thought sent a jolt of surprise through him.

"Listen, Levi. There's something I've been wanting to discuss with you."

"Okay."

"I know you came here for temporary work. But my orders are not slowing down. Right now, I have half a dozen landscape and nursery companies owned by *Englischers* looking to stock my sheds, in addition to Troyer's big nursery right here in Clymer. And I've got more asking about the sheds."

Pushing his hat back on his head, Levi said, "You've been blessed, my cousin."

"I have been. These people don't want stock assembly line–type products. They are clamoring for Amish made."

Levi sat up taller in the chair. "I'm not sure what you're asking here, Jacob."

Steepling his fingers, Jacob speared him with a look of determination. "I want to share my blessings with you."

"I don't know what that means, exactly."

"It means I want you to go into partnership with me."

Levi settled against the back of the chair in shock. Though he'd known Jacob and Rachel had been discussing this, he'd no idea that a full partnership was what his cousin had been thinking about. Levi had expected the possibility of more hours, taking on more responsibility within the shop or maybe even overseeing projects, but this… He'd not seen this offer coming.

A partnership.

This could be life changing. Of course, it would mean relocating here permanently. He knew one person who would be delighted with this bit of news. He so wished this opportunity had come along even a year ago. But then, he reminded himself, a year ago he wasn't even considering leaving his community to start fresh. Now with his life in limbo, he had no idea what he wanted. Could this be the answer to his prayers, or would taking Jacob up on his offer only bring more heartache?

"Hey, Levi. I can see from the look on your face that my offer hasn't brought you the happiness I'd hoped for."

"*Nee, nee.* It's not that. I've so much on my mind,

Jacob. So much to consider. And you and Rachel have been so kind to me these past weeks."

"Well, we like having you here. And you've been a tremendous help for me. And my Rachel likes having me home a few nights a week in time for supper." Jacob leaned forward. "Is there something else I don't know about?"

Levi knew the gossip concerning him and Sadie was quietly making its way around Miller's Crossing. Things like the prospect of a new couple never stayed quiet for long in any close-knit town, particularly an Amish one. Right now, he told himself, there was nothing more between them than a growing friendship, though he knew Sadie wanted more. Levi didn't know if he had it in him to give her that. He'd tried to explain that to her when he'd seen her last.

Maybe he was nothing but a coward when it came to love.

"Levi?" Jacob's voice interrupted his musings. "What do you think?"

"I'm not sure."

"If this helps any, I'm aware of the undercurrent between you and Sadie. I know it's none of my business, but if that's holding you back—"

"Jacob, I came here because I needed time to put my life back in order." Levi gave his cousin the short version of what had transpired between him and Anne. "I thought I'd found the love of my life last year and she ended up leaving me. I'm not sure I can be this man Sadie is searching for."

He knew he'd hurt her feelings the other day. He felt terrible about it.

"For what it's worth," Jacob said at last, "I think the

Lord knows what He's doing and He sent you here for a reason other than to help out a family member and a friend."

"Funny those are the words you chose. Sadie said the same thing... Well, the part about the Lord bringing me here for a reason."

"You should listen to her." Jacob smiled. "So, you'll think about my offer?"

"I will."

"Levi, I really want to make this work. If you decide to leave, then I'll have to seek out someone else to buy into a partnership. I really want to keep this business in the family."

"I understand."

"One more piece of advice—you need to let go of your past. Otherwise you'll never find the happiness you deserve."

Levi knew the bigger part of this would be not only letting go of the past, but letting Sadie in. He wondered if he could find the courage do that.

Sadie stepped out the front door of the schoolhouse, taking in the glorious sight spread out before her. The fall semester had gotten underway a few days ago, and Sadie had been thankful for the distraction of preparing for this week. It kept her mind off of Levi. She hadn't seen him since the day he'd told her he couldn't be the one for her.

So now Sadie filled her time with teaching. Watching her students, both young and old, playing in the schoolyard filled her heart with gladness. The swings were full with the *kinder*. And the older ones ran around the bases playing a raucous game of kickball. She hated to end their freedom, but the lessons were calling. She yanked a braided string and rang the bell.

"Come on, everyone. The quicker you get inside, the quicker you can get to your work!"

Mary stepped out of the line, asking, "Miss Sadie, did you see how high I went on the swing?"

"I did, Mary. You've really improved."

"*Danke*, Miss Sadie."

She ushered the rest of the *kinder* inside. "I hope you all enjoyed your time outside. And now that we've settled in our seats, I want to go over the chore list with you." In addition, she had a special project for them to work on.

There were a few groans. She stayed behind her desk, waiting for them to quiet. "I've assigned the tasks based on what I think you can do best. You'll find your name on the sheet and then be responsible for that chore."

Mica's hand shot up. "What if we don't like the chore?"

"Then you'll do your best to complete it. Now, today I'd like us to start on our first class project of the school term. As you know, our building and shed sustained some damage over the summer from that storm. I'd like to break off into groups—the boys in one, the girls in the other. We are going to make thank-you cards for Mr. Byler and Mr. Herschberger. The girls will work on one for Mr. Byler and the boys will do the one for Mr. Herschberger. They did a great deal to make sure your classroom was ready for you. In addition, Mr. Byler built us a brand-new shed. When the cards are finished, you can each take a turn signing your name."

Sadie had already set up large pieces of paper on the project table located along the side wall. "Perhaps some of you older boys can help move the table away from the wall so there is space for you to gather around. "We'll have the girls work first since there won't be room for all of you at once. In the meantime, I'd like the boys to get out their chapter books and begin reading silently."

After she got the girls set up with paper, crayons and colored pencils, she walked around the room, helping the boys with their reading. She stopped by Josh's desk and worked with him to sound out a word, but when she got to Mica's desk, she noticed he hadn't even opened his book.

"Mica, why aren't you reading?"

He gave a shrug. "I have a headache."

Concerned, she inspected his face, then lay her hand lightly against his forehead, looking for any signs of a fever. "Would you like me to get you a cold compress to put on your forehead? That might help."

"Nee."

"All right. Stay here and rest at your desk. I'll keep an eye on you."

"Danke, Miss Sadie."

Moving down the line, she stopped a few more times to work with the other students. Noticing a half hour had passed, she switched the groups out. The girls were quick to open their books.

"Mary Ellen, could you please take little Mary and Beth over to the reading corner and read out loud to them?"

"Yes, Miss Sadie."

Mary Ellen was one of her oldest students and soon she would be aging out of the classroom. Next year, she'd finish up eighth grade. Sadie intended to have her assist her with the other *kinder* this year. The girl loved to learn and had an abundance of patience. Sadie hoped she might go into teaching.

She heard chatter coming from the craft table and went over to check on the progress the boys were making with their card. Oddly enough, Mica was bent over the table with a crayon in his hand coloring in some lettering. He elbowed Josh, who leaned in, cupped his hand and whispered into Mica's ear.

She found Mica's behavior odd, considering he'd just told her he couldn't read because he had a headache. She'd believed him and allowed him to skip his reading time. She might come off as a kind and easygoing teacher, but Sadie didn't like being lied to.

She needed to nip this in the bud.

"Mary Ellen, I need you to stop reading to the girls and keep an eye on the class."

Stepping behind Mica, she gave him a pat on the shoulder. "Mica, I'd like to have a word with you, outside."

She knew from the look on his face that he understood he was in trouble. A hush fell over the room as she led him out the back door, where her steps faltered as she came face-to-face with Levi.

"Levi! What are you doing here?"

"I'm finishing up with the painting on the shed. How are you doing, Sadie?"

"I'm fine. And yourself?"

She wanted to shake some sense into him. Here they were speaking to each other like they were polite strangers, when they both knew better. Mica squirmed. She'd nearly forgotten he was standing beside her.

"Mica, sit on the step, please, while I speak to Mr. Byler."

Doing as he was told, the boy sat on the bottom step awaiting his fate.

"I'm doing okay."

Longing to ask if he missed her as much as she'd been missing him, Sadie forced herself to watch Mica as he brought his knees up to his chest. Wrapping his arms around his legs, he rested his chin on his bony little kneecaps. Sadie didn't like to think that he might be afraid of his punishment. She had no intention of being overly strict. That wasn't her way.

She glanced over his head at the shed. It looked mighty nice with the spotless windows flanking either side of the door, and the whitewashed siding. Levi had done a fine job.

"The shed looks wonderful, Levi."

"*Danke.* I have one last thing to do and then I'm done."

She wondered if he felt the same pain she felt. A knot had formed in the pit of her stomach. She didn't know what to do with the sensations rippling through her. How could she, upon seeing him here, feel joy and sadness at the same time? Even after their last conversation, even after the days of feeling hurt and empty inside, why did her heartbeat still kick up at the sight of him? Sadie knew then and there whatever was between them hadn't ended as Levi had wanted.

The sound of the *kinder*'s voices coming from behind her jolted her back to reality.

"I'd like to drop by Jacob and Rachel's on my way home," she said to Levi. "Could you let them know to expect me?"

"*Ja.*"

"Miss Sadie, can I go back inside?"

"*Nee*, Mica. We need to talk." She looked back up to find Levi watching her, the expression on his face carefully guarded. Sadie fought hard to tamp down her frustration with the man. This situation infuriated her and she didn't know how to fix it.

"I'll leave you to your day," Levi said.

He walked off, leaving her to watch his retreating back. The breeze ruffled the dark locks of hair skimming the top of his blue work shirt. Sadie took in his tall, lanky form, remembering the first day they'd met and what a mess she'd been.

She wanted to cry.

"Miss Sadie? Are you okay?" Mica asked.

She took in a deep breath, bolstering her courage. Looking down at the boy, she gave him a shaky smile. "I'm fine, *danke*." Gathering her skirt, she sat next to him. "Mica, I know you understand that lying, even a tiny fib, is wrong."

He nodded.

"I'm going to let you off easy this time around by sending your reading home with you tonight. You can read the pages and we'll discuss them tomorrow. I'll send a note to your parents so they'll know. I won't mention why."

He swiped a hand across his eyes. It broke her heart to see any of her students in pain.

"Mica, do as I've asked and all will be well."

"Okay, Miss Sadie. I'll try."

She patted him on his thin shoulder as they stood. Holding the door open, Sadie let Mica go inside ahead of her. She had one foot on the threshold when she thought she'd heard her name.

Turning, she saw Levi about to swing his hammer

against a piece of wood. She waited, hoping he'd stop and look at her. But he didn't.

Squaring her shoulders, she followed Mica inside, closing the door behind them. She wanted to do nothing more than sit at her desk and lament over Levi. But there wasn't time to do that. She had a class to tend to.

The rest of the day flew by with math lessons and their first English assignment, which was to write about what they did over summer break. While they worked on that, she wrote the note to Mica's parents. She let Mary Ellen lead the class in the closing scripture, and then made sure each of them had signed their name to the thank-you cards.

Once the *kinder* were gone, Sadie neatened up her desk, grabbed the cards and, locking the door behind her, went to where she'd left her bicycle. She put the cards in the basket on the handrails and headed for Jacob and Rachel's.

The trip took about half an hour, and Sadie had been preparing herself for the final hill the entire time. Back in her younger days, she'd been able to ride up the steep incline with little effort. But now it loomed like an unscalable mountain in front of her.

Resting her feet on either side of the bike, she pondered the situation. She could easily get off and walk the bike up the hill, or she could take on the challenge to ride. While she stood there debating, she heard the creaking of a wagon coming up behind her. She turned to see if it might be someone she knew.

"Hey, do you need a lift?"

The bobbing of her head said one thing while her mouth said, "Nope. I'm *gut*."

Cocking his head to one side, Levi asked, "Are you sure? Seems like you're having trouble deciding."

She scuffed the toe of her foot along the side of the road, trying to make up her mind. If she remained stubborn and pushed the bike up the hill, it would be at least another twenty minutes before she arrived at Rachel and Jacob's place. Then the time for a visit would be shortened because she still had to pedal back to her house, which would get her home just in time for supper. But if she took Levi up on his offer, she'd have more time to visit with Rachel.

On the other hand, she didn't understand why he wanted to be with her. He'd made his feelings on their relationship clear. She didn't need to spend any more time with this man. A man who didn't want her to be a part of his life.

"Come on, Sadie, let me give you a ride."

Chapter Fourteen

He could almost see her mind working at coming up with a reason not to go with him. But finally, she got off the bike and took some papers out of the basket. She let him take hold of the handlebars. While she got herself seated in the wagon, he loaded the bike in the back.

Grabbing hold of the side rail to hoist himself up, Levi observed, "Maybe your *vader* should let you get one of those motorized scooters." Settling next to her, he added, "The youngies go whizzing by me all the time."

"*Nee*. He thinks they are too dangerous. And they sort of frighten me. Today I'm heading to see Rachel and to drop off a surprise for you and Jacob," she explained, keeping her eyes straight ahead on the road.

"What sort of surprise?"

"If I told you, it wouldn't be a surprise." She held her hands neatly over the papers in her lap.

Apparently, she would not be elaborating, so he asked, "Did Mica get into trouble?"

"I wouldn't call it trouble. We had a misunderstanding."

"I see. He's a *gut* boy."

"He is."

Levi understood Sadie's stiff attitude toward him and yet it still stung. He knew he'd been the one to put a halt to their feelings. It had been the right thing to do for both of them. She'd be free to find someone who could love her with his whole heart, and Levi...

Well, he didn't know what any of this meant for him. He'd done a lot of thinking about what Jacob had said.

Putting aside the hurt and pain of betrayal had taken a toll on his soul. And now he had this offer of a partnership from his cousin. An opportunity that, if he accepted, would mean he'd be living near Sadie. He'd see her at church services and picnics. He didn't imagine she'd be single much longer. Levi might have to reconcile himself to seeing her with someone else. Then again, he'd told her to move on, to accept the man her *vader* had chosen.

Knowing Sadie, though, he doubted she had any plans to settle on a choice that wasn't of her own making. His heart ached. Somehow this ache didn't feel the same as what he'd felt when Anne had left him. *Nee*, this pain held something different. A longing that didn't seem to go away. Sadie was literally within arm's reach. He knew all he had to do was turn and tell her his words had been a mistake.

He wouldn't do that. Sadie deserved someone who could love her with their heart intact. Levi didn't trust himself with his feelings. The hurt and pain of Anne's betrayal still lingered, and he couldn't seem to let go.

"Levi?" Her warm, sweet voice broke through his musings. *"Bischt allrecht?"*

"Ja," he answered, even though he felt far from all

right. Clearing his throat, he noted, "We're here. Shall I drop you at the house?"

"I'd like that, *danke*. But I do have that surprise for you. So, come inside with me."

She waited for him on the porch as he tied the horse to the hitching post. The afternoon sunlight spilled across the house, bathing her in a warm glow making his heart ache all over again. Sadie had to be the prettiest woman he'd ever seen.

Rachel burst onto the porch. "Sadie! I'm so happy to see you. I just made some iced *kaffi*. Jacob and Levi have been partaking at the end of these hot days. Would you like a glass?"

"Just water, please, Rachel."

"I'll bring out some of my sugar *kichlins*, too. I'm afraid they do not compare to your snickerdoodles," Rachel admitted with a laugh.

She headed back into the house, and Levi heard her call out to Jacob, telling him they were here. A shadow appeared behind the screen. Jacob swung the door open and came out to join them.

"*Gute nammidaag*, Sadie. Levi."

"*Gute nammidaag* to you, Jacob," Sadie replied, sitting in one of the rockers on the porch. "I've brought you and Levi a surprise from the *kinder*."

"*Ach*. We don't need a surprise." Jacob raised his hands in front of his chest.

"This is one you will cherish, I promise."

After pulling two folded sheets of paper out of an envelope, she handed one to Jacob.

Levi stepped around him to collect the remaining one Sadie held out to him. His fingertips skimmed hers. For the briefest of moments, her soft skin brushed against his roughened hands. She pulled away, casting her eyes downward. His stomach clenched. What had he done?

"Rachel. Come see this card the *kinder* made." Jacob's face lit up with joy. "Show me yours, Levi."

Levi held the paper between his fingers. The *kinder* had indeed done a fine job with their artwork. The front of his card had a rather rustic drawing of the shed. He smiled when he saw the stick figures alongside. Each one had an arrow pointing at it. One had the name *Mica* written over it and the other *Josh*. Levi shook his head. He'd never forget working with those boys. Opening the card, he read each name. *Thank you* was written in block letters.

He'd never gotten a gift such as this. He looked up to find Sadie watching him. Her blue eyes taking in his face, she gave him a slight nod.

"I told you, you would like this surprise."

"You were right."

"Here's our refreshments!" Rachel came out onto the porch carrying a tray of drinks and the plate of *kichlin*.

"Sadie, did Levi tell you his news?" she asked, as she handed out the drinks.

Accepting the ice water, Sadie answered, *"Nee."*

"Jacob has officially asked him to become a partner in the business. This is such *gut* news for us. Of course, he has to say yes first."

Sadie's mouth opened and then closed. Setting her glass on the low table between the rockers, she rose, brushing past Levi.

"I'm afraid it's later than I thought. I'd best be getting home. *Danke* for the water, Rachel."

Setting his glass next to hers, Levi hurried down the porch steps after her. "Sadie, let me take you home."

She spun around so fast they bumped into each other.

* * *

She started to push him away. "I can get myself home. Don't worry about me. My house is downhill from here."

"Sadie, I know you're upset with Rachel's news."

Keeping her voice low so Rachel and Jacob couldn't overhear, she barely got out, "Rachel's news? Is that how you think of this? Jacob offered you the partnership, Levi. You." She poked a finger against his chest.

He started to take hold of her hand. Feeling as if her skin had been scorched, she took a step back, out of his reach. It seemed that no matter what he did and said to her these days, it only ended in pain and hurt. Sadie didn't know how to get him to see that together they could make anything work. Why did he continue to hold back?

"I have to go." With that, she made her way to where he'd left her bike leaning up against the side of the wagon.

"Don't go off angry."

Slowing her pace, she turned to face him.

His hands were clenched at his sides. Sadie longed to take hold of them, to feel his strength, to offer him hope. But she stood there, waiting for him to say something, anything, realizing if he were to stay here in Miller's Crossing that their lives would become intertwined.

Her heartbeat settled into a calmer rhythm as her anger dissipated. If Levi took Jacob's offer, he would be here, near her. She dared to meet his gaze, wondering if any of this had occurred to him. Wondering if he even cared. His steadfastness told her he did.

"I can't be late for dinner again."

And she rode off, arriving home to find her *vader*

waiting for her. He sat on the front porch in his favorite chair, sipping from a glass of lemonade. She noticed his hands and the calluses etched in them from the years working in the fields. A straw hat covered his graying hair. His mouth was pulled into a grim line. Stepping up onto the porch, Sadie avoided his gaze.

"*Dochder.* Come, *sittsit unnah.* It's time for us to talk."

She knew better than to disobey him, even though she knew full well what he wanted to talk about. She sat on the hard bench next to the door.

"I can't wait any longer for you to make up your mind. I want a union between you and Isaiah Troyer. It will be good to bring both households together."

Her stomach twisted at his words. "Please, *Daed.* I only need a little more time."

"I've given you time. Sadie, you are the teacher at the local *schul.* You have a reputation to think about." He slapped the palm of his hand on the flat arm of the rocker. "I can't have this behavior of yours continue."

"But I don't love Isaiah."

"You will grow to love him in time."

She shook her head so hard she felt the prayer *kapp* loosen. Fighting back tears, she straightened her *kapp.* "I can't do as you ask." Not when her heart belonged to someone else.

"Sadie! I'll not have you disobeying me!"

Sucking in a breath, her mind worked to find another way to convince her *daed* that this was not the right choice for her. Isaiah Troyer could never be her Amish man.

"I'm going to speak to him tomorrow," her *vader* warned.

She covered her mouth with one hand, pushing back the sob that threatened to escape. Her stomach roiled as her heart pounded inside her chest. This couldn't be happening, not when she and Levi were so close to… *Close to what?* she wondered. She let her eyelids drop, saying a silent prayer that her *daed* would give her more time. Sadie believed with all her heart and soul that Levi had been sent here not to help out Jacob but to find her.

Behind her, she heard the creak of the screen door.

Hoping to sway her *vader* once more, Sadie said, "I need more time."

"Nee."

"Wait!"

They both jumped at the sound of her sister's voice. Sara flew out onto the porch like a dog was nipping at her heels.

"Sadie isn't the right Fischer *dochder* for Isaiah," she blurted out. She stood in front of them, wringing her hands together. "I am."

"What is this nonsense?" their *vader* bellowed.

Sadie jumped up off the bench to stand with her sister, the life nearly scared right out of her. "Sara, what are you talking about?" Though thrilled her sister had intervened, Sadie worried that she might have gotten them both into more trouble than they were already in.

"Sadie isn't the one for Isaiah." Sara flung back her shoulders and speared their *vader* with a confident look. "I am."

Her *vader* narrowed his eyes. "You better explain yourself, Sara."

"Isaiah and I hit it off at the picnic. *Daed*, I've had feelings for him for a long time."

This admission made sense to Sadie, who'd been

seeing the signs of Sara's affection toward Isaiah for months now. She recalled that Sara had been the one upset when the special dinner had to be canceled due to the storm. And Sara had been the one to put on her special dress the day of the picnic. And Sara had been the one to talk to Isaiah after church services.

Silence descended as the sisters collectively held their breath waiting for the final decision.

Their *vader* stood and walked to the far end of the porch. Placing both hands flat on the railing, he bowed his head. Sadie took hold of Sara's hand, giving it a squeeze. Even their *mamm* had come to stand in the doorway.

Sadie let out a nervous sigh. He was taking too long.

Finally, he turned to face them. "I will speak to Isaiah about you, Sara."

Sara broke away from Sadie, running to give their *vader* a hug. *"Danke!"*

Then she stepped to the side so their *vader* could deliver Sadie's fate.

"I know you think you have feelings for Levi Byler."

She didn't think it. She knew she'd fallen in love with the man.

"This should come as no surprise to you, Sadie. News like this travels fast in close-knit communities. Before you ask me, I think you know why I've wanted this for you and Isaiah. I know very little about Levi, other than he is Jacob's cousin and appears to be a good worker."

"Jacob has officially offered him a partnership." Sadie thought this bit of news might help her *vader* to see that Levi was not simply passing through Miller's Crossing. There was a good chance he might settle here.

"Again, I will remind you that you have a reputation to uphold."

"I understand." Sadie knew she'd just been given her last chance to find her true love.

Chapter Fifteen

Sadie got to work early the next morning, her mind filled with yesterday's conversations with both her *vader* and Levi. She couldn't help thinking they all wanted the same outcome. Being a woman of faith, she knew the Lord had plans. The words of her *grossmudder* Fischer popped into her head.

For faith to prosper, it must experience impossible situations.

Sadie let out a morose laugh. Her love for Levi had certainly brought her an impossible situation. But she knew as sure as the sun would rise and set each day, her faith was as solid as a rock. And just as strong as her faith in the Lord, she'd faith that she and Levi would find their way. The signs had been there yesterday when she could see his concern for her after she'd learned about his offer. At first, she'd felt betrayed that he hadn't told her, then she reminded herself that Levi assumed they were finished.

She knew different.

Glancing out a window of the schoolhouse, she saw the *kinder* coming down the road. It was a sight that never got old. They came in groups of three and four, filtering out from their family's houses. The little girls wearing their blue *schlupp schotzli* over their dresses. Siblings and cousins helping one another to stay safe on the shared road. As soon as they hit the schoolyard, they ran across the grass and in through the basement entrance. All except for Mica. He straggled behind his group, scuffing his shoes through the tufts of grass.

Sadie hurried downstairs to the coatroom. *"Gute mariye, everyone!"*

Here and there, the children responded with their own, *"Gute mariye."*

She kept watch over the tops of their heads, until she saw Mica join them. "Everyone, let's put your lunches in your cubbies and then settle at your desks, please."

Mica avoided making eye contact with her, which Sadie didn't like.

They filed upstairs in order of youngest to oldest. Each student took their seat and Sadie had them read aloud the morning Bible verse, then begin working on their math lessons.

The morning passed without incident. At eleven o'clock, she sent one of the older girls down to start the oven to warm the hot lunches. By noon everyone had eaten and was ready to go outside to play.

Mica had never been far from her sight. She noticed again that he didn't seem to want to read from his book. Though she did not like to stress it, obedience was one of the things they practiced here at the school. For the most part, her students behaved. Very rarely had she had to call upon a parent to come in, and heaven forbid, she'd never had to have the school board intervene on her behalf when it came to matters concerning parents and their children.

Still, her concern for Mica was growing.

"Mica, could you stop by my desk after you're done with your lunch, please?"

"Yes, Miss Sadie."

It pained her to see his mouth downturned. Sadie couldn't imagine what had gotten into him. Last year he'd been one of her best students. She didn't understand what had changed. She needed to get to the bottom of this and quickly.

She asked Mary Ellen and one of the other older girls to chaperone recess time. At twelve thirty on the dot, Mica arrived at her desk.

"Did you have a *gut* lunch?" she asked.

"Peanut butter and jelly, again." He rested his elbow on her desk, giving her a forlorn expression.

"I take it you don't like peanut butter and jelly?"

"It's okay. Not my favorite."

"I see. Now, tell me about last night's assignment. Did you get one of your parents to help with your reading?"

He shook his head.

"Why not?"

"They had chores to do."

"What about one of your older *bruders* or sisters?" Two of Mica's siblings had graduated last year, so Sadie knew they could help.

"Nee."

Bringing herself down to his eye-level, she reached across her desk and laid her hand gently on his arm. "Mica, can you tell me why you don't want to ask for help when you're at home?"

Again, he shook his head. She decided to try another tactic.

"How about you and I spend ten minutes during each recess working on your reading until you've caught up?"

"I can't do that either."

Sadie could almost feel his pain. Whatever was bothering him and keeping him from reading had to be pretty serious. "Mica? I need you to explain this to me."

"I can't do that."

His answer caused her to sit back in her chair. She watched him struggling and could tell he wanted to share his problem with her. Was he afraid of something at home? She prayed not.

An idea came upon her. "How about this. I'll read the pages from yesterday and you can follow along with me. Does that sound like a *gut* plan?" When he didn't respond, she added, "We have a test coming up on Friday, and it's going to have questions from these chapters. I know you want to do well."

His head moved up and down without looking up at her.

Satisfied that she had gotten through to him, Sadie asked him to bring his book up to her. Glancing at the clock, she saw there were fifteen minutes left of playtime. Mica would have to miss being outdoors with the other students today. Sadie felt bad about that, but it was important he kept pace with the others in his group.

While he got the book, she pulled another chair alongside hers. He sat down next to her and handed her the book. Sadie opened to the chapter he should have read and began reading to him. Every once in a while, she'd glance over to see if he were following along. At one point she paused. It seemed as if he were having problems seeing the words. Mica was leaning in close, squinting at the page.

Sadie nibbled her lower lip in thought.

The outside bell began to clang, signaling recess had come to an end. She would have to thank the girls for being so punctual with the time. Closing the book, she patted Mica on the shoulder. "Are you liking the book so far?"

He perked up a bit at her question. "I like when the boy tries to teach his sister how to fish."

Joy filled her heart. That was really *gut* to hear. It meant Mica had been paying attention even though he appeared to have trouble seeing the words. But she couldn't read to him every day. If her suspicions were correct, Mica was having trouble with his sight. She would send another note home and this time make him promise to show his parents.

The rest of the day flew by with ease. Sadie followed the routine, passing the trash can around the room for each student to toss out any papers they didn't need, and then escorted them to the coatroom, bidding them all a *gut* evening. She packed up and went home.

The next day dawned to begin the routine all over again, with Sadie arriving at the schoolhouse an hour before the *kinder*.

Judging from the buggy parked in front of the school, Sadie assumed Mica's parents had read her note. *Gut.* The sooner they figured out his problem, the quicker they could resolve it.

She noticed a familiar wagon parked out back. Levi must be doing some final touches on the shed.

Pushing her bike to the side of the building, she gathered the lesson plans she'd brought home last night and headed inside. The Kings were sitting in two chairs facing her desk. Sadie paused, gathering her thoughts, preparing to greet them.

"It's about time you arrived!" Robert King turned to face her and stood behind his wife's chair.

From the doorway, Sadie said, "Mr. and Mrs. King. I didn't expect you."

Robert's *bruder* Amos owned the stationery store. Sadie realized they were quite different. Amos had always been kind to her, but she'd never gotten the feeling Robert was the same.

"Well, you should have after that note you sent home with Mica yesterday!" Robert's voice boomed through the room.

Calm. She needed to remain calm. Part of her job was to act on behalf of her students. She had to keep Mica's needs at the forefront. Bringing her papers with her, Sadie walked down the middle aisle. She rounded her desk and carefully set her things down. Then, raising her eyes, she faced Robert and Elenore King.

"What's this nonsense about him having problems reading?"

Sadie knew she had to tread lightly because Robert King sat on the school board. But that did not mean she wouldn't fight just as hard for Mica. As a matter of fact, Robert's stature made her want to dig in her heels to prove to him that she could handle this problem.

"Robert, Elenore. I noticed a few days ago that Mica seemed to have lost interest in doing his reading assignments."

"I'll speak to him about listening to you," Robert said.

"It's more than not listening. That's not it."

She decided it best not to mention Mica's complaint of the headache just yet. Sadie was quite certain Mica had told her that so she wouldn't push him to read in front of the class. She kept the part about the first note to herself, as well. If she needed extra leverage to convince the Kings to help him, she would tell them about the headache.

Sadie continued, "Yesterday I had him stay inside during recess to work with me. I decided to read out loud to him."

"I don't want you coddling my *sohn*," Robert admonished.

"I'm not doing that. I'm doing my job, trying to help him."

"His mother can help him."

"Robert, with all due respect, I believe that Mica's problem isn't that he can't read. It's that he's having struggles with his vision."

"What are you talking about?"

"I noticed that while he was following along, he had to lean in close to the page and then I saw him squinting. I think he needs to have his vision checked."

"You are no *doktor*! You are a teacher. Your job is to teach!"

"Robert!" Elenore put her arm on her husband's arm, stilling him. "Sadie has Mica's best interest at heart, I'm sure."

Pushing her hand away, he scolded, "Be quiet, Elenore." Continuing, he admonished Sadie, "You would do well to remember that you are still on probation here. Even if last year went fine, the school board hasn't ended their search for a new teacher."

Sadie stood there in shocked silence. She'd done nothing to deserve this kind of censure.

* * *

From outside the building, Levi heard what sounded like a male voice, raised in anger. Setting down the frame for the window box he'd been working on, he hurried to the schoolhouse.

Entering through the front door, he made his way to the threshold, just in time to hear a man say, "Perhaps it's not Mica's problem with his vision but the way you are teaching him."

Stunned, Levi walked into the classroom to see Sadie standing behind her desk visibly shaken. Her face ashen. It took every effort not to sprint over to the desk, take hold of the man at her desk and toss him outside. Coming to her defense seemed like the natural thing to do.

"Sadie Fischer is a *gut* teacher and you should consider yourself very fortunate to have her."

Sadie looked up, surprise registering on her face when she saw him standing there. She hadn't heard him come in.

The man glared at him. Levi immediately recognized Mica's *vader*. They'd met briefly after the storm. He wondered if the man remembered him. As the two of them stared at each other, Levi saw the anger simmering in Robert. The man's dark eyes narrowed, and his hands clenched at his side. Levi wondered why Robert didn't understand that Sadie only wanted the best for each and every one of her students, and Mica was no different.

Finally, Robert spoke. "I'm fairly certain you have no *kinder* in this school?"

"I do not."

"Then you have no business speaking here."

Levi stood there, weighing his options. He could

apologize, or he could go back outside. Or he could strengthen Sadie's defense, not that he thought for one minute she couldn't defend herself.

"Miss Sadie does a fine job of seeing to the needs of her students."

"I imagine you know this because of all the time you've been spending here."

This was exactly why he'd told Sadie there couldn't be more between them. As long as he was around here, and they were alone working together, there would continue to be problems for her. Levi hadn't come to Miller's Crossing to find love. He'd come to rebuild his life, as a single man. Even though there had never been anything untoward between them, he knew in their community appearances were everything.

"As you know, I've been working with her since the storm blew through. As a matter of fact, your *sohn* Mica has been one of our helpers. He did a fine job with the painting and helping me build the new shed. You should be right proud of him."

Robert's ire over the reading issue seemed to soften. "*Danke.* I'm surprised he stayed focused long enough to get any work done."

"The painting he seemed to take to, but the work on the shed, not so much." Levi chuckled, hoping to break the tension in the room.

"He likes to horse around when he's outside." Robert swung his gaze back to Sadie.

"Robert, Elenore, I only want what's best for Mica," Sadie began. "As I'm sure you both do. Could you at least think about getting his eyes examined? If there is an issue, I imagine that soon it will carry over to other parts of his life. He's already complaining about headaches."

Elenore took hold of her husband's hand. "Please, Robert. We can at least think about what Sadie is saying."

"We'll discuss this at home." He stood up and then, nodding to Levi, said, "I'd like a word with you, outside."

Sadie's eyebrows rose.

Levi waited for Robert to join him and then took him down the stairs and out the basement door into the morning sunshine. Turning to face Mica's *daed*, he planted his feet about a foot apart, folded his arms across his chest and waited.

Robert's beard skimmed the top of his chest, and his gray hair reached almost to his shoulders. The man stood a good three inches taller than Levi. But even the steel gaze bearing down on him didn't intimidate him.

"Levi, I'm not one to beat around the bush, so I'll get right to the point of the matter. There's been gossip about you and Sadie Fischer. Part of my job on the school committee is to make sure the reputation of the teacher is a *gut* one, beyond reproach."

"I understand. My time with Sadie has been innocent. You can trust my word on that."

"You've been here working with her. Others saw you with her at the picnic. There may have been other times I've not been made aware of."

Levi felt his hackles raise. There had never been anything inappropriate between him and Sadie. He did not take these hints of accusation lightly. Moreover, he would never do anything to jeopardize her teaching job. Still, he found himself not liking the feeling Robert gave him. *Ja*, he knew how closely the Amish guarded their *dochders* and how many *vaders* worked hard to make the best arrangements for the good of the family. Sadie's *vader* hadn't been any different. But Levi had done nothing wrong.

This conversation left him with a sour taste in his mouth.

"I know Sadie understands this," Robert went on, "but I want to be certain that you do, too. It does not matter to me the work you've done to help out. And even though you are a relation to Jacob, you're a stranger here."

Levi continued to hold his stance even though he felt as if he'd been sucker punched.

Robert left him standing in the shadow of the shed, and Levi watched him walk back into the schoolhouse. Only when Robert was out of sight did he let his hands fall to his side. He spun around, and his eyes fell on the window boxes. His latest surprise for Sadie. Why did he keep torturing himself when he knew he wasn't going to accept Jacob's offer of the partnership?

How could he? He'd be living near Sadie. And Levi simply couldn't trust his heart or his feelings again. The pain Anne had wrought had left him deeply wounded. And even though some of those wounds had begun to heal, Levi still didn't think he could trust himself to make the right choice. This encounter with Robert King only reinforced the reasons why Levi couldn't stay in Miller's Crossing and why he wasn't the right man for Sadie.

In all the weeks he'd been working side by side with her, he'd seen how she loved her *kinder*. Her days were devoted to making their lives better. He wouldn't be the one to destroy her happiness. He didn't want to rush headlong into another relationship.

Levi didn't know how to fix things.

He felt the ache growing inside him. He just wanted to do his work. Lord knows, he hadn't come here planning on falling in love. And yet that was exactly what had happened.

Pushing aside the pain and despair, Levi knew that the time had come for him to give Jacob an answer to his offer. But first he would finish what he started.

Picking up a two-by-eight plank, he placed it on the sawhorses, measured and cut the plank to size, two inches longer than the front of the windows. He did that one more time, and then, laying the tape measure along the wood, he measured out six inches in length and proceeded to cut four of those.

As the morning wore on, the *kinder's* voices floated through the open window. Every once in a while, he heard the sweet sound of Sadie's voice either giving instruction or offering encouragement. When he heard the singing, he stopped his work to listen. The song, a familiar one, reminded him of home and family and of his love for the Lord. The hymn called to mind all the good that life could bring a person.

He didn't want to wallow. Shaking himself out of the doldrums, he hammered the pieces of wood into place until they resembled two long boxes. Then he hung one box beneath each window. Going to his wagon, he hefted the bag of potting soil onto his shoulder and brought it over to the work area. He filled both boxes with dirt, then gathered the pots of mums from his wagon.

He'd been first in line at Troyer's nursery this morning so he could pick out the prettiest plants. He'd chosen purple, yellow and white petunias.

Their blooms danced in the breeze. The purple reminded him of the way Sadie's eyes changed color depending on her mood. The pots of white mums brought to mind her strength, and the yellow ones made him think of how she embraced whatever came her way. And he'd not forgotten yellow was her favorite color.

Levi hoped she would like this final gift.

He placed one plant of each color in the window boxes. Patting the soil into place, Levi listened to the sounds of the *kinder* and realized he would miss them, almost as much as he would miss Sadie. Stepping back, he brushed his hands together, letting the loose dirt fall. He gave one last look to his handiwork and, satisfied that he'd done his best, began packing up the wagon.

A selfish part of him wanted to stay so he could see the look on her face when she stepped outside to see these flowers.

He'd started to untie the horse from the hitching post when he realized he'd left his tool belt on the ground by the shed. He jogged back over, picked it up and turned to see the *kinder* streaming out the coatroom door.

"Mr. Byler! How are you?" Mica ran up to him.

Patting the boy on the head, Levi said, "I'm *gut*, and how about yourself?"

"I'm doing okay, I guess." His face took on a glum expression. "I'm having trouble with my reading, so Miss Sadie has been helping me."

"I see. Well, it's important to know how to read."

"I understand, but I'd rather be outside playing."

Levi imagined he did.

"Mica!" Sadie's voice carried over on a breeze.

Levi took his hand off Mica's head and watched Sadie come out of the coatroom into the brilliant day. She raised a hand to shield her eyes from the sunlight. He saw her scan the area, looking for Mica.

Mica's *vader*'s words came back to Levi. As long as he remained here, her reputation could be at stake.

The Amish rules of courtship were strict. Levi knew them well. Sadie's *vader* had chosen for her. Watching her, he wondered what would happen if he decided to stay.

"I'm over here, Miss Sadie, talking to Mr. Levi."

Mica ran past her as she walked toward the shed, then Sadie stopped dead in her tracks.

Chapter Sixteen

"Wow!" she breathed out.

She stared at the beautiful petunias in the planter boxes hanging beneath each window on the front of the shed. She placed her hand on her heart. Levi's gesture was so thoughtful it brought tears of happiness. He'd been so stubborn about wanting to even give her the windows and now he'd gone and done this.

It almost made up for the earlier upset between him and Mica's *vader*. Almost. But she'd get back to that in a minute. First, she had to get a closer look at these flowers.

She couldn't keep the grin off her face as she went over to inspect the boxes. Up close the plants were even prettier. The vibrant purples along with the clean-white and sunshine-yellow flowers made her heart sing. She wondered how Levi had known to pick out her favorite colors.

She spun around to tell him how grateful she was for this gift. "Levi. *Danke. Danke* so much! You don't know how much joy this will bring the *kinder*. In the spring we can put different flowers in these boxes. And

I know you didn't think any of my ideas were worth keeping in the beginning. But I can tell from the look on your..." She had to stop herself from blurting out *handsome face*.

Calming down, she said, "I can tell from the look on your face that you think these boxes and the windows look wonderful."

"I think you look wonderful."

The words had come out so softly that she thought she might have imagined them.

Her heart skipped a beat. Levi had paid her a compliment. The first one since they'd known each other. Though she tried not to get her hopes up, she wondered if this meant he wanted to move forward in their relationship. She dared not speak.

"I'm glad you like the flower boxes," he said a little louder. "And, *ja*, you were right. The windows are a *gut* fit."

Sadie didn't like his brusque new tone.

Levi took a step away from her. As sure as a dark rain cloud came over the horizon to spoil an otherwise perfect day, she watched Levi's mood shift. Sadie didn't understand what was happening.

"Well, I'm done here," he said. "I'd best be getting back over to Jacob's shop."

"Wait!" Sadie started after him. She needed to find out what Robert had spoken to him about.

Levi stopped and turned to look at her. Sadie didn't like what she saw, not one little bit. It appeared that a wall had gone up around him, worse than all those times before when she'd tried to break through to him. And when she'd so recently called him out on not telling her about the partnership offer.

Plunging ahead, she said, "I suppose I should thank you for intervening with Mica's *vader*. Honestly, I could have handled the man by myself. Dealing with distressed parents is part of my job."

His chin came up at her words. "Robert King had no business raising his voice to you."

"I agree. But he thought I wanted to tell him how to parent his *sohn*. Which I did not." Lowering her voice, so as not to have the *kinder* overhear, she confided, "I believe Mica is having trouble with his vision. He needs to see an eye *doktor*. I'm afraid Robert doesn't seem to agree with my assessment."

"That's not all he doesn't agree with."

"What are you talking about?" Sadie had a terrible feeling this had something to do with Levi.

Putting up his hand, he shook his head. "I can't talk about this."

"*Ja*, I think you need to. Tell me what Robert said to you."

"*Nee*. It will only cause trouble."

"Levi, if you are worried that I can't handle the situation, you'd be wrong. Just like when you walked in on my meeting earlier. You were wrong to interrupt. I didn't need your help. Although I appreciate your kind words on my behalf, I had the situation under control."

He leaned against the wagon. Shaking his head, he pointed a finger at her. "I don't think you did. Robert King was upset and he was standing over you and his wife, trying to intimidate you. *Es dutt mir leed*, Sadie, but I'm glad I came into the classroom when I did."

Sadie's frustration with him boiled over. The situation with this man had been tenuous for days, ever since he'd told he couldn't be the one for her. Sadie knew better. She could also tell that he was in no mind to listen to reason but that still didn't stop her from voicing her opinion.

"Levi, you can't have this both ways. You can't push me away one minute and then want to protect me the next. You can't leave me with this wonderful gift—" pausing, she looked at the window boxes "—and not think that I wouldn't see it as a sign of your affection."

They seemed to be at an impasse. Sadie fought back the heartache. This man, the only one she could ever love, stood here in his blue chambray work shirt, with his straw hat covering his light brown hair, leaning against the wagon, rubbing his hand down his face. She knew he wanted to wipe away his frustration. She clasped her hands together, not knowing what else to do. She felt her faith wavering.

Finally, Levi said, "I didn't want to tell you what Robert said. But I don't see any other way to protect you, to protect your job. He warned me to stay away from you. He said your reputation is at stake."

She started to tell him that was just Robert spewing nonsense when she heard one of the *kinder*'s cries. Her gaze quickly scanned the schoolyard to see who needed her.

Little Beth sat on the ground in front of the swing set, holding her right knee.

Without a thought, Sadie rushed over and kneeled in front of the girl. "Beth, *bischt allrecht*?"

Beth let out a sob as tears streamed down her face. "I fell off the swing," she wailed.

"There, there. Let me take a look." Sadie pushed Beth's *schlupp schotzli* off her knee and saw where her stockings had torn. Near as she could tell, this was nothing more than a scrape. But to be on the safe side, she would take Beth inside to clean it and put on a Band-Aid.

"Do you think you can walk?"

Beth's lower lip trembled. "I don't think so. I think it might be broken."

"Beth, I can assure you your knee is not broken. Now, come on and try to stand up," Sadie coaxed.

Doing as she was told, the child started to stand, and then let out a shout. Sadie knew the scrape wasn't serious. Still, she pushed herself off the ground, preparing to gather Beth in her arms to carry her inside. But before she could move, she felt a hand on her shoulder.

"Let me help." Levi's shadow covered them.

Sadie stood up the rest of the way, allowing him to move past her to scoop Beth up off the ground as if she were light as a feather. Levi cradled her in his arms as Sadie ran ahead to get the coatroom door opened.

"I've got a first-aid kit over by the sink." Sadie led them to the small kitchenette.

Levi sat Beth on the countertop.

"*Danke*, Mr. Levi." Beth batted her tear-soaked lashes at him.

Sadie thought her heart would melt at the sweet look on that little girl's face, so she could only imagine what Levi had to be thinking. He turned to her and Sadie sighed over the fact that he still appeared to be carrying that dark cloud with him.

"I'll leave this to you," he said in a brusque tone.

Sadie recognized that their situation would have to wait. Offering him her thanks, she gave her attention to Beth. For the first time since she'd met Levi and fallen in love with him, Sadie felt her resolve cracking.

Nee. She prayed for patience and strength. *I have to stay strong.*

* * *

As Levi made his way back to the shed company, he tried not to dwell on the situation with Sadie. But how could he not? At every twist and turn, no matter how hard he tried to keep them at bay, thoughts of her floated through his mind.

And it didn't help that the ride back to Jacob's seemed to take forever. The road was crowded today, with cars and eighteen-wheelers everywhere. With the fall season coming, the tourists were out and about earlier in the week. Here in Miller's Crossing, the leaves were just beginning to turn colors, the green leaves tinged with oranges and reds. A part of him wished he'd be here to see the colors at their peak.

He waited for the traffic to clear at the intersection of Clymer Hill Road and Route Ten. When it came his turn, he turned right onto Clymer Hill.

The horse slowed as it started the ascent up the long hill. The wagon rattled along, cresting at the rise where the church stood. He remembered the day he'd first met Sadie. What a sight she'd been stuck in the mudhole. From the top of her head to the tips of her toes, she'd been a soggy mess. Even then he'd been struck by her presence and her personality.

A buggy careening around the corner at the bottom of the hill interrupted his musings.

"What on earth? Hey!" He gave a shout as the buggy came full speed up the hill. "Hey! *Was iss letz* with you! Slow down!"

The buggy pulled to a halt beside him. Levi immediately recognized one of the workers from the shop.

Mark Miller barely got the words out. "Levi! I'm so

glad I found you! There's been an accident. You must come quickly!"

"Slow down. Tell me what's happened."

"Jacob took a fall outside his house. Rachel said he needed to go to the hospital."

Concern filled Levi. He prayed his friend's injuries were not serious. "All right." Seeing the young man was upset, Levi asked, "Did Rachel call for an ambulance?"

"*Nee.* Jacob insisted they call one of the neighbors. They came by and drove him away. I think he injured his arm."

"Okay, let's get back to the house."

Levi waited for the lad to turn around in the church parking lot, and then led the way back to Rachel and Jacob's. He saw some of the workers standing around in a circle outside the shop. Their heads were bowed, and Jacob knew they were praying for their boss. He grew worried. If they had all stayed, then Jacob's condition must be serious.

Leaving the horse with some water and a bit of grain, he walked across the lot to join them.

"Levi. *Gut* you came back when you did. Jacob took a tumble down the steps coming out of his house. Rachel thinks he might have broken something."

"Did anyone else see what happened?"

"*Nee.* Most of us were inside."

"How long do you think they've been gone?" he asked.

"About half an hour."

That was too soon for any news. Levi looked at the men, who were all watching him. It took him a minute to realize they were waiting on some sort of instruction from him.

"I think it's best if we all go back to work," he said. "I'll go check to make sure Rachel didn't leave anything cooking on the stove. I'm sure she left in a hurry."

"*Ja*, she looked very upset."

The men made their way back inside the shop while Levi headed up the small incline to the house. He paused at the bottom of the porch steps. He could see multiple footprints where he guessed Jacob had fallen. He also saw the crack in the second step from the bottom. Not a *gut* thing. Skipping that step, he went on into the house.

Immediately, he could smell freshly baked bread and chicken. Hurrying through the great room, he saw two loaves of bread on a wire rack near the stove. And sure enough, simmering away on the back unit was a large black pot. Lifting the lid, he waited for the steam to clear, then peered inside. A whole chicken languished in the bubbling liquid along with celery, carrots and onions.

No doubt the beginning of the evening meal, and probably stock for later. He decided to turn it off. If he got busy outside, he didn't want to forget the pot and have the liquid cook off, scorching the chicken to the bottom. Better to be safe than sorry.

Now that he'd gotten the cooking under control, he turned his attention to fixing the step.

He went out the back door to the small outbuilding where Jacob stored his personal tools. He slid the door open, surprised to find everything neatly organized. The shovels, rakes and hoes were all hung neatly on the right side. He found a big red multi-drawer toolbox and opened a drawer marked Hammers. He picked up a medium-size one and selected a few large nails that would easily hold the repair.

Back at the porch, he tore the old step off the risers, then walked over to the scrap pile outside the shop to see if he could find something that could work as a replacement. After a bit of rummaging around, he managed to find a board that looked close enough in size. He hammered it into place, then tested the tread with his weight. This would suffice. With the job done, he returned everything back to its place in the outbuilding.

The sunlight angled through the branches of the maple trees circling the yard. Levi walked through the coolness of the shadows. He needed to check in on the workers. The end of the day was nearing, and they'd all be going home soon.

"Levi! We're wrapping up here."

He met Saul Yoder just inside the doorway. "Is there anything I need to be worried about on behalf of Jacob?"

"*Nee.* We're set with the biggest project, which is for Troyer's Nursery and Garden Center."

"*Gut.* When do you think that will be finished?"

"I'd say by the end of next week. Do you think Jacob will be out of work long?"

"I can't say until we see what his injuries are."

"For what it's worth, the others and I, well, we think you'd be a *gut* fit for Jacob's company."

Levi's eyes widened. He had no idea anyone else knew about the partnership offer.

"I can tell by the look on your face I spoke out of turn," Saul said. "I'm sorry. Nevertheless, we'd all be happy to have you join the company."

Levi decided to let the comment go. Saul had intended no harm. No one knew of his indecision when it came to accepting Jacob's offer. This was Levi's battle.

Saul and Levi made their way around the shop, checking to be sure each station had been shut down correctly and readied for the next day. He noticed a light on in the office. Like many other Amish businesses in the area, this one was powered by a combination of propane, generators and solar power. Bidding Saul goodnight, Levi entered the office.

He saw the lamp on the desk and started to turn it off when his hand hit a stack of papers, sending them onto the floor. He bent down to pick them up and stopped when he saw a lawyer's letterhead on one of the papers. Knowing this was none of his business, he started to shuffle them in place. And that was when he saw his name.

Squinting, he mumbled, "What is this?"

Chapter Seventeen

He cast a quick look over his shoulder to make sure no one had seen him. This didn't make sense. Why was his name on a legal document? He stood from the floor and sat down with the paper in Jacob's chair. Going through his friend's legal papers made him feel like a criminal. But he had to see what Jacob had done.

Levi took his hat off and laid it on the desk next to some crisp white stationery. He ran his hands through his hair in frustration, and then, taking the plunge, he started to read through the document.

The top page appeared to be a cover letter. It stated the reason Jacob had contacted the attorney and detailed the scope of what Jacob would need done in order to secure a partner in the Herschberger Shed Company. One of the pages talked about the possibility of changing the name of the company to Herschberger and Byler.

As flattering as this idea was, Levi didn't understand why Jacob would go to all this trouble and not discuss this with him first. He'd seen enough. Putting the papers back in place, he turned the light off and went back up to the house to wait.

He took some leftover roast beef out of the refrigerator and made a sandwich. After pouring himself a glass of iced *kaffi*, he grabbed his plate and headed out to the front porch. While he ate, he wondered how Jacob was faring. And he mulled over this idea of the partnership. Clearly the employees didn't mind him coming on. And truth be told, the idea of finally settling down held some appeal. But could he stay here and not have contact with Sadie?

Once again, he wished he'd met her earlier in his life. Leaning back in the rocker, Levi pondered the situation. This partnership with Jacob would mean he'd leave his family permanently. He'd become a member of the Miller's Crossing church community. *Ja*, he'd see his *mamm* and *daed* on occasion, and writing letters to them helped them stay connected. He knew his parents always had his best interests at heart. They were as devastated as he had been over what had happened with Anne.

He finished the *kaffi* and sandwich, then set the plate on the table. Levi tipped his head back, closed his eyes and let the sounds of nature wash over him. Off in the distance he heard a hawk screeching and the frogs croaking in a nearby pond. Life could be *gut* here in Miller's Crossing.

He heard gravel crunching under tires and opened his eyes to see the beam of headlights sweeping across the driveway. Pushing up from the chair, he hurried off the porch.

Rachel was getting out of the back seat of a blue sedan. "Oh, Levi! I'm so glad you're here."

"How's Jacob?"

"Come and see for yourself." Rachel scurried to the passenger-side front seat.

Levi followed, anxious to see how his cousin had fared. He let out an *"ach"* when he saw Jacob's right arm in a cast and a sling.

While Rachel held the car door open, Levi helped Jacob out of the car as best he could. His friend seemed to be a bit wobbly on his feet. When Jacob swayed, Levi held on to his good arm. "Whoa. I've got you."

"Dan...ke."

Coming up behind them, Rachel advised, "He's been given a mild painkiller."

Levi nodded, taking care to guide Jacob up the porch stairs. "I fixed the step."

"Danke! Danke, Levi. That's the one that caused Jacob's fall," Rachel said, racing ahead of them to hold open the front door. "Take him into our bedroom. He needs to lie down and raise the arm up above his heart. The doctor said it will help keep the swelling down."

Again, she pushed her way ahead of the men, getting Jacob's side of the bed ready with extra pillows. Levi guided Jacob to sit on the bed.

"Ah." Jacob let out a relieved sigh. "I've had quite the time of it, I'm afraid. I noticed the step had cracked earlier today. I was actually coming out to fix it when I fell. Can you believe that?"

"Ja. These things happen," Levi answered as he helped him lie back in the bed.

"Jacob, I'm going to make you some toast," Rachel said. "The nurse said you have to take the medication with food. And how about some tea?" She tipped her head to one side, gazing down at her husband.

"Ja, that will be fine."

Thinking Jacob might need to rest, Levi started to follow Rachel out.

"Levi, wait. Let me have a word with you before Rachel comes back."

Levi paused at the foot of the bed, noticing the lines of fatigue around Jacob's eyes and the occasional grimace of pain on his face.

"I'm worried. The *doktor* said I fractured two bones in my wrist. One is what they called a hairline and the other is a bit more serious. They don't think I will need an operation to fix it, but the next few weeks will decide the course. I have to have this on for four to six weeks," he said, tapping on the hard cast. He started to give Levi a grin, but failed miserably.

"Look," Levi assured him, "I don't want you to worry about anything. You concentrate on resting and healing. It's getting late. I'll leave you to Rachel's care."

Softly, he closed the bedroom door behind him as he went to join Rachel in the kitchen.

"*Danke* for taking care of the pot, Levi," she said. "I completely forgot about it being on. Everything happened so fast. He was going down the steps one minute and the next he was on the ground calling out for me."

"He seems to be doing well and the *gut* news is he came back home without a stay in the hospital."

She nodded. "We were lucky that the urgent care could do everything. He needs to see a specialist in a few days. Those are all *gut* things. Did he tell you about the injury?"

"*Ja.*"

"I'm not sure he told you everything. The nurse was very clear to me. He needs to keep that arm still. They want the fractures to heal well so they don't have to do an operation to fix them."

He saw the distress on her face and wanted to let her know that he would be here for them. "That makes sense. You know you both can count on me to help run things while Jacob heals."

"I'm glad you'll be here, is all."

The teakettle let out a shrill whistle. Rachel took it off the heat and went about fixing the tea and toast for her husband. "I know you can see to the running of the business while my Jacob recovers." Rachel put the teacup and saucer on a tray next to the plate of toast.

Remembering the papers he'd seen in the office, Levi knew he couldn't leave, not under these circumstances. He would get back to the idea of the partnership when Jacob was feeling better. But for now, temporarily, he'd stay put. A *gut* man did not walk out on his family when they were in need.

"Lizzie and I have come up with a plan to get you and Levi together."

Sadie stared dumbfounded at her sister. Sara, who had been beaming like a ray of sunshine for days now, was sitting here giving her advice on matters of the heart. Ever since their *vader* had given his blessing on her courting Isaiah, she'd been walking around with a happiness that appeared to be never ending. Meanwhile, Sadie had been existing in limbo. But today Sara had invited their friend Lizzie over for afternoon tea when all Sadie wanted was to wallow in a bit of self-pity.

She picked at the needlepoint she'd brought out to the porch to work on. There might not be enough rose-colored thread to finish. The design was a simple one:

Love is the reason behind everything God does. She'd planned on making this for herself, hoping to hang it in her own home one day. Now she would finish it and give it to her sister as a wedding gift.

Picking up the threaded needle, she poked it through the fabric, working on the letter *o* in *Love.*

"We're going to have a potluck dinner." Sara clapped her hands together in delight.

"Rachel wants us to come to her place," Lizzie added. "She said her refrigerator is overflowing with casseroles. Everyone who stops by to visit Jacob comes with a dish in hand. I stopped by yesterday to leave a loaf of my homemade banana bread."

"And I'm to come as the extra?" Sadie hated the bitterness in her voice. Her frustration with Levi boiled over.

Both Sara and Lizzie had stricken looks on their faces.

"Sadie, you listen to me," Sara demanded. "Levi will be there."

"You seem awfully sure of yourself, Sara."

"*Ja,* I am. He's staying there, for goodness' sake. This situation between the two of you has to be resolved. The dinner will be tomorrow."

Sadie's stomach churned. "Tomorrow."

"That's right," Lizzie said, exchanging glances with Sara.

This turn of events had Sadie nibbling on her lower lip. She knew that Levi wouldn't be happy with this setup.

She wanted to confess something to Sara and Lizzie but didn't quite know how to form the words. Finally, knowing that getting this off her mind would be better than keeping it inside, she said, "I believe something is holding Levi back. I'm not exactly sure what the problem might be, but something from his past is clearly troubling him and keeping him from moving on with his life."

"Have you spoken to him about this?" Sara asked.

"Sara, I have tried every which way to get him to open up to me. This burden he is carrying is great. He doesn't trust what I know is in his heart."

"Hmm." Lizzie sipped thoughtfully at her tea. "I know one thing for sure, Sadie. God's plans should never be questioned."

"Are you thinking I should let Levi go?" Sadie got choked up just thinking it.

"That is not what I'm saying at all. Do you remember how hard I fought my love for Paul?"

Sadie laughed. "*Ja.* You were being so stubborn."

"That I was. I didn't think any man could ever love a woman who looks like I do." Lizzie rubbed her hand over the scar on her face. "But I finally gave into what my heart was telling me and what Paul knew all along. We were meant to be together."

Sadie's friend had been through a lot. The death of her *bruder* in a tragic accident, when they were young *kinder*, had left her scarred inside and out. But Lizzie had persevered and found her true love.

Setting her glass down on the low table between them, Lizzie leaned over and patted Sadie on the knee. "You will get this figured out."

A restlessness filled her. Putting the needlepoint down on the table, she stood up, stretching her arms. Nothing she did these days seemed to erase the tension that had taken root between her shoulder blades. "I'm going to go into the village to see if Decker's has the thread I need."

"Do you want company?" Sara asked.

"*Nee.* A walk might do me some good. Maybe the time will clear my head." Sadie went inside to grab her wallet. She said goodbye to Sara and Lizzie, then headed out.

She did enjoy the walk and the fresh air. By the time she arrived in Clymer, she had worked up a bit of a thirst. Going into the grocery store, she found the thread she needed in the home goods section and decided to treat herself to some root beer. She paid for the two items and stepped out onto the sidewalk.

"Yoo-hoo! Sadie!"

Chapter Eighteen

Elenore King came rushing up to her. "Oh, Sadie, I'm so glad I ran into you. I was across the street at the café."

"*Gute nammidaag*, Elenore."

"*Ja. Ja. Gute nammidaag* to you."

The woman seemed to be in a bit of distress. She was wringing her hands and could barely keep still. Sadie worried that something might have happened to Mica. "Elenore, *was iss letz*?"

Shaking her head, Elenore replied, "Nothing is wrong. At least I hope not."

This didn't sound *gut*. Sadie didn't think she could handle any more stress in her life. Clearly, this woman had something she wanted to tell her. Sadie thought asking about Mica might get her to talking. "How is Mica doing with his reading?"

"That's one of the things I wanted to tell you about. First, let me apologize again for Robert's treatment of you the other day."

"There's no need for that."

"I think there is. You are a *gut* teacher. I think one of the best Miller's Crossing has had in a long time.

Robert was having a bad day. And that's no excuse for his behavior."

"I understand."

"He's been busy with work and of course providing for our family. This problem with Mica came at a bad time is all," she explained. "But I want you to know I convinced him to let us take Mica to the eye *doktor*."

"Elenore! This is wonderful news!" Sadie knew that Mica's reading would be back on track soon.

"Mica's eyes are weak. He's going to be wearing glasses while he's in school and for doing his reading and homework."

Sadie realized it had taken great courage and strength for Elenore to convince her husband to let this happen. Though she never doubted that the man cared for his family, he was known to be strict with them.

"I'm so happy for Mica."

Elenore fidgeted with the drawstring on the bag she was carrying. Her gaze didn't quite meet Sadie's eyes as she said, "There's one more thing I need to tell you."

"What is it?"

"The school board is meeting tonight. They are going to be deciding on your position."

Elenore's words hit her hard. Sadie had known this day would come. She'd understood from the beginning that this job might be temporary. Still, the idea of her fate being in the hands of three members of her community worried her.

"*Danke* for letting me know."

"*Willkomm,*" Elenore replied, and then went off, leaving Sadie standing near the intersection of Main Street and Route Ten.

She didn't know what to make of this news other than realizing she didn't want to leave the *kinder*.

The stoplight was on its third cycle of green, yellow, then red when she heard a very familiar voice say, "Are you going to stand here all day or are you crossing the street?"

She looked at Levi, blinking back tears.

"Sadie? Is something the matter?" He stepped toward her.

She backed away, blurting out, "The school board is meeting tonight."

"I see."

"They are going to be talking about me. Deciding *my* future." She poked herself in the chest. "What if I'm not the person they want to teach their *kinder*?"

"Sadie, I don't believe for one minute that they will let you go. Nor should you."

"Levi, Robert told me just last week that he'd be watching me closely. And I think he told you the same." She swallowed. "I took the job because I was looking for something to do to fill the time until I found..." She stopped talking.

Levi took a half step toward her and reached out a hand to her. But then, realizing they were in public where anyone could see them, he let the hand drop.

"Until you found what?"

"You know what I've been searching for."

He did.

"The *kinder* adore you." *I adore you.* "I've seen how they look up to you. And you bring such life into their lives. How can you think the school board won't see that?"

"I only know that my heart was in the wrong place when I began teaching last year. My reasons for accepting the temporary position were selfish. I simply thought I could walk into that classroom, do my teaching and leave. I wanted to fill this void in my life. And you know what? The *kinder* do fill my life. I love to see the expressions on their faces when they solve a problem. And one of my older students, Mary Ellen, why, she's growing up so fast and is a *gut* helper to me. Every night I go home thinking about the next day and all the new things we'll learn together."

She paused, as if remembering they were having this conversation in a very public place. She put her shoulders back and tilted her chin up to give him one of the fiercest looks he'd ever seen. "I can't lose them."

He almost cracked a smile, thinking there was the woman he loved. Levi longed to take her in his arms, to give her the comfort she so desperately needed. But he couldn't. He had decisions of his own to make. And only when he settled things in his own life would he be able to open his heart to her. A woman who richly deserved so much more than he could ever give her.

Tipping his hat back, he asked, "Will I see you tomorrow at Rachel and Jacob's?"

She seemed surprised by his question. "You know about the potluck?"

He nodded. Why wouldn't he know about the plans Rachel had made with Lizzie? "Rachel is very excited about having company. She's been so busy worrying over her husband that she's making herself crazy."

"But you've been there to help."

It wasn't a question but he answered anyway. *"Ja."*
"Gut."

Levi could almost see her mind wandering back to her problem. He hoped the board wouldn't use his friendship with her against her when making their decision. That wouldn't be fair. As far as he was concerned, they'd done nothing inappropriate.

"Listen, whatever happens at this meeting tonight, you've got your friends and family who will support you no matter what," he said.

"I know. I wish I could be there at the meeting. I'm not the most patient person."

He winked at her. She didn't need to remind him of that.

She gave him a half smile. "I guess I need to be getting back home. I'll see you tomorrow."

He wanted to offer her a ride but knew she'd turn him down. He watched her walk off, praying tomorrow would bring the answers she'd been hoping for. As for himself, he knew the time had come to settle things concerning the partnership.

He got back to the shop and was surprised to find Jacob sitting behind the desk in the office.

"So, you've finally grown tired of being cooped up?" Levi asked.

"As much as I love her, my wife has been driving me crazy with all of her coddling," Jacob admitted. "I know she's worried, but the trip to the specialist went better than we could have hoped."

"Is the cast coming off anytime soon?"

"*Nee.* Three more weeks, I'm afraid. But the bone is healing."

"I'm glad. You don't seem to be in as much pain either."

"I'm not. And that's a *gut* thing and another reason I

want to get back out here—" Jacob nodded toward the shop area "—to work."

"You've got a lot of really dependable employees. They were all praying for you to have a speedy recovery."

"*Ja*, they are *gut* men. If we expand, I'll have to go outside of Miller's Crossing to find helpers. Would you be okay with that?"

The *we* part of his statement wasn't lost on Levi. His friend had been patient with him long enough. Jacob slid the contract Levi had found a week ago across the desk to him.

"I've had an attorney work on some papers. Do you want to take a look at them?"

Sitting down, Levi crossed one leg, resting the heel of his boot across the other knee. He took his time, tempering his words. "I already saw these papers."

Jacob raised an eyebrow.

"I came out here the day you fell to close up the shop, and noticed a light on in the office. When I came in, I found the documents."

"I'm assuming you looked through them."

Levi would never hold back the truth from his cousin. "I saw my name and looked at a few of the top pages."

Resting his good arm on top of the desk, Jacob studied him. Levi toyed with the cuff on the bottom of his pant leg.

"Levi, what do you think of what you've seen so far?" Jacob asked at last.

"I think it seems like a fair deal. But I'm wondering why you would want to add someone else's name to the business. The change would incur another expense. You'd have to change your branding."

"I think it's the right thing to do. My attorney advised waiting to see how a new partnership would work out before putting through that particular paperwork." Jacob leaned in, pushing the contract almost to the edge of the desk.

Levi chuckled. The man was determined. He grabbed the contract before it landed on the floor and sat back in his chair, reading through each page.

Jacob wanted a very nominal buy-in. Levi suspected it was because Jacob wanted Levi to bring something to the table other than financial strength. He got to the part about the company name change. His name looked *gut* on paper.

Still, he worried Jacob was being too generous. If this arrangement did not work out, then he'd be left with a company that bore someone else's name. The impact of the decision struck him. If he stayed here in Miller's Crossing, this would become his home. If he gave in to his feelings for Sadie, there would be no turning back.

And would either of these choices be so bad?

"I hear we're having company for dinner tomorrow night. I think the women have something planned." Jacob's voice broke the silence.

Levi shot a glance at him, thinking back on the conversation he'd had with Sadie earlier. She'd had a funny look on her face when they talked about the dinner. He began to grow suspicious.

"I don't know about your theory," he said. "I think they wanted to have a gathering is all."

Jacob shrugged. "If you say so. I still think they're up to something. You about done with your reading?"

"Give me another minute." Levi wanted to look over

the last page one more time. The page with the signature line.

Jacob slid his pen across the desk.

"Sadie, did you start the bratwurst?" Sara asked.

"I'm not sure why you want to bring this. Didn't Rachel already say she has a lot of food?"

"Yes. But I think Isaiah might like it."

"Then why aren't you the one making the dish? I'm busy baking my cookies," Sadie snapped.

The day had been wearing on and still there was no word of the school board's decision. But she hadn't meant to take her frustrations out on her sister.

"Sadie! You apologize to your sister right this instant," their *mamm* ordered. Turning around from the sink, she speared Sadie with a look she hadn't seen since she was a *kinder*.

"*Es dutt mir leed*, Sara. Forgive me, please." Wiping her hands on a towel, she added, "I don't know what's gotten into me."

"This is so unlike you, Sadie," her *mamm* added.

"*Es dutt mir leed, Mamm.*" Dropping the towel on the counter, Sadie ran out of the kitchen and onto the front porch.

The pressure of waiting for the news was too much for her. So much of her life hung on the edge. Her job. Her relationship with Levi. Whether or not Levi would choose to become a partner and stay in Miller's Crossing. She leaned against a post at the top of the steps, trying to calm her nerves. But the thoughts kept coming. She feared her life would never hold the happiness she sought. She thought about her encounter with Levi yesterday.

Something about him had changed. She couldn't put her finger on exactly what, but he hadn't pushed her away. *Nee.* If anything, she'd felt closer to him.

She saw her *vader* coming up the pathway from the barn.

"*Dochder*, I have a note for you."

Sadie ran down the steps to meet him. This could be the news she was waiting for. With a shaky hand, she took the envelope he held out to her and saw her name in neat block lettering.

"Is this something important?" her *vader* asked.

"*Ja.*" Sadie's nerves were rattling so much she barely got the word out.

A million thoughts ran through her mind. If the school board was keeping her, surely they would have sent someone by to tell her in person. On the other hand, if they were going to let her go, she imagined Robert King might have taken great pleasure in delivering that news himself. She didn't know what to do.

And then a thought hit her. As sure as the sun rose and set, there was only one person she wanted with her when she opened this envelope.

She left her *vader* and ran back inside the house. "Sara, do you have everything ready to go?"

"Sadie, what's gotten into you now?" her *mamm* asked.

"Nothing. And everything." Sadie gave her *mamm* a hug, then picked up the red cookie tin with her snickerdoodles.

Sara was just putting the foil on the bratwurst. "Are we leaving? Isaiah isn't here yet. Did you forget he's driving us?"

Sadie had forgotten. "Okay, let's wait for him at the top of the driveway."

"Sadie!"

"Come on, hurry up!" She tugged her sister by the arm toward the door.

She needed to get to Levi.

Chapter Nineteen

Levi was helping Rachel put the dishes out on the picnic table in the side yard. She'd told him evenings like this were not to be wasted eating indoors. He set a dish of baked chicken in the middle of the table, along with the green bean casserole, baked macaroni and cheese, another pasta dish and a large tossed salad. The neighbors had been generous with their offerings during Jacob's recovery. And he couldn't even begin to think about the number of pies and cakes that filled the second shelf of the refrigerator.

Speaking of desserts, he hoped Sadie might bring her blue-ribbon snickerdoodles. Levi hoped she'd have good news, too.

He'd been thinking about her all day long. He prayed the school board had made the right decision, because he had a bit of his own news to share with her.

Moving to the other side of the table, he fixed the thin cushion over the bench. Rachel had insisted they use them. While the menfolk didn't mind sitting on hard benches, she assured him the ladies preferred a bit more comfort.

A buggy pulled up in front of the house, and Levi stood taller, waiting for Sadie to get out. Surprise ricocheted through him when he saw Isaiah Troyer climbing down from the front seat.

How could Sadie do this to him? Was this some sort of bad joke that life had decided to play on him a second time? He didn't think he had it in him to bear heartbreak once again.

His arms went rigid as he fisted his hands at his sides. Why on earth had Sadie brought Isaiah here?

"Levi."

The stern tone of Rachel's voice halted his dark thoughts.

"Whatever you are thinking, don't."

Sadie got out of the back seat. He watched as she tipped her head back, laughing at something her sister said. *Her sister.* Sara and Isaiah were walking side by side with Sara's arm linked through his.

Not believing what he was seeing, he glanced at Rachel, who was looking very smug. "I don't understand."

Rachel gave him a pat on the arm. "I think it best if Sadie explains the situation to you."

He left the table and crossed the lawn, meeting Sadie halfway between the buggy and the picnic area. "I think we need to talk."

She nodded.

"Let's go around to the back of the house. On the way you can tell me about your sister and Isaiah."

"The short version is Sara has always been the Fischer *dochder* for Isaiah," Sadie said with a shrug. "I suspected her feelings for some time."

"And you didn't say anything sooner?"

"Because I needed to be sure. Look, Levi, you've

known my *vader* had his mind set on a match between Isaiah and myself. I knew better."

"I see," he said, even though he didn't.

Sadie went on to explain. "Once we convinced our *vader* that Sara was meant for Isaiah, and Isaiah decided that Sara was indeed the better fit, he gave his blessing to them."

Levi still didn't understand how he hadn't seen any of this coming. "Interesting. And what about you? Has he given his blessing to you?"

Sadie stopped along the path. The look on her face told him everything. "I'm afraid not yet." She lifted her eyes to meet his.

Levi wanted to wipe away her doubt.

"He's not sure about you, Levi. But I am. I know there are things in your past—things you've kept from me. Perhaps it's time to let me in."

"Can you tell me what the school board said first?"

"All right. I have some news to share. Except I'm not sure if it's bad or *gut*. I've got the envelope here in my pocket. Someone gave it to my *vader* to give to me."

Stopping along the path, he looked down at her. He could almost read the doubt about her future in her eyes. Reaching down, he caught her hand. Her skin felt warm and soft beneath his calloused fingertips.

Giving her hand a reassuring squeeze, he said, "Remember what I said to you yesterday? How no matter what happens, you'll still have all of us to get you through?"

"I do remember." Sadie dropped his hand and took the envelope out of her pocket. She nibbled on her lower lip.

Levi felt his heart lurch. If the news was not what

she'd hoped for, she'd be upset. One thing he knew for certain was her strength would get her through.

She took a deep breath, then ran her finger under the flap of the envelope. Exhaling, she pulled out a note. "I'm almost too afraid to look."

"Do you want me to read it to you?"

"Nee."

Her gaze skimmed the page. And then her face broke out into the widest smile he'd ever seen.

"*Gut* news, I take it?"

"Yes! Yes! I'm staying. They want me to stay!"

Levi brought his arms around her, hugging her close, feeling her trembling with excitement. He let her go, saying, "Oh, Sadie, this is the best news for you."

"The only thing that would make it better is if you were going to tell me that you've decided to stay."

He'd decided more than that. "I have something I need to tell you."

Sadie wanted more than anything to hear Levi tell her that he loved her and that he would never leave her. She let him take her hand once more, relishing the warmth and security his touch brought her. She loved this man more than life itself. She wished this trepidation she felt every time they drew closer would leave. Only Levi could make the sensation go away.

"Does this something have to do with Jacob's offer?"

"*Ja.* And there's more." He led them to a bench under a big maple tree. "Come sit. I want to tell you about what brought me here."

She tilted her head to see him better. "I thought you came to help your cousin."

"That was part of the reason, but not all of it."

Sadie put a hand on either side of his face. Rubbing her thumbs along the hard plane of his cheekbones, she felt his strength. "Levi, in order for us to work, you need to tell me what is in your heart. I know you've been holding a pain deep inside. I saw it the first day I met you."

Sadie remembered how businesslike he'd been with her then, practically ordering her out of the wagon, and how mad he'd gotten when she didn't tell him right away where she lived. And the other times when he'd pushed her away...

But the day Robert King had come into her classroom, intent on making her at fault for Mica's learning problems, that day had been the turning point. Levi had been there for her, and now she wanted to be there for him.

"Tell me what happened to you."

Putting his hands around hers, he said, "This isn't easy for me. None of this has been easy for me." Touching his forehead to hers, his voice broke. "Falling in love with you should have come easily. And yet, I've tried to fight those feelings from the moment I set eyes on you."

"Why?"

"Because my heart had been broken." He shifted away from her, resting his hands on his knees. "This situation is difficult for me to talk about."

Sadie's heart began to race. What if she were forcing him to relive something too painful? "I'm so sorry."

"I've been in love before." He stopped and then started speaking again. "That's not right. I thought I'd been in love. I wasn't."

Sadie let the words sink in. There had been someone else before her.

"A young woman. A lot like you." He turned to look at her then. "Pretty and impetuous."

"I'm not—" She was about to say *pretty*, but Levi held up a hand, stopping her.

"Sadie, you asked me to tell you. Please, let me continue."

Folding her hands in her lap, she nodded.

"We fell in love quickly. Again, I thought at the time the feeling was love. I'd known Anne for a long time. We grew up in neighboring communities. I met her at a picnic. The time seemed right, and my family might have been pressuring me to find a wife. I know you understand."

"I do."

"To this day I'm not sure what thoughts were in Anne's head. I only know she left me a note, telling me she'd decided to leave the community."

"You mean she wanted to move?"

"*Nee*. She wanted to leave the Amish life."

Sadie gasped. She couldn't imagine walking away from the only life she'd ever known. The thought of being shunned brought tears to her eyes. The idea that she'd have to leave her family, friends and the *kinder* she taught to be all alone in the *Englisch* world? *Nee*. She couldn't fathom how someone would want to do that.

Swallowing a sob, Sadie, barely got out, "Why? Why would she want to leave?" Worse yet, why would she push a man as wonderful as Levi away?

He looked out over the yard, unable to meet Sadie's gaze. "She was in love with someone else. An *Englischer*."

"Oh, Levi. I'm so very sorry."

"You must understand how hard this has been for

me. I wanted to start a new life with her, and she had met another man and fallen in love. I can forgive her, because she never would have found happiness with me. But when it first happened, I was angry and hurt. I know now that Anne and I weren't meant to be together. But I can't forget how her actions made me feel."

"But, Levi, I'm not that woman." Sadie shook her head. "I would never treat you like that."

"I know."

"And the situation with Isaiah, well, that was my *vader*'s doing from the very beginning."

"I know that. Though I have to tell you I wasn't sure what to think when I saw him getting out of the buggy just now."

Sadie realized her mistake not telling him about Isaiah and Sara when she saw him yesterday. "I guess I should have told you about the change in plans."

"That would have been helpful."

He stood up, shoving his hands in his pockets. "I wasn't sure I'd ever be able to trust my heart to love anyone again. And then I met you, Sadie Fischer. You turned my world upside down and right side up."

Sadie's heart soared. But she had to be sure he understood, no matter what, that she wasn't like this other woman.

"Levi, I would never be like Anne who broke your heart."

"You can't deny you've had an idea of the kind of man you wanted to spend the rest of your life with. Not too old, not too young..." His voice drifted off.

She knew those words might come back to haunt her for the rest of their days together. Defending herself might not be an easy thing, but she had to at least try. "I've *never* thought of you as such. You are a kind and decent man. One who is *gut* with the *kinder*. One who delivers on his promises."

"As little as a week ago, I would have told you that none of those words matter," Levi said. "Then I heard Robert King raising his voice to you, and the only thing I could think was I needed to keep you safe."

"I told you the other day, I had the situation under control."

"I remember. But I knew then that if I left here, I might very well be leaving something *gut* behind. I've been fighting this feeling for too long." Splaying his hands wide, he said, his voice broken, "I didn't want to risk my heart again. Do you understand what I'm saying?"

This time the wrenching sob came from her. Standing, she almost couldn't bear to ask him, "Levi, then you don't deny there is something between us?"

"Oh *ja*, there is more than something between us. I've fallen in love with you, Sadie."

Sadie clung to his side. Looking up at him, she needed to know if they had a future.

"Does this mean you're staying? Before you tell me what you're about to do, let me tell you how much I love you. Levi, my world righted the day I met you. You weren't too old or too young or heaven forbid already spoken for."

Levi let out a laugh. "You're not going to let that go, are you?"

"Nope."

"I don't know why I thought I could ever leave you."

"Wait!" she said suddenly. "You need to tell me your other news."

"My other news?"

"*Ja*... Jacob's offer. Are you going to accept it?"

"I signed the papers this morning."

"*Ach!* That's wonderful!" Sadie fell into his arms. "I love you, Levi Byler."

"I love you, too, Sadie Fischer. More than life itself."

Tipping her chin up, he looked down into her eyes. Sadie's heart melted at the love she saw reflecting back at her.

Levi bent his head low. His mouth brushed against hers, his touch sending her heartbeat soaring.

"If you don't mind," he said quietly, "I want to give you a proper kiss."

She didn't mind at all. Standing on her tiptoes, Sadie met him halfway, their lips touching.

Lifting his lips from hers, he asked, "Can I tell you again how much I love you?"

"You can. Over and over and over." Sadie didn't think she'd ever been happier.

"I've finally found my home," he said with a smile.

"And I've finally found my perfect Amish man."

* * * * *

WE HOPE YOU ENJOYED
THIS BOOK FROM

LOVE INSPIRED
INSPIRATIONAL ROMANCE

Uplifting stories of faith, forgiveness and hope.

Fall in love with stories where faith helps
guide you through life's challenges, and discover
the promise of a new beginning.

6 NEW BOOKS AVAILABLE EVERY MONTH!

LOVE INSPIRED

Stories to uplift and inspire

Fall in love with Love Inspired—
inspirational and uplifting stories of faith
and hope. Find strength and comfort in
the bonds of friendship and community.
Revel in the warmth of possibility and the
promise of new beginnings.

Sign up for the Love Inspired newsletter
at **LoveInspired.com** to be the first
to find out about upcoming titles,
special promotions and exclusive content.

CONNECT WITH US AT:

Facebook.com/LoveInspiredBooks

Twitter.com/LoveInspiredBks

Get 4 FREE REWARDS!

We'll send you 2 FREE Books plus 2 FREE Mystery Gifts.

FREE
Value Over
$20

Both the **Love Inspired**® and **Love Inspired**® **Suspense** series feature compelling novels filled with inspirational romance, faith, forgiveness, and hope.

YES! Please send me 2 FREE novels from the Love Inspired or Love Inspired Suspense series and my 2 FREE gifts (gifts are worth about $10 retail). After receiving them, if I don't wish to receive any more books, I can return the shipping statement marked "cancel." If I don't cancel, I will receive 6 brand-new Love Inspired Larger-Print books or Love Inspired Suspense Larger-Print books every month and be billed just $5.99 each in the U.S. or $6.24 each in Canada. That is a savings of at least 17% off the cover price. It's quite a bargain! Shipping and handling is just 50¢ per book in the U.S. and $1.25 per book in Canada.* I understand that accepting the 2 free books and gifts places me under no obligation to buy anything. I can always return a shipment and cancel at any time. The free books and gifts are mine to keep no matter what I decide.

Choose one: ☐ **Love Inspired**
Larger-Print
(122/322 IDN GNWC)

☐ **Love Inspired Suspense**
Larger-Print
(107/307 IDN GNWN)

Name (please print)

Address   Apt. #

City   State/Province   Zip/Postal Code

Email: Please check this box ☐ if you would like to receive newsletters and promotional emails from Harlequin Enterprises ULC and its affiliates. You can unsubscribe anytime.

Mail to the **Harlequin Reader Service:**
IN U.S.A.: P.O. Box 1341, Buffalo, NY 14240-8531
IN CANADA: P.O. Box 603, Fort Erie, Ontario L2A 5X3

Want to try 2 free books from another series? Call 1-800-873-8635 or visit www.ReaderService.com.

"What do I need to know?" Hannah faced him then, her big blue eyes full of expectation. Randy liked that about her. She didn't hide anything.

Well, everyone hid something. He'd certainly been hiding something for years—from this town, from his friends, even from his brother.

So what? It was nobody's business.

"Let's start with the basics." He gave her a quick tour. Her presence was making his pulse race. He didn't like it or the reason why it was happening.

Hannah's cell phone rang. "Do you mind if I take this?"

"Go ahead." He backed up to give her privacy, busying himself with a box of nets, but he could hear every word she said.

"You're kidding," she said breathlessly. "That's great news. Yes…Right now? I'd love to…You're serious? I can't believe it…"

Finally, she ended the conversation and turned to him with shining eyes. "That was Molly. She has a dog for me."

"Another puppy?" He placed the box on the counter.

"No, a retired service dog." She looked ready to float through the air. "I've been on the adoption list forever. The ones that have become available all went to either their original puppy raiser or someone higher on the list."

"Won't the dog be old?" Why would she want someone's ancient dog that might not live long?

"Some of them are. This one is eight. Too old to be placed for service, but he's still got a lot of good years left."

Something told him that even if the dog had only a couple of good months left, Hannah would be equally enthusiastic.

"I'm going to go pick him up." She lightly clapped her hands in happiness, and he kind of wished he could go with her.

"Let me get you the store key, then."

"Oh, wait." She winced. "I didn't think this through. Is there any way I can bring him with me to the store? He passed all of his obedience classes years ago. I'm sure he wouldn't cause any trouble. I just can't imagine bringing him home and then leaving him by himself all day before he has a chance to get to know me. He's used to being with someone all the time."

"Of course. Bring him." He'd always liked dogs. His customers wouldn't mind. In fact, they'd probably linger in the store even more because of him. Maybe he'd get a dog of his own after he moved into the new house. It was a thought.

"Thanks." She came over and gave him a quick hug. "I'll open the store tomorrow at nine. You're closed on Sundays, right?"

"Right." He stood frozen from the shock of her touch as she hurried to the back. The sound of the screen door slamming jolted him out of his stupor.

Hannah almost made him forget he wasn't like any other guy.

And he wasn't.

He had a secret. And that secret would stay with him until the day he died.

When that day came, he'd be single.

He had to be more careful around Hannah Carr. There was something about her that made his logic disappear like the morning dew. He couldn't afford to forget he couldn't have her.

Don't miss Guarding His Secret
by Jill Kemerer, available June 2022
wherever Love Inspired books and ebooks are sold.

LoveInspired.com

IF YOU ENJOYED THIS BOOK, DON'T MISS NEW EXTENDED-LENGTH NOVELS FROM LOVE INSPIRED!

In addition to the Love Inspired books you know and love, we're excited to introduce even more uplifting stories in a longer format, with more inspiring fresh starts and page-turning thrills!

LOVE INSPIRED

Stories to uplift and inspire.

Fall in love with Love Inspired—inspirational and uplifting stories of faith and hope. Find strength and comfort in the bonds of friendship and community. Revel in the warmth of possibility, and the promise of new beginnings.

LOOK FOR THESE LOVE INSPIRED TITLES ONLINE AND IN THE BOOK DEPARTMENT OF YOUR FAVORITE RETAILER!

LITRADE0422